Praise for Orson Scott Card

"Orson Scott Card makes a strong case for being the best writer science fiction has to offer."

—The Houston Post

"[An] intriguing medical thriller from bestseller Card (*Ender's Game*) and screenwriter Johnston."

—Publishers Weekly on *Invasive Procedures*

"A relentless thriller, which couldn't be timelier . . . Intriguing plot wrinkles . . . There are many deftly shaped supporting players, and major shocks explode in a split second (no Stephen King slo-mo for Card!). Moreover, all the action doesn't obscure the author's message about the dangers of extreme political polarization and the need to reassert moderation and mutual citizenship; indeed, it drives it home."

—Booklist on *Empire*

"Violent infighting has the American Empire on the brink of destruction in this look at a possible future."

—Library Journal on *Empire*

INVASIVE
PROCEDURES

ORSON SCOTT CARD
AND AARON JOHNSTON

TOR®

A TOM DOHERTY ASSOCIATES BOOK
NEW YORK

INVASIVE PROCEDURES

Edited by Beth Meacham

A Tor Book
Published by Tom Doherty Associates, LLC
175 Fifth Avenue
New York, NY 10010

www.tor-forge.com

Tor® is a registered trademark of Tom Doherty Associates, LLC.

ISBN-13: 978-0-7653-5282-8
ISBN-10: 0-7653-5282-6

First Edition: September 2007
First Mass Market Edition: August 2008

Printed in the United States of America

0 9 8 7 6 5 4 3 2 1

To Peter Johnson,
friend and fellow storyteller

CONTENTS

ACKNOWLEDGMENTS

by Aaron Johnston

This novel is based on my screenplay adaptation of Orson Scott Card's short story "Malpractice," which was first published in *Analog Science Fiction* in 1977.

Scott and I were working together at the time, developing some of his literary properties for the film industry, and we both agreed that "Malpractice" was a short story worth exploring. We exchanged countless e-mails—the sum of which, should they ever be compiled and printed, might actually exceed the length of this novel—to discuss how best to expand the story into a feature-length narrative. Later, when we began to expand the story a second time into this novel, we wrote another volume of e-mails with additional story possibilities. Occasionally Scott would fly out to Los Angeles for business, and we'd pass an afternoon rehashing it all and filling our stomachs with gourmet ice cream.

In addition to our time collaborating, several books were particularly useful in writing this novel. Richard Preston's *The Hot Zone* gives the true account of a highly contagious, deadly virus that appeared in the suburbs of Washington, D.C., in 1983. It also happens to be one of the most terrifying books I've ever read. My hat goes off to the military staff at the United States Army Medical

X ACKNOWLEDGMENTS

Research Institute of Infectious Diseases (*USAMRIID*), at Fort Detrick, in Frederick, Maryland, who do more than we know—and probably *want* to know—to keep us safe from deadly biological threats.

I was also fascinated by *Beating Back the Devil: On the Front Lines with the Disease Detectives of the Epidemic Intelligence Service,* by Maryn McKenna. The BHA is loosely based on the EIS, but our fictitious agency doesn't do justice to the true heroism and selfless service given by the men and women of the real federal organization. When the rest of the world flees an outbreak, the EIS runs *to* it.

Beth Meacham, our editor at Tor, contributed substantially to our work—she is a good friend to us and every writer she works with. Thanks also to Barbara Bova, our agent, for giving tireless encouragement, not to mention many good suggestions.

Dagen Merrill, one of the most talented film directors I know, was integral in adapting the original short story to a screenplay. It was he who suggested that the Healers be genetically modified giants, and therefore deserves credit for many of the story's best scenes.

Thanks to Chris Wyatt, a producer on *Napoleon Dynamite*—a film that makes me laugh just thinking about it—for reading the screenplay and for giving smart notes. Chris knows suspense as well as he does comedy and his insight was invaluable. I'm also grateful to Captain Ben Shaha, currently serving a second tour in Iraq, who gave me a basic understanding of military weaponry. Jonathan Frappier shared what he had read of the homeless in Los Angeles, and his findings guided me further in my research.

Kathleen Bellamy, Orson Scott Card's assistant, made sure that the manuscript shipped when it needed to, and helped me, a first-time novelist, understand the many steps of the publishing process.

Other friends and family members read the screenplay and novel in various stages of completion and gave suggestions and encouragement throughout the process. Particular thanks go to Eric Artell, Ian Puentes, Sara Ellis, Emily Card, Peter Johnson, Karl Bowman, and my parents, Dave and Marsha Johnston.

My wife, Lauren, deserves the greatest credit because she was kind enough to read every draft and every page—often several times each—and lovingly tell me what did and didn't work. A more supportive and patient wife the world has not known. And to Luke and Jake, my two rowdy boys, who were understanding enough to let me work when they would much rather have had me by their side, on the carpet, playing Thomas the Tank Engine—Boys, I'm ready now with my train if you are.

February 6, 2007

INVASIVE

PROCEDURES

1

HEALERS

Dolores never met a Healer she didn't like until the night they took her away. It happened at the playground on Santa Monica Beach at about two o'clock in the morning. Dolores slept in the metal tube that connected the jungle gym to the swirly slide. For a homeless woman of forty, it wasn't that bad of an arrangement. She had privacy here, and the garbage cans at the playground usually had enough juice boxes or snack packets to tide her over until morning.

A passerby would, no doubt, think Dolores older than her forty years. Time on the street had a way of aging a person in much the same way war did. Her greasy brown hair hung in knotted clumps beneath a black knitted cap. Her eyes were gray, distant, and tired. Years of wind and sun had leathered her face and left dark circles under her eyes. Beneath her heavily soiled trench coat were several layers of other clothing: T-shirts and sweatshirts and all kinds of shirts—far more than normal people would wear but just enough for someone who slept out in the cold.

Tonight the cold was especially cold, the kind that snaked its way into Dolores's metal tube and then into the holes and folds of her clothing. It was a cold that had kept her up all night. And by the time the uninvited drunk man arrived, Dolores was in a particularly sour mood.

He stumbled into the playground, smelling like a vat of cheap liquor. From where she lay, Dolores couldn't see him, but he was making plenty of noise and sounded like trouble.

Go away, she wanted to scream. Take your booze smell and the vomit smell that's bound to be right behind it and go away.

Instead he collapsed onto the slide, and the metal rang with the sound of his impact.

Dolores inchwormed her way to the end of the tube and looked down. There he was, sprawled on his back in the sand, his arms spread wide, his mouth slightly agape. He must have slid right off the slide after falling onto it.

Dolores shook her head.

Whatever you been drinking, mister, you must have burned a lot of brain cells, because no poorly buttoned flannel shirt and holey pair of blue jeans are going to protect you from this wind. You need layers, peabrain. Layers.

She wriggled back inside the tube. Not dressing for the weather was about the stupidest, most inexcusable reason for dying Dolores could think of.

She was debating whether to move elsewhere for the night, just in case drunk man here woke up and caused trouble, when she heard voices.

"Here's one, sir."

It was a man's voice, strong, probably a cop. Good. Get that stinking heap away from my slide before he throws up.

"He's drunk, sir."

Of course he's drunk. You got a clothespin on your nose?

"He'll do," another man said. An older man, by the sound. And quieter. Like somebody used to being obeyed without having to push. The kind of person who shouldn't be in an empty playground on the beach after dark, in the winter.

She knew the smart thing to do. Lie low, don't make a sound. They obviously hadn't noticed her. And that was always a good thing.

"Help him to the van," the older man said.

The van? Cops don't take drunks "to the van." They either book them or roll them.

So who were these guys? She had to get a peek. If she moved really slowly, she could keep silent. Then again, if she moved too slowly, they'd be gone before she got to the end of the tube where she could see. So she needed just the right balance of speed and stealth.

Got it wrong. They must have heard her, because someone started climbing the ladder.

Dolores's grip tightened around her tennis racket. She'd never be able to swing it, of course. There wasn't room. But she could at least raise it warningly if she had to.

A face appeared. "Hello there."

It was the old man. White hair. Trim white beard. And a smile so wide, you'd think he had just walked into his own surprise birthday party.

Dolores kept silent. If she ignored him, he might think her crazy and leave. Always better not to take chances with a stranger than to open one's mouth and let them hear the fear in your voice.

"A little cold to be sleeping outside, don't you think?" the old man said, lifting a hood over his head as the wind picked up.

It was the hood that gave him away. He was a Healer. Only Healers wore capes with hoods like that. It was their calling card. Dolores thought the capes and hoods rather silly-looking but understood that they were more functional than fashionable. The cape was like a flag, a neon sign, drawing anyone who needed a Healer directly to one. It said, Hey, I'm a Healer. Come to me if I can help you, and I gladly will.

They were the Good Samaritans of the street. Healers made it their mission to give out free food and to treat people who were sick or injured—getting in trouble sometimes because they had no medical licenses, but not in really bad trouble because nobody could ever prove that they were actually practicing medicine and because they only helped the homeless anyway, people who couldn't help themselves or get help anywhere else.

The only thing odd about this Healer, however, was his age. Dolores had never seen an *old* Healer before. The ones she had seen, strolling along the Third Street Promenade helping the homeless there, were all young, healthy, body-builder types. Big guys. Always guys. And always big. Muscle big. Don't-mess-with-me-because-I-can-break-your-face big.

But this Healer was anything but a young Arnold Schwarzenegger, though he didn't look particularly weak.

"You'll freeze to death if you stay out here," he said, still smiling.

Dolores kept her expression blank but was inwardly happy to see him. Free food was free food.

The only catch was that Healers could talk your ear off if you let them. Wellness of the body and soul and all that, helping the species reach its potential. Whatever. Dolores didn't care what religion they were preaching. She just listened and pretended to care, until they gave her the food. Then she'd politely thank them and be on her way.

"I'm George Galen," he said. As if that was supposed to mean something to her.

Maybe he was waiting for her to tell him her name, but she wasn't about to, so she got to the point instead. "You got any food?" she said.

"We do," he said. "Sandwiches in the van."

"I ain't in the van," she said. "Fat lot of good your sandwiches do me."

His smile widened. "Turkey or ham?"

"Turkey," she said.

Galen looked behind him and called down the ladder. "She wants a turkey sandwich, Lichen."

Dolores craned her neck a few inches, just enough to see who it was he was speaking to.

A young Healer—the normal kind of Healer, with big

bulging muscles and wearing one of those capes over his shoulders—nodded and hurried away. Another Healer had an arm around the drunk man and was helping him hobble away from the playground.

Galen looked back at her, gesturing to the Healer who had run off to fetch the sandwich. "Lichen is one of my young associates."

"Lichen? That's his name? What, he from Europe or something?"

Galen laughed. "No, no, I gave him that name. He is like lichen, able to grow strong even when the wind blows hard."

Dolores rolled her eyes, not caring if the old man noticed. Crazy religion mumbo jumbo.

Galen didn't look fazed.

They waited there in silence a moment until Lichen came jogging back with a sandwich in a small plastic bag. He handed it to Galen, who handed it to Dolores.

She unwrapped it and began to eat. It was good. The Healers always had good stuff. Turkey, yes, but lots of lettuce and tomato, too, and sprouts, and mayo—a real sandwich, the kind somebody might pay for, not the slapped-together crap that homeless people usually got. "Thank you," she said. She might be gutter trash to most people, but she still had manners.

That didn't mean she was a pushover, though. "I'd rather skip the sermon if you don't mind," she said.

Galen tilted his head back and laughed again. As he did, Dolores saw a glimpse of the gold ribbon stitched on the inside band of his cape collar. All Healers had some color there, she had noticed, usually red or blue.

It surprised her to see a Healer laughing. All the ones she had ever talked to were stiff as boards and always spoke in reverent tones, like the street was a chapel getting ready for mass.

"I'm not here to give any sermons, ma'am."

She nodded. "Good to hear."

"You've heard our message before, I take it?"

She took another bite. "I could give it myself. Keep the body and soul pure. Yadda yadda yadda."

He laughed again. He was a jolly one, there was no questioning that. She even smiled back this time. The street had given her edge, but the charm of this George Galen was melting that away like warm sunshine. She even considered apologizing for not wanting the sermon.

He beat her to the punch.

"You have my apologies," he said, "if my Healers preach a little overzealously. I hope they've treated you well otherwise."

"Oh, they're always nice. I had me a bad sore on my foot a few weeks back, and one of them gave me some ointment and a nice bandage."

"And it helped, did it?"

"Healed up nice and quick." She wadded up the empty sandwich bag. "That was good."

"I have plenty more where that came from."

The edge came back instantly. Dolores didn't like the sound of that last statement. It sounded like those strangers who offered candy to children. "What's that supposed to mean?"

"It means that we're offering you a hot meal and a warm bed to sleep in tonight."

"*Whose* bed?" she said immediately. "I'm not that kind of woman, if that's what you're—"

He laughed heartily, throwing his head back so far that his hood slid off and his bushy mane of white hair was exposed again. "No no no," he said. "Nothing like that. You'll get your own bed. Trust me."

A warm bed. A soft one. And more food. "Free of charge?" she asked.

"Free of charge."

She stared at him a long moment, waiting for the punch line or catch. When one didn't come—

"All right," she said. "Mind getting off that ladder so I can snake out?"

Galen obligingly descended. Dolores wriggled out and carefully climbed down after him.

They drove north along the Pacific Coast Highway. That was the first bad sign. Dolores had assumed they'd be heading back into LA, toward downtown, where a lot of the nonprofits had their offices, not north toward Malibu.

She was sitting between Hal and some other guy. Hal, she had learned, was the drunk man who had collapsed at the playground. Galen had asked him his name rather nicely when they had pulled over to let him throw up.

If Dolores thought he smelled bad before, it was nothing compared to the odors he was giving off now. No hot meal is worth this, she thought.

At least the homeless kid on her left wasn't drunk. He seemed pretty normal, in fact. Fifteen or sixteen at the most, with black stringy hair tied back in a ponytail and thrashed black combat boots. Most punks his age would be running at the mouth and complaining about something. But not this kid. He just stared out the window and kept to himself.

"I'm Dolores," she said. The idea of free food and a warm bed had suddenly put her in a good mood.

The kid in the ponytail looked at her. "Nick."

Dolores smiled. "Nick. Now that's a name. Can't say I know many Nicks. Course there's Jolly Saint Nick. You know him. Man, I love me some Christmas. Presents, stockings, those fancy decorations in all the store windows. Course some people have forgotten why we have it. They forget it's the Lord's birthday. It's a shame, don't you think?"

Nick returned his gaze to the window and said nothing.

So much for polite conversation, thought Dolores.

Behind her, sitting alone in the very back seat was another boy, Nick's friend, also homeless by the looks of him, with the face of a junkie if Dolores had ever seen one. Kid probably wasn't a day over fourteen, although the drugs made him look much older. He had shaggy black hair, wore a tattered trench coat, and sported a tattoo of a snake, which began somewhere under his collar and extended up the side of his neck.

"Your friend Nick don't talk much," said Dolores, turning in her seat to face him.

"Not much to say, I guess," said the boy.

"What about you? What's your name?"

"Why? You taking a census?"

Dolores made a face. "You're the funny one, huh? The Teller?"

"The what?"

"Teller. You know? Penn and Teller. Magicians. One of 'em talks and the other one doesn't. Maybe it's Penn who talks. I can't remember which. Marx Brothers had the same gag. Harpo never said a thing, just played the harp and honked this little horn."

"I'm Jonathan," the boy said.

"Like Saint John. From the Bible."

"No, just Jonathan."

"Fair enough. You and your friend Nick come along for the free food too, I take it?"

Jonathan looked out the window. "Yeah. We could use some free food."

You and me both, thought Dolores. You and me both.

Up in the passenger seat, Galen sat whistling and tapping his fingers on the armrest. The driver was one of the big Healers, possibly the biggest Dolores had ever seen, nearly seven feet tall and thick as a horse. Unlike Galen, he seemed on edge, both hands on the steering wheel, leaning forward slightly as if the van wasn't going fast enough for him. The Healer named Lichen sat behind Galen near the sliding door. He wasn't nearly as large as the driver, but he was big enough to make Dolores wonder how many hours a day he spent in a gym.

"Where's this place we're headed?" Jonathan asked.

Galen turned around in the passenger seat and smiled. "Close, Jonathan. We should be there shortly."

"Seems awful far," said Nick.

Galen merely smiled again. "I hope everyone likes pot roast," he said. "It's been simmering for hours now. And twice-baked potatoes."

Well that sounded right tasty to Dolores. She couldn't remember the last time she had pot roast. Nowadays it was just whatever looked edible, put it in your mouth and chew. Don't ask what it is. Don't ask where it came from. It's got nutrients you need. So eat it.

Yes, sir. I could go for some juicy pot roast about now.

Hal was of another opinion. "Pull over," he said. "Gotta puke."

The van immediately pulled over and the door slid open. Hal was out in flash, dry heaving over some sagebrush.

Dolores wasn't sure which kind of vomiting sounded worse, wet or dry.

"Shouldn't drink so much," said Galen.

"You don't say," said Hal.

Dolores shook her head. This was downright unappetizing.

"You'll feel better once we get some coffee in you," Galen said.

Hal nodded. "Just give me a second." He was still on his knees on the asphalt as he bent over and retched again. If it weren't for the soundtrack, you'd think the guy was praying.

It was pathetic, really. Dolores couldn't help but feel sorry for the man.

Hal stayed there for the longest time, not moving.

The other two Healers didn't like this one bit. The driver kept looking at his watch and then up the road, like he was expecting someone or had an appointment to keep. Lichen stood outside with Hal, standing over him like a fidgety prison guard.

"It's late, sir," the driver said.

Galen put a finger to his lips. "Patience, Stone." He rolled down the passenger window. "Are you all right, Hal?"

"Fine," Hal said. Then he slowly got to his feet. Galen got out of the van and helped him back inside. It was kind, the way the old man treated him—paying no attention to the smell and not minding having to touch his filthy clothes. Like the Lord, Dolores thought: reaching out and healing the blind and the lepers.

They hadn't driven two miles when they pulled over yet again. This time for a hitchhiker.

Are we driving or not? Dolores wanted to scream. All this talk of pot roast has worked up a hunger. Let's get a move on.

Galen rolled down his window. "Need a ride?"

"More than you know," the hitchhiker said, jogging up to the passenger window. "Thank you for stopping."

"The pleasure is ours," Galen said. "What's your name, son?"

"Byron."

Dolores thought him a scruffy-looking fellow. Byron carried no bags, but he looked like a drifter. Three-day beard. Dirty blue jeans. A baseball cap with the Mack truck logo on the front. A denim jacket.

Galen, however, didn't seem to mind the man's appearance. He looked Byron up and down, as if measuring him for a suit, and said, "Get in. We'll give you a lift."

"Thank you."

The door slid open, and Byron climbed in, taking a seat behind Dolores, next to Jonathan. As soon as Lichen had the door closed, Stone had the van in gear and on the road again.

Galen turned around in the seat. "I'm George Galen," he said, then, pointing to the driver and the Healer behind him,

"These are my companions, Stone and Lichen. My other guests are Hal, Dolores, Nick, and Jonathan there beside you."

Byron gave a vague wave and smiled at everyone, not looking particularly comfortable with the crowd or the smell. "Nice to meet you," he said. Then he addressed Galen. "My car broke down, and I couldn't find a phone. Nothing's open at this hour."

"Your car?" Galen asked, as if he was surprised the man owned one.

"You probably passed it a mile or so back." he said. "I would've used my cell phone, but it ran out of juice. How's that for luck?"

"We have a phone back at the shelter," Galen said. "You're welcome to use that one."

"That's very kind. Thank you."

Dolores caught Stone, the driver, eyeing Byron through the rearview mirror with a look of suspicion, like he suspected him to be trouble.

After a long silence Byron said, "You're Healers, right?"

"That's right," said Galen.

"I've seen you around," said Byron. "You do a lot for the community. That's very commendable."

"We heal what needs mending," said Galen.

They passed two all-night gas stations, and Byron asked to be let out both times.

"Don't be silly," Galen said. "It's warmer at the shelter. You'll be much more comfortable there." When they left the Pacific Coast Highway and started driving up into the mountains, Dolores got nervous.

"Must be a pretty secluded shelter," Byron said. "I hope whoever I call can find it."

Galen said nothing. Nor was he whistling anymore.

After a half a dozen turns up unlit roads, the van pulled onto a gravel drive.

Finally, Dolores thought. Finally we're going to stop. This driveway can't be long.

But it *was* long. They drove for another ten minutes, twisting and turning, the tires grinding the gravel. Dolores was beyond nervous now. She was the only woman in a van of six men, more than a day's walk from the pier. She shouldn't have agreed to go. She should have stayed in the cold. This was too far away, too strange.

She gripped the tennis racket tucked in her bag between her feet.

She wanted to make a break for it, push Hal and Lichen out of the way, slide open the door, and jump.

"I want to get out," Nick said.

"No kidding," murmured Byron.

Galen said nothing.

Then the gravel road widened and they pulled up to a building. The driver stopped the van and Galen turned around to face them.

"Here we are," he said.

They all looked out the window. Dolores's heart sank. This was no shelter. And no home either.

She turned back and saw that Lichen was holding a gun, or something that looked like a gun. "Everybody out," he said.

Beside her, Nick began to cry.

2

RECRUIT

Lieutenant Colonel Frank Hartman stepped into the decontamination room, wearing his biocontainment suit and feeling his heart rate quicken. Despite having crossed this threshold hundreds of times before, Frank still occasionally felt the sickening knot of dread in his stomach or the quickening of his pulse as he prepared to enter Biosafety Level 4. It was a natural reaction. Level 4 was possibly the most dangerous man-made environment in all the world and certainly the most dangerous here at the United States Medical Research Institute of Infectious Diseases at Fort Detrick, Maryland. It was here that the military housed and studied the world's deadliest viruses, viruses like Ebola or Marburg, microscopic devils that had the tendency to turn one's innards into black gooey messes and for which there was no known cure or treatment.

Frank checked the air valve on his suit and took a few deep breaths of fresh oxygen.

The breathing calmed him, and the sound of his breaths echoed in his helmet as the doors closed behind him.

The decon room, no larger than an elevator, was the last wall of defense between Level 4 and happy-go-lucky taxpaying Americans. As the lights went out, Frank became very still. Tight beams of ultraviolet light emitted from the walls and scanned him for contaminants. He thought it a silly exercise to be scanned *before* entering Level 4 as well as after, but such was the military. Everything had its order and tradition, be it ass-backward or not.

The ultraviolet light dancing around him suddenly went out, and the bright fluorescent light above him illuminated.

A computerized female voice said, "Decontamination complete. Please enter your access code."

A row of numbers composed of light appeared on the wall.

Frank extended a gloved finger and entered a complex series of digits.

His yellow biosuit, which covered every inch of him, was made of a thick, puncture-resistant rubber that weighed heavily on his shoulders and looked about three sizes too big. A utility belt at his hip held several pouches and a holster sporting a shiny injection gun. The helmet had a single pane of Plexiglas across its front with a comlink just below Frank's mouth. The inside of the suit smelled strongly of baby powder.

"Welcome, Dr. Hartman," the computerized voice said. "You are cleared for entry."

Frank felt and heard the rush of air as the fans behind him turned on, blowing fiercely. The entry doors opened, and Frank stepped over the threshold and into Level 4. The fans were a precautionary measure, preventing airborne pathogens from escaping Level 4 during entry. Once the doors closed behind him, the fans slowed until all was silent.

Frank looked down the long empty corridor that stretched before him and felt the twinge of fear again, tickling at his spine. Two more breaths and all was well.

The floor, like the ceiling and walls, was a blinding spotless white, the one exception being the large red biohazard symbol painted on it at the entrance.

Frank waddled down the corridor. Moving in the suit, with its size and weight and rubberiness, was always awkward. Frank had made a joke once that researchers here looked like the offspring of an astronaut and a rubber duck.

He passed through another series of doors, each with its own security access, until he came to a room lined with glass holding cells.

The cells were four feet deep, four feet wide, and stretched floor to ceiling, like tall glass lockers. Inside each, suspended from the ceiling at eye level, was a cage. Inside each cage sat a small, bleary-eyed monkey. Frank approached the first cell and tapped the glass. At the sight of Frank, the monkey sprang to its feet and shook the cage bars violently.

"Well, aren't you a fireball this morning?" Frank said.

He turned to a computer terminal mounted on the wall and entered a command.

The monkey looked up as blue gas poured into the cell from an air vent in the ceiling.

The gas swirled and billowed into multiple tendrils of vapor as it slowly descended toward the cage.

The monkey, wide-eyed with terror, shook the bars again vigorously, screaming in a panicked frenzy.

Frank felt a pang of guilt. It wasn't often that he used animals as test subjects, but sometimes the occasion required it. When it did, the cold detachment necessary for such work somehow eluded him. He found himself liking the animals, giving them names, even—the cardinal sin of science.

"It's only a sedative," he said, annoyed for feeling the need to explain himself. "It's not going to kill you."

The monkey continued screaming.

"I can't have you biting me. If you'd keep your trap shut when I'm in there, we wouldn't have to do it this way."

The gas billowed into the animal's face.

After a moment, the monkey staggered, then slumped lazily to the cage floor, fast asleep.

Frank entered another command into the computer, and the ventilation fan stopped and spun in the opposite direction, sucking the gas back up into the air shaft. A loud buzzer followed, sounding an all clear, then the holding-cell door hissed open. Frank waddled inside, opened the cage, and clipped a heart monitor on one of the monkey's fingers. The monitor beeped, and a bead of light, bouncing up and down rhythmically, appeared on the LCD screen.

Good, he thought. Heart rate's normal.

He set the monitor aside and lifted the monkey's limp right arm. Then, being careful not to prick himself, he uncapped a needle, found a suitable vein, and took a small blood sample. When done, he dropped the used syringe into the biohazard chute at the back of the cell and slid the vial of blood into a pouch at his hip.

The monkey sighed quietly but didn't move.

Almost done, girl.

Frank removed the injection gun from his holster and turned off the safety. A vial of red serum sloshed inside the injection tube. He placed the tip of the gun against the monkey's thigh and squeezed the trigger. The serum shot into the monkey's leg. When the needle retracted, Frank holstered the gun and gathered his things.

"This could be your last dose, girl. If you keep getting better, I'll get you a really big banana."

He exited the holding cell and went through a series of doors until he reached the main lab and heart of Level 4. It was an expansive room, filled with humming diagnostic machines centered around a twelve-foot-tall electron microscope in the middle of the room.

Frank put the vial of monkey's blood into a glass containment box and vacuum-sealed the lid. Then he sat in front of the box and inserted his gloved hands into the gloves attached to the box. It was cumbersome working this way, gloves on top of gloves, but he couldn't risk contaminating the sample.

Carefully he uncapped the vial and, using an eyedropper,

placed a drop of blood onto a slide. A robotic arm whisked the slide away and slid it into the electron microscope.

Moments later, the electron micrograph appeared on the monitor.

It looked clean. There were no virions that Frank could see. The blood appeared completely virus free.

Frank knew better than to get too excited. The monkey was only a single subject. He couldn't be certain that it had been the red countervirus he had been administering that was responsible for eradicating the virus.

Still, after all the success he had had in eradicating the virus in petri dishes using the same red countervirus, Frank felt optimistic.

There was a beep in his headset, and a woman's voice sounded. "Dr. Hartman?"

Frank recognized the singsonginess of the voice at once and resisted the urge to sigh audibly. It was General Temin's secretary, and her calling meant only one thing.

"This is Dr. Hartman," he said.

"Your presence is requested in General Temin's office immediately," she said. The words came out of her so sweetly that it was almost as if she considered the message the best of news, as if Frank did nothing more than sit around all day idly waiting for the good general to bless him with his presence.

Rather than explain to her how incredibly inconvenient it would be for him to leave Level 4 after just entering it, not to mention all the time he would lose in having to disrobe from his biosuit, Frank thanked her politely and ended the conversation.

Twenty minutes later, he arrived at General Temin's office, showered and in full uniform. At thirty-nine, Frank was slim but toned, the result of adhering to the daily exercise regimen that had been drilled into him during officer's training: get up, run, swim, run some more, throw up maybe, shower, go to work.

His black hair was cropped short, graying slightly at the

temples. His jaw was square and clean shaven; his cheeks ruddy; his lips tight as if smiling were a pleasure they only rarely indulged in.

His khaki-brown uniform was well pressed and lightly adorned with a few colorful bars of achievement and rank over the pocket of his left breast. An officer's hat was tucked under his right arm, and his black shoes were polished to an impressive shine.

The secretary, wearing a uniform a little tighter than regulation would permit, didn't look up from her computer when he entered.

Frank drew closer and cleared his throat.

She stopped typing, lifted her eyes to him, and smiled warmly.

"Why, Dr. Hartman," she said, batting her eyelids, as if his presence somehow embarrassed her and yet was an unexpected surprise.

A true Southern belle, he thought. "General Temin asked to see me?" he said.

"And see you I shall," a gruff voice said behind him.

Frank felt a heavy hand on his shoulder and turned to look into the weathered and smiling face of Major General Ned Temin.

He was a round man, with the kind of gut that came from age and prolonged time behind a desk. His hair was white, heavily receded, and buzzed to a stubby shortness. His nose was wide and red, which, combined with the roundness and wrinkles of his face, made him look like W. C. Fields without the jaunty hat.

Despite the inconvenience of the visit, Frank couldn't help but smile. Temin was the kind of man who brightened a room just by being in it, laughing more perhaps than etiquette would allow, but never so much that anyone minded, since his laughter was so contagious and his demeanor always pleasant.

"You don't eat enough, Frank," he said, louder than

Frank thought necessary. "Look at you. You've lost five pounds since I saw you last."

"It's the long trek to your office, sir," Frank said. "I think it's the farthest room from Level 4."

Temin laughed. "Bet your butt it is. I stay as far away as possible. I'm not letting one of those viruses in here to shrivel *my* pod."

Frank glanced surreptitiously at the secretary, who was typing again and didn't look up, clearly accustomed to Temin's choice vocabulary.

"You asked to see me, sir? It sounded urgent."

Temin put an arm around Frank's shoulders and led him toward the conference room. "You got company." He opened the door and led Frank inside, not taking a moment to warn Frank who that company might be. "Gentlemen, I'd like you to meet our leading virologist, Lieutenant Colonel Frank Hartman. He's the man who's got that virus of yours against the ropes, so to speak."

Two conservative-looking men in dark suits stood and smiled cordially.

BHA, Frank thought. Here for a status report.

The taller of the two men, black, handsome, and broad shouldered, extended a hand.

"Oh, I wouldn't shake Frank's hand just yet," Temin said. "He's been down in Level 4 and doesn't wash up too thoroughly."

There was an awkward pause as the man looked questioningly at Frank's hand.

Temin chuckled.

"He's joking," Frank said, taking the man's hand and shaking it.

The man smiled. "Yes, General Temin is quite the prankster. I should have known better. It's an honor, Dr. Hartman. I'm Agent Tyrese Riggs of the Biohazard Agency, and this is my associate, Agent Carter."

Frank noticed that they both carried sidearms beneath

their suit coats. Carter was clearly the younger of the two, in his early thirties perhaps, thin and blond, wearing fashionable black-rimmed glasses over a sharply angled nose. To Frank, their suits seemed too stylish for federal agents, as if they had just come from an Armani photo shoot. Then he remembered that the headquarters of the Biohazard Agency was in Los Angeles, and perhaps LA feds didn't dress like Washington feds, preferring a touch of Hollywood in their wardrobes.

At Temin's suggestion, everyone sat at the conference table.

"Your reputation precedes you, Doctor," Agent Riggs said. "Your accomplishments in antiviral research make you a leader in your field."

"Research?" Temin said with a laugh. "Hell, I wouldn't call it research. Frank here is a virus killer."

"So it would seem," said Riggs, smiling. "We feel fortunate that you agreed to examine the virus we submitted several months ago."

Several months was actually five months. Frank had received the sample of the virus in a containment box with no explanation as to its origins except that it came from the Biohazard Agency and was to be considered extremely virulent. Initial tests in Level 4 had confirmed that fact. Rapid cell degeneration. Aggressive spreading. This was an ugly virus, as malignant and as dangerous as anything Frank had ever encountered.

Since being given it, he had worked tirelessly to develop a countervirus that could annihilate the virus on contact. He had done so, or at least, he hoped he had done so. Whether it would prove effective among the monkeys, whom he had intentionally infected with small doses of the virus, was yet to be seen.

Agent Riggs opened a manilla folder and casually flipped through it. "We've reviewed the results of your initial lab tests, Doctor, and we think this countervirus you've developed looks very promising."

"Thank you, gentlemen," Frank said, "but I would remind you that the results of those tests are not necessarily an assurance that the countervirus will be effective on humans. In the early trials I merely eradicated small samples of the virus in petri dishes. I'm sure I need not tell you that achieving the same degree of eradication in a living animal is a different matter altogether."

"And yet you've already moved on to that phase, I hear," Riggs said.

Frank was surprised. He hadn't yet submitted a report on the monkeys; the BHA was apparently keeping closer tabs than he had thought.

"Yes, but I've only recently begun testing," he said. "It's too early to make any definitive conclusions."

"What are your preliminary findings?" Riggs said.

"Positive as well. But trust me, gentlemen, we're still six months away from knowing if this is something we could eventually move to clinical trials."

"I'm afraid we don't have six months, Doctor," said Riggs. "Time is against us here."

Frank didn't know how to respond, so he merely folded his hands in front of him and waited.

"What else can you tell us about the virus?" Riggs said, still all business.

"What else do you want to know?" Frank said, not particularly appreciating being put on the spot. If they had given him some time to prepare his notes, maybe he could have thrown together a formal presentation.

"Anything you've discovered in your research would be helpful," Riggs said.

Frank sat forward and shrugged. "All right. The virus is a highly aggressive, highly contagious retroviral vector with a rather brief incubation period. As far as how dangerous it is, only Ebola rivals it in virulence. However, unlike Ebola, it moves fast—inconceivably fast, really. Should you be infected, you'd have about two to seven minutes before it kills you."

The agents looked unsurprised by this.

Temin, however, swore. "You boys know how to find a virus, don't you?" He looked back at Frank, pulling at his collar. "And you got this ... uh ... thing sealed tight down in Level 4, Frank?"

"Safely contained, sir," Frank said.

"And this countervirus you've developed," said Riggs, "how is it that it's able to stop the virus?"

"It's an antiviral compound that includes a benign strain of the virus, allowing it to function as both a vaccine and a treatment."

"Impressive," Riggs said, nodding.

"Theoretically," Frank said quickly. "Again, this hasn't been tested on human subjects."

"Still," Riggs said, examining the file again. "This is quite a feat in a relatively brief amount of time."

"I'm telling you, boys," Temin said, laughing and slapping the table. "A virus killer. You couldn't have picked a better man."

"Indeed," said Riggs, smiling along with him.

"Where did you find it?" Frank asked suddenly.

The broad smile across Riggs's face slowly waned.

"It was engineered, obviously," said Frank. "A retroviral vector doesn't simply spring from the jungles of Africa. Someone made it. Who?"

Agents Carter and Riggs exchanged glances during the silence that followed.

Frank pressed on. "With all due respect, gentlemen, you've been jerking me around ever since you politely dropped off the sample. You give me very little preliminary data. You don't tell how the sample came into your possession, nothing that could have directed my research. Then you ignore my repeated requests for additional intelligence. This seems counterproductive to me. The more I know about the virus, the better able I am to combat it."

There was a moment's silence, then Riggs shifted uncomfortably in his seat.

"Is it a weapon?" Frank said.

Temin's brow wrinkled, and he looked scowlingly at the agents. "Weapon?"

"Retroviral vectors have two purposes, General," said Frank. "They're either medicinal or a very cruel biological weapon."

"What the hell is he talking about?" Temin said to the agents. He pointed an accusatory index finger. "Have you boys been harboring a bioweapon in this facility here without my knowledge? Because if so, so help me—"

"It's not a weapon, sir," Riggs said.

"No?" Temin said, his index finger frozen in air, his expression both deflated and confused.

"Our purpose here today, sir," said Riggs, "is not to give an intelligence briefing. Much of what we know about the virus is still highly classified."

"Classified?" Temin said, throwing a hand up. "Hell, I got more clearance than most of Congress."

"I'm sure you do, sir," said Riggs. "But our visit today concerns Dr. Hartman and his future role in our fight against V16."

"V16?" said Frank.

"The name we've given the virus," said Riggs.

"You say my *future* role," Frank said. "You sound as if it's larger than perhaps I am aware."

Agent Riggs looked knowingly at General Temin, who grunted and folded his arms in an obvious show of disagreement.

Frank caught Temin's eye, but the general quickly looked away.

Agent Riggs leaned forward in his chair and pressed his hands together as if in prayer. "Dr. Hartman, you have my apologies if our secrecy on this matter has in any way hindered your research. The fact remains, however, that, despite our concealment, you've discovered how to treat V16. That makes you a very important person to us." He looked down at the folder a moment and cleared his throat. "As

I'm sure you're aware, Dr. Hartman, this facility is a critical component of the US Biological Defense Program. General Temin here works closely with the Defense Department's interagency counterterrorism effort, of which our agency, the BHA, is also engaged. When the need arises, and with the approval of the Defense Department, we can recruit from this facility."

Frank glanced at General Temin, who seemed to be expecting this, then turned back to the agents. "Are you implying, Agent Riggs, that you're here to inform me of my recruitment into the BHA?"

"Temporarily, yes. We wouldn't be asking for your help, Doctor, if we didn't believe American lives were at stake. V16 is a serious threat. And currently your countervirus is the only leg we have to stand on."

Temin spoke next. "I got the call this morning, Frank. This is straight from the top. I got no pull on this one."

Frank wasn't too surprised. Interagency assignments like this were common. CIA. FBI. NIH. Fellow researchers left all the time, some for months on end. It was part of the job. Some even jumped at the opportunity, seeing it as temporary escape from the rigor of military service. Extended shore leave, they called it.

Riggs said, "We ask that you bring with you all existing samples of the countervirus as well as all data relative to its creation."

Frank nodded. He understood clear and simple. He wasn't being asked. Going with the BHA was an order, and if General Temin was truly as powerless as he had said, it would do Frank little good to argue. "I see," he said. "Well, I suppose I should pack, then. I have time for that, I assume?"

Riggs smiled. "Our plane leaves in the morning. But you need not pack much, Dr. Hartman. The BHA will see to it that all of your needs are met."

There was something about the plasticity of Riggs's smile that made Frank doubt him. He seemed suddenly like a greasy car salesman who knew more than he was letting on. Frank looked at Agent Carter, who, behind his stylish glasses, only stared back with a blank expression. General Temin, still with arms folded, looked angrily defeated. All traces of his characteristic cheerfulness had evaporated. Frank pursed his lips and drummed his fingers on the table. The whole situation unnerved him. The secrecy. The virulence of the virus. The flashy suits. The rush to action. It all felt slightly off, like a distant alarm ringing in his head. Just as he decided to voice his concerns, Agents Riggs and Carter rose, said their good-byes, and told him where to report in the morning.

Then they were gone.

"Don't let them screw you," Temin said with brash finality as he got up and left the conference room. "Suits like that will always screw you."

Frank sat there alone a long moment, feeling as if the screwing had already begun.

3
TRANSPLANT

Dr. Monica Owens realized she was a bad parent six years after becoming one. The thought had been nagging at her conscience for years, but the truth and weight of it didn't sink in and take root in her mind until she rose early one morning, went down to the kitchen, and tried to make pancakes for her son Wyatt.

I can do this, she told herself, scanning the instructions on the back of the pancake box and feeling overly confident. If I can perform a quadruple bypass, I can certainly whip up a few pancakes.

She set the box aside and began looking for a frying pan.

At forty, Monica still looked as young as some of the residents who shadowed her at the hospital. Many of her patients, mostly the bawdy older men, took great pleasure in telling her how attractive she was and how if anyone was going to see them naked on the operating table, it might as well be her. It was her eyes they talked about most, those strikingly green eyes, followed by her brown hair, which extended to her shoulders in layers and curled slightly upward at the tips. Her face, free of makeup—because her father had told her as a teenager that she didn't need it—was narrow, angular, and spotted lightly with freckles. She wore black slacks, a white cotton blouse, perfect for the perpetual spring of Los Angeles, and a gray pair of running shoes.

Most of the cabinets now stood open. It stung Monica slightly to be reminded how unfamiliar she was with her own kitchen, but soon the right cabinet was found and the frying pan secured. She placed it on the stove and turned the dial to what she guessed would be an appropriate setting.

Next came the mixing bowl.

She found that rather quickly, but couldn't find a whisk, so she settled for a fork. After five minutes of stirring, she convinced herself that the batter was *supposed* to be lumpy and poured the first pancake into the pan.

Several minutes later she was fanning the smoke away and wondering how something so brown and so liquid could have gotten so black and so hard so quickly.

"What's that weird smell?" Wyatt said, crinkling his nose as he came into the kitchen.

"Have a seat, Wyatt, Mom stayed home and made pancakes for you."

He climbed up into a seat at the table.

He was short for a six-year-old, but Monica didn't worry. Boys sprouted at the most random of ages. His sandy blond hair, still wet from the shower, hung limply across his forehead. He wore a pair of dark blue cargo pants with far too many zippers and pockets on the sides and a yellow T-shirt Monica didn't recognize.

She scooped the pancake up with the spatula and laid it deftly on Wyatt's plate. She might not know how to cook, but she was always deft.

"This is burnt, Mom," he said.

"It got a little dark on one side. But the other side is fine."

"I can't eat just one side of the pancake, Mom. Where's Rosa?"

The question she didn't want to hear and didn't want to answer. Rosa was Wyatt's nanny. A better nanny the world had never known. Despite a weak grasp of the English language, Rosa seemed to have ESP at times, knowing precisely what Wyatt wanted or needed and having it ready for him before he even asked for it—not to the point of spoiling him, but in a way that made him feel involved and special. "I told her I was fixing your breakfast this morning," said Monica. "I think she's doing the laundry right now."

As if on cue, Rosa came into the kitchen, carrying dishcloths and dish towels for the linen cabinet.

"Rosa!" said Wyatt. "Buenos días! Mom burnt the pancakes."

Monica playfully shook a finger at him. "Hey, be grateful I only burned one side."

Wyatt grinned and took a big, drippy, syrupy bite. Immediately his face went sour. "This pancake is weird. It's like there's dust in it."

"Dust?"

"Dry places. Uck."

Before Monica could stop him, he spat a half-chewed mouthful back onto his plate.

Monica's shoulders sunk. "Well, so much for that."

"I make him eggs?" said Rosa. "He likes the scramble egg."

A moment passed before Monica said, "Yes, thank you."

Rosa must have understood or sensed something of how bad Monica felt. Because she reached over and patted Monica on the forearm—not condescendingly, but kindly, reassuringly—and said, "Oh, no thank me, Señora Owens, is my *job*. I should be thank you. If you no give me the grocery money, we would have no eggs and Wyatt go school hungry." She smiled. "And you have nice frying pan, good stove—easy to do right because you have everything ready."

Monica nodded. She would have answered, but as she was about to speak, she could feel in her throat that it would come out as a sob.

Again, Rosa apparently sensed not only what Monica felt, but why.

"You are *good* mother, Señora Owens, very good. Wyatt is lucky little boy to have mother like you."

Monica wanted to say, Yes, what a fine mother I am for having a frying pan I can hardly find myself.

Soon Wyatt was eating a plate of scrambled eggs with shredded cheddar cheese on top. Just like he liked it. Cooked by Rosa, of course.

"Just so you know, Wyatt," Monica said, "I am secretly an excellent cook. I used to cook all the time for your dad."

"Maybe that's why he left," said Wyatt.

The words froze her to the heart.

Rosa, too, understood what this meant. She was already washing the frying pan, but she stopped at once and turned to look at Wyatt, probably unsure whether it was her place to rebuke him when his mother was present.

Only Wyatt was clueless. He turned around, grinning. He must have thought he had made a joke.

Of course he saw at once that he had made a mistake, from the look on Monica's and Rosa's faces.

"I didn't mean . . . I was just—"

"You were just joking," said Monica. "I understand that. But your father and I got a divorce. That's why he left."

"I know," said Wyatt. "He told me that it wasn't your fault. Nobody's fault."

Nobody's fault—yeah, the guy who had a mistress for the whole last year of our supposed marriage, he *would* say that it was "nobody's fault." But Wyatt couldn't know that everything he said was only making it worse. Besides, it was the parents' job to shield the child, not the other way around.

"Oh, Wyatt, it probably *was* my cooking. At least *you* had the sense to spit it out!" Then she tickled him and he laughed.

He was still cheerful later at the door as he got ready to

set out with Rosa, who walked with him the few blocks to school. Monica helped him on with his jacket—so small a thing, his jacket, and yet so much bigger than his clothes used to be—and gave him a hug and a kiss.

Then Wyatt faced Rosa and the two of them clasped hands and bowed their heads, as if in prayer, but not saying anything aloud.

Monica had no idea they did this. And her puzzlement must have shown on her face, because Rosa looked a little embarrassed afterward, and Wyatt looked at her and said, "Rosa says a prayer about me, and I say, God bless Mom and Dad and Rosa, and keep us all safe. Only I just say it in my head."

"Well, that's . . . very nice," said Monica. She didn't mind at all. It was a good thing for them to have that custom. And if Monica had her doubts about God, she also had doubts about her doubts . . . it wasn't as if she knew there *wasn't* a God, either. And Rosa wasn't having him do anything particularly Catholic, like praying to a saint or fingering a rosary, anything Monica would disapprove of. And it was obviously a ritual that meant something important to Wyatt.

If I had been home, Monica thought, I wouldn't have done *that*. And yet, it was clearly something Wyatt needed before he went to school. Rosa had been the one to see that need and devise a way to satisfy it. Just as she had been the one to cook breakfast. The breakfast that Wyatt preferred.

Monica was *glad* that Wyatt had Rosa. So glad that she could hardly drive up the PCH to the clinic for the tears that kept clouding her eyes. Stupid, irrational tears.

She was actually early to the clinic. So her first scheduled appointment wasn't for a while yet.

"Good morning, Dr. Owens."

Monica looked at the receptionist. It was the new one. The bubbly one. What was her name? Kathy? Katie? "Good morning. Is Dr. Mankewitz in yet?"

"Dr. Mankewitz began his vacation today," she said, giggling. "Looks like it's just you and me today."

Monica smiled. Lucky me. "I'll be in my office. Let me know as soon as my first appointment arrives."

"Actually, he's already here," the receptionist said, handing Monica a folder.

"I didn't see anyone in the lobby."

"He insisted on waiting in a room. I tried to explain our policy, but he said he needed a place to lie down." She shrugged. "He's in room two."

Monica quickly opened the folder and headed down the hall—she'd lecture the receptionist on letting patients in early later. As she turned the corner and approached room two, however, she stopped in her tracks. The name on the patient questionnaire she was holding said Mickey Mantle. She checked the file tab: Mickey Mantle. Was this someone's idea of a joke or a legitimate coincidence? She quickly scanned the rest of the file and saw that Mantle, or whoever he was, was a new patient and had given them very little information. No address. No contact information. Even his age was a mystery. In the designated box he had written, "old enough."

Monica reached the door and opened it. Mantle wasn't lying down. He was at the window, tapping the glass. "Mr. Mantle?" Monica said.

He looked at her and smiled warmly. "You have hummingbirds."

He was a rather fit-looking man in his late sixties. Thick white hair, trim white beard, and he wore a conservative gray suit with a red handkerchief in the breast pocket and matching red necktie.

"Yes, I put those feeders in myself," she said.

He tapped the window again. "Fascinating creatures."

"The receptionist said you wanted to lie down. Are you feeling ill, Mr. Mantle?"

"Galen," he said, turning to face her again. "George Galen. Pleased to make your acquaintance." He took her hand and shook it vigorously. "I'm not in the habit of giving receptionists my real name. I hope I didn't startle you." Then he chuckled softly as if it had all been done in good humor.

Monica grinned, not sure how to take it all. "I see. All right. Are you feeling ill, Mr. Galen?"

"Me? No no no no. No, I'm fine. Fine. Fit as a fiddle. At least, I hope so." Then he patted his stomach like Santa Claus.

Or maybe Monica only thought that because he looked like Santa Claus. Only thinner. "Well, I hope that's true," she said. "I'm Dr. Owens."

"Oh, I know who you are, Doctor. I've researched your career extensively."

"Really?"

"Yes, and you've got quite the impressive résumé, too. Top of your class at Stanford. Top of your class at Duke Medical. The highest evaluations during your residency and cardiothoracic training. A staff position at the Heart Institute at St. John's Health Center here in Santa Monica. Then a director's position, which you resigned after your divorce. And now you're here, in one of the smallest but most respected cardiology clinics in Southern California."

"Wow. I don't know if I should be frightened or flattered."

"Flattered. I value my heart, Dr. Owens. If someone's going to be tinkering with it, I might as well get the best." Then he smiled and sat down on the edge of the examining table.

"Well, hopefully no one will need to tinker with your heart at all, Mr. Galen. If you're as fit as you say you are, you won't need my help."

"Oh, I need your help. I'm sure of that."

Monica tucked the file under her arm. "All right. What seems to be the problem?"

"I need a heart transplant."

Monica raised an eyebrow. "A heart transplant?" Galen

had said it as calmly as if he were ordering a glass of water. "That's a pretty severe diagnosis, Mr. Galen. Normally a transplant is a last-resort procedure. It's a very risky operation. If you're fit as you say you are, I'd strongly advise against it."

He smiled again. "Oh, it's not for me. It involves me, yes. But the transplant is for someone else. I'm just the donor."

"I see." Monica knew where this conversation was going. Anyone who needed a new heart was placed on a special waiting list. A long waiting list. In fact, last year nearly eight hundred men, women, and children in America had died while waiting for a suitable donor heart.

And the worst part of Monica's job, the most gut-wrenching, painful experiences of her life, were the moments in which she had to tell a patient and his or her family that a heart would not likely be found in time. There was always hope, yes. But at this point, hope was slim.

The reaction was always the same: tears, grief, confusion, anger. Why wasn't the hospital doing more? We've waited so long, why hasn't one come through yet? You mean you're just going to do nothing?

Then the anger passes. And in its place comes desperation. Like the time last year when the patient's sister cornered Monica at the hospital. "Take mine," she had said. "I want you to take my heart and put it in my sister. We have the same blood type. We come from the same parents. Her body won't reject it. She can have it. I want her to have it. Please, I beg you to take it." And then Monica cried, just embraced that woman and cried like a baby. Because they both knew she couldn't do it. She couldn't kill one person to give life to another.

And now here was this old man, sitting on her examination table, asking her to take his heart out. Who was it for? His wife? His son? A lifelong friend, perhaps?

"Mr. Galen, I'm truly sorry for your loss. I really am.

But I cannot take the heart of a living person and put it into someone else. By doing so I'd forfeit my right to practice medicine and subject myself to severe criminal prosecution. It's against the law."

Galen didn't flinch. "I thought you'd say that. I anticipated it, in fact. And I respect your integrity. I really do. It's one of the reasons why I chose you in the first place. You're a kindhearted woman."

Monica didn't know how to respond, so she simply nodded. At that point she expected Galen to stand up, express thanks for her time, and leave. But he didn't. He just sat there, staring at her.

"Is there anything else I can do for you?" she asked.

"I'm a very determined man, Dr. Owens. And I value my life greatly. I wouldn't be asking you to do this if I didn't think it would help me and all of mankind."

Help mankind? Suddenly Monica felt uncomfortable.

"You may think I'm incredibly self-centered by saying so," he said, "but I'm a very important person, Doctor. The preservation of my life is my highest priority."

Monica nodded. "Mr. Galen, I don't mean to sound condescending, but donating your heart will not preserve your life."

Galen chuckled. "You think I'm crazy, don't you? I can see it in your eyes. You're looking at me and thinking, This old man has got to be sniffing gas fumes. But don't worry, Doctor, I won't hold it against you. If I were in your shoes, I'd think I was crazy too." He hopped down. "That's why you have to see everything for yourself. Unless I show you, you'll never believe it. Being a doctor, I think you'll appreciate what I'm doing." He opened the door and waited for her.

Monica stood there. "I don't understand. You want me to come with you?"

"Of course. I have a car waiting."

For a moment Monica was speechless. This man really was crazy. "Mr. Galen, I can't go anywhere with you. I have other patients to see, other appointments. I have to stay here. It's my job. But I will happily recommend another doctor." She pulled out her prescription pad and started writing. "He's a friend of mine. I'm sure he'd be very interested in talking with you and learning more about whatever work you're doing. This is his office number. You can tell him I sent you." She tore off the paper and handed it to him.

He looked at it. "Let me guess, a shrink?"

She smiled politely.

Galen folded the paper slowly. "Dr. Owens, I'm a civil human being. I respect the mind and talents of intelligent people like yourself. I know you only have my best interests in mind. So I won't get annoyed. But you should understand that my asking you to accompany me is not an invitation."

Monica stiffened. He was threatening her. And what was worse, he was blocking the only exit. I have to get out, she thought. I shouldn't be alone with this man. He's obviously disturbed.

"I see," she said. "Forgive me if I gave offense. It was not my intention. Allow me to speak with the receptionist and see if I can cancel the rest of my appointments."

"That won't be necessary," he said.

"I'd hate to leave my patients waiting. Now if you'll excuse me." She moved toward the door, and instead of trying to stop her, Galen stepped out of the way. She hurried down the hall and was looking over her shoulder at him when she turned the corner and bounced off something. A man. A very large man. Abnormally large. Built like an ox, wearing all black. He looked down at Monica but didn't move.

"This is my associate, Stone," said Galen, moving down the hall toward Monica and introducing her to the giant as casually as if they were at a dinner party. "He won't harm you."

Monica backed away from Stone, her heart hammering.

"We're not here to frighten you," Galen said. "I'm only asking you to do what you do every day of your life."

Monica looked past Stone and saw the receptionist lying on the floor, not moving.

"What did you do to her?"

"A mild narcotic," said Galen. "She's sleeping. She's not hurt. In fact, when she wakes up, she won't even remember having fallen asleep. Or having talked to me. Or having seen you. Her memories of the last few hours will simply be absent from her mind. So rather than be alarmed, she'll feel right as rain. And instead of notifying the authorities, she'll go about her business same as always. Because in her mind, you never came into work today. And if we're all adults about this, no one will get hurt. No one but me, that is."

Monica saw the used syringe in Stone's hand and backed away from him until she reached the wall. "Stay away from me," she said.

Galen held his hands up, palms out, in a calming gesture. "You're not in danger, Doctor," he said. "I only ask for your cooperation. We will not harm you. I only need your talent for a very important procedure. One that will, if effective, revolutionize medicine. I'm giving you the opportunity of a lifetime here, Doctor. Trust me. With my help, you can cement your name in the history books."

Monica looked at them both. She was still terrified, but they weren't crowding her. They were giving her space. They were letting her think. "If I say no?" she said.

Galen frowned. "I'm not a violent man, Doctor Owens. But the work I'm doing is invaluable. So I won't allow a few obstinate people, including yourself, to get in the way of my success."

Monica wanted to cry. Her chest felt constricted. She wanted to speak, but fear held her tongue.

"If I can't persuade you," said Galen, "then perhaps someone else can." He flipped open a cell phone and dialed. "Put him on," he said presently. Then he handed the cell phone to Monica.

She put it to her ear. "Hello?" she said reluctantly.

"Mommy?" the voice said.

Monica's heart skipped a beat. It was Wyatt. And he sounded very afraid.

4
COUNTERVIRUS

A jeep picked up Frank in the morning and drove him to the airfield. The driver was a young, gangly enlisted man with a Southern accent and heels that clicked together when he saluted. A real by-the-booker. "Morning, sir. Help you with your bags, sir." He must have said *sir* ten times before the bags were loaded into the bed of the jeep and then another two hundred times, or so it seemed, during the brief drive.

"So where are you from?" Frank had asked.

"Yes, sir, I'm from Tennessee." He had his hands on the steering wheel in a ten-two position, arms stiff, eyes never leaving the road.

"Where were you stationed before Fort Detrick?"

"Yes, sir, I was at Fort Benning, sir."

And on and on with the *yes sir*s and the *no sir*s. Frank found it all slightly amusing and appreciated the momentary distraction from his concerns about his new assignment. Truth be told, he had slept little the night before. The more he considered a temporary stint with the BHA, the more uneasy he felt, even though he had no legitimate reason to feel that way.

The BHA, or Biohazard Agency, was a relatively new federal organization. Frank knew little about it, except that it had its origins in the Epidemic Intelligence Service, a group of agents from various federal agencies like the FBI and the Centers for Disease Control. Members of the EIS had prepared and trained for biological attacks and potential epidemics. But their involvement with the EIS had not been their full-time job. They still worked as doctors or field agents or virologists or whatever else they did to pay the bills. So the EIS was like an elite club of tactical white-collar do-gooders.

Two years ago, someone of rank and importance had decided that the duties of the EIS deserved more attention than that given by a few part-time volunteers. So the EIS was dissolved and the BHA was born. Agents of the BHA worked only for the BHA.

The jeep passed through all the necessary checkpoints until it reached the airfield and drove out onto the tarmac. Agents Riggs and Carter were waiting outside a small, sleek private jet beside two men in red jumpsuits.

Frank thanked the driver, which got him three more *sirs*, and got out of the jeep to greet Agents Riggs and Carter. The two men in jumpsuits busied themselves loading Frank's bags into the jet's cargo hold.

"Morning," Riggs said, extending a hand to Frank's and shaking it. "Good day for flying." He shielded his eyes from the morning sun and looked heavenward.

Frank was too riveted to the jet to follow Riggs's gaze. "We're flying in that?" he said, surpised. "That looks like a luxury aircraft, not some taped-up military bucket with wings."

Riggs laughed. "Gulfstream jet. I think you'll find it accommodating."

The men in jumpsuits lifted a large metal trunk out of the jeep.

"Careful with that one," Frank said.

"Are the samples of countervirus in it?" Riggs asked.

Frank nodded.

"Set that down a second," said Riggs.

The men complied, and Riggs unlatched the lid and opened it. Several dozen vials of countervirus were positioned in neat rows within thick black foam. Riggs removed one of the vials and held it up to the light. The sun's rays reflected off its edges. Riggs shook the vial gently, and the red serum inside sloshed. "So this is magic stuff, eh?"

"That's it," said Frank, "though how magical it is has yet to be determined."

"Why's it red?"

"It's a countervirus, meant to stop the spread of the virus, so I colored it to make it easy to identify."

Riggs nodded. "Red means stop."

"Right."

Riggs returned the vial to its hole in the foam and repeated Frank's instructions to the men in the jumpsuits. "Careful with this one."

They latched the lid closed, then loaded the trunk into the cargo hold.

"Let's hope it works," Riggs said.

Sensing the right moment to press for information, Frank said, "I hope that my coming with you makes me privy to certain intelligence. You're visibly concerned about the efficacy of the countervirus, and I'd like to know why."

Riggs nodded gravely, then gestured to the aircraft. "Let's have a seat."

Agent Carter led them up the few stairs and into the jet's interior. Frank had ridden first class on commercial airliners before—usually because of a fluke upgrade—but those experiences had done little to prepare him for what he faced now. The interior of the Gulfstream was like a posh waiting room, with a dozen or so wide leather recliners, lush carpet, and cherry wood trim. Several flat-screen computer monitors, on which the BHA insignia lazily bounced, hung from the ceiling or were suspended from the wall, designed to accommodate those sitting in the recliners. Frank was half tempted to remove his shoes.

He stepped inside and took a seat while Agent Riggs sealed the door and Carter spoke briefly with the pilot.

As the plane began taxiing to the runway, Riggs sat opposite Frank, facing him. Carter took a seat somewhere in the back, alone.

"You boys fly in style," said Frank, craning his neck around to get another look. "I dare say Uncle Sam loves the BHA more than he does the Army."

Riggs grinned and handed Frank a large envelope.

"What's this?" Frank said.

"All our secrets."

Frank pulled out a stack of documents, all rubber-stamped CLASSIFIED, as well as several eight-by-ten color photographs. The photo on top was so gruesome that Frank nearly dropped what he was holding.

It was a crime-scene photo. A close-up.

In it, a police officer lay dead on the asphalt, a pool of blood behind his head—or rather, what was left of his head. It looked as if his face had turned to putty and slid downward off his skull, the flesh still attached to him, but only casually so. Dark black splotches covered what was left of the skin.

Frank had seen this before, albeit not on a human. The first round of monkeys, which had received a hearty dose of the virus, experienced a similar reaction: rapid cell-degeneration, massive internal hemorrhaging, skin lesions, followed by death. It had been a frightening, gut-wrenching ordeal to witness. And this, a photograph, a mere visual record of a person having undergone the same ordeal, was just as nauseating.

White chalk outlined the corpse, and a folded index card beside the man gave the place and date: Long Beach, California, six months ago.

"We first discovered V16 about six months ago," said Riggs, "in an abandoned warehouse in Long Beach. A few shopkeepers near the warehouse heard some commotion inside it, thought it was being vandalized and called local police. Two cops showed up. One went inside, and two minutes later he came out screaming, his face in his hands. Moments later he was dead."

"How was he infected?" Frank asked, looking up from the photograph.

Riggs pointed to the other photos in the stack.

Frank flipped through them quickly. They had been taken inside a dark building, presumably the warehouse, and showed what looked like a laboratory, complete with beakers and burners and centrifuges and various diagnostic machines. Beside a computer terminal sat a white refrigerator-sized box.

"What's that?" Frank asked, pointing to it.

"A gene sequencer."

Frank's expression must have shown his surprise.

"Yes, not exactly what'd you expect to find in an abandoned warehouse in Long Beach." Riggs pointed to a photo of a row of test tubes. "We believe the police officer opened one of these test tubes and somehow spilled the contents on himself."

"The tube contained the virus?"

"We found thirty-one test tubes in all," said Riggs, "all carrying a different strain of the virus. Meaning they were intended for thirty-one different patients."

"Patients?"

"You said so yourself, Doctor. Retroviral vectors like this are either a weapon, or they're medicinal."

"This virus is medicinal?" Frank said.

"Yes. Or at least, that's what we *believe* it was designed for."

Frank gestured at one of the photos of the warehouse. "You're telling me this was some kind of secret gene-therapy clinic?"

"Back-alley cures, underground healings, call it what you will."

Gene therapy was a rather recent advance in medicine, Frank knew. The idea was simple. Genetic diseases were the result of either a defective or a missing gene in the DNA. Sickle-cell anemia, hemochromotosis, Parkinson's disease, and others were all the result of missing or defective genes. Gene therapy was simply a way of giving the right genes to the person who needed them. The trick was to figure out how to insert a cloned, healthy gene into the DNA where it belonged. Doctors could never operate on such a cellular level. But a virus could. That's what viruses did, after all; they penetrated cell walls and deposited genes, typically viral genes that made people sick. But if those viral genes could be removed and replaced with *good* genes, then the virus suddenly became a good kind of virus. A healing virus.

Frank rubbed his eyes. "You're telling me that someone figured out how to put cloned genes inside a retrovirus in the hopes of healing a genetic disease?"

"Hard to believe?"

Frank shrugged. "Well, considering that geneticists have been trying to accomplish this for decades with only marginal success, I find it rather amazing, if not amusing, that someone would be so bold as to believe that they could accomplish what science had not, using a few test tubes and a gene sequencer bought on eBay."

Riggs grinned. "When you put it that way, I suppose it does seem a little amusing."

Frank looked down at the photo of the police officer again and thought that it wasn't so amusing, after all.

By now, the plane had reached its cruising altitude.

Frank said, "So the gene therapy virus they created was a bust? I mean, what this guy found in the warehouse, this virus in the test tube, it was a failed attempt at a gene-therapy virus."

"Not necessarily," said Riggs. "Remember, a gene-therapy virus is only good for the person it was engineered for. It has genes he or she needs. You and I don't need those genes. Our bodies reject them."

Frank now understood. The police officer had found a

virus intended for someone else; his body did not need whatever genes it contained. But since the virus spread so quickly and so aggressively, his body didn't have time to combat the foreign gene, and his cells degenerated as quickly as if someone had thrown acid on his face.

"And you have no idea who was responsible for this?" Frank said. "Who the warehouse belongs to?"

"We didn't until forty-eight hours ago," Riggs said, swiveling in his chair so that he faced one of the computer monitors. He touched the screen and called up a program. A video began. It was news footage. A seven-story building in Los Angeles was burning. Firefighters were working to put out the flames, but much of the top floors had already been destroyed by fire.

Frank recognized the scene. "Gas leak, right?" he said. "I saw something about this building on CNN a few days ago."

"Gas had nothing to do with it," said Riggs. "That was what we fed the press. The truth is, the top floor of the building was another lab, just like the one we found in Long Beach six months ago."

"A gene-therapy lab?"

"Right. Only, whoever built it had apparently learned a lesson from the warehouse in Long Beach. This one was wired with explosives."

"Explosives? They blew up their own lab?"

"No. The building was an old abandoned apartment complex. It hadn't been used in years. The city had condemned it, and it was scheduled for demolition. Someone from the demolition crew was walking through the building, checking for squatters before they started tearing it down, and we think he might have triggered the explosives."

Three people had died in the blast, if Frank remembered correctly.

"And this fire told you who the lab belonged to?"

"Not entirely," said Riggs, "but we got a decent lead. The blast blew some debris from the building. Including this." He touched the screen, and an image replaced the video. It was of a large burned piece of dark fabric.

"What's that?" Frank asked.

"That, Dr. Hartman, is a black cape."

"You mean Zorro is . . . dead?" asked Frank.

Riggs sighed. "You know exactly what it means."

5
WYATT

Galen removed the blindfold from Monica's eyes, and she blinked, momentarily blinded by the light. As her eyes adjusted, she saw that they were standing inside what looked like a hospital corridor. There were patient rooms and a gurney pushed against the wall nearby. Galen stood beside Stone, facing Monica, his hands on his hips, grinning widely, like a little boy just let loose in a candy store.

"I apologize if the ride was at all inconvenient," he said, "but secrecy on this matter is paramount. I'm sure you understand."

Monica didn't understand. Whatever Galen was doing that he thought important enough to give up his heart, it was irrelevant to Monica. All that mattered was Wyatt. Nothing could distract her from that preoccupation. He had been taken. He was frightened. And he needed her.

They had driven her around for an hour and a half, taking far more twists and turns than she knew was necessary, in an effort to disorient her. She was certain they were outside Santa Monica, but she had no way of knowing where or how far away from the city. The incline of some of the roads led her to believe that they had driven up a mountain, or at least a foothill, probably north of Los Angeles, but she couldn't be certain.

They had left the receptionist sedated on the floor in the clinic, and Galen had assured Monica that one of his associates would remove her car from the parking lot, so as not to arouse any suspicion. The message he was giving her was clear. No would be coming for her or Wyatt.

Galen handed the blindfold to Stone, and Monica looked hard at the giant in an effort to memorize his face. When this was over and she found the police, she wanted to give them a perfect description of Galen and Stone.

Of course, Stone wouldn't be too hard to pick out of a lineup. He was at least a foot and a half taller than Galen and so bulky that if he walked onto any professional football field, he'd have a contract shoved in his face. His cropped silver hair suggested a man of older years, but his wrinkle-free, flawless skin made Monica think otherwise. He was a man without age. And his gray eyes never left her.

She stared him down, unblinking, wondering where this new courage had come from him and deciding to give credit to Wyatt.

"You don't like Stone, do you?" said Galen, that twinkle in his eye again.

She didn't. But saying so wouldn't help her position and certainly not help Wyatt, so she didn't answer.

What startled her, however, was that she saw no malice in Stone. His size was intimidating, yes, but in his gaze was a softness that made him look almost innocent, childlike even. It made her shudder.

Perhaps sensing that he had unnerved her, Stone bowed his head and said, "It is an honor and pleasure to meet the physician so fortunate and skilled as to treat the prophet."

Galen chuckled and waved Stone quiet. "Now, now, Stone, the good doctor doesn't know of such things yet." Then he winked at Monica.

"Where's my son?" she said.

Galen smiled. "You *are* a loving mother, Doctor. I have seen how much you dote on young Wyatt. That impresses me. Parents can become so busy these days. He's lucky to have you."

"Where is he?" she said.

"Patience, Doctor. Patience. Wyatt is well taken care of and unharmed. I'm not a cruel person. Children are precious and should be handled so. I only took Wyatt in the first place because I knew it absolutely necessary to win your compliance. I despised having to frighten him. That was not my intent. It should make you proud, however, to know that he has been the perfect guest and a most respectful gentleman. He's such a sweet boy, really. Few children are so well behaved, don't you think?"

It made Monica sick to hear Galen speak of Wyatt like this, as if Galen were some kind, elderly neighbor who had invited Wyatt over for cookies and milk.

"I want to see him," she said.

"And so you shall. But first things first." He removed a syringe from inside his suit coat and began filling it from a small vial of unmarked medicine.

Monica stiffened. "What is that?"

"A vaccine. And believe me. You want to take it."

"No. I'm certain I most definitely do not."

Galen smiled, carefully filling the syringe to the right dosage. "Wyatt didn't make a peep when we gave him his, Dr. Owens. Now come on, you're a doctor. Don't tell me you're afraid of needles."

Monica felt her face turn red hot with anger. "You gave that to my son?"

Galen patted the air with his hand. "Relax, relax. It's perfectly harmless. No side effects whatsoever. I told you, it's a vaccine. It protects you both from the virus. And since you'll be handling the virus, this is as good a protection as you're going to get. Now come on, roll up your sleeve."

Monica looked at Stone, who watched her without expression.

"I give you my word," said Galen. "No harm will come to you from it. You'll thank me later. Believe me."

Monica's mind raced. The needle could contain anything. Galen's word wasn't worth much.

"It's just a little shot, Dr. Owens. Nothing to it. Easy as cheesy. Take it and I'll bring you to Wyatt. You have my word on that as well."

Monica felt her muscles relax. She would do anything to be with Wyatt, even relent to whatever drug Galen had concocted. She exhaled deeply and rolled up her sleeve.

"That's the spirit. Now, you'll only feel a little sting."

Monica winced as the needle went in. Once the vaccine was expelled, Galen removed the needle and handed it to Stone, then wiped away a tiny drop of blood that formed over the needle prick using a handkerchief from his suit coat pocket. Then he unwrapped a Band-Aid and crudely stuck it over the spot on Monica's arm. "There we are. That wasn't so bad, was it?"

Monica readjusted her sleeve. "Now take me to Wyatt."

Galen pointed to a door not ten feet away. "He's right in there. But you only have a few minutes to visit, I'm afraid. We have so much work to do."

Monica stepped to the door cautiously, fearing some trick.

"Go on then," Galen said, shooing her forward. "He won't bite."

She pushed open the door. There was Wyatt, standing in the middle of the room alone. Monica rushed to him and took him into her arms.

"Mom!" he said, the tears coming already.

"I'm here, sweetheart. I'm here."

She heard the door click behind her, turned to look, and saw that Galen had shut it, giving them their privacy.

She immediately looked around the room for another exit or a window.

There wasn't one.

Wyatt buried his face into her shoulder and clutched her tightly. He was still wearing his coat, and his school backpack sat beside him on the floor, unopened.

"Did they hurt you?" she asked. "Are you hurt at all?"

He shook his head.

She took his face in her hands and examined it closely. There were no visible signs of mistreatment. No cuts, scrapes, bruises. "You sure you're not hurt?"

He nodded.

Monica sighed and pulled him to her again. He seemed so small and frail to her all of a sudden. His chest was so thin, his arms so short and weak. She had forgotten what a little boy he still was, how much growing up he had left to do. Why had she lost her cool with him so many times? Why had she allowed herself to ever raise her voice or send him to his room or refuse to allow him to watch TV when he wanted? He was only a child. And now, in a single morning, she had nearly lost him.

Without intending to, she broke into sobs.

Wyatt was startled. He stepped back and looked at her, his own tears stopped. "Mom, I'm okay. Really. I'm not hurt, see?" He wiped his cheeks and forced a smile.

Monica managed to smile back. She was kneeling, which made them equal in height. She pulled his forehead to hers and took a deep calming breath.

The sobs ceased. Her breathing slowed.

Be strong, Monica, she told herself. That's what Wyatt needs right now. Strength. He's pretending to be brave because he sees that you're distraught. He's trying to help you. You need to do the same. Focus.

She looked into his eyes and felt her muscles relax. "I'm just happy to see you," she said. "That's all. I was worried about you."

"I wasn't sure you were going to come," he said.

"Of course I was going to come."

"You sounded scared on the phone."

She glanced back at the door. "I was scared."

"You were?"

"Yes, very much."

"Me too."

She brushed the hair out of his eyes. "Well, I'm here now. And nothing is going to happen to you."

Wyatt smiled again, and this time it was genuine. They embraced.

"They gave me a shot," he said when they parted. "I told them I wasn't supposed to have any shots, not by anyone who wasn't a doctor, but they gave it to me anyway."

She put her hand on the side of his face. "It's okay," she said, not knowing if it was true. "I'm not angry. They gave me one, too. We're going to be fine."

He nodded his head, visibly relieved to have her reassure him.

"Do you want to talk about what happened?" she said.

He looked at the floor and spoke quietly. "We were walking to school, Rosa and me, and this van . . . it pulled over and . . ."

His bottom lip quivered.

Monica pulled him close again. "Shh. It's okay. We don't have to talk about it now if you don't want to. It's okay." Galen had recounted to Monica on the drive how his associates—which Monica interpreted to mean "large men like Stone"—had taken Wyatt that morning while Wyatt and Rosa were walking to school. But to hear Galen describe it, it had been a pleasant experience for everyone, and Wyatt had practically been a willing participant. Monica knew better.

She rubbed Wyatt's back and held him for a minute in silence. When they parted, he was calm again.

Monica looked around the room. It was clearly intended to resemble a child's bedroom. The walls were painted a pale blue. The twin bed in the corner had blankets and sheets printed with colorful dinosaurs. Wyatt loved dinosaurs. The rug on the floor was in the shape of the United States, with each of the state boundaries and capitals clearly marked. In the corner sat a widescreen, high-definition television, the kind that Monica had seen in electronic stores with ridiculous price tags. Three long cords twisted from the back of it and connected to a video-game console, which sat on the floor beside a precariously tall stack of un-opened video games.

"Did you play a game?" she asked, motioning toward the television.

"They have Potato Commandos," Wyatt said with a sniffle. He reached over and retrieved the case.

"You've been wanting this one," Monica said, flipping the box over and looking at the screen shots on the back. It was a silly game. Armed potatoes waddled around dirt fields shooting each other and exploding into mounds of mashed buttery carnage. It was far less violent than some of the other games Wyatt had asked for, and Monica had intended to get it for him for his birthday.

"Did you try it out?" she asked. The plastic wrapping had been removed and lay on the ground beside him.

"Where's Rosa?" he asked. Monica saw that he was twisting his right forefinger. It was a nervous habit he had.

"I don't know, sweetheart. I don't think they hurt her." She took his hands in hers.

"They gave her a shot," he said.

"Yes, they told me."

"Is she dead? Did the shot . . . kill her?" His voice was soft again, almost a whisper.

"No no no, Wyatt. The shot made her sleep. She's not dead. She's fine. She's probably awake by now." Monica didn't know if it was true, of course, but Galen had said as much, and right now it did Wyatt good to hear it.

"Is she going to come get us? I want to go home."

Monica put her hands on his arms. "I know you do, sweetheart, but—"

There was a knock on the door, and Galen poked his head in. "It's time, Doctor. We should get going."

Monica didn't look at him. Let him wait.

Galen disappeared into the corridor, and the door closed.

"Who's that?" Wyatt said.

"Nobody." She felt her voice getting high again. It did that when her throat tightened and she felt the urge to cry. She exhaled again and kept her cool. "I need to go right now but—"

"No." He clung to her, suddenly panicked.

She took his face in her hands again and spoke gently. "Wyatt, I need you to be brave. I need you to be strong. Can you do that for me? I have to go now, but I'm not leaving the building, all right? I'll be back very soon. Nothing is going to happen to you. I promise you."

"But I don't want to be by myself."

Monica's heart ached. "I'll be back to check on you soon. You can count on it."

"When can we leave, then? When can we go?"

"Soon. We're going to go soon. Here, let's give this Potato Commandos a whirl, what do you say?" She pushed the eject button and dropped the game disc into the slot. The machine took a moment to recognize the disc, and then the music began. A potato wearing an Uncle Sam costume pointed at the screen and called for recruits.

"I don't want to stay here. I want to go with you," Wyatt said.

"You can't, sweetheart. Besides, look at this great room. It's got dinosaurs, games, lots of cool stuff. We can't go without you trying some of it out, right?"

He didn't look persuaded.

"I'm coming back," she said. "I promise."

"Pinky swear?" he asked, holding up his little finger.

She hooked it into hers. "Pinky swear."

Outside in the corridor Galen greeted Monica happily. "Well, what do you think? Quite the little boy's room, isn't it? I designed it myself. At first, I had a big rocking horse brought in, but some of the men thought Wyatt might be a little old for that. I see now that they were right. He's very tall for his age. Fascinating games, though, don't you think?

Potatoes shooting potatoes. It's wonderfully immature, I know, but I can't help but laugh at it." He gave a giddy chuckle.

Monica felt sick again. She wanted nothing more than to go back into the room, grab Wyatt, and run. Stone was no longer around. She was alone now with Galen and felt fairly confident that she and Wyatt could outrun him.

But Stone couldn't be far. Plus she had no idea where she was exactly, which direction led to an exit, and how far away help might be once she found it. If she was in a hospital, maybe help was closer than she realized.

Then again, Galen had said he had designed the room for Wyatt himself. If it *was* a hospital, it wasn't a functioning one.

"Well, no need to diddle daddle," he said. "I imagine you'll want to meet them as soon as possible."

"Meet who?"

"Your patients," he said, rubbing his hands together. Then he turned on his heels and headed down the corridor. After a few steps he turned back and motioned for her to follow. "Well, come on then."

Monica took a final look at the door. Even with it closed she could hear the sounds of the video game. Wyatt was occupied. And for now, more importantly, he was safe. If she did what she was asked, he'd remain safe. Or so she hoped.

"Time is precious, Doctor," Galen said, walking backward and waving her to come quickly.

With no other option but to obey, Monica followed.

6
SCRIPTURE

The Gulfstream was somewhere over the Midwest, heading toward Los Angeles. By now, Frank felt even more unsettled by the image of the dead police officer and the rest of the V16 report. If what Agent Riggs said was true, these Healers, as they called themselves, had two identities. The public knew them as civil servants, a fringe religion based more on human kindness than on any specific theology. They wore black capes, gave out free food, and treated simple surface wounds with bandages and Neosporin. A walking first-aid kit with a meal to boot.

But in the shadows, unbeknownst to most, Healers had a much more complex agenda. There they built a virus in hopes of using it to heal those with genetic diseases.

"And the cape," Frank said, "this cape you found in the rubble after the explosion, that's the only bit of evidence you have to link these . . . Healers to the labs and the virus?"

"No," said Riggs. "We also found this." He opened a briefcase and removed a plastic evidence bag. Inside the bag was a badly burned book, no bigger than a thin paperback. He offered the bag to Frank.

"What is it?" Frank said.

"Open it."

Frank unsealed the plastic bag, removed the book, and examined its cover. It was made of brown suede and had been damaged by both fire and the water that had extinguished the fire. Frank checked the spine and gently wiped some of the soot off the cover in hopes of finding a title. There wasn't one.

Carefully, so as not to damage the pages any more than they already were, Frank opened the book. Most of the pages were burned at the corners or heavily wrinkled from water damage. At first Frank thought this a journal, since the text was handwritten instead of printed.

Then he found the illustrations.

Glued into the book at what seemed a random order were hand-drawn illustrations that reminded Frank of drawings found in monastic manuscripts. Except instead of featuring saints and angels or pious-looking cardinals, *these* drawings all depicted the same young, dark-haired man in a white shirt and red necktie. In the first illustrations the man had a hand extended, raising someone from a sickbed.

He was a Healer in the traditional sense.

One of the illustrations was much more difficult to decipher. In it, the young man in the red necktie stood in the center of the page, his hands pressed together as if in prayer. Held between his hands was a syringe with the needle pointed heavenward with gold rays of light shooting forth from the needle's tip. Flanking the man in the red necktie were two naked men nearly twice his size, their muscles massive, their necks thick. Rays of light from the syringe rested on selected parts of their body: their arms, their legs, their chest, their nose, their feet. Frank was clueless as to the drawing's meaning.

Continuing on, he flipped to the final illustration. It was wider than the others, filling two full pages and only slightly damaged by fire. Here there were five men in red neckties, all identical, like quintuplets, standing in a circle, arms linked. Their hands were pressed together in front of them. Light shot from their fingertips and converged into a single orb of golden light glowing above them. The caption at the bottom of the illustration read: *The Council of the Prophets.*

Frank looked up at Riggs, an eyebrow raised. "Council of the Prophets?"

Riggs shrugged. "Your guess is as good as ours. What *is* clear is that these Healers are a few doughnuts short of a dozen. If you think the illustrations are weird, you should try reading the text."

"What is it?" Frank said, turning the book over in his hands.

"As far as we can tell, it's the Healer Bible, so to speak. Their book of scripture."

Frank flipped back to the beginning. The title page had survived the fire.

THE BOOK OF BECOMING
Helping Man Reach His Full Potential
by George Galen

"George Galen," Frank said, looking up at Riggs with a tone of recognition. "Why is that name familiar to me?"

"He's a geneticist," said Riggs. "Something of a scientific legend, I'm told. Years ago he served as one of the principal researchers on the Human Genome Project."

Ah yes, thought Frank. Pompous George Galen. He had enjoyed a brief flash of fame following the completion of the Human Genome Project in 2003. What was supposed to have taken researchers fifteen years to complete, Galen and the others had done in thirteen, two years ahead of schedule. The project successfully identified the thirty thousand or so protein-coding genes in human DNA and determined the sequences of the three billion chemical base pairs that make up human DNA. The resulting database was to be used as the foundation for further genetic research and sequencing. All life sciences were affected by it: biology, medicine, even sociology to some extent. It was the supposed beginning of the genomic age.

But the project was not without its obstacles, Frank remembered. Galen clashed often with colleagues, arguing over what researchers called ELSI, or the ethical, legal, and social implications of the human genome. According to some accounts, one argument became so heated that Galen threw a chair, which struck and broke a research assistant's nose. No charges were ever filed, but Galen thereafter brought a contentious mood to the project. The *New York Post* even ran a cartoon in which two lab assistants were strangling each other with strands of DNA.

It was a public relations nightmare.

The situation only worsened when the project concluded and Galen returned to his post at the National Human Genome Research Institute (NHGRI), a small component of the National Institutes of Health (NIH). There Galen discovered that his annual budget was still a paltry two percent of the NIH's annual allotted spending.

Galen claimed he had been cheated. With the genome mapped, he was ready to translate the sequence information into potential health benefits. But to do so he needed money. And lots of it.

Rather than take his case to the NIH, however, Galen did the unthinkable: he hit the talk-show circuit, slandering the NIH and blaming it for all the medical maladies Galen believed would be cured should he be granted the proper resources and funding. What he said about the presidential administration and those in Congress responsible for allocating the NIH's funding was no less scathing.

It was professional suicide. Galen was thereafter ignored in all scientific circles. The NHGRI sent him packing and stripped him of all standing. Even universities, which had always extended an inviting hand, now turned a blind eye. *Time* magazine even ran a front cover article entitled "Fallen from Grace." After that, Galen slipped from the public radar.

That was seven or eight years ago.

"Galen is a Healer?" asked Frank.

"So it seems," said Riggs.

"I suppose that makes sense," said Frank. "If you're going to attempt to make a gene-therapy virus, and do what modern medicine has not yet achieved, you're going to need the talents of someone like George Galen."

"Yes," Riggs agreed.

"What about the guy in all the illustrations?" said Frank. "The guy with the tie."

Riggs shrugged. "Not sure. But whoever he is, Galen and the Healers consider him their prophet."

"And the Council of the Prophets? These men that look like five versions of the same guy. What about them?"

"Like I said, your guess is as good as ours. The book raised more questions than it answered. But it did help in one respect."

"And that is?"

Riggs gestured for the book, and Frank handed it to him.

"Here in the back." He flipped to the end of the book. "We found a list."

Frank looked. There, handwritten on the page, was a list of names and addresses. Some of the addresses were burned away or only partially legible, but some remained unscathed. Beside each name was written a genetic disease.

"Who are these people?" Frank asked.

"Patients," Riggs said. "People whom the Healers have treated with the virus."

Frank felt his stomach tighten. "What do you mean 'treated'? They were *given* the virus?"

"After we found the book—and remember this was all in the last forty-eight hours—we went to one of these addresses to talk to this person." He pointed to the first name on the list. "Patrick Caneer. Sickle-cell anemia."

"And?"

"And we found him, in bed, with an IV in his arm and

with several large sheets of plastic hanging from the ceiling in a circle around his bed. Like the boy in the bubble."

"A containment curtain?"

"A do-it-yourself containment curtain," Riggs said. "Healers had hung the plastic, given him the virus, and then told him to stay in bed for three days while the virus ran its course and cured his sickle-cell anemia."

Frank was momentarily dumbfounded. The audacity of a homemade curtain, the idea that a little tarp and some duct tape could keep a virus like V16 in check, made the hair on the back of his neck stand on end. Compared to all the many doors and precautions that existed in Biosafety Level 4, a few sheets of plastic was practically nothing.

"And when you found him, how was he?" Frank said.

"Scared out of his mind," said Riggs, "not because of the virus, but because he thought we were going to arrest him. Decent kid. In his early twenties."

"He wasn't harmed by the virus?"

"Remember, the virus can be engineered for a specific person. In this case, it had been engineered for Patrick Caneer. The strain of virus carried exactly what *he* needed, the genes to cure *his* sickle-cell. To everyone else, however—Patrick's family, his neighbors—the virus was a terrible threat. Lethal, even. Let's not forget our friend here." He tapped the image of the dead police officer. "And the Healers are obviously aware of the threat. Otherwise, they wouldn't bother to build a containment curtain. Patrick also informed us that the Healers explained to his family the need to steer clear of the kid while the virus ran its course."

Insane. Absolutely insane. So irresponsible in the handling of a lethal virus that it took Frank a second to gather his thoughts. "And when you found him," he said finally, "he was okay?"

"We went in in full biogear, contained the whole apartment. Then we took him to our infirmary. He's been there ever since. But that's not even the really bizarre part of the whole story. The bizarre part is this. According to tests we've conducted, he no longer has sickle-cell anemia."

Frank couldn't hide his surprise. "You mean . . . he's cured?"

"I mean he no longer has sickle-cell anemia. Whether it was the virus or not, I don't know. But the kid ain't sick with sickle-cell anymore. That much I *do* know."

Frank put a hand to his head. This wasn't making sense. A crazy religion, made up of bodybuilders, no less, had enlisted the help of a blacklisted geneticist and whipped up a gene-therapy virus that by one account, at least, might actually work.

"You're telling me this kid is in your infirmary right now?"

"Right now."

"And he still has the virus inside him?"

"That's what I'm telling you. And that's why we needed the countervirus you created immediately, whether it was fully tested or not. We have to get it in this kid, not to mention the other patients we've picked up from this list."

"The others?"

"There are eight names on this list. We've collected all eight of them. They've all been to our infirmary. All in the last forty-eight hours. And they're all waiting for you."

Frank sat forward in his seat. "You mean they all still have the virus in them, whatever strain they were given?"

"No," said Riggs. "Some of them were patients weeks ago—months ago, even."

"And they've been lying in bed in a containment curtain all this time?"

"No, they've been living their lives normally," Riggs said. "Better than normal, because they don't show any symptoms of the genetic disease they once had."

"So they've been healed?"

"So it seems."

Frank looked down at the list of names and then back

up at Agent Riggs. "But how are they able to move about and interact with people in the world if they have the virus in them?"

"That's just it," said Riggs. "They don't have the virus in them. Three days after giving someone the virus, Healers return and administer *their* version of a countervirus, which cleans the virus out of the person's system. They take down the plastic. The Healer leaves. And the person goes about his or her life again."

"So the Healers have a countervirus?"

"A version of one. Apparently. That's how they stop the virus in the people they treat. We, however, for the past six months, have only had a sample of the *virus*. We haven't had a countervirus. Now, thanks to you, we do."

"Maybe," said Frank.

"Don't say maybe," said Riggs. "We're counting on you."

Frank felt overwhelmed. "Okay. Let me get this straight. Healers walk into a person's apartment. They hang a bunch of plastic around the bed and put an IV in the person's arm."

"Right," said Riggs.

"Then they administer the virus."

"Which has been engineered for that person, so it helps them, not hurts them."

"Engineered for that person, yes," said Frank. "Then the Healer tells this patient that the Healer will return in three days to administer a countervirus and stop the treatment."

"You got it."

"And all this you've learned in the last forty-eight hours?"

Riggs handed the book back to Frank. "We have George Galen and his little book here to thank for that. Everything we've learned started there."

Frank leaned back and silently flipped through the book

again, this time paying attention to any legible text. One passage read:

Man has evolved into the captain of all living things, the product of time. And yet in his current state he is blind to his potential and enslaved to diseases that need not beset him. Only the Prophet can open him up and allow him to become something greater than himself.

The Prophet

This prophet, whoever he was, obviously thought very highly of himself. Here he was prophesying about his own future achievement: helping man reach his evolutionary potential.

Frank shook his head. How could George Galen, the author of this book and a genius by anyone's definition, believe this crap? How could he believe that such a prophet existed? Sure, Galen had run on hard times, but had his fall from fame been so severe that he had gone mental?

They landed at LAX and got into a government-issued town car and drove north on the 405. Frank's luggage and the case of countervirus were stored safely in the trunk of the car.

Frank sat in the back, staring down at the closed charred copy of the Healer book of scripture.

"If you know these Healers are responsible," he said, "why not hit the streets and arrest the first Healer you find, take him in for questioning?"

"We thought of that," Riggs said. "Unfortunately, Healers have all but vanished since the explosion, like they knew we were on to them. We've got the LAPD keeping an eye out for them, but as far we as we can tell, they've all gone back to whatever hole they crawled out of."

They took the Wilshire Boulevard exit and immediately came upon the Federal Building, a massive, white,

impenetrable-looking structure. They drove past the long
row of flagpoles out front and headed for the back parking lot.

In minutes they were walking through the building's
entrance in the rear, passing through a security check-
point designated for armed governmental employees.
Frank flashed the ID card Riggs had given him to the security guard and followed the two agents to the elevator.

As they waited for it to arrive, Frank realized that no
one else was approaching this elevator. The lobby was
fairly crowded with people, but everyone else used the elevators across the hall, the main elevators of the building,
the ones going up.

A chime sounded, and the elevator Frank and the agents
were waiting for opened. They stepped inside, and Carter
produced a key, inserted it into a hole, and turned. The
doors closed and the elevator descended.

"Welcome to the BHA, Dr. Hartman," Carter said with
a smile.

Frank looked at the console and saw that there were no
buttons for floors. Wherever they were going, there was
only one stop.

7

CORE

Galen led Monica down a series of corridors, talking constantly. Monica was doing her best to keep up, but the man had more energy than she'd expect of someone his age.

"You'll have to excuse the mess," he said, waving his arms vaguely in the air. "It's a work in progress. We plan on finishing all the construction eventually."

A long sheet of plastic hung across the hallway in front of them. They stepped through it, and Monica saw the mess to which he referred. This whole wing of the hospital, if it was indeed a hospital, was still under construction. Walls were unfinished. Electric sockets were open and unwired. Building supplies littered the floor: conduit, sheetrock, nails, buckets of plaster. Nor had any tile been laid. The floor was rough concrete.

"Watch your step," Galen said, leading her through the maze of hanging plastic sheets.

"I know it doesn't look like much now," he said, "but you should have seen it before we got here. Awful. Just awful. Graffiti, trash. Really disgusting. We've come a long way. And we're not normally this disorganized either. We wanted to have it all finished before you arrived, but we had an incident a few days ago, lost one of our labs, and we thought it safer to speed up the project. We stopped renovating out here and put all of the staff in the Core."

"Of course," Monica said, as if this were all to be expected.

In truth, she had no idea what he was talking about. But she didn't want to let on. The man was clearly unstable. Angering him with unwanted questions would only worsen her situation.

"Ah, here we are," he said, parting the last sheet and approaching a pair of doors.

He pulled one open and motioned her inside.

It was a vast room with vaulted ceilings. Blue lights hung along the walls and bathed everything in a deep blue hue. There were at least twenty people in white paper lab suits, moving about, looking into microscopes, sitting at computer terminals, labeling test tubes. Some looked up and noticed them, but most went about their business without paying them any attention.

Galen smiled wide. "Impressive, don't you think?"

Monica said what she thought he wanted to hear. "It's amazing."

He gave a soft laugh. "You're humoring me. Please, Doctor. You're safe now. You can speak your mind with confidence. I brought you in because I respect your opinion. What do you think?"

She looked around at the workers. "It's very . . . clean," she said finally.

He laughed heartily this time. "You amuse me, Dr. Owens. I suppose I can't expect you to know what we're doing here just by giving you a peek." He spread his arms wide. "This is the Core. It's where we work our magic, so to speak."

He lifted a test tube off one of the shelves and read the label. "Gary Miner. Santa Clarita, California. Thirty-six years old. Huntington's disease."

He handed it to her. She looked at the label. "What is it?"

"That, Dr. Owens, is Gary Miner, a young man with Huntington's disease."

Monica looked at the milky liquid inside the tube.

"Don't look so concerned, Dr. Owens. We didn't melt Mr. Miner down. What you're holding is a tissue culture, a sample of Mr. Miner's DNA. From the date on the side here I see that we extracted it only a week ago."

He took the sample from her and placed it back on the shelf. "Our sequencers here will identify the composition of his DNA and locate the faulty gene. Here, take a look." He took her hand and led her to a large boxy computer where several men stood working. His hand lightly tapped the side of the computer. "It may not look like much, but these models pack quite a punch."

He pointed to a video monitor, where four letters raced repeatedly across the screen in random order. *A, C, G, T.*

Monica understood what she was looking at. DNA was composed of four chemical components: adenine, cytosine, guanine, and thymine. Each of the letters on the screen corresponded to one of those components. The order of the letters as they appeared must be the order of the chemical components along a single strand of DNA.

"I see the wheels inside that head of yours turning, Dr. Owens."

"You're decoding someone's DNA."

He smiled. "At lightning speed. We have to dye the tissue sample prior to loading it into the sequencer. Each of the four base molecules reacts differently to the dye and turns a separate color. That's how the computer knows what it's looking at. The software then recognizes the colors of the sequence and, voila. Fascinating, don't you think?"

Monica nodded obediently.

Galen rubbed his chin and looked at the sequence thoughtfully. "Hm, let's see. It looks like we've got a female here. Red hair. Tall. A little on the heavy side . . . Oh no. Oh dear me. Poor girl." He looked at Monica with a frown. "She's got a bad liver," he said sadly.

Monica looked skeptical. "You know that just by looking at it?"

He laughed loudly again. "I can't fool you, can I, Doctor? I'm sorry. I couldn't resist. No, we can't tell all that by simply looking at the sequence. In fact, we can't tell much of anything from one segment. You see, about ninety-seven percent of it is fluff, or what we call non-coding DNA. Junk. It doesn't seem to do anything. It's just there. It's the same with your DNA as well, not just this sample. Most of it doesn't have any function at all. No, what we're looking for are those special sections that control and organize necessary human functions."

"Genes."

"Precisely. The genes. But did you know that only a few of our genes are unique? It's true. Ninety-nine-point-nine percent of your genes are exactly like mine. Most people don't know that, but it's a fact. Genetically, all humans are nearly identical. Just a few little specks of you *makes* you you. And only a few little specks of me *makes* me me. That difference could be minute, even down to a single letter in the code. We refer to them as SNPs, or snips. That's short for 'single nucleotide polymorphisms.' Many of these snips lead to genetic diseases. And if we can identify the snip as the source of the disease, we can replace it with a cloned, correct gene."

"Gene therapy."

Galen rubbed his hands together. "It's very exciting, isn't it? And it's not that difficult. The slightest alteration in someone's genetic sequence can make all the difference in the world."

"What are you looking for in this strand?" Monica said, surprised to find herself interested.

Galen conferred with one of the workers. "Sickle-cell anemia, he tells me. This is the sequence of a little girl named Kimberly. We're going to cure her if we can. And trust me, we can."

Monica didn't know what to think. The lab seemed legitimate. The gene sequencers looked real. The lab workers sounded competent. But this was Galen, a criminal, a crazy old man. Could any of this be believable if he was running the show?

She watched as Galen took a moment to speak to the workers manning the sequencer. He was kind to them, expressing gratitude for their hard work, patting them on the shoulder and telling them how fortunate he felt to have them involved. Monica could see how much his words meant to them, how they beamed with pride and valued his praise. He was more than the man in charge here. These people revered him.

There was a sudden commotion at the other end of the lab. Monica heard footsteps, shouting, breaking glass.

"Stop him!" someone shouted.

Suddenly a teenage boy appeared, running around the lab equipment, knocking over workers, bumping into tables, desperate to get away, and heading straight for the doors Monica and Galen had entered through. He wore hospital scrubs and had a tattoo on his neck.

"Jonathan!" Galen said. "What are you doing?"

Another man was chasing the boy, a large Healer like Stone. He stopped, aimed a handgun, and fired.

Monica screamed.

The dart struck Jonathan in the back of the neck just as he was approaching the doors. His body went limp immediately, and he fell forward onto the tile, sliding across it and crashing into the doors with a terrible thud.

Galen was furious. "Lichen! What the devil are you doing?"

Lichen lowered his gun, looking suddenly embarrassed.

Galen ran to Jonathan, who wasn't moving, and cradled

his head. "He could have fallen and broken his neck," he said. "A lot of good he'd do us then."

"He was trying to escape, sir," said Lichen.

"Escape where? Into the hallway? He's lucky you didn't shoot him in the eye." He waved Monica over. "Doctor, if you will."

She approached reluctantly. Lichen stood near Jonathan, and she wasn't thrilled about the idea of getting any closer to him. She looked at the dart gun in his hand, his finger still resting on the trigger.

Galen pointed a stern finger. "Put that away, Lichen, before you shoot someone else."

"Yes, sir." He pocketed it.

Monica knelt beside Galen and opened her pouch, which he had instructed her to bring with her from the clinic. She took out her stethoscope and listened to Jonathan's heart. It was beating fast, but that was to be expected—he'd been running at top speed. Monica was simply relieved his heart was beating at all. She looked at his face and cleaned a cut on his forehead. There were probably scratches elsewhere, maybe even a broken bone, but she wasn't about to begin a full examination right now.

"He's alive," she said. Then she slowly turned his head and removed the dart. "What was in this?"

"Ketamine," said Lichen. "It's a tranquilizer."

"Of course it's a tranquilizer," said Galen. "And it was completely unnecessary. You put everyone in this lab at risk chasing him in here. You could have damaged the sequencers. That was foolish."

It was obvious Lichen hadn't intentionally led Jonathan in here. Jonathan was the one leading, not the other way around. But Lichen said nothing.

"And you frightened Dr. Owens as well. I doubt she appreciates that."

"Forgive me, Doctor," said Lichen, bowing his head.

"Here am I trying to give her a nice introduction to our work," said Galen, "and you go and scare her silly. What kind of impression does that give? Look at her. Now she's all flustered."

"Again, my apologies, Doctor," said Lichen.

Everyone in the lab had stopped what they were doing and stood staring.

Galen stood, raised a hand, spoke in a loud voice. "Go on now. Back to work. All of you. Don't be distracted. We have much still to do."

As the workers obeyed and shuffled back to their stations, Galen lowered his voice to Lichen and pointed to Jonathan. "Pick him up. I want him back with the others."

Monica tensed. Others? There were other people here like this boy? Other people being held against their will? Other prisoners like me and Wyatt?

She watched as Lichen bent down and lifted Jonathan as if he weighed nothing.

"Come, Doctor," said Galen, "I'll introduce you to the others."

Monica followed. Then came Lichen, carrying Jonathan. It made her nervous to have Lichen walking behind her. Not only was he large, but he also carried a weapon, one he clearly knew how to use with deadly accuracy. After all, Jonathan had been a moving target. And from Lichen's reaction, Monica could tell it hadn't been a lucky shot.

Then there was the issue of ketamine. It must have been a dangerously high dose to knock the boy out so quickly. It made her wonder, What would a dose that high do to a smaller person?

She put the thought out of her head. No one was going to shoot Wyatt. Not if she could help it. She would do precisely what Galen asked, anything and everything he wanted. If men like Lichen and Stone were at Galen's disposal, then Monica wasn't about to take a single risk.

8

PATIENTS

Monica drew a map in her mind as she followed Galen
down another series of corridors. Wyatt's room was a
good distance away now, and Monica wanted to know exactly how to return to it unaided if she had to. It was
doubtful, she knew, that Galen would allow her to go anywhere without an escort, but the opportunity might arise.
And even if it didn't, she couldn't stand the thought of not
knowing precisely where Wyatt was in relation to her. The
map was a mental string tying the two of them together.
To lose herself in the labyrinth of the building was to lose
Wyatt. And that was not going to happen.

"What is this place?" she said. "This building, I mean.
Before you came here."

"Not too much look at, is it?" said Galen.

It wasn't. Most of *these* halls, unlike those nearest the
Core, were not under renovation—although they desperately needed it. These were old walls. With peeling wallpa-
per and grime and smelling heavily of mildew. The building
still had the appearance of a hospital, but now of a hospital
left empty and neglected for decades. The ceiling had water
damage. The linoleum was cracked and badly stained in
spots. And instead of bright fluorescent lights, a string of

naked lightbulbs had been jerry-rigged to the ceiling, as if this weren't a hallway, but a mine deep within the earth.

"This used to be a retirement home," said Galen. "Or in other words, a place for middle-aged people to drop off and forget about their aging parents." He didn't laugh.

Behind Monica, Lichen still carried Jonathan, limp in his arms. Had she not checked Jonathan's vitals herself, she'd think him dead.

Two men in hooded black capes approached, each with his face buried in a book. The costume looked vaguely familiar to Monica. She had seen capes like this before but couldn't place them. One of the men noticed Galen approaching and elbowed the other. They both stopped and stepped out of the way, making room.

Galen nodded to them as he passed. "Brothers."

They nodded in return, then focused their attention on Monica. "That's her," she heard one of them whisper.

She avoided their gaze and quickened her pace, looking over her shoulder twice to see if they were still there staring at her. They always were. She shuddered. It wasn't until Galen turned down another corridor that the men in capes disappeared from sight and Monica relaxed.

"Be at peace, Dr. Owens," said Lichen. "You need not fear them. They will not harm you. And nor will I."

She studied his face and could see that he meant it. Like Stone, Lichen looked almost childlike. It was an odd conclusion, considering his size, and yet Monica couldn't deny the gentle sweetness there.

"What are you?" she said. "You and Stone?"

"We are Healers," Lichen said. "Men brought to their full potential. The prophet has made us stronger than evolution has made man."

She didn't understand. Didn't want to understand, really. But for some reason she felt certain that he would not, as he had said, hurt her.

At least, not until Galen tells him to, she thought, coming

to her senses. If the old man ever gave the order, she had no doubt that Lichen would obey.

"Your patients are still a little shaken up, Dr. Owens," said Galen, stopping at a closed door and dropping his voice to a near whisper. "It was quite a shock to their systems to be brought here, so a few of them are fairly resentful right now, especially Jonathan." He gestured to the limp body hanging in Lichen's arms. "This is the fourth time he's tried to run off. It's silly, of course. He has nowhere to go. It's the drugs, I suspect. He can't stand the withdrawal. It makes him desperate. I'm not too worried, though. He'll come around eventually."

He paused for a moment to study Monica's face. "You think I'm cruel, don't you?" he said.

Monica said nothing.

"We've rescued him, Doctor. Think of that. We took a young man who was dead to the world and we gave him a second chance at life. I know you may think our methods are a little unorthodox, but consider what we're accomplishing here. The world has turned its back on these people. We're giving them a life they never thought possible."

He smiled.

"Of course, they don't see that yet. They don't comprehend what we're doing for them. And frankly, I suspect neither do you. But again, I don't fault you for it. It's too new. It's too different from the world of medicine you know. But believe me, Dr. Owens. When all is said and done, I feel confident you'll agree that we were in the right all along."

He opened the door and led them inside.

A group of Healers, all large and all wearing black, were huddled near the door. They parted and grew quiet as Galen entered. Monica avoided looking directly at them but could feel them staring down at her.

At the other end of the room stood four people, three men and one woman, all wearing matching green hospital scrubs.

Galen pointed at each of them. "Dr. Owens, I present Byron, Nick, Dolores, and Hal."

The youngest of the bunch, Nick, a boy about Jonathan's age, saw Jonathan's limp body and ran toward him.

"What did you do to him?" he said, looking fiercely at Galen.

One of the Healers standing by, perhaps in an attempt to protect Galen, grabbed Nick and held him firmly.

Nick kicked and thrashed and tried to free himself.

"Let him go," Galen said.

The Healer released Nick, and he fell hard to the floor.

Galen approached him and offered a hand to help him to his feet, but Nick pushed it away.

"Get away from me," he said.

Byron came over and helped Nick stand up.

"Thank you, Byron," said Galen. "Now, I want everyone to calm down. Jonathan is fine. We had to give him a little dose of something so he'd sleep, but he's not hurt. Lichen, put him in his bed and let him rest."

Lichen carried Jonathan to one of the many beds in the room and set him gently on it.

Monica noticed how the patients gave Lichen plenty of room and then some.

"This is Dr. Monica Owens," said Galen. "She's working with us now, and I want you all to give her the respect she deserves."

"If she's working with you," said Nick, "then she doesn't deserve spit."

Galen looked at him coldly. "I'll ignore that remark, Nick. And so will the rest of us."

Nick turned to Lichen, who now stood tall and erect beside him. He was clearly whom Galen was referring to. Nick hung his head and said nothing.

Galen sighed. "Brothers, dear sister, let's stop this behavior. Have I not given you more food than you could eat? A bed to lie on? Hot water to wash with? Clean clothes to wear? Dolores, did I not give you the feminine products you requested?"

Mortified, Dolores turned away. The others kept silent.

After what seemed to Monica like an eternity of awkwardness, Galen smiled. "There. See? Isn't that better? We can all get along wonderfully if we simply try."

This was the real George Galen, Monica thought: not the one who talked fancy about gene sequencers, but the one who kidnapped and used people and acted as if he were doing them the biggest of favors. He was the most dangerous of men, because in his actions, he saw only good. He saw himself as a hero.

Galen turned to Monica. "Check their vitals, Doctor. Let me know if they need anything. Medication, rest, exercise. I want them as healthy as possible. Lichen, stay and supervise. And see to it that Jonathan remains comfortable."

Lichen nodded, and Galen left with the other Healers.

Lichen found a chair near the door. Monica stood alone in the middle of the room, all of her supposed patients staring at her, waiting.

She tried to make sense of it all but couldn't. Why were they her patients? Galen had said he needed a heart transplant. Did one of these people need a new heart? She doubted it. They were all relatively young and—with the exception of Dolores, who was slightly overweight—looked fairly fit. Nick and Hal were a little thin for their height, yes, but that could be the result of high metabolism, not a weak heart.

Monica smiled meekly and was about to speak when Hal threw his arms up. "I knew he wasn't going to get anywhere," he said with exasperation. "I knew it. The kid runs like a girl. It's pathetic."

"Like a girl?" Nick shouted, getting in Hal's face. "Well, at least he's running. I don't see you trying anything."

"Because I'm not an idiot. You think any of us is getting anywhere with him around?" Hal pointed to Lichen, who was watching the whole exchange without expression.

Hal's face softened. "No offense to you of course, Mr. Lichen," he said. "Personally I find it appalling that Jonathan would even attempt such a thing. It shows a complete lack of respect for authority."

"Oh, you're one to talk," said Nick. "It was your idea to send someone for help in the first place."

Hal shoved Nick hard in the chest. The boy fell backward but was up in a flash, pushing Hal back, twice as hard. They were at each other's throats when Byron pulled them apart. "Hey. Back off. Both of you." He was between them now. "We won't accomplish anything if we kill each other."

"Then you tell the little brat to keep his hands off me," said Hal.

Nick made a move to charge again, but Byron held him at bay. "That's enough. Both of you. Now cool it."

Hal pushed Byron's hand away and stalked off to his bed.

"Contention is of the devil," said Dolores. "I hope y'all know that. We won't get no blessing with the two of you acting this way."

"Shut up," said Hal. "We want a sermon, we'll ask for it."

Dolores shook her head and spoke to Monica. "Men." Then she crossed to her bed and lay down.

Nick stormed off also and plopped down on the bed beside Jonathan's. Only Byron remained. He put his hands together and smiled. "Well, Dr. Owens, let's get this over with."

Monica wasn't sure how to proceed. They were all watching her again, waiting for her to take action. She spotted a chair beside the nearest bed, but was hesitant to ask anyone to sit in it for an examination.

"You want me to sit down?" Byron asked, following her eyes to the chair. "It might be easier to check my vitals if I sit down."

She nodded. "Yes, please."

He sat. She grabbed another chair and put it beside him. "Would you roll your sleeve up please?"

She got out her equipment and checked him. His blood pressure was great. His temperature was normal. His heart rate was good. There was hardly an ounce of fat on his body. She asked him all the appropriate questions. He was thirty-five. He didn't smoke, drink, or use drugs. He exercised regularly, watched his diet, and had no history of heart disease. Both of his parents were still living and healthy. In short, he was one of the healthiest persons Monica had examined in years.

Byron was pleased to hear it. He even smiled and thanked her.

Monica felt more comfortable now, in her element. Byron was a normal person. He wasn't a Healer. He wasn't a crazy, bearded old man. He was just a guy. And to top it off, he was no friend of George Galen. Monica gathered enough courage to speak with him openly.

She lowered her voice. "You're being held here against your will?"

He looked surprised by the question. "Yes."

"Why? What do they want from you?"

He whispered, "I don't know. My car broke down a few days ago and I was hitchhiking to get to a phone when—"

A deep voice boomed from the corner. "Examine them only please, Doctor."

Monica didn't turn to look at Lichen. She worried that if she did he would take her expression as a show of defiance. Instead she bowed her head submissively and asked Byron to leave. He got up and went to his bed without another word.

Dolores was in the examination chair before Monica even had a chance to ask the next person over. She had been waiting for Byron to leave apparently, but standing behind Monica so that Monica hadn't noticed her.

"I'm Dolores Arlington, in case you didn't know already, and I figure you don't know, since you don't have a folder or any papers that I can see. Or do you have files on us that we don't know about?" She looked suspicious.

Monica was momentarily at a loss for words. "No, I don't have any files on you, Dolores. But I *am* interested in your health. Would you mind answering a few questions for me?"

Dolores laughed and shook her head. "Questions? Goodness." She became quiet then, considering this. "You know, no one's asked me any questions in a long time. And you know why nobody ever asks me any questions? Because nobody cares, that's why. Because what I got to say and what I think don't mean a hill a beans to nobody."

Monica stared at her, suddenly feeling sad. Dolores spoke with such simple conviction that it was clear she believed what she said. She wasn't looking for pity. She was simply stating fact, as if reading from a textbook of her own life.

"I care," Monica found herself saying. And she meant it.

Dolores looked at her oddly, as if Monica had spoken Chinese, then shrugged. "Ask away."

"Okay. Do you exercise?"

"Oh, we're getting right to it, are we? I mean, I know I could lose a few pounds. And I know what you're thinking. You're thinking how can a homeless woman have a belly at all, right? I should be skinny as a rail, right?"

Monica cocked her head. "Homeless?"

"Homeless," repeated Dolores. "As in without a home. I live on the street. We all do, except Byron over there. He's a big-shot lawyer, only Galen thought he was a drifter and picked him up same as the rest of us. He needed people who wouldn't be missed, know what I mean? Who's gonna miss a few homeless, right? Answer: nobody. Only Byron *isn't* homeless. Or at least so he says, and I believe him even if Hal doesn't. You see, Byron's car broke down. I used to own me a Chevy Nova, but the man who ran the trailer park, he had it towed after my Earl burned himself."

"All of you are homeless?" Monica said.

"You got wax in your ears? Galen picked us up *because*

we're homeless. Nick over there thinks Galen's got something in store for us. Something bad. Otherwise, why wouldn't he just let us go?"

Monica's head was spinning. What did Galen want with five homeless people, or at least five people he *thought* were homeless? Why was he holding them here? Why was he holding *her* here? None of it made sense.

She asked Dolores more questions and concluded that she had a good heart. So it couldn't be Dolores that needed the transplant.

She politely dismissed Dolores without giving her a full examination, and Dolores went back to bed.

No one was waiting to take her place. In fact, neither Nick nor Hal moved from his bed or showed any desire to be examined at all.

"So who's next?" Monica asked.

No answer.

"It doesn't hurt one bit," said Dolores. "I don't know what y'all are afraid of."

"Shut up," said Hal. "Nobody asked you."

"You shut up," Dolores said, her smile replaced with a snarl. "You keep barking like you own the place. But you're just mad because you don't have a bottle of liquor to suck on."

Hal hopped out of bed with clenched fists. "You're going to have a fat lip if you don't shut your mouth."

Lichen rose to his feet, and the mere movement of his massive frame changed the mood of the room immediately. Hal lowered his fists, and Dolores lay on her bed, deliberately turning her back to Hal.

Monica stood. "It's all right. I'll check Jonathan. They can relax for now. I'll examine them afterward."

Lichen considered this a moment before finally sitting back down.

Monica relaxed and took her bag to Jonathan's bedside. She rolled up his sleeve and saw over a dozen needle wounds. Most of them were swollen, and many of

D AND JOHNSTON

, we should get to know each other. I
back to see Wyatt, so I waited here."
nows how to play Potato Commandos,

protective arm around Wyatt and studied
n looked perfectly content. If he was be-
e didn't seem distressed about it. Plus, she
ere alone, unescorted, which meant Galen
eed to monitor him too closely. He wasn't
inst his will.
ou a doctor of?" she asked.
siology," he said, pointing to the side of his
brain function and neural interaction, how we
cord memories, how groups of neurons com-
nother and respond to certain stimuli.
art transplant.

them had been scratched to the point of bleeding.
Heroin.

She glanced at Nick, who was watching her closely
now.

"Jonathan is a friend of yours?"

"What do you care?"

"I just ask because you seemed eager to help him before."

Nick said nothing.

Monica checked Jonathan's temperature and blood
pressure. "He has a fever. Was he hot like this before he
tried to run?"

Nick wouldn't look at her.

"I need to know because he may be having a reaction to
the tranquilizer."

No response.

She pulled back Jonathan's eyelids and saw that his
pupils were highly dilated. Lichen had given him quite a
dose of ketamine, no question.

"He gets the shakes at night," Nick said softly. "Sweats
a lot, too. He's been hot for two days now."

Monica nodded and took out her pad and wrote a prescription. It surprised her that she still remembered the
names of drugs she hadn't even thought about since her
stint in the ER during her residency.

"You're going to give him some medicine?" Nick
asked.

"Jonathan is going through withdrawal. He's very sick.
If you're a friend of his, and I think you are, I'd appreciate
your encouraging him to get some rest. He shouldn't
scratch these sores. I'll try and get a cream he should rub
on them. That will ease the itching."

Nick looked at the floor. "What do you people want
from us, huh?" he whispered. "Why you keeping us here?
We didn't do nothing to nobody. We weren't hurting anything. But you got us as prisoners here. Why?" His eyes
were welling with tears.

Monica wanted to cry also. She wanted to tell him that she was a prisoner as much as he was. She wanted to tell him about Wyatt, how they had taken him and frightened him and how she didn't know if they were going to let her and Wyatt live once she had finished whatever it was they had brought her here to do.

But she said nothing because suddenly Lichen's voice boomed from across the room.

"No more questions!"

After that, Monica examined Nick and Hal in silence, which was perfectly fine with Hal, who Monica could see was in no mood to talk anyway.

They were both malnourished. Nick, like Jonathan, had a few needle marks on his arms, but far fewer than Jonathan, and his looked healed—he hadn't shot up for some time now, apparently. Hal checked out fine except that his hands shook slightly. If he was indeed an alcoholic, he was eager for a drink.

"You are finished?" Lichen asked her.

"Yes, and I would like to see my son now, please."

"Of course. I will take you to him."

"I remember the way."

Instead of responding he went out the door and held it open for her. She understood. He was going to take her there whether she wanted an escort or not.

They walked the halls in silence. Finally Lichen said, "You are not happy here, I see."

That caught her off guard. Of course she wasn't happy. "You're keeping my son and me prisoner. How can I be happy?"

"What you see around you you do not yet understand. What may appear evil to you is good, the wisest of wisdoms. Once you understand what the prophet is giving to the world you will be happy. You will feel peace as our brothers and sisters find an end to their suffering."

Monica could tell he was trying to calm her, but his

words
more un

"My w
Her face
forward and

"What I m
son are safe h

"Then why
back there? Why
whatever you ask

Lichen nodded,
come clear shortly.
a chosen one."

"What does that
brought me here? Gale
Am I supposed

together so closel
knew you'd come
"Dr. Yoshida
Mom."
Monica put a
Yoshida. The m
ing held here, h
had found him
didn't feel the
being held ag
"What are
"Neurophy
head. "I stud
make and re
municate with
That sort

words had the opposite effect. The more he spoke the more unsettled she became.

"My words frighten you, I think," he said.

Her face was giving away her true feelings. She looked forward and said nothing.

"What I mean to say, Dr. Owens, is that you and your son are safe here. No one will harm you."

"Then why threaten me? Why threaten those people back there? Why hold my son as a hostage, force me to do whatever you ask?"

Lichen nodded, appreciating the question. "All will become clear shortly. You will see how your mission here is a chosen one."

"What does that mean?" she said. "Why have you brought me here? Galen said he needed a heart transplant. Am I supposed to give him one?"

"That is for the prophet to explain."

She was frustrated now. He was either cryptic or evasive or both.

"What about the others? Byron, Dolores, and the others? What about them? What does Galen want with them?"

"They are the vessels."

This was hopeless. "Vessels for what?"

He stopped walking. "We have arrived, Doctor." He pointed to the door.

Without realizing it, she had walked all the way back to Wyatt's room. She could hear the video game and laughter inside. She opened the door. An Asian man in a white lab coat was sitting on the floor beside Wyatt. Each of them held a game controller and was laughing at the monitor. Frederica was furious. A stranger alone with her son.

The man smiled, set down the controller, and stood.

"Mom," Wyatt said, running to her.

"Forgive me for startling you, Dr. Owens. I am Dr. Kouichi Yoshida. I figured that since we'll be working together so closely, we should get to know each other. I knew you'd come back to see Wyatt, so I waited here."

"Dr. Yoshida knows how to play Potato Commandos, Mom."

Monica put a protective arm around Wyatt and studied Yoshida. The man looked perfectly content. If he was being held here, he didn't seem distressed about it. Plus, she had found him here alone, unescorted, which meant Galen didn't feel the need to monitor him too closely. He wasn't being held against his will.

"What are you a doctor of?" she asked.

"Neurophysiology," he said, pointing to the side of his head. "I study brain function and neural interaction, how we make and record memories, how groups of neurons communicate with one another and respond to certain stimuli. That sort of thing."

She didn't blink.

Yoshida waited, then said, "From the look on your face, I can see that you have a lot of questions."

"You could say that," Monica said.

He gave a little laugh. "Well, I'm your man. If you have questions, I can answer them. No one understands the mind of George Galen better than I do."

9
BHA

The elevator doors slid open, and Frank stepped out into a brightly lit chamber. Agents Riggs and Carter followed. A guard in a tight-fitting black uniform greeted them and pointed to spots on the floor where red footprints were painted. "Stand here, please."

Frank aligned his feet with the footprints, then watched as the guard unstrapped a long baton from his hip and twisted the handle. The baton hummed to life and glowed white, looking to Frank like a handheld bug zapper.

"Contaminant rod," said Carter, extending his arms and allowing the guard to scan him. "It looks for any biohazards you might have accidentally picked up in the field."

The guard scanned Carter and Riggs fairly quickly before turning to Frank. "Arms out, please."

Frank remained still as the guard slowly and methodically scanned him. The guard paid special attention to the creases and folds of Frank's uniform, as if expecting to find some secret stash of hazardous material wedged there.

"You boys don't take any chances, do you?" Frank said.

"We can't afford to," said Riggs. "You of all people should understand the importance of containment."

The guard turned off the baton and told them they were clear to proceed inside.

Frank followed the agents down the chamber to a dead end. Carter swiped a card through a reader, and a small window on the wall slid open, revealing a keypad and monitor. He entered a code and then stood motionless as a red light emitted and scanned his face. There was a beep as identification was verified, and then the wall split, revealing an expansive room on the opposite side where hundreds of people moved about; bustling to workstations; speaking into headsets; monitoring large, high-definition video screens. The scene reminded Frank of a big-city newsroom—loud, urgent, and a blur of motion.

BHA headquarters.

They descended a short flight of stairs as the door sealed shut behind them. Carter pointed to a wall where a computer-generated map of Los Angeles County appeared. "The blinking lights represent the places where Healers have attempted gene therapy, those addresses in the book."

Frank counted eight lights.

"We're looking for any patterns in the distribution of the addresses," said Riggs. "We're hoping they can give us some idea as to where Healers may go next."

They reached the main floor and weaved through the commotion until they arrived at a row of offices at the rear of the room. Riggs stopped at a door labeled EUGENE IRVING, DIRECTOR. "Director Irving asked to meet you and welcome you to the agency."

What was that in his tone? Frank wondered. Sarcasm?

Inside, the secretary greeted them with a whisper and told them to go through a second door to Irving's office, where he would be waiting.

Riggs tapped the door twice before entering.

Director Eugene Irving, a thin man with slick black hair and a suit to match, was hunched over his desk, examining some documents with a much younger agent. Frank recognized Irving from the photos he'd seen of him in the press and thought he looked much older in person—in his late fifties, perhaps, with pale skin, a long neck, sharp jaw, hollow cheeks—like a man who had just recently gone on a crash diet and was in need of some electrolytes.

Without looking up, Irving waved them to the empty chairs opposite his desk.

"And this is all from a single hospital?" Irving said to the young agent.

"Children's Hospital on Sunset, sir."

The young agent was portly with short auburn hair that stuck up the front—whether by design with the help of hair gel or simply because of a cowlick, Frank couldn't tell. He wore a gray suit with a black necktie so narrow that it only barely covered the line of buttons down his white oxford shirt. A BHA ID tag was pinned to the breast pocket of his suit coat.

Irving looked at Frank and gestured to the young agent. "This is Agent Marcus Atkins," he said. "One of our analysts. Recently he's been spending his time studying hospital databases. Atkins, this is Dr. Frank Hartman from Fort Detrick, the virologist."

Agent Atkins nodded. "Pleasure."

"Why hospital databases?" Frank said.

Atkins brightened at the question. "Well, since we learned that it was the Healers making the virus and that they were using it to attempt to cure genetic diseases, we've wondered, How do Healers identify potential patients? How do they find someone with a genetic—" He stopped midsentence. "You know who the Healers are, right?"

"He's been briefed, Marcus," said Riggs.

Atkins blushed. "Of course. Excuse me, Doctor."

"No problem," said Frank. "Please, continue."

Atkins cleared his throat. "Well, we've been wondering how Healers find people who suffer from genetic diseases. How do they know, for example, who, if anyone, on your block has Parkinson's disease or sickle-cell anemia or cystic fibrosis? They've been operating in secrecy, after all. It's not like they're knocking on random doors asking if there's a genetically diseased person inside."

"Get to the point," Irving said, rubbing his eyes.

Atkins turned a deeper shade of red. "Right. Anyway, Healers have obviously found a way to identify who needs gene therapy. So we examined a few hospital databases and discovered that one of them, at least, had been hacked."

Director Irving cut in. "Someone's been cracking the system and downloading patient information."

"Stealing medical records?" Frank said.

"Not just any medical records," said Atkins. "All the records downloaded belonged to patients with a diagnosed genetic disease, precisely the type of people Healers would want to contact."

Director Irving handed Frank a slip of paper. "These are the names that were downloaded."

Frank scanned the list. There were a dozen names in all. "So these could be potential targets for a Healer?"

Atkins shrugged. "Maybe. Who knows? It might not even be the Healers hacking the system."

"It's worth following up on," said Carter. "We should contact these people, see if any Healers have come by. If so, we can be fairly confident that it was the Healers who hacked the database."

"Or," said Riggs, "we *don't* contact these people but instead post a few agents at these addresses and have the agents watch for any suspicious activity. That way, if a Healer *does* show up, we can take him on-site."

There was silence as Irving considered this. Then he asked for the list, and Frank returned it to him. Irving gave the list to Atkins. "I want a team at each of these addresses. Don't talk to these people. If they know we're looking for Healers, they might warn the Healers and tell them to steer clear. The moment our boys see anyone who could possibly be one of these wackos, they call it in and we rush the place."

Atkins nodded. "Yes, sir." Then he hurried out of the room.

Irving leaned back in his chair and put his hands behind

his head. "Word on the street is that you have this virus of ours licked, Frank. You don't mind if I call you Frank, do you?"

"No, sir."

"Good. So, this countervirus of yours, it's the answer to our prayers?"

"As I explained to Agent Riggs and Agent Carter," Frank said, "the countervirus has not yet been tested on human subjects."

Irving shrugged. "There's always a first for everything. Riggs and Carter have told you about the crowd we have in our infirmary?"

"Yes, sir."

"I want the ones still infected with the virus to be treated immediately. After you've had a chance to settle in, that is."

"Of course."

Irving swiveled in his chair and picked up an ink pen off his desk, twirling it in his fingers. "We're taking a giant risk on you, Frank. I'm not one to let outsiders in here to fiddle with our business. Makes me nervous."

"I understand, sir. I'll do my job and be as unintrusive as possible."

"I'm glad to hear it," said Irving. "We take our work very seriously. These Healers are keeping us up at night. They're very disturbing people."

"I agree, sir."

"You've seen their little book of scripture, then, I take it?"

Frank nodded.

"Quite the read, isn't it?"

"Yes, sir. It's the piece of this puzzle I find most surprising, in fact."

"Oh? Why's that?"

"Because it puts the Healers way outside the mainstream, sir. Normal people would shy away from this kind of thing. New scripture. Prophecies and prophets. It's all very mystical. People typically find that off-putting, frightening even. I find it hard to believe that anyone would allow a Healer to treat them."

"Oh, I agree. But keep in mind who these patients are, Frank," said Irving. "We're talking about genetic diseases. Most of these people have already been through the wringer. They've tried every medical option, seen every doctor, taken every drug. And nothing worked. They're out of options. But the pain is still there. They still suffer. So when a Healer comes along they think, What have I got to lose?"

"Well that's just it, sir. They have a great deal to lose. Healers aren't offering a bottle of Tylenol. This isn't some proven treatment that four out of five doctors recommend. It's a virus, completely without credentials, as far as I know. Not to mention extremely dangerous."

Irving set the ink pen back on the desk and looked at Frank intently. "Have you ever known someone with a genetic disease, Frank? Intimately, I mean. A loved one? A friend?"

"No, sir."

"Then I suspect you've never had them open up to you, tell you what it feels like to be stuck with something medicine can't fix? Never had to watch them wiggle in pain? Never wondered to yourself why there wasn't a damn thing you could do about it?"

"No, sir."

"Then you've never seen true desperation, Frank. You've never felt as helpless as these people and their families do."

Frank tensed. Was Irving needling him? Surely the BHA had researched Frank's service records before giving him access to their operations. Irving must know that Frank *had* suffered a great loss, that Frank *had* experienced true desperation, that Frank knew *exactly* what it felt like to watch someone dear to you suffer. Rachel hadn't had a genetic disease, but leukemia was just as severe a diagnosis. Was

Irving so callous a person that he'd wave Frank's loss in front of him just to make a point? Or had he truly never seen Frank's files? Either way, Frank wouldn't let the man rile him.

"I see your point, sir," said Frank. "I merely meant to suggest that it's surprising a street medicine engineered by a fringe religion could proliferate at all."

Irving surprised Frank with a laugh. "Street medicine. I like that." His laughed tapered, then he stood and came around the front of the desk, his hands in his pockets. "Don't get me wrong, Frank. I'm not defending these Healers. I think they're as cracked as you do. They wear black capes, for crying out loud. First time I saw photos, I thought we were dealing with vampires." He laughed again and looked to Agents Carter and Riggs, who took his glance as a cue and tossed in a few laughs of their own. Frank merely forced a smile.

"My point," Irving said, "is this. Don't concern yourself with the psychology of these people. That isn't your job. You're here as a medical advisor. I will value your counsel on that subject and that subject only. I want to make that point very clear."

"Of course, sir."

"And you will operate within the parameters that I define, and not interfere with any other aspect of this agency. I can't afford to have someone telling us how to do things around here. That's *my* job. I was appointed to this position by the president for a reason. Do we understand one another?"

"Completely, sir."

"Excellent." He clapped his hands together. "Then let's get to it."

Frank followed Carter and Riggs out of Irving's office and into a bright cylindrical corridor.

"He likes you," said Carter.

"Who?" said Frank. "Director Irving?"

"No question," said Riggs. "He only had to tell you once that he was a presidential appointee."

"First time I met him," said Carter, "he told me four times in as many minutes that he was a personal friend of the president."

"He seemed pleasant enough," said Frank.

They reached a set of closed doors. Carter swiped his card through the reader, and the door opened.

"You caught him on a good day," said Riggs. "He threw a stapler at me once."

Frank looked to Carter for confirmation, who nodded solemnly and then led them out onto a loading dock. A sleek subway car waited on a track in front of them. It extended down a dark tunnel to the right and disappeared from sight.

"How big is this place?" Frank said with wonder.

"We've just left the Command Center," said Riggs. "This will take us to T4, our operational facility. The nuts and bolts of the BHA."

"Where the real work is done," Carter said with a wink.

A uniformed guard slid open the subway car door and motioned them inside. Frank and the two agents each found a seat and fastened their safety harnesses. The guard slid the door closed and went to a computer console on the loading dock. A female automated voice sounded inside the car. "Please be seated. This train is about to depart."

With a slight jolt the subway car pulled away from the loading dock and then quickly picked up speed down the track.

Riggs said, "T4 houses the infirmary and our Level 4 containment site. We keep them as far away from the Command Center as possible as a safety precaution."

That made sense to Frank. In fact, if he had his way at Fort Detrick, Level 4 would be a separate building on the most isolated plot of earth on base, thus minimizing the risk of an outbreak should, heaven forbid, containment fail.

The subway ride lasted a good ten minutes, and since the car had moved at a brisk clip, Frank figured they were well outside the city by now. The loading dock they stopped at was identical to the one they had left, and if not for the change in guard, Frank would have thought the car had simply traveled in a huge circle.

The guard saluted Riggs and Carter and looked genuinely pleased to see them. "Welcome home, sirs." He saw the small suitcase Frank was pulling. "May I take your bag, Dr. Hartman?"

So they were expecting him. "No, thank you. I can manage."

The guard escorted them to another door and returned to his station. Carter repeated the security check yet a third time, and the doors opened, revealing another expansive room nearly equal in size to the Command Center but far more tranquil. No computers, no monitors, no furniture at all, just stark white walls and bright white light. A few BHA employees in matching black uniforms walked by, the heels of their boots clicking on the polished floor and echoing through the chamber.

"Welcome to T4," said Riggs, leading them inside. "Everything you need is housed here, Frank, including your barracks."

"Barracks? Your staff live here?"

"We're completely contained in this facility. Mess hall, barracks, combat training, and workout gyms. Even an on-site sewage-treatment plant and enough water tanks to last us at least ninety days. Basically, we could stay down here for weeks without ever going to the surface."

"Why underground?" asked Frank. "Containment?"

"Millions of people live in LA County," said Carter. "You can imagine the disaster that would result if a Level 4 substance leaked into the open. The earth between us and the surface is simply another shield of protection."

"And this way," said Riggs, "if there *was* a leak, the only people who would die would be us. And since we're already underground, no one has to bury us." He winked at Carter.

"Right," said Carter, smiling. "We'd be in the world's biggest coffin. All they'd have to do is a make a little gravestone above us. 'Here Lies the BHA.'"

Frank allowed himself to grin but didn't feel particularly amused. The thought of having no escape should a leak occur wasn't comforting. To change the subject he stepped forward and took in his surroundings. A series of corridors was in front of them, each extending at least a hundred yards, with multiple connecting passageways that led off in every direction. It was a massive underground complex, larger than any federal facility Frank had ever seen, aboveground or below.

"Come on," said Riggs, checking his watch. "We had the countervirus taken to the infirmary. Let's see if you're worth the trip."

10

YOSHIDA

Monica wasn't sure which bothered her more—that she had found a stranger in Wyatt's room playing video games with him or that the stranger in question, this Dr. Kouichi Yoshida, was being so friendly. It felt off. So far the only people she had met here were Galen, the Healers, and other prisoners like herself. Of those, the only people who had seemed happy were the bad kind. And right now, Yoshida had a smile right out of a Colgate commercial, all teeth, ear to ear. He creeped Monica out.

"Perhaps we could talk in my office," Yoshida said. "Wyatt can stay here and play video games with Lichen."

Monica looked over her shoulder at Lichen, who, big as a bear, stood watching from the hallway. She felt Wyatt's fingers dig into her side and knew that Wyatt considered hanging out with Lichen as bad an idea as she did.

"Some other time, perhaps," she said. "Wyatt and I have had a traumatic day. I'd rather be alone with him right now, thank you."

"Don't be silly," Yoshida said, waving his hand dismissively and moving for the door. "You two will have plenty of time to see each other. Besides, I should bring you up to speed on all the equipment before the surgeries."

He stood in the doorway now, facing her, that same vacant

smile on his face. With Lichen looming behind him, Yoshida looked embarrassingly small. He was about five-and-a-half feet tall with straight black hair parted down the middle. A pair of small, round silver spectacles framed his unblinking eyes. Beneath his white lab coat he wore a tacky Hawaiian shirt with about twenty colors more than necessary.

"What surgeries?" said Monica.

"You see?" said Yoshida. "You *do* have a lot of questions. Come on, I'll lead the way." He turned away from the doorway and disappeared from view.

"Don't go, Mom," said Wyatt quietly, still clinging to her. "Don't leave me alone with him." He was peeking around her at Lichen.

Monica took both of his hands in hers and knelt in front of him.

Lichen said, "Wyatt can stay here by himself. He doesn't need me to watch over him. I will accompany you and Dr. Yoshida."

Monica felt light-headed. She wanted nothing more than to be with and comfort Wyatt. And yet she feared that if she wasn't completely compliant, it might have negative repercussions for them both. The memory of Jonathan's limp body with a tranquilizer in his neck was too vivid a one to forget.

She rubbed a hand down Wyatt's arm, straightening his shirtsleeve and giving him what little comfort she could. "I'll only be gone a few minutes," she said. "I'll make sure no one bothers you. When I get back, we'll play head-to-head." She nodded at the TV. "You can blast me with a potato gun."

He glanced at the screen, then turned back. "Five minutes?"

"Five minutes," she said.

Yoshida was waiting out in the hall, the grin on his face not the least bit diminished. "Your Wyatt's a real charmer," he said. "Fast with his fingers, too." He mimed using a game controller.

"Where's your office?" Monica said, changing the subject. The less attention given to Wyatt, the better.

"This way," said Yoshida, going in a direction Monica had not yet explored. She followed and heard Lichen's heavy footsteps behind her.

They went down a dimly lit hallway, through a large room that looked as if it could have once been a cafeteria, and down a flight of stairs.

Yoshida held open the rusty metal door at the bottom of the staircase, and Monica stepped inside. It was like stepping into another world, going from darkness to light, leaving the grungy, mildew-infested halls of an abandoned retirement home and entering an immaculate laboratory— the kind of lab one would expect to find at a multinational electronics corporation: bright, modern, and static-free. Robotic arms with needle-sharp points at their tips lined a narrow conveyor belt that ran the length of the room. Elsewhere were computer terminals of various shapes and sizes. Miles of cable extended to every machine and device and then to the twenty or so computer servers lined against the wall. The servers hummed quietly and blinked with so many tiny dots of colored light that they looked like boxed Christmas trees.

"Welcome to my office," Yoshida said, clearly pleased with himself. "Come on, I'll show you around." He held the door open long enough for Lichen to enter and then crossed the room to where the conveyor belt ended. When he saw that Monica hadn't followed, he waved a hand and shouted her over.

Reluctantly, she went to him, eyeing each of the robots as she passed. They stood like frozen little soldiers, each about the length of Monica's arms, and looked like the kind of machines you might expect to find on the assembly lines of auto manufacturers, only much smaller.

She found Yoshida standing at a folding table near the end of the conveyor belt. On the table, lined in a neat row atop a piece of felt, lay four small computer chips.

Extending from one side of each of the chips were several dozen strands of fiber optics, making it look as if each chip had a spiked haircut roughly two inches long.

"I was going to make the last one earlier," Yoshida said, "but I thought you might want to see it for yourself. So I waited. You ready?"

"Ready for what?" she said.

Yoshida's already-stretched-to-the-limit smile widened, and he flipped a switch.

The room came to life. All the robotic arms and drills and machines hummed and whirred and moved into position over the conveyor belt—the army of electronic soldiers was getting into formation. Monica leaned forward and peered down the length of the conveyor belt and saw that the machines and arms at the opposite end were already at work, poking and soldering something on the belt. Then the conveyor belt jerked forward, and Monica stepped back, startled.

As the object moved down the belt, the arms and devices stretched and poked and did their brief business, then shrunk back out of the way, allowing the next cog in the machine to poke or stamp or do whatever it was designed for.

Finally the object being created came into view.

It, too, was a computer chip, identical to the other four on the table. Yoshida, now wearing white cotton gloves, picked up the chip as delicately as he might pick up a volatile explosive and placed it gently beside the others. He sighed, cocked his head to side, and admired his creations. "They're beautiful, don't you think?"

"What are they?" Monica said.

"Well, they're not exactly ready yet," Yoshida said. "I still haven't downloaded all the data onto them. Galen wants to wait until right before the surgeries to do that."

"What are they?" she repeated.

He looked at her, still all smile, and put his hands in his lab coat pockets. "These, Dr. Owens, are George Galen's mind."

11

LEVEL 4

Frank followed Agents Riggs and Carter through the halls of the BHA's underground facility until they reached the locker room. As far as locker rooms went, it wasn't anything to write home about. Rows of tall metal lockers with thin wooden benches between them.

Riggs made a sweeping gesture with his hand. "This locker room connects to our Level 4 containment area, where the infirmary is housed. All of your patients are waiting in there. Director Irving wants you to treat them with the countervirus as soon as possible, so I'll shut up and let you get down to business. You'll need to go in wearing full biogear. Agent Carter here will give you all the equipment you need and then accompany you inside and help out however he can."

"And the countervirus?" Frank said.

"If our luggage boys followed instructions, your trunk should be waiting for you inside Level 4. Any other questions?"

Frank shook his head.

"Good. And don't sweat it. We brought you here because you're the best." He gave Frank an encouraging tap on the arm and left.

"Well," said Carter, "let's get you suited up."

He led Frank down one of the aisles of lockers. Once he found the locker he was looking for, he stopped and tapped it with his finger. "This one's yours. Everything you need is inside. Strip down to your underwear. Put on the suit and helmet. If you have any questions, I'll be over there changing." Carter left Frank and went to his own locker only ten yards away.

Frank opened the locker. A black rubber suit hung neatly under a single beam of light. Frank took it out and held it up to his body. Instead of being loose-fitting to allow for air circulation, like the suits he was accustomed to, it was tight, like a wetsuit.

Frank undressed, hung his military uniform on the hooks inside the locker, placed his shoes and socks on the floor of the locker, then stood there in his boxers, not sure how to proceed. The biosuit was a single piece of rubbery fabric, like a glove. As far as Frank could tell, there were no zippers or holes in the back for opening and allowing someone to step into it.

"Stretch the collar," Carter said, watching from a distance. To demonstrate, Carter stretched the rubbery collar of his own suit, making a wide hole. Then he stepped into the hole and slowly worked the suit up his body and over his shoulders.

It took a little doing, but Frank eventually got his on as well. It fit him like a glove, as if it had been made to his exact size and specifications. He did a few knee bends. The fabric was snug but not restrictive.

The helmet came on next. It slid over Frank's head easily and connected to two air tanks in the bottom of the locker via a long air hose. Frank opened the air valve, and cool oxygen flowed into the helmet. He slid the air tanks into the backpack clearly designed to carry them and slung the backpack over his shoulders, tightening the straps.

He looked at himself in the mirror hanging at the back of his locker and felt more like a scuba diver than a virologist.

A compartment below the mirror caught his eye. He

opened it. Inside hung a contaminant rod, a pistol, four cartridges of ammunition, and a Kevlar vest. He lifted the pistol and pulled back on the hammer. It was light, made of durable plastic, and fit snugly in his rubbery grip. He returned it to its stand and lifted the vest. It was heavy, with a large hump in the back to fit over the user's air tanks and backpack.

Carter appeared at his side dressed in his own biosuit.

"Why do I need this?" Frank said, holding up the vest and speaking loudly to be heard though the helmet.

Carter pointed to an electronic device on the wrist of his suit. "Hit your comlink," he said.

Frank found his own and touched it. Carter's voice became clear and audible inside his helmet. "We wear those vests only when we're in the field," Carter said. "Same for the sidearm. Hopefully you won't need them."

"I wouldn't think so. I'm here as a medical consultant, remember?"

Carter shrugged. "I'm not the quartermaster." Then, eyeing Frank's suit, he said, "How's the fit?"

Frank rotated his shoulders. "Feels good."

Carter did a quick check for leaks, then pressed a button on Frank's shoulder that sealed the bottom of Frank's helmet to the neck of his suit, making it airtight.

"Ready?" said Carter.

"As I'll ever be," said Frank.

Carter led the way to Level 4, passing through a series of glass doors that required security clearances. Finally they reached the entrance.

INFIRMARY

AUTHORIZED PERSONNEL ONLY

WARNING: LEVEL 4 CONTAINMENT

DO NOT PROCEED WITHOUT

PROTECTIVE CLOTHING

They went inside. The entry room was wide and sterile and lined with medicine cabinets. Frank's metal trunk sat on the floor near the wall. Carter went to a cabinet and found an injection gun and a handful of syringes. Frank opened the trunk, removed several vials of red counter-virus, and gently put them in a pouch on his hip.

"The patients' rooms are through here," said Carter, leading the way.

They went to an adjacent room with a line of doors on one side.

Frank walked to the door nearest them and peered through the window in it. Inside, an old man slept on a hospital bed surrounded by a wall of life-monitoring machines. He looked to be in his seventies, with wrinkled, saggy, liver-spotted skin. His jaw was covered with white stubbly facial hair that matched the wispy white hair on his head. He wore a red hospital johnny with the letters *BHA* embroidered over the right breast and a pair of white ankle socks.

"Who is he?" Frank said.

"Name's Richard Schneider," said Carter. "He was the second one we brought in. Healers had treated him the night before we found him, so it hasn't been three days yet. The virus is still in him, spreading through his system."

"Agent Riggs said the Healers have their own version of the countervirus. Were they scheduled to give it to him?"

"That's our guess. Mr. Schneider isn't being too forth-coming with the details, so we can't be sure. But from what we've gathered, Healers typically return three days after giving the treatment to administer a countervirus of their own creation. We've got two of our boys watching Schneider's house in case the Healers come back."

"What were they treating him for?"

"Parkinson's disease. It's monogenetic, meaning it's caused by a change in the DNA sequence of a single gene. Healers target that type of disease because technically it's the easiest to cure. Fix the one bad gene and the disease goes away." He pushed open the door. "Come on, let's give Mr. Schneider his dose of countervirus."

As it turned out, Schneider wasn't asleep after all. His eyes snapped open when Frank and Carter entered, and he sat up in his bed, looking suspicious.

"You can't hold me here," he said. "I got rights."

Carter touched a button on his comlink, and his voice was broadcast from a speaker on his helmet. "Mr. Schneider, this is Dr. Frank Hartman. He'll be giving you some medication today."

Schneider scooted to the far side of the bed. "I don't need any medication. Not from you."

Now that they were close, Frank could see that the old man's hands and face were trembling; it was an advanced case of Parkinson's disease.

"I'm afraid you don't have a choice in the matter, Mr. Schneider," Carter said. "So I'll appreciate your being cooperative." He gestured at Frank to proceed.

Frank looked down at the trembling old man and felt increasingly uncomfortable. Not only did he have serious reservations about administering the countervirus before proper testing had been conducted and FDA approval had been granted, but he also disliked treating patients suffering from so much anxiety.

He hesitated, then removed a vial of countervirus from his pouch and stepped to Schneider's IV. When it became obvious to Schneider that Frank intended to attach the vial to the IV tube, Schneider pulled the IV needle from his wrist.

"You're not putting that inside me," he said, angry now. "You don't have the right to put nothing inside me. Not unless I say so. I'm in the middle of something. I can't have you putting stuff inside me right now. You'll mess it up."

"Mr. Schneider," Carter said, remaining calm. "You are making this more difficult than it needs to be." He gave Frank the injection gun. "You will remain still so that Dr.

Hartman can give you this injection, or we will be forced to restrain you."

"The hell you will. I want my lawyer on the phone. You people can't hold me here."

Carter held his ground. "Actually, Mr. Schneider, we can. You have an illegal substance in your body which puts those around you in danger."

"I took precautions. I hung the plastic like they told me. I stayed in bed. I wasn't going to get out. No one was in danger. It was only going to be for a few days, until the treatment ran its course, see?" He held his hands out. "Look, I got the Parkinson's, all right? I need this treatment they gave me. I can't have you putting stuff in me."

Frank loaded the vial into the injection gun.

"What's the matter, you deaf?" said Schneider. "I said I don't want any of your meds."

Carter held up a hand to quiet him. "I'm not going to argue with you, Mr. Schneider. Right now, you will follow instructions and remain still. Had you not pulled out your IV, we could have done this the easy way."

Schneider pointed a trembling finger. "You're not sticking me with that, you hear? In the IV or otherwise. Not unless you tell me what it is."

Carter hesitated.

"It's a countervirus," said Frank simply. He wasn't going to lie to the old man.

"Countervirus?" said Schneider, suddenly looking horrified. "You mean it'll stop the treatment?" He didn't wait for an answer. He pressed himself against the bar on the opposite side of the bed. "You stay away from me, you hear me? I'll be cured in a few hours. Once it runs through my system. You stay away from me."

The beeping of the heart monitor began to increase. Frank stiffened. The old man was working himself into a frenzy.

"You're going to ruin everything," he said. "You're going to ruin it. I can feel myself getting better, do you hear me? I can feel myself getting whole again. You can't stop that now, not when I'm this close. I beg you, please."

He broke into sobs and covered his face with his hands.

Frank was at a loss. Why couldn't they wait a few hours? What harm would it do? The man was isolated already. Who could he infect? Why not wait, see if the virus heals him, and if it doesn't, give him the countervirus then?

Carter must have sensed something of what Frank was thinking because Frank heard Carter's voice in his helmet, speaking privately so that Schneider couldn't hear. "We don't have a choice, Frank. We have to do it, if for no other reason than to find out if the countervirus works. Healers are criminals. They may appear to have a benevolent agenda, but they've killed people, they've destroyed property, they've turned this entire region into a biological hot zone. You've seen what this virus can do to people it wasn't intended for. We can't let that go unchecked. We *have* to have a method for treating people. And we'll never know if this countervirus is the answer unless we put it to the test. We can't wait for formal human trials, not when the threat is this immediate. We've got to stop these Healers now. If we can use the technology they've created to help people, we will. But we'll do so legally, safely, without putting others at risk."

Frank nodded. "You're right. Of course you're right." The logic was inarguable. And yet it still seemed cruel to Frank to snuff out the man's hopes like this, to leave him with the disease with the end so close at hand.

"Let's do it," said Frank.

They faced Schneider again and saw that he was brandishing his IV needle like a knife, a single drop of blood visible at its tip. "Stay away from me or so help me, I'll stick you with this. Don't think I won't."

They both froze. The needle was clearly strong enough to puncture their biosuits.

"Mr. Schneider," Carter said calmly, "you will put the

needle down and act civilly." He took a step forward and Schneider waved the needle at him violently, narrowly missing Carter's stomach.

"Mr. Schneider," Carter boomed, "this is your final warning. You will cooperate or you will be *forced* to cooperate."

But he wouldn't cooperate, and it was ten minutes before two orderlies in biosuits showed up to restrain him. Frank gave him the injection in the arm, and the old man howled in agony, not from the needle prick, but from losing what he had so longed for.

When they left him he was curled up in the fetal position on his bed, crying like a child.

After that experience, Frank decided not to inform the other patients what the vials contained. They were getting the treatment whether they wanted it or not, and upsetting them by telling them it was a countervirus would only make the process more difficult. At Frank's request, the orderlies accompanied him and Carter to each room and stood quietly by their sides while the countervirus was administered. With the orderlies present, no one else put up a fight.

There was the young black man suffering from sickle-cell anemia Riggs had described on the airplane; a thin boy of twelve or thirteen with visible symptoms of Marfan syndrome; and five others, who technically were clean of the virus, having been given a countervirus by the Healers three days after their respective healings, but whom the BHA wanted to keep in isolation until they were certain these people didn't pose a threat to the outside world.

"You can't keep me locked up like this," said one middle-aged woman who was clean of the virus. "The treatment's been out of me for months. I'm not a threat to anybody. You can't hold me like this."

"Could you describe what the countervirus they gave you looked like?" Frank asked, hoping to get some shred of information that might help him guess at its composition.

"Why would I tell you?" the woman said. "You only

want to stop them. You think I'd turn on them like that? After what they did for me? They healed me. I owe them everything. I don't have to tell you anything."

Frank didn't press the issue.

Once all eight patients had been visited, all Frank and Carter could do was wait. The countervirus would need a few hours to be integrated into each patient's system.

After those hours had passed, Frank took a blood sample from each of the patients.

The orderlies took the samples away to an adjacent lab and then came back in a few minutes with the answer. In all cases, the blood tested negative for the virus. There was no trace of it in anyone's system, including the three patients in whom the virus had still been active before treatment.

Carter took Frank's hand and shook it. "Well, Mr. Countervirus, General Temin was right. You're a genuine virus killer."

Frank somehow managed a smile. He knew he should be pleased—five months of work had gone into creating the countervirus, and this should be a moment of relief and satisfaction. Yet he felt none of that. Instead, he thought of Schneider coiled on his bed, crying and clutching the sheets, his hands still trembling from Parkinson's.

After decontamination, Frank showered, wrapped himself in a towel and returned to his locker. Carter was there on a bench, waiting for him. Rather than put his flashy business suit back on, Carter had dressed in the black uniform of the BHA. In his lap was a folded uniform identical to his own.

"Here," he said, offering the uniform to Frank. "Welcome to the club. Change and meet me outside. Then we'll get you something to eat."

Carter left the locker room, and Frank put on the uniform. It fit nicely. Black slacks. Black shirt, with the insignia of the agency over the left breast pocket. White stripes down the length of the sleeve suggested rank. A pair of new shoes and socks sat on the bench, and Frank put those on as well. When done, he tossed his towel in a hamper and joined Carter in the cafeteria.

The food was surprisingly delicious. Like every other aspect of their organization, the BHA had spared no expense. Dinner consisted of steak, grilled potatoes, asparagus, and a peach cobbler.

"So," said Carter, cutting into his steak, "is there a Mrs. Frank Hartman?"

The question caught Frank off guard. Broaching the subject of family seemed taboo. He was here on business, not to make intimate friends.

"There used to be," he said. "I'm divorced."

"Oh," said Carter. "That's none of my business, I guess. Sorry."

Frank shrugged. "Such is life."

"Such is life," Carter repeated. There was a moment of awkward silence. Frank tried to think of a segue to a different subject, but Carter got there sooner.

Sort of.

"I'm a child of divorce myself," he said. "My parents spilt when I was ten."

"That must have been tough," Frank said, not really knowing what else to say.

"My father wasn't the greatest of men. Part of me was glad to see him go, truth be told."

Not knowing how to respond to that, Frank became interested in his peach cobbler.

"Once he was gone, though," continued Carter, "I felt worse than I had when he was around. He had ignored me when my parents were still together, but at least he had *been* there. During those times, I could pretend, at least, that he was there because he cared about me. But when he was gone, I had nothing to hold onto. He didn't come around, so I knew he didn't give a rat's ass."

Carter waited, giving Frank an opportunity to contribute to the conversation. For his part, Frank didn't feel particularly motivated to chime in. To have a stranger—for Carter still was one—divulge his childhood relationship with his father seemed odd.

"It's tough being a parent," Frank said simply, hoping that would end the conversation.

It had the opposite effect.

"Oh?" said Carter. "You speak from experience? You got kids?"

Somehow the question Frank avoided at all costs had snaked its way into the conversation. And once asked, it could not be ignored. To ignore it demanded an explanation. It was better to simply answer and move on.

"I did," said Frank. "A daughter. She died of leukemia."

The response to this was always the same. People were mortified to discover that they had broached an unhappy, deeply personal subject and felt guilty because they assumed that by bringing up a death they were making the person experience the grief of it all over again.

Carter blushed. "I'm . . . sorry," he said, fumbling. "I didn't mean to . . ."

"It's okay," said Frank, forcing a smile.

But it wasn't okay. Not really. And as Carter quickly steered the conversation to safer ground, Frank found himself thinking only of Rachel. She had been six when she died, following a long hard fight. When the end had finally come, Frank and his wife had felt some measure of relief—not because there was no grief (there was plenty of that), but because nothing had been more excruciating than to watch Rachel slowly slip away, to watch her suffer.

Despite these memories, Frank put on a good face throughout the remainder of dinner and even afterward while Carter showed him to his room in the barracks.

The room was what he needed and nothing more: a bed, a bathroom, and a soft pillow. There was a computer terminal in the wall, and Carter showed Frank how to access the system and notify him or Riggs if Frank found the need. They then made arrangements to meet again in the morning, and Carter left him for the evening.

Frank still had the burned book of scripture, George Galen's *The Book of Becoming,* and he lay on the bed flipping through it. Since many of the pages were damaged by fire, Frank had to fill in a lot of blanks.

It was clear, however, from what remained that Galen had been careful in writing it, leaving out anything that could be considered incriminating. No mention of the virus. No mention of Healers or any specific group at all, in fact. Galen simply explained the need to reach out to the less fortunate, particularly those whom the world had forgotten: the homeless, the hungry, gangs, even small business owners were to be kept on a good servant's radar.

Occasionally Galen quoted the prophet, who always adopted a more biblical form of speech. Then there were chapters on healing oneself, how to rid the body of those habits and vices that kept one from reaching one's full potential. Drugs were shunned. And alcohol. Idleness was frowned upon. A continued practice of learning was encouraged. Regular exercise. Healthy diet. The chapters that followed were dedicated to those with genetic diseases, how science had dropped the ball, how the solution to these ailments was within grasp but ignored by those who could make it readily available. This was the Galen Frank had read and heard about, the pompous Galen, the quick-to-throw-blame Galen. Although the NIH was never named, it was clear who Galen was pointing a finger at.

The final chapters of the book were the most unnerving. They spoke of unlocking a healthy person's "genetic potential." No methodology was suggested, but the essence of it was clear: Galen believed that improving *healthy* DNA was as worthy of the reader's attention as healing *diseased* DNA. After that, there were several quotes from the prophet alluding to his own death and resurrection, which Frank, finding nothing of interest in them, merely glanced over.

With everything read, Frank turned to the last illustration, the Council of the Prophets. The young man in the red necktie, this supposed prophet, whoever he was, stood with four men identical to himself. The detail of the drawing was good, but the face of the man left room for interpretation. It wasn't a face Frank recognized, and yet some of the features felt familiar to him. The jaw. The nose. The roundness of the face. He had seen these features before.

As he stared at it, a thought came to him, and he quickly put the book aside and turned on the computer terminal. He signed onto the Net and did a search for George Galen. The first hundred hits or so were exactly what he expected: articles on the Human Genome Project, reports of Galen's tirades on a few talk shows, a few scientific journals containing studies written by Galen. But then Frank found what he was looking for: a photo of Galen in younger years, long before he had gained notoriety, long before the notorious white hair. It was a newspaper photo, taken back when Galen was doing some postdoctoral work at Stanford. Galen and a few graduate students were huddled inside a children's hospital, surrounded by many of the children from the ward. Galen had apparently organized some charity event that had raised money for the hospital and made the local paper. He was smiling wide, full of youthful idealism. The similarities were unmistakable. Dark hair, brown eyes, even the posture was the same. There was no questioning it, the drawing in the book was of Galen in his youth. The man in the red necktie featured in all the illustrations was George Galen. Author and prophet were one and the same.

12

CONTROL

Monica sat on the bed in Wyatt's room, watching him sleep. It was past midnight, and the hall outside their room was quiet. She had been listening for footsteps or voices for over an hour and had heard neither in that time. When she had checked the door earlier, she found it unlocked with no one outside it guarding it. The Healers either didn't suspect Monica would try to escape or they simply knew escape was impossible.

She looked down at Wyatt. He slept on his stomach, still wearing the clothes he had dressed in that morning. For the first time today he looked at peace.

Monica got up and pulled the sheet over his shoulders. She didn't want to leave him alone, but now was the best opportunity she was going to get to explore and find a way out. If she found one, a safe one, she'd come back, wake Wyatt, and the two of them would go together.

Stepping softly so as not to disturb him, she went to the door, opened it, and walked out into the hall. The lights were on, but the hall was empty. She stood there, listening, but heard only the ambient hum of the overhead lights and the air-conditioning.

She thought about what she might say if they caught her

out of her room. She couldn't claim to have been looking for the restroom, since there was one near Wyatt's room she had been using all day. She *could* say she was looking for food. Their meals had been brought to them on trays, so she wouldn't be lying if she said she didn't know where the kitchen was.

She walked in the direction of Yoshida's office . . . no, his laboratory, where he was building what he believed to be Galen's mind.

She shuddered. Yoshida was no more sane than Galen was.

She remembered passing a set of double doors on her way to his office and decided to try them. She reached them without incident and pushed on them tentatively. They swung open. The hall beyond was no different from the one she now stood in. Taking a final glance over her shoulder, she stepped into the unknown.

After thirty yards the hall turned to the left. It was then that she heard voices. She stopped, pressed herself against the wall, and listened. The voices were faint—whispery, almost, and sounded as if they were saying the same thing over and over again, like a recording that had been looped. Monica peered around the corner but saw no one. Down that direction, however, light spilled from a doorway into the hall.

She took a few cautionary steps closer and as she did, the voices became more distinct. Closer still, and she realized that what she had perceived to be two voices was actually one. Yoshida's voice.

Staying out of sight, she drew close to the doorway.

In hushed tones, Yoshida was whispering, "There is no master but the master. I must obey the master. There is no master but the master. I must obey the master."

He screamed then, and a loud crash sounded. A metal serving tray flew out the doorway and clanged against the opposite wall, clattering to the floor near Monica's feet.

She put a hand over her mouth to stifle a scream.

Yoshida grew louder, more desperate. "There is no master but the master. I must . . . obey the master."

His voice strained with every word, as if it required all of his strength to speak them.

"There is no . . . master . . . but . . . I will . . ."

Another crash as metal objects fell to the floor.

Monica looked back the way she had come. Someone would hear this. Healers would come. They'd find her here. She had to get back before she was discovered.

Just as she turned to go, Yoshida stumbled out of the room. He was a wreck, the perpetual smile gone, his eyes wild, his hair unkempt, and worst of all, his whole body was shaking, a trembling that began at the top of his head and extended to the tips of his extremities.

Monica recoiled from him.

He lurched for her and seized her by the arm. "There is no master but the master."

Monica tried to push him away, but his grip was like iron. He muttered the words again and again, not to her, but through her. She stumbled a step backward but somehow stayed on her feet.

"There is no master but the master."

She reared back to strike him, to break his hold on her by force, but then his shaking suddenly became violent. His head arched back, his eyes grew slack, and he released her. Then, like a puppet cut from its strings, he fell to the floor with a sickening crack and began flopping like a fish out of water.

He was having a seizure.

Monica's heart hammered in her chest, but she put the panic aside and acted on instinct. She had been an ER doctor. She knew trauma. Her movements now were automatic. She got down beside him and cradled his head so it wouldn't strike the floor again.

"Help!" she cried. "Somebody help me!" She had to get

him to a bed, off the hard floor. But she couldn't do it alone. She needed help.

Heavy footsteps sounded, and in seconds Lichen appeared.

"He's having a seizure," Monica said. "Help me."

But instead of helping her Lichen turned on his heels and ran back the way he had come.

"Wait! What are you—"

But he was already gone. Monica sat there stunned as the sound of Lichen's footsteps died away. She looked back at Yoshida. His body twitched and rattled and banged itself against the linoleum. She held him tightly, using all her strength to minimize the harm he did himself. But it was no good. His head still struck the floor. His back still arched. His legs still kicked.

There was shouting and more footsteps, and then Lichen reappeared, this time with Galen, who wore silk pajamas, slippers, and a bathrobe.

"He was shaking," Monica said, "talking to himself. Then he fell—"

Galen got down beside her and gently nudged her away. He grabbed Yoshida's head, cradled it in his hands, licked his lips, and then bent down and pressed his lips against Yoshida's forehead.

Monica watched, mystified, as Galen held that position.

Then, to her astonishment, Yoshida's body began to relax. His feet stopped kicking. His arms slunk to his sides. His body went limp. He was like a machine being turned off with all of its parts slowly pulled to the ground by gravity.

The kiss ended, and Galen sat back on the floor, head cocked to the side, watching Yoshida with concern.

Yoshida blinked his eyes open. For several seconds, he was perfectly still, staring up at the ceiling. Then, ever so slowly, the corners of his mouth turned up into that familiar smile. He turned his head to the side, saw Galen's face and said pleasantly, "Hello, master."

Monica ran back to her room in a sprint. She didn't stop when Galen called to her. She didn't stop when she nearly ran into Stone in the hall. She didn't stop until she reached Wyatt's room, threw open the door, ran inside, and locked the door behind her.

Wyatt woke with a start. "Mom?"

She went to the bed, got under the covers, and held him tightly.

No one came to the door.

Wyatt didn't speak.

And after what felt like hours, Monica fell asleep.

13

IRVING

Director Eugene Irving was not a man to be trifled with. To serve as the director of a federal agency such as the BHA, one needed balls of steel, plenty of ambition, and a few friends of political importance. Irving had all three— or all four, depending on whether you counted the steely balls separately.

His appointment as director had been partially due to his performance at the FBI, where behind his back his colleagues had called him the Charmer, as in snake, and partially because his cousin was a Republican congressman from Kentucky with plenty of pull on the National Intelligence Committee. Irving had a gift for making his superiors believe that he was the only man below them who recognized their greatness. And since such a man made for good company, Irving's superiors were eager to take him along with them as they rose through the ranks of the FBI. In short, he had ridden several men's coattails to a position of power.

Now, if only he could show the *current* powers-that-be—that is to say, the administration—how effective he was in his current post, he might actually have a future beyond it. As it was, he was only days away from a forced resignation. These Healers were going to destroy him.

He had not yet actually told anyone outside the agency all they had learned about the Healers, and he had given his agents strict instructions to the do the same. They would comply. None of them wanted another agency to start a turf war. But secrecy, Irving knew, could only be maintained for so long. The FBI, which leaked to the press like a sieve, had taught Irving that the almighty printed page could topple a man's career in a single day.

He had a plan. A good plan. It had been to deal with the threat himself, alone, and *then* go to the administration to show them that he had not only discovered a serious problem but also handled it so deftly that they would see in him the potential for greatness. We need not worry our pretty little heads with Eugene Irving on the job. Why isn't he the defense secretary, Mr. President? Why isn't he on your cabinet, Mr. President?

It had been a scenario Irving had played out many times in his mind. He had been waiting for the Healers. Or at least something *like* them. Something dangerous. Something that he could throw a lasso around, wrestle to the ground, and subdue appropriately. A trophy. A means to express his might, his competence.

But as he sat through the status meeting that morning, it was becoming increasingly clear to Irving that the Healers were *not* the golden ticket he had long been waiting for. In fact, they were becoming just the opposite.

"I thought you said Healers were going back to this man's house," Irving said, keeping the fury in his voice only barely contained so that they thought him civil but still feared him.

The BHA agents around the conference room table looked at him and then back at Agent Riggs, who stood at the front of the room, giving the report.

"You said," Director Irving went on, giving each syllable the proper emphasis, "that Healers were going to go to the home of this . . ." he looked down at the paper in front of him and found the name, "this Richard Schneider to give him a countervirus. That's why I had agents stake out the place. That's why they've been sitting there around the clock for three days now. Because *you* told me that Healers would be going to this location. And yet Healers have *not* gone to this location. Am I hearing you correctly?"

As Agent Riggs nodded, Director Irving thought how unfortunate it was that Riggs was African American. Irving had no bias against his race, of course, but he did enjoy making people blush. And right now, the blackness of Riggs's skin was denying Irving the sweet pleasure of seeing someone's face go from white to beet red at having been taught his place in the universe of Eugene Irving.

Riggs cleared his throat. "Sir, the patient in question was the source of our intelligence. Our suspicion—"

"Your suspicion?" Irving cut in, his voice icy. "The God-fearing government of the United States of America does not pay you to have suspicions, Agent Riggs. Suspicions do not solve crimes. Suspicions do not put bad people in prison. Suspicions do not allow old ladies to feel safe and sleep well at night. This"—he pounded on the table for emphasis—"is an agency of action. We do not waste time on unsubstantiated conjectures or unfounded intelligence. These Healers are a threat. All of our efforts should go into finding them, not sitting around waiting for them to come to us. They're as big as horses, for crying out loud. They shouldn't be too hard to pick out of a crowd. And until we find them, until we stop them and contain this virus, this nation is in danger. Now, I want results. I want Healers in custody. Yesterday. Do I make myself clear?"

Irving's face was as stern and demanding as he could muster, but inside, he was beaming. The speech had been a bit melodramatic in places, but overall it showed great political promise. I can work a crowd, he thought. He imagined himself standing at the pulpit of the Republican National Convention, his arms outstretched, his fingers giving the *V* for victory, the deafening roar of the crowd below him, and tens of thousands of balloons and confetti raining down around him. He would have to give some thought to a running mate.

"Perhaps we should ask other agencies for help."

Director Irving was brought back to reality. Someone at the table had spoken. He looked around and saw that everyone was staring at the virologist from Fort Detrick. Frank Hartman.

"Excuse me?" Irving said.

Frank leaned forward. "I said, maybe it's time to involve other agencies. We might have some more luck locating the Healers if we had more warm bodies out there looking for them. We could notify the FBI, the LAPD, even the NSA. I'm sure with their help, we'd have a better chance of success."

Irving was so shocked by the audacity of this man, by the very idea that someone would think it appropriate to counsel the director of the agency in front of other agents, that Irving sat there, mouth agape. What he wanted to do was reach across the table and smack the man. But after such a moving speech, he didn't want to spoil the moment, and so he remained as cool as possible. "Dr. Hartman, you're new at the agency. You've only been here a few days, so I will forgive your speaking out of turn. If I want the advice of someone unfamiliar with the operations and capabilities of this agency, I'll ask my mother-in-law. If you have opinions, I ask that you keep them to yourself."

To Irving's even greater surprise, this did not shut the man up.

"What Riggs was trying to say," Frank said, "about his suspicion, which is also my suspicion, is that Healers did not go to the home of Richard Schneider because they knew agents were watching the house."

The agents around the table looked from Frank to Irving as if expecting Irving to pull a gun and use it.

"What I mean is, I think someone told the Healers that agents were watching the house. Somehow they know the BHA is looking for them."

It was Irving's turn to blush, not from embarrassment but from barely contained fury. "Perhaps you weren't listening, Dr. Hartman, but what you *think* and what you *suspect* is of no importance. *We* will solve this problem. *We* will find the Healers. I think I speak for my fellow agents here when I say that we don't appreciate you telling us we're incompetent."

"That's not what I—"

"That's precisely what you said. To imply that we need to ask for help is to imply that we can't do the job ourselves." Before Frank could respond, Irving stood and faced them all. "Unlike our visitor here, I know that each of you is capable. I have full confidence in you. We will do our duty. And we will do it our way, the right way.

Irving left the room before another word could be spoken. Always leave them wanting more, he thought.

As he moved down the corridor back toward his office, he couldn't get Frank Hartman out of his mind. The man was becoming more of a burden than a help. If this kept up, he'd have no choice but to remove him from the agency. That would take a little doing, of course. The Defense Department had cleared Frank's temporary reassignment—even though they hadn't understood exactly what that assignment was—and sending Frank packing back to Fort Detrick without a legitimate reason would be a tricky business indeed.

That problem gnawed at him as he sat in his office, staring at the pile of paperwork that demanded his attention. I can't work like this, he thought. I can't work under this stress.

So he did the only thing one could do when the rigors of one's job became too demanding. He went to the golf course.

Eighteen holes has a way of making one's problems go away, and by day's end, Director Irving was feeling up again. Which might have been the reason why his guard was down when he returned home that evening. He pulled into his driveway without noticing the strange white van parked at the curb a block away from his house. Such abnormalities typically raised flags of suspicion, but Irving was in too good of a mood to suspect anything.

He took the golf bag from the trunk of his Mercedes and went inside. He set the golf bag by the door and, out of habit, went straight to the refrigerator. It wasn't until the refrigerator door was closed and the Coca Cola can opened in his hand that he saw the man sitting on his sofa.

Irving dropped the soda and reached for a holster that wasn't at his hip. Instead his hand found a golf glove protruding slightly from his pocket.

"Director Irving," George Galen said. "I hope you don't mind us coming in and making ourselves at home."

There was motion to Irving's right, and he spun around to see a man too large to be a normal man. Another one of slightly lesser size now blocked the door.

Galen gestured with his hand. "These are my associates Stone and Lichen. They will not harm you, Director Irving. Nor will I. I gather you know who I am."

"George Galen," Irving said, pleased at himself for keeping his voice so steady.

Galen got up from the sofa and approached him. "Yes. I am George Galen. But I am more than that as well. I have been for a very long time. I am a prophet."

Irving felt his muscles tense. In his peripheral vision he saw nothing he could use as a weapon. The only item currently at his disposal was the golf glove, and that would do little against men this size.

"A prophet because I see truth," Galen said. "A prophet because I see a future for all of us that no one else believes in. No one else but those like Stone and Lichen here, whose minds are open. To believe in this future requires faith. You're a man of faith, are you not, Director Irving?"

"What do you want?" Irving said, his hands forming into fists.

"I want you to believe, Director Irving. I want you to have faith. And above all, I want you to be happy."

Irving felt massive hands pin his arms to his side. A sharp kick to the back of knees sent him to the floor. Then the hands holding him lifted him slightly to a kneeling position.

Galen stepped forward, looked down into Irving's face, and gently put his hands on the side of Irving's head. "It would have been better if you had left us alone, Director Irving. As it is, you're getting in the way. I'm even told that you have a countervirus of your own now. This disappoints me greatly. I can't have you impede us. Not now. The best part is about to begin."

At this point, Director Irving suspected that his neck would be snapped or that a gun would be pointed. But no movement to his neck was made and no gun produced. Instead, George Galen did the last thing Director Irving would ever suspect. He licked his lips, bent down, and kissed Irving on the forehead.

14

ARENA

Jonathan sat upright in bed and watched the door. It was nearly six in the morning, which meant Dr. Owens would be coming around to check their vitals any minute now. She did so several times a day, and in the few days since her arrival, Jonathan had grown to savor their encounters.

They weren't allowed to speak, of course; Lichen had asked that she examine them in silence. But that was probably for the best—if he spoke, he'd only say something stupid. And Dr. Owens seemed like the kind of woman who could recognize stupid as soon as she heard it.

No, for Jonathan it was enough just to look at her, to watch her while she checked his temperature, blood pressure, and whatever other crap they wanted to know about him. She had a way about her, he had noticed, a quiet determination that he had never seen in a woman before.

Not that Jonathan had known many women, none that would pay him the time of day, anyway. When you were homeless, other people had a way of pretending you didn't exist, walking by without looking you in the eye or otherwise acknowledging you. And if their eyes *did* meet yours, they were always filled with disgust and contempt, the look you might give a rat or a cockroach or a steamy bag of trash.

It was a look Jonathan knew all too well. He had seen it often ever since he and Nick had stolen Jonathan's stepfather's Plymouth and driven it to California last year.

It had been a dumb thing to do. Both he and Nick knew this, though neither would admit it.

The drive from Alabama had been a long one, and the car hadn't lasted the trip. They had hitched the rest of the way and arrived in Los Angeles with only a few bucks between them.

Temporary relief came when Nick lied about their ages and got them work on a construction crew. But the foreman fired them the moment he discovered them sleeping in the very houses they were building. After that, things went bad. People pretending to be friends kept showing up. First the drug pushers. Then the pawnshop owner, the one who gave them a crowbar and dropped them off in the rich neighborhoods. Then the drug pushers again.

Liars, all of them.

In fact, liars were the only type of people Jonathan knew. Even Galen had proven to be one. Jonathan wanted to kick himself for being foolish enough to believe that for once he had found a genuine human being, somebody who wasn't smiling all sweetly on the outside yet plotting something sinister on the inside.

Nick was the exception, of course. He was no liar. Nick was true. Always had been, even when they were kids growing up in the same trailer park Nick had stuck by Jonathan when no one else had.

And now Dr. Owens was another exception. She wasn't like Galen at all. She was good, clean. She even made Jonathan forget at times how badly he needed a hit, how badly he wanted to scratch himself, to peel the flesh off where the needles had touched him last. And now she was coming again, right on schedule. He could hear her footsteps approaching.

The door opened. It wasn't Dr. Owens. It was the big guy, Lichen. He walked directly to Jonathan's bed and spoke quietly so as not to disturb the others, who were all still asleep. "You will come with me, Jonathan."

"To hell with you," said Jonathan. He still feared Lichen, but the fear had diminished. Lichen was only dangerous when he had a tranquilizer gun in his hand. He hadn't struck any of them yet and probably wouldn't.

"You will not disobey the prophet," Lichen said.

"You can tell the prophet to kiss my little white ass."

Lichen's massive hand wrapped around Jonathan's mouth and he lifted him out of the bed. Jonathan kicked and fought and tried to scream, but it was useless. He was no match for Lichen.

Lichen carried him out into the hall and set him on the floor. "You can walk or I can drag you," he said.

"Touch me again and it will be the last thing you do." It sounded ridiculous even to Jonathan, but he felt better for having said it.

"Very well," said Lichen. He reached down and grabbed Jonathan by the ankle.

"All right. All right. I'm walking. I'm walking. Chill."

Lichen released him. "This way." He turned on his heels, and Jonathan begrudgingly followed.

They walked for several minutes in silence, weaving their way through many long corridors of the building. It struck Jonathan as odd that they didn't encounter anyone. Usually there were people up at this hour.

"Where is everyone?" he said, being sure to keep his voice as casual-sounding as possible; he would not give Lichen the satisfaction of knowing how afraid he was.

"All will be explained to you," said Lichen, without looking back. "All of your questions will be answered."

Jonathan grew more anxious with every step. They walked down corridors under construction. They walked past walls of hanging plastic and rooms filled with building supplies. Finally they reached what looked like the wing of a new hospital, although Jonathan knew it *couldn't* be the wing of a new hospital; they hadn't left the *old* building. No, this new-looking part was merely the same old, grungy part, only slicked up with bright lights and a few coats of paint. This was Galen, the crazy old man, pretending to be something he wasn't. *Pretending* to be a hospital. A liar, just like all the other liars.

They passed stacks of open boxes filled with gauze and tubes and medical equipment, all still wrapped in plastic.

"This way," said Lichen firmly. He had stopped and was looking back at Jonathan.

Without realizing it, Jonathan had stopped at one of the boxes and picked up a bag of syringes—clean, sterile, syringes. He was holding them tightly in his hand and staring at them vacantly when Lichen's voice had snapped him back to reality. He dropped the syringes back in the box and quickly fell back into step behind Lichen.

"You are foolish to lose your free will to drugs," said Lichen. "You would be wise to keep your body pure and undefiled."

Jonathan thought of half a dozen slicing retorts but kept them all to himself.

Lichen pushed open a pair of steel double doors, and Jonathan stepped inside.

It was an operating room. Or so it appeared. Under a pool of light stood three people, all dressed in green scrubs. There was Galen, Yoshida, and Dr. Owens, who looked like she might be crying.

The doctors stood between two gurneys, one empty, one occupied. Jonathan couldn't see the face of the person lying on the gurney, but whoever it was, he wasn't moving.

"Welcome, Jonathan," said Galen. "Don't be afraid now. Come in. Come in."

Jonathan felt a light shove from behind as Lichen urged him forward. He stepped into the light and looked up. The operating room was at the bottom of a small arena. On a floor above him, in a wide circle, and behind glass windows, sat at a dozen or so Healers. They all looked down at him like Roman citizens calmly acknowledging the poor sap who would soon be a lion's meal.

"It's a big day for you, Jonathan," said Galen. "A day we've been waiting for. You'll be the first, a sort of trial run to see if this works as well as we all hope it does."

Jonathan said nothing. Galen was watching him, waiting for a reaction, and Jonathan refused to give him one.

"I know this is a little unfair of us to spring this on you unannounced," said Galen cheerily, gesturing at the crowd, "but we thought you might run for the hills if we told you about it ahead of time. You've been a wily guest, after all. You slept well, I hope?"

Jonathan looked intently at Dr. Owens. Now that he was closer to her he could clearly see the tears in her eyes.

Galen nodded and Jonathan felt Lichen's strong grip again, this time pinning his arms to his side and lifting him into the air. Lichen carried him to the empty gurney and laid him on his back. Jonathan didn't resist, even when they restrained him with leather straps.

He turned his head and looked at the man asleep on the gurney beside him. The man lay on his stomach, his head turned to the side facing Jonathan with his eyes closed. Jonathan didn't know his name, but he recognized him. He was the Healer who had brought Jonathan and the others food before. He had been wearing all black then. Now he was naked. On the left side of his lower back someone had drawn a dotted line with a black marker. The skin around the black line had been shaven.

"He volunteered," said Galen, following Jonathan's gaze. "He knew how important this test would be, so he volunteered. I thought that rather brave."

Jonathan wasn't listening. He was looking up at Dr. Owens now, who hovered over him, still crying. She had taken his hand into hers, and Jonathan found her touch warm and soft, exactly as he had imagined it would feel. Even with her cheeks streaked with tears, Monica was beautiful to him—twice his age, maybe, but more a woman than ever he had known.

Or so he had thought.

The last thing he remembered before they put the IV in him was how stupid he had been to believe that someone other than Nick could be his friend. If Dr. Owens was his friend, she would be fighting for him right now, pushing Lichen away and removing the straps that restrained him. But she did nothing, and Jonathan knew this meant that she was only *acting* upset. She was *pretending* to be his friend, even now. Even as they put him to sleep. And that, Jonathan thought, made her the biggest liar of them all.

15
ESCAPE

Curtains opened abruptly and blinding rays of a setting sun fell onto Jonathan's face. He blinked twice, but his eyes couldn't focus. He tried to sit up, but a stabbing pain in his stomach put him on his back again.

"Don't move," a voice said. "You'll only hurt yourself. Here, drink this."

Jonathan felt a hand behind his head and a cup at his lips. He opened his mouth as someone gently poured water inside. It was cold and wet and relieved the aching dryness he suddenly noticed in his throat. When he had his fill he lay back again.

"Now lie still," the voice said.

Jonathan opened his eyes, and the blurry image before him slowly cleared. Dr. Owens stood beside his bed, a syringe in her hand. She stuck it into a short tube that protruded from his IV and spoke quietly. "This should help with the pain. Just give it a moment."

"What do you care?" he managed to say, but not nearly as forcefully or angrily as he had hoped.

In seconds, whatever she had given him started working. The pain was subsiding; his head was clearing; he felt awake, energized. He threw back the bedsheet and pulled up his gown, caring little if she saw him undressed. The bandages covered his entire midsection.

"You've had surgery," she said calmly. "You need to rest, but I thought you might like a little sunshine."

"Where are my clothes?"

She pointed to a stack of clean scrubs on the table. "I can help you dress if you feel up to it, but I wouldn't suggest you wear pants just yet. The waistline might put unneeded pressure on your wound. How are you feeling?"

"Get out," he said in whisper. The sight of her made him want to cry for some reason, and he couldn't bear the thought of her seeing him cry.

"Jonathan," she spoke softly, "you have every right to be angry, but please listen to me."

"Get out!" he screamed, finding his real voice now, his grown-up voice.

She discarded the bottle that had contained the narcotic and moved for the door. She stopped there. He didn't look at her, but he knew she was watching him and crying quietly.

"I know nothing I can say will make a difference to you, Jonathan. And it shouldn't. But know that I'm as sorry as you are that any of this ever happened." She walked out.

He lay in bed, watching the sun disappear over the tree line and listening to the activity outside his door. Besides the occasional passing footsteps, all was quiet.

When the sky finally darkened and the stars appeared, Jonathan pulled out his IV, got out of bed, and locked the door. Keeping the lights off, he went to the wastebasket and retrieved the empty bottle of narcotic. Then, searching through the cabinet, he found four bottles of the same medication. He took the pillowcase off the pillow and made it into a sack, stuffing the bottles inside it. Then he packed syringes, clean bandages, scissors, and a blanket. The clean scrubs Dr. Owens had pointed out to him would give him only scant protection against the cold, so he cut a small slit in a blanket, making a poncho. He then changed into the clean scrubs and pulled the poncho over his head.

What he couldn't find or make were shoes, and after a vigorous search, he decided to go without.

The ground outside was about ten feet below the window. He lifted the windowpane and was momentarily panicked to discover that it only opened halfway, meaning he would have to squeeze through a smaller space than he had expected. The sack fit through easily. He tossed it to the ground below. Then, after several attempts, the last of which forced him to suck in his chest more than he had thought possible and to turn his head awkwardly to the side, he squeezed through and reached the ledge outside. He lowered himself as much as his arms were able, then dropped the remaining few feet to the ground.

When he landed, a pain from his abdomen shot through his body so explosively that he nearly passed out. He crumpled to the ground and grabbed his side, constricting his muscles in an attempt to minimize the hurting. It was as if someone was hovering over him, stabbing him repeatedly with a hot blade.

He writhed in the dirt a moment and then somehow, after catching his breath, got to his knees. He pulled back his clothing to examine the bandage. Small splotches of red had soaked through. He was bleeding.

He considered unwrapping the bandage and looking at the wound closely, but he feared he wouldn't be able to wrap it as tightly when he was done, so he left it.

He heard a jingling noise, and his heart skipped a beat when saw the source of it: dog collars. Two Doberman pinschers appeared around the side of the building and ran toward him. The instant they saw him they began barking ferociously. Jonathan recoiled against the wall, trapped. The dogs surrounded him, their jaws snapping, thick saliva spraying.

But they didn't come too close. They were guard dogs, not attack dogs. Jonathan, who had hopped many fences in his days, fleeing from police, knew the difference. Attack dogs bite. Guard dogs are all talk, no action.

Keeping his expression as calm as possible, Jonathan got to his feet and shuffled toward the back fence. The dogs circled him, barking constantly. But they didn't charge. They kept their distance.

When he reached the chain-link fence, he felt exhausted. Every step took more energy than the last. The medication, he realized, had fooled him into thinking he had more strength than he did.

One of the dogs lunged and snapped dangerously close to his thigh. They were getting more confident now, building their aggression. He had to move.

He tossed the sack over the fence and began climbing, ignoring the tearing he felt in his abdomen. The pain was nearly unbearable, but the frantic will to survive was even stronger.

He reached the top and managed to position himself on the other side of the fence without falling. They would hear the dogs. They would come after him. He had to hurry.

He lowered himself to the ground. The dogs barked and pawed at the fence.

Scooping up the sack, Jonathan padded away.

He hadn't gone twenty feet into the forest before cutting the bottoms of both feet. He had decided against taking the road they brought him in on, thinking they would find him easily on it if they discovered him missing. Now he wasn't sure he had made the right decision. It was dark under the trees, and the forest floor was littered with twigs, pinecones, protruding stones, and a thousand other sharp things.

He considered giving himself another shot of narcotic. The pain in his side coupled with that of his feet was almost too much to bear.

What he didn't know, however, was if it was safe for him to *take* another dose so soon. Dr. Owens had given him an injection only twenty minutes ago. Would another dose now knock him unconscious, or worse, stop his heart? As a junkie, Jonathan had seen overdoses before. Was he willing to take that risk? No, he decided. He'd wait. He could handle the pain.

A few minutes later, after a heavy thorn pierced his foot, he changed his mind.

He sat at the base of a tree and prepared a syringe, remembering how full the syringe had been when Dr. Owens had given him the last dose. Then, without hesitating, he stuck himself in the arm.

The relief came faster this time. Jonathan closed his eyes and relaxed, enjoying the process of giving himself a hit as much as the hit itself. His body tingled. His feet turned numb. He grabbed a low branch, pulled himself up, and, shouldering the sack, began walking again.

Soon his eyes adjusted to the light, or lack thereof, and he could step without cutting his feet further. He continued to stumble every so often, however, and when he did, the pain in his side shot through him like a bolt of lightning. Each time it happened, he had to stop and rest.

After half an hour, the ground sloped downward. Walking downhill proved more difficult than walking on level terrain. The slope forced him to put more weight on each foot as he stepped, and doing so aggravated the wound. For a moment he considered doubling back and looking for another route, but he knew that he had a better chance of finding a road at the bottom of the hill than at the top.

As he moved he checked the bandages. They were wet now, partially from sweat, but mostly from blood. What had been a few splotches of red before was now a single spot of blood the size of a dinner plate.

A branch snapped in the distance behind him.

Jonathan stopped and looked back up the hill. Several flashlight beams cut through the darkness at the hill's crest.

They were coming for him.

Jonathan felt panic rise inside him. He scurried down

the hillside, slipping on a patch of gravel and landing on his side. He almost cried out in pain, but he gritted his teeth and held in the scream.

At the base of the hill he came upon a shallow creek bed and gladly stepped into it. The cold mountain water soothed the soles of his bare feet as he stood there catching his breath. He looked back, and the sight of the flashlights coming down the hill motivated him to move again.

Rather than cross the stream directly, he walked with the current for a hundred yards in an attempt to throw off his trackers.

When he left the stream, his heart was pounding, and the bandages were completely soaked through. He dug into the sack, found a syringe, and gave himself another dose on the move, worrying little this time about the exactness of the amount or the dangers of giving himself too much of it.

He could hear their voices now. They were faint still, but they were getting closer, gaining.

Jonathan pressed a hand against his wound to minimize the bleeding and picked up his pace.

Branches snagged at his face and clothes as he went. There was no time to step delicately now, no time to choose the best path. What he needed now was speed. He took off the poncho and threw it aside. It was wet, heavy, and slowing him down.

His foot hit a rock, but the agony in his side was so striking and so constant that he hardly noticed. Even the narcotic wasn't strong enough now. He winced at the thought of how he would feel as soon as it wore off.

Then he shook the thought from his mind. Fear would only slow him down. All that mattered now was speed.

Lichen watched the two Healers with scent sniff the air around the creek bed. "Well?" he said.

"He entered the water here," one of them said. "The smell of blood is still strong."

"I want a direction, Pine," Lichen said, "not a travel log. Where did he cross?"

"Difficult to say," the Healer named Pine said. "I don't detect a scent on the opposite side."

"Nor tracks," said another. They were shining their flashlights along the creek bank, searching for footprints or traces of blood.

"I should have brought the dogs," Lichen said. "They at least can track."

It was the deepest of insults. Dogs were weak. They tired easily.

"Perhaps he went downstream," said Pine.

Lichen had already considered that, but he hadn't thought Jonathan intelligent enough to have come up with the idea himself. Perhaps the boy was smarter than he gave him credit for.

Or perhaps his mind had turned already and he had acquired the intelligence of the donor. But then, if that was the case, why was he running?

Lichen spoke quickly. "You three go upstream. The rest come with me."

The group parted, Lichen taking the lead and running downstream, water splashing from each of his giant steps.

After a distance, Pine grabbed Lichen's arm. "Wait."

Lichen stopped.

Pine tilted his head back and inhaled deeply through his nose. "He went out here."

"You're sure?" Lichen said.

Pine shined his flashlight on the bank and found Jonathan's tracks.

Lichen turned to another Healer. "Get the others."

The Healer ran back upstream while Lichen charged headfirst in the direction of Jonathan's tracks. Pine ran behind him, desperately trying to keep up.

• • •

At first Jonathan thought he might be hallucinating. Flashes of red and blue light were dancing on the trees above him. He was on his back, lying in the dirt and staring upward. He didn't remember falling or passing out, but he couldn't think of any other explanation for why he was suddenly in this position.

He rolled over onto his stomach and immediately wished he hadn't. The pain was throbbing now. He didn't know exactly how much blood he had lost, but he knew it was a lot. The bandage was doing little to stop the flow of it now. He could feel the thin trickle of it running from the wound and down his leg. And he felt lightheaded. It was becoming difficult to concentrate.

He struggled to his feet and saw that the light was coming from a source still obstructed by the trees ahead of him. He staggered forward and to his relief reached the end of the forest.

Before him was a wide grassy clearing, and beyond it and up an embankment was a police car. It was parked on the opposite side of a narrow country road with its lights flashing. A state trooper was standing with his back to Jonathan at the driver's-side window of another parked car, probably writing a ticket.

It was more than Jonathan could have asked for. Here, precisely where he needed one, on an otherwise desolate country road, was a cop. He was going to get help. He was going to make it.

He tried to cry out, but only a hoarse whisper escaped him. His throat felt raw again. He needed a drink. Why hadn't he drunk water from the creek?

Then he remembered the Healers. The Healers were coming.

He moved through the clearing as quickly as possible, his gait staggered and awkward. The footprints he left behind him were red and wet. Every muscle in his body screamed for him to stop, to give up, to lie down here in the grass and let sleep take him. He wouldn't wake up, he knew, but sleep would be an end to the pain.

The greater part of him, however, pushed on, the part of him that remembered Nick. Nick was still in trouble, he told himself. Nick needs me to make it.

Soon he could hear the faint twang of country music coming from the car radio. It made him smile. He was only a few steps away now.

The embankment was so high and steep that Jonathan lost sight of the state trooper when he reached it. No matter. He only had to ascend a short distance and there the state trooper would be again, ready and able to help him. He began to climb when a heavy hand grabbed his shoulder. It flipped him over and pinned him against the embankment. Lichen stood over him, hunched so as to be concealed from the road. He put his other hand over Jonathan's mouth.

Jonathan wanted to kick himself free, but Lichen's knee held him against the ground. Jonathan's hand fumbled in the dirt beside him until it unearthed a large stone. Swinging it in an arc he struck Lichen on the side of the head.

Lichen fell backward, releasing him, and Jonathan scrambled free, clawing his way upward, expecting Lichen's heavy grip to return at any moment. But it didn't. Jonathan reached the top and staggered onto the roadside.

"Help," he heard himself say.

Across the street the state trooper turned abruptly, his hand whipping to his holster. He was young, barely twenty, and when he saw Jonathan his eyes widened.

Jonathan rushed forward into the street, almost falling, arms outstretched.

Blinding white light flooded Jonathan's eyes. He turned and saw the grill of the approaching semi truck the instant before it struck him. Tires screeched and smoked as Jonathan's limp body flew through the air and fell hard onto the asphalt twenty feet away.

The truck came to a screaming halt, and the driver was out in an instant, the engine still running. He put his hand to his forehead and ran to Jonathan's body. The state trooper was right behind him.

"He came out of nowhere," the driver said, pale and terrified. "Ran right into the road. I didn't have time to swerve or nothing. He ran right in front of me. You saw him. He ran right in front of me."

"I think he's alive," the state trooper said.

The truck driver bent down to inspect further.

"Don't touch him," the state trooper said, grabbing his radio. "Nine fifteen to county. Request ambulance on US Highway 49, mile marker 67, over."

The dispatcher was acknowledging the call when the state trooper saw a flash of movement in the clearing below him. He unbuckled his flashlight and pointed the beam over the field. A big man in black was running back toward the treeline.

"Hey!"

The man in black didn't stop.

"Freeze!"

The state trooper pulled out his pistol just as the man in black reached the shadows of the forest and disappeared.

Sirens wailed as the ambulance bounced down the highway, rushing to the hospital and rattling the patient inside. Jonathan lay strapped to a stretcher, his neck in a brace, his face broken and bloody. The EMT hovered over him, assessing the damage and moving quickly.

It didn't make sense: the kid was already dressed like a hospital patient, wearing hospital scrubs but carrying no identification. Even more puzzling, according to witnesses, the kid had walked out of the forest miles from anywhere.

The EMT cut away Jonathan's shirt and found a bandage sopping with blood. He continued cutting, pulled back the dressing, and looked with horror at the gaping wound. What appeared to have once been a well-stitched incision was now mangled, torn, bleeding. The EMT applied appropriate pressure and in moments his gloved hands were dark red.

"He's got massive abdominal hemorrhaging," he shouted to the driver. "If I don't stop this he could go into cardiac arrest."

As if on cue, the machines monitoring Jonathan's vitals gave an unending beep. He was flat-lining.

"I'm losing him."

The driver hit the gas; it was late, the road was deserted, and every second counted. They could afford to go a little faster.

The EMT stuffed gauze into the wound and grabbed the defibrillator. Unless he could shock the heart into action, Jonathan would die in moments. He waited for the light to indicate a full charge, then put the pads to Jonathan's chest. With a jolt, Jonathan's body jerked, and miraculously the heart sprang to life, pumping rhythmically again.

Suddenly Jonathan's eyes shot open, and his hand reached out and grabbed the EMT's collar, pulling him close. The EMT was only inches from Jonathan's face when fluid erupted from Jonathan's mouth and splattered across the EMT. Immediately the heart monitor flat-lined a second time.

Instead of helping again, however, the EMT grabbed his own face and stumbled back against the wall of the ambulance. It felt as if his skin was on fire. Everywhere the fluid had touched him was burning hot.

He tore through his supplies; found a large, sterile gauze; and vigorously began wiping at his face.

"What's the matter?" the driver shouted.

But the EMT didn't answer. The liquid felt as if it was

boring into his flesh, drilling straight to the bone. He fell to his knees, covered his face, and screamed.

The driver momentarily lost control of the ambulance, the scream had startled him so badly. With a quick jerk of the steering wheel, he righted them again. "What is it?" he asked, his voice panicked.

"Burning my eyes. I can't see. My eyes."

The driver hit the brake and pulled over. With the lights still flashing, he got out, hustled to the back, and threw open the rear doors. The EMT collapsed into his arms.

The driver gasped. The EMT's face looked severely burned, as if it had been held over an open flame. He lowered him to the ground, and the EMT coughed, spraying the driver with blood and saliva. The driver wiped his face on his sleeve, then watched helplessly as the EMT began to convulse violently on the roadside.

In seconds the twitching stopped, and the EMT's chest deflated. He lay there limp, mouth open, face charred. Even without checking for a pulse, the driver knew the man was dead.

Frantic now, the driver dragged the EMT to the tailgate. If he could get him back inside the ambulance, maybe he could resuscitate him.

But try as he might, he couldn't lift him. The EMT was too heavy. And since the stretcher was occupied, his only hope was to call the other ambulance.

He ran back to the driver's seat and reached for the radio, and that's when the pain hit him. Suddenly his face stung with heat. The EMT's saliva burned like acid, stabbing like a needle, cutting through the fleshy tissue of his cheeks. He cried out and stumbled to the ground.

Panicked, he clawed his way into the driver's seat, put the ambulance in gear, and hit the accelerator. Gravel sprayed from under the tires as the vehicle rocketed back onto the highway, covering the forgotten EMT in a cloud of chalky dust.

The rear door of the ambulance was still open, and the stretcher bounced against the ambulance walls, banging into medical equipment, knocking some of it loose, sending it flying out the back. Tubs and packages, boxes, and straps all tumbled out onto the highway, leaving a trail of medical debris. If not for the harness anchoring the stretcher to the ambulance's interior, it too would have shot out the back and crashed onto the highway.

Moving at eighty miles an hour, the driver clutched the steering wheel with one hand and wiped at his face with the other. The road was becoming increasingly more difficult to see. His vision was going. Even the windshield in front of him was hazy and unfocused.

All that mattered little, though, compared to the searing pain in his face. He was tempted to let go of the wheel completely and claw at his face with both hands, but he didn't. He held firm. He was closer now. He could make it.

In an instant, that optimism vanished. The road turned sharply, and he hadn't seen the curve coming.

The front end of the ambulance smashed inward as it hit and then ripped through the metal guardrail. The driver was already through the windshield, flying outward and over the ravine before plummeting two hundred feet to the rocky bottom below. The ambulance was right behind him, a crumpled mass of disfigured metal and broken glass. It bounced twice against the cliff face before rolling to a stop near the driver, its emergency lights still flashing.

16

HEALER

The alarm sounded high and shrill and woke Frank from a deep sleep. He sat bolt upright in bed, disoriented, and blinked at the red flashing siren mounted on the wall near his barracks door.

There was noise and commotion out in the hall. Frank got out of bed, hurried to the door, and opened it. Four men, all agents of the BHA and all still dressed for sleep, were running out of their barracks and down the hallway toward the locker room.

The wail of the siren stopped, but the lights continued to flash.

Carter ran past.

"What's going on?" Frank said.

"Looks like another drill," Carter said, not slowing down.

Frank leaned against the door frame and rubbed his eyes wearily. The last few days had been exhausting. Riggs was on the warpath. After learning that Frank's countervirus had been effective, Riggs had formed an assault team to deal with the Healer threat. The team consisted of six tactical field agents, one communications expert, and one medic: Frank. It would be Frank's job to treat any infected person they found in the field and to assist the team in containing the virus. "You know and understand V16 better than any of us," Riggs had said. "If we find it, be it in its raw form or inside someone, I want you there to either annihilate it or contain it on-site."

Frank hadn't objected, but it did bother him to be thrown so suddenly into a tactical team with whom he had no experience. Plus, he had come to the BHA with the understanding that he would be conducting research or treating patients in an infirmary, not strapping a sidearm to his hip and kicking in doors.

And yet, there was a part of him that craved action like that, the rush of adrenaline, the heavy march of boots. He was a soldier first and a doctor second, or so his commanding officers had always told him.

What he didn't crave were the constant drills that inevitably came with any field assignment. Riggs had seized this principle with gusto and had been running drills nonstop for the past four days: forming a perimeter around a suspected hot zone, storming the home, subduing the infected person, containing the virus, and on and on and on and over and over and over again until Frank, who had thought himself in top physical condition, found himself crawling into bed each night, aching from muscles and bones he didn't know he had.

Overall, Frank had been impressed with the members of the team. Most were ex-military or ex-intelligence and had come to the agency with top credentials and service records. Some even had combat experience. And although Frank was the only one among them who was currently on active duty, he found himself hard-pressed to keep up with them.

The only exception was Peeps, the team's youngest and slowest member.

Peeps was the team's communications expert and had warmed to Frank immediately, since he considered Frank as much an outcast as he did himself. Since their first meeting, Peeps had made it his duty to tag along with Frank to every meal and explain the do-eats and don't-eats of the cafeteria. Normally Frank would have felt smothered by the attention, but for the time being he didn't mind the company.

"You coming?" Peeps said.

Frank blinked and raised his bowed head. He was falling asleep just standing here. "It's a little late to be running another drill, don't you think?"

Peeps shrugged.

He was a young kid, barely out of high school, tall, thin as a post, with a somewhat goofy expression. His curly brown hair suffered from a bad case of bed head at the moment, and a few pimples dotted his face. He wore a white pair of cotton pajamas with a comic book hero printed on them and looked as if he had just been teleported from a third-grade slumber party.

Frank said, "What would they do if I went back into my room, put my pillow over my head, and went to sleep?"

Peeps laughed, then looked as if he wasn't sure this had been intended as a joke. "You better come," he said.

"Right."

They jogged together down the hall toward the locker room.

"You're a little old to be wearing that, don't you think?" Frank said, gesturing at Peep's pajamas.

"They're comfortable. Besides, women love a man in pajamas."

"I didn't know you were a ladies' man, Peeps. Aren't you a little young to be chasing members of the opposite sex?"

"I'm eighteen, thank you very much. That's voting age. If I'm old enough to vote for the president, I'm old enough to chase skirts."

Frank grinned, feeling looser now—awake, even. "I thought *videotaping* skirts was your specialty."

"That too," Peeps said with a wink. It was common knowledge that Peeps had been recruited out of high school after rigging the varsity girls' locker room with surveillance cameras and then broadcasting the feed over a local cable channel. After he was convicted, men in nice conservative suits had come to offer him an alternative to prison time. Peeps, who was no idiot, had taken the offer.

The press, which had followed the trial and made Peeps somewhat of a folk hero among the twelve- to twenty-four-year-old male demographic, had called him Peeping Tom, and the name had stuck. Peeps had recounted the whole story at length to Frank immediately after introducing himself.

When they reached the locker room, some of the men were already in their biosuits, rushing toward the elevators.

Frank and Peeps opened their lockers and began changing. As soon as their suits were on, Agent Carmen Hernandez appeared, fully dressed and ready to go.

"Taking your sweet time, I see, boys," she said. "You might want to step it up a bit. Most of us finished dressing a full minute ago."

Peeps clapped. "Well, whoop-dee-doo and congratulations to you. I'm sure the agency has a medal or something for getting dressed so quickly."

Hernandez smirked. "If *you* go slow, we *all* go slow."

Frank recognized this as one of Riggs's catchphrases. As the leader of the assault team, Riggs had shouted those words a hundred times over the past few days. More often than not, he was shouting them at Peeps, who was almost always last at every drill. Frank couldn't tell if Agent Hernandez was mocking Riggs now or simply reemphasizing the principle.

Peeps obviously assumed the latter. "And what are you going to do about it, 'Nandez? Shoot us if we don't dress fast enough?" It was more a tease than a provocation.

She smiled, snapped a cartridge in her pistol, and holstered it. "Come on, Peeps, you think I'd make it that easy for you? If I was going to kill you, I'd do it nice and slow-like, gut you or something, tie your insides in a knot, and hang you out the window."

"There aren't any windows. We're underground."

"So I'd make one by tossing your skinny ass through the wall."

"See, Frank?" Peeps said. "I told you. She's knows it's skinny. She *has* been looking at my ass."

Even Hernandez laughed at that one.

Frank liked Hernandez. Her parents had immigrated from Mexico before she was born, and she had been raised in a home that cherished America. Choosing to defend it had been a no-brainer, and Hernandez had enlisted right out of high school. College had eventually worked its way into her plan, and after a stint at the Bureau of Alcohol, Tobacco, and Firearms, Hernandez had taken a post at the BHA. She had straight black hair cut short to accommodate a biohelmet, a face that could comfortably appear on the cover of a fashion magazine, and a rough don't-mess-with-me exterior. From what Frank had seen so far, Hernandez felt it her duty to constantly prove herself, as if she assumed that everyone expected less of her or was on the verge of questioning her abilities because she was a woman. No one did, of course—she was always the first person prepped and in formation; and while not always the first to finish a task, she made sure she was never the last. She did her duty well. The men on the team had warned Frank, however, "Whatever you do, don't make a pass. Hernandez might be a looker, but if she catches you looking, you're liable to find yourself on your back nursing a bloody nose."

They were dressed now. Frank and Peeps had their helmets, packs, and air tanks in place, and Hernandez led them to the elevators at a run.

When they reached topside, the helicopter blades were already spinning. They were the last on board, and the pilot took off the moment they seated themselves and the door closed.

Riggs addressed them. "This is no drill. Two of our boys have been watching an apartment in West LA. The medical record of the young girl who lives there was downloaded from Children's Hospital. We suspected that Healers would try to contact her, and it looks like we were right. Our boys watching the apartment said a suspicious character entered the building eight minutes ago."

"How suspicious?" Carter said.

"A distance scan indicated that the man is carrying the virus on his person. So there's a hot agent in the open. No screwups. This is our first chance to catch one of these guys, so let's do it right. Peeps, I want you connected with the team on the ground. The rest of you pay attention."

A schematic of an apartment building appeared on the wall monitor beside Riggs.

"We're going to the third floor, apartment 309. The target is seven-year-old Kimberly Turner. Our hope is to get there before the Healer exits the building and engages our boys on the ground. Agent Carter, Dr. Hartman, and I will enter from the front, here. Agent Hernandez, you will come in once we've subdued the Healer and help Hartman contain the virus. Agent Shaha, you will take the others and take a position in the back here below the balcony. Any questions?"

No one moved.

"Good. Then snap up and check your gear. We drop in less than two minutes."

Peeps did a quick radio check and confirmed that everyone's comlinks were operational just before the pilot announced that they were approaching the drop zone.

Riggs's voice sounded in Frank's helmet. "How you feeling?"

"I don't remember this being in the brochure," said Frank.

Riggs smiled. "You brought the countervirus?"

Frank tapped the pouch at his hip.

"What is it they tell you in the military?" Riggs said. "Keep your head down?"

"And don't run away," said Frank.

"Shoot first and ask questions later?"

"Actually, the military never gets around to asking the questions. We just shoot."

Riggs smiled. "You'll be fine. This is old hat for you. Carter and I will incapacitate the Healer. You go in and contain the victim. When the countervirus is in her, give Hernandez the clear. Piece of cake, right?"

The helicopter stopped its forward motion, and the pilot announced that they had reached the drop zone. Everyone stood and moved in a line to the door. Riggs slid it open and dropped the ropes. The helicopter blades were of a design that produced less noise than a car engine, so if they were lucky, they could drop without the Healer hearing them and being alerted to their presence.

Two undercover BHA agents stood on the asphalt below, ready to greet and assist the team as they descended. Peeps was the first man out, and since sliding down the rope was the one field exercise at which he excelled, he reached the bottom smoothly and without incident. The other agents followed quickly. Frank hit the rope after Riggs and slid down a little faster than intended. Luckily, his gloves took most of the heat.

In seconds the ropes were retracted, and the helicopter was pulling up and away.

The apartment building was three stories high and no different from the other overpriced apartments in West LA. Riggs gave the signal, and everyone moved into position. Frank joined Riggs and Carter at the building's entrance and saw Peeps follow the two undercover agents into a black van parked at a curb nearby.

Riggs pointed up at one of the windows on the third floor. "Plastic."

Frank looked and saw the sheets of plastic hanging

inside the apartment. What Riggs had said was true: Healers had their patients build makeshift containment curtains and used them to quarantine the patient during the gestation period. Frank shuddered at the sight.

Riggs touched his comlink. "Peeps, how we looking?"

"These guys got footage of the suspect entering the building twelve minutes ago."

A surveillance video appeared on the inside corner of Frank's visor. He watched as the Healer ducked his head to enter the building, the very spot where Frank now sat. The man was enormous, bigger than Frank had imagined Healers to be.

Peep's voice said, "Target, again, is Kimberly Turner, seven years old, sickle-cell anemia, only daughter of Roland Turner." Photographs of a young black girl and her father appeared on Frank's visor.

"Frank. That's your girl," said Riggs.

Frank gave a thumbs up.

"GPS is up and running," said Peeps. "Team is locked and in position."

The schematic of the apartment appeared, followed by flashing red dots that indicated the position of every member on the team. Kimberly's apartment glowed yellow.

"Target is set," said Riggs. "Recording, now." He reached up and turned on a small camera set in the side of his helmet. Frank and Carter did the same.

Peeps's voice said, "All right. I'm getting all of your visuals. Cameras are rolling. Riggs's video should be coming in now."

On the inside of Frank's visor above the schematic appeared a small window of video, Riggs's video feed. Frank and everyone else on the team could see exactly what Riggs, the team leader, saw.

"Whenever you're ready," said Peeps.

Riggs took a deep breath, drew his gun, opened the front door without a squeak, and went inside. Frank saw how the red dot representing Riggs moved through the schematic on his visor as the real life Riggs moved through the building. Carter went next. Frank unholstered his sidearm and followed the two toward the staircase.

Seven-year-old Kimberly Turner sat in a chair in her room, clutching her favorite stuffed animal and trying to hear what the giant man was whispering to her father. She wished the man would hurry up and leave. She didn't want him here, even after Father told her it that was okay and that she would feel much better once he left.

"But he doesn't smile," Kimberly had whispered to him. "He looks grumpy, like a mean person."

Father must have told the man this because now the man smiled constantly. But not a sincere smile, not the kind of smile she got from Ms. Perkins, the school librarian. That was a real smile, one with teeth and happiness behind it. This man had a wide, forced grin that made him look like he needed a restroom and quick.

And though she couldn't prove it, Kimberly suspected that it was the giant doctor who had made Father hang all this plastic in her room. It was silly. She couldn't even get to her dresser now.

"But you won't need to get anything," Father had told her when he hung it. "I'll get whatever you need and slide it under the plastic."

"But why can't I get it myself?"

"Because you'll need to stay in bed."

"For how long?"

"Three days."

"Three days? How can I go to school if I'm stuck in bed?"

"You don't have to go to school. We're taking a little vacation."

Kimberly wasn't one to argue with that. "What will I do in bed all day?"

"I'll bring the TV in here. You can watch it all day if you like."

This was sounding better by the minute, and finally Kimberly had agreed. But now that the giant doctor was here, she wanted more details. Why was this doctor coming to their house instead of Kimberly and Father going to his clinic? Didn't he *have* a clinic? And why come so late at night? Why couldn't he come during the day? And why was he so big?

The only other doctor who had come to her house had been normal-sized. That had been a week ago. Kimberly had been very still as he wiped a Q-tip inside her mouth to get some sample he needed. DMA, or something.

Father came and knelt beside her. "Dr. Stone is going to give you a shot, Kimberly. You'll only feel a little prick, and then it will be all over."

Father said it like she had never had a shot before, like he expected her to cry or refuse. Maybe he wanted her to. Maybe it made Father happy if he thought he was helping. "Can I hold your hand while he gives it to me?" she said.

Father smiled and took her hand. "I'd be crazy to say no to the hand of a princess."

"An ice princess?" she said.

"With magic skates and a golden dress."

She smiled. It had been a story Father had made up a long time ago—one he always told her whenever he came and stayed with her in the hospital. Sometimes he forgot some of the details, but Kimberly always filled in the holes and reminded Father which parts he'd missed. It made Father happy to see how much she enjoyed the story. So much so, in fact, that Kimberly began to believe he forgot parts on purpose just so she would open her eyes and participate instead of only listening.

Dr. Stone reached into his briefcase and pulled out a syringe filled with a medicine so bright green that it glowed. Kimberly stared at it.

"It will only hurt for a second, Kimmie," Father told her.

She looked at him and smiled to show she wasn't afraid.

"Please wait behind the plastic, Mr. Turner," Stone said.

"I can't hold her hand?"

"Behind the plastic, please. It's for your own protection. A matter of life and death. I will see to it that Kimberly gets into bed."

"Yes, of course." Father squeezed her hand tighter. "I'm going to be just over there, Kimmie. Everything is going to be fine. Dr. Stone will see to it that everything is fine."

She nodded and watched Father reluctantly move behind the plastic.

Stone knelt beside her. Kimberly rolled up her sleeve without being asked. She knew the drill. Stone cleaned a spot on her arm with a swab of cotton, then uncapped the syringe.

There was a bang, and the door flew open. Three men in what looked like space suits charged into the room, holding guns. Kimberly screamed.

Riggs pointed his weapon at Stone. "Federal agents! Put the needle down!"

Frank held a bead on Mr. Turner, his finger off the trigger. The little girl stopped screaming but looked on the verge of tears. Mr. Turner put his hands up. Stone didn't move.

"I said put the needle down. Now!"

Stone continued to hold his position. Frank almost gasped at the sight of the man. His head nearly touched the ceiling, and his arms were as big around as Frank's legs. His expression was blank, and he didn't appear the least bit concerned that three armed men were about to take him into custody.

"I'm going to count to three," said Riggs, "and if I reach three and that needle is in your hand, it's going to get very loud and you're going to get very dead."

The little girl ran to her father and threw her arms

around his waist. The sudden movement spooked Frank, and his finger went to the trigger, not squeezing it.

Relax, he told himself. Get a grip.

"One," said Riggs.

Stone looked at Kimberly just a few feet away, as if judging the distance from the needle to her arm.

"Two."

Stone held his hands out, showing he would comply.

"Put it on the bed. Nice and slow."

"No," said Turner. "Wait a minute. Who are you people?"

Riggs never took his eyes off the Healer. "We're federal agents of the Biohazard Agency, Mr. Turner, and you are in great danger."

Stone lowered the needle to Kimberly's bed.

"Now step away from it and put your hands behind your head."

Stone began to obey, but in one fast movement grabbed the briefcase and slung it at Riggs. It spun like a Frisbee through the air and hit Riggs square in the chest, knocking him backward off his feet. Before Frank or Carter even flinched, the Healer backhanded Carter, launching him to the side like a rag doll. Carter smashed through the closet doors and fell hard to the floor. Toys, clothes, and boxes fell from their shelves on top of him.

Riggs was on his back and fired. The bullet ripped into the Healer's shoulder, the force of it knocking him off balance. To Frank's surprise, however, the Healer's face showed no pain. His expression was unflinching, which meant his body had responded to the forward motion of the bullet only, not the pain it inflicted, as if he had merely been shoved unawares.

Before Riggs could fire again, Stone was on him, wrenching the gun from his hand and picking him up, using his wounded arm as much as the healthy one.

Frank aimed to fire, but Stone was faster. Inhumanly fast. He threw Riggs's body directly at Frank with such force that when they collided, Frank fell back into the hall, the wind knocked out of him. Riggs rolled to the side, unconscious, his helmet visor cracked.

Turner grabbed Kimberly and hovered over her, protecting her.

Frank struggled to his feet, found his gun, and saw Stone lift Turner off Kimberly and toss him aside. Turner crashed into a framed mirror on the wall and fell to the floor, not moving.

Kimberly screamed.

"Don't move," said Frank.

Grabbing Kimberly, Stone lifted her in front of him, using her as a human shield. She kicked and cried and winced with fright.

Stone said, "Why must you interfere? What I give this girl will make her whole again."

"Put her down!" said Frank. He knew he couldn't fire. Even though Kimberly only covered a portion of Stone, Frank didn't trust his aim. He might hit the girl.

Again with lightning speed, the Healer moved, grabbed the syringe off the bed, and stuck the needle into the meat of Kimberly's arm. Again, she screamed, this time from pain.

"Catch," said Stone, then pitched Kimberly into the air toward Frank.

Instinctively, Frank dropped his weapon and held out his arms. It was an awkward catch and Kimberly was heavier than he had expected, but when they fell to the floor, she seemed unhurt.

Stone, still clutching the syringe, spun around, pushed through the plastic, and jumped through the sliding glass door that led to the balcony. The door exploded outward, raining shards of glass down onto the alley three stories below.

The agents on the ground immediately opened fire, some hitting Stone, but most hitting the building. Stone was too fast. He jumped off the balcony and fell directly toward his attackers. The shooting and sounds of a struggle continued as Frank opened his pouch and produced the countervirus. At the sight of another syringe, Kimberly wailed louder.

"Kimberly, I need you to listen to me. My name is Dr. Hartman. I have to give you this medicine."

She recoiled from him, looking afraid.

"I'm not going to hurt you. I want to help. This medicine will help you."

She wouldn't stop crying. She was too distraught. Nothing he could say would calm her.

"I'm sorry," he said, then took her arm and, despite her pulling and panicking, gave her the shot. She screamed again, tears streaming out of her eyes.

Frank spoke into his comlink. "Target deactivated. I need a bag in here."

Carter shook his head, brushed away the debris that had fallen on him from the closet, and got to his feet. "Where is he?"

Frank pointed to the gaping hole where the sliding glass door had been. Carter ran to it and looked over the side, just in time to see Stone clear the back fence and sprint up the alley.

Peeps's voice sounded in their helmets. "He's running. Suspect is headed north toward Santa Monica Boulevard. And we have agents down. Repeat, agents down."

Carter ran out the door, yelling to Frank as he passed him, "I'm going after him." He disappeared down the hall just as Agent Hernandez arrived with the containment gear.

She knelt beside Kimberly and waved a contaminant rod around her. The rod glowed red. "She's hot."

"She will be for a few hours," said Frank. "It takes a while for the countervirus to take effect.

Hernandez pulled a clear plastic bag from her pack and shook it open. It looked like a long clear trash bag with arms, legs, and a breathing apparatus at the head. "Kimberly, my name is Agent Hernandez. You're not going to like this, but you need to put this on."

"Carter needs backup," Peeps said. "Repeat, Agent Carter is in solo pursuit."

Frank looked at Riggs, who lay unconscious on the floor.

"Go!" Hernandez said.

Frank took off at a run, maneuvering through the apartment and down the stairs, taking two, three steps at a time. "Peeps, I need a wider visual."

"Roger that."

The schematic of the building inside Frank's visor disappeared, and a satellite map of a four-block radius took its place. Carter's blinking red dot was superimposed over the image, showing his position moving fast toward Santa Monica Boulevard.

Peeps said, "They jumped a fence behind the building and are now moving north up an alley."

Frank ran outside and around the building. The agents who had held a position here below the balcony now lay on the ground, spread over the parking lot. One of them was slowly getting to his feet, but the others were deathly still.

Frank didn't stop. He jumped the fence behind the Dumpster and took off up the alley. "Give me Carter's visual."

"Roger."

Carter's video feed appeared as a thumbnail on Frank's visor. As if looking through Carter's eyes, Frank could see Stone in front of him, running. Carter was apparently moving fast as well; the video image jostled violently.

Frank reached behind him as he ran and opened the valve further on his air tank, giving himself more oxygen. He was breathing heavily and needed a greater supply. Plus, the visor was fogging, making it difficult to see. Cool air poured in, and the visor cleared.

He killed them, Frank thought. The Healer had killed members of the team: Shaha, Mayo, Kim, and the others.

They all lay dead back in the parking lot. Or if they weren't dead, they were at least hurt very badly. Even Riggs, whom Frank considered indestructible, was down.

And the Healer had done it with his bare hands. No weapon. Just his hands.

Frank heard the screeching of tires ahead as Stone left the alleyway and ran out onto Santa Monica Boulevard, turning west toward the ocean and sprinting down the middle of the road into oncoming traffic. Cars swerved to avoid him.

Carter was right behind him, moving fast. More tires screeched. Horns blared.

Frank's chest felt like it might burst, he was so out of breath. The problem wasn't the air valve now. The problem was Frank. Even after several rigorous days of training, he still wasn't ready for a run like this.

"Peeps," he heard Carter say, "my visor's fogging, losing visibility. I'm removing my helmet."

"Negative," said Peeps. "Negative. Suspect could still be hot, over."

Carter's video feed suddenly went to static, and the red dot representing Carter on Frank's map became stationary.

"Peeps," said Frank, between heavy breaths, "what's happening?"

"I lost him. He took off his helmet. I got no visual, nothing to track."

Frank reached Santa Monica Boulevard and turned west on the sidewalk. Cars were stopped in the road. A half a dozen of them had collided. Drivers were out of their vehicles, yelling at each other, and people were coming out of restaurants and stores to see the source of the commotion.

Frank hit the speaker on his comlink. "Out of the way," he said.

The crowd on the sidewalk in front of him dispersed as people scurried to the side to let him pass. A woman screamed with fright at the sight of him in his suit.

Frank ran three blocks before he found Carter's helmet on the roadside. He picked it up and continued running. The pain in his chest was now so intense that he wanted to vomit. No matter how wide he opened his mouth, he couldn't get enough oxygen. He felt completely drained of energy. His legs were wood.

He heard ambulance sirens behind him in the distance and hoped they were going to the apartment building and not the crash scene. No one he ran by on Santa Monica Boulevard looked hurt, but he couldn't say the same about the apartment.

He turned the corner, and there was Carter, hunched over with his hands on his knees, catching his breath. Alone. Frank stopped running, ripped off his helmet, and threw up into a garbage can.

A young couple out for a late-night stroll saw him heaving and hurried away in the opposite direction.

Frank felt a hand hitting him softly on the back. "You, okay?" said Carter.

Frank dry heaved a final time before calming and standing erect, the bitter taste of vomit still in his mouth. "What happened?"

"Car was waiting. But even if there hadn't been, I never would have caught him. He never slowed down, only got faster."

"You get a license plate?"

"It was too far away. I couldn't even tell what color it was in the dark."

Frank spoke into his comlink. "Peeps, we need a ride."

A fleet of ambulances surrounded the apartment building when Frank and Carter returned. Medics with BHA insignia on their backs were lifting team members onto stretchers. There were no body bags as far as Frank could see, which was a relief.

Riggs was awake but badly shaken, walking to and from

the wounded, assessing their damage. A doctor tried to examine him, but Riggs brushed him off. Police were setting up a barricade to keep back the neighbors who were gathering around the building and craning their necks to see the scene.

Frank found Kimberly and Agent Hernandez in the back of an ambulance. Kimberly was inside the containment bag with the breathing apparatus near her mouth. She glanced at Frank and abruptly looked away.

The medics arrived with Roland Turner on a stretcher and pushed him into the ambulance. Kimberly brightened at the sight of her father, but then grew still when she saw the blood-soaked bandages around his arm.

"I'm okay, princess," Turner said. "It's just a scratch. Come here and let me look at you."

"I'm afraid that's not possible, Mr. Turner," said Hernandez. "Kimberly needs to remain sitting here. She can't have any contact until she's been fully tested and treated."

Turner's face grew ugly. "Who do you people think you are, huh? First you come into my home, pointing guns at us, putting my daughter and me in danger."

"Mr. Turner," said Frank, "the man you let into your home was carrying a virus that—"

"You think I don't know that?" said Turner. "Do you think I'm such a fool that I would let a man into my home without knowing full well what he was bringing with him? My daughter is sick, you hear me? Sick. And hurting. Pain you can't imagine. And she's my daughter, not yours. I know what's best for her. And now you've gone and ruined everything. If she isn't healed because you interfered, so help me you'll pay for it. I swear to you."

Frank felt a hand on his shoulder and turned to see Carter beckoning him to step away from the vehicle. When the doors of the ambulance closed, Turner was still shouting.

"You can't reason with them, Frank. Don't even try."

Carter left him alone after that, and Frank stood there, staring up at the apartment building. Agents he didn't recognize marched inside with contaminant rods. They would scan for the virus and quarantine the building. Other agents were escorting the building's other bleary-eyed tenants outside to a table, where they would be tested for possible infection.

News helicopters flew overhead, their bright search-lights sweeping the entire city block.

Sirens blared as more police vehicles arrived, and neighbors and news crews jockeyed for position at the police barricade. If the world didn't know about Healers before now, they were about to find out.

"You okay?" said Peeps.

Frank faced him. "Yeah. You?"

"I feel like I *should* be hurt, but I'm not." He shook his head. "We had four men on the ground out here, Frank. All armed. That Healer was *unarmed*. One guy. Unarmed. And these guys . . ." he motioned to the agents being loaded into ambulances, ". . . they didn't stand a chance. That Healer could've killed them, I think, if he wanted to. With his bare hands. Just his hands. And did you see how fast he was running? He had four rounds in him and he was running like the Six Millon Dollar Man. His body was doing things it shouldn't have been able to do."

"Yeah, I saw."

"You know what I think?" said Peeps, adopting a conspiratorial tone. "The guy's got CIPA."

"What?"

"CIPA. Congenital insensitivity to pain with anhidrosis. It's a genetic disease. Rare as hell. People who have it don't feel pain. They can fall off a roof and not know they're hurt until they find their arm in the bushes."

"A genetic disorder?"

"CIPA. Look it up, if you don't believe me."

"And you think this Healer may have this condition? You think he's incapable of pain?"

Peeps shrugged. "What's to say they don't *all* have that disease? Think about it. These guys produce a virus that fiddles with your genes, right? Heals you of some disease? But who's to say they can't do the opposite? Who's to say they can't take a healthy person and *give* them a genetic disease?"

Frank considered that. He remembered *The Book of Becoming*. Galen wasn't averse to manipulating healthy DNA. He had embraced the idea, in fact.

Riggs approached, holding a long-range communicator. "Peeps, we're going to need that van. Tell the ground crew we're borrowing it for a while. The whole setup. If they give you any lip, tell them I gave the order."

"What's wrong?" said Frank.

"I just got off with headquarters. The sheriff up in Agoura Hills called in. An ambulance crashed up there. Three dead bodies."

"What's that got to do with us?" said Peeps.

"Sheriff said it looks like something melted their faces off."

"Melted their faces?" said Frank.

"His words. Not mine."

The photograph of the dead police officer that Frank had been shown on the plane came to mind.

Riggs said, "The helicopter's flying some of our boys out there now. We'll catch up with them. Get your gear."

He walked off, and Frank closed his eyes. His head was pounding. His biosuit was heavy with sweat. His muscles ached from overexertion. And from the sound of things, the night was only going to get worse.

17

SITE

The incessant ringing of the doorbell woke Director Eugene Irving from an otherwise peaceful slumber. He rolled over, looked at his wife, who continued to sleep undisturbed, and realized that she wasn't getting up to answer it. Cursing under his breath, he threw back the covers and got out of bed. He found his slippers and his bathrobe and shuffled down the hall.

The doorbell buzzed again.

"I'm coming. I'm coming."

He passed the grandfather clock and saw that it was two in the morning. He found the light switch, flipped on the blinding lights, and slowly descended the stairs to the front door.

Someone knocked.

"I'm coming," he said angrily. He flipped on the porch light and peered through the peephole. He immediately recognized the white-haired figured looking back at him. Stone.

Irving felt a momentary panic. He unlatched the deadbolt, freed the chain, and opened the door.

"What are you—"

Before Irving could finish, Stone's hand was at his throat, constricting it, pushing him back into the house as

Stone entered and kicked closed the door behind him. "You set your men on me," he said in a low growl.

Irving's mouth was open, gagging. He tried to speak but no sound escaped him. Desperate, he pulled at Stone's hands. He could've been pulling at a mountain for all the good it did him. His lungs screamed for air. He could feel his face turning blue. Just when he began to see spots, Stone released him. Irving fell to his knees, gasping and sputtering.

Then Stone's hands moved again, inhumanly fast, this time clutching Director Irving's bathrobe and lifting him off the ground, bringing him within an inch of Stone's nose.

"Explain yourself."

"I don't know what you're talking about." He could feel Stone's hot breath on his face.

"Your men. They came while I was treating one of our patients. They were watching the apartment."

And then Irving remembered the list. The list of downloaded names. "We found a list. A list of names that you had downloaded from Children's Hospital. I had some of our people watching those addresses."

"Why didn't you tell us?"

Irving whimpered. "That was several days ago. When I gave the order I didn't think they'd watch this long. I forgot that—"

Stone dropped him. "Humans are weak. I should've expected as much." He pushed past Irving and made his way to the kitchen.

As Irving followed, he paused at the banister to glance up the stairs to make sure his wife wasn't standing there watching. She wasn't.

In the kitchen, Stone found a glass, filled it at the sink, downed it, filled it again, and downed it a second time.

"I need bandages," he said.

"You shouldn't be here. You can't stay here. You have to leave. Now."

"I need bandages first," Stone repeated. "And a new shirt."

Irving looked at Stone's black shirt and noticed for the first time that it was soaked with blood. Stone pulled the shirt off, and Irving put a hand to his mouth. Four deep puncture wounds—bullet wounds, maybe—dotted Stone's chest. They had stopped bleeding, but they were big enough for Irving to poke his finger into.

"Bandages," Stone said, a little more urgently this time. "And pliers."

"Pliers?"

"For removing the bullets."

Irving felt the dinner of the previous evening start to venture back up his esophagus. He put his hand back to his mouth, swallowed, and tried to calm himself.

"Your home is the only one I know in the area," said Stone. "I didn't come here to bully you. I need your help. Now please find me pliers and some bandages so that these can heal."

Irving composed himself, stood erect, and looked as menacing as possible. "I don't answer to you. Now get out of my house."

Stone looked at him blankly and spoke calmly. "Do you see these holes in my chest? If I can withstand this, do you think I would be remotely intimidated by you? You will either find me what I need or I will be forced to harm you."

A minute later, after sterilizing the needle-nosed pliers with hot water and alcohol, Irving handed the requested items to the Healer in his kitchen.

"A bowl, please," said Stone.

By the time Irving found a silver mixing bowl, Stone was already pulling the first slug out of his chest. He dropped it into the bowl, where it landed with a *ka-tink.* Irving stood there, staring at the bloody slug in the bowl still clasped in his hands. He didn't dare lift his eyes to watch Stone remove the others. It wasn't until the third bullet that he realized that Stone made no sounds, no cries of anguish. If it pained him to dig deeply into himself with a pair of needle-nosed pliers, Stone gave no sign of it.

Finally, the fourth bullet dropped into the bowl.

Next came the bandages. Irving cut tape as Stone applied the sterile gauze to the areas. By the time they patched up the fourth hole, it looked as if it was healing already. Heavy red scar tissue was forming where a gaping hole had been only moments ago.

When they were finished, Stone said, "May I have a shirt now, please?"

Rather than point out that he had nothing in Stone's size, Irving tiptoed back up to his room and found a T-shirt in his closet. His wife stirred, and Irving froze, daring not to make a sound, fearful that she would wake and suddenly have the urge to go downstairs to the kitchen for a late-night snack. Instead, she rolled onto her side and continued sleeping.

When Irving returned to the kitchen, he was horrified to see Stone on the phone. For an instant he thought someone had called and that Stone had answered. But then he realized that the phone would have rung first. Stone recounted to whomever he was speaking what had happened to him and how he had run the two miles or so to Irving's home. When he was finished, he offered the receiver to Irving.

"Hello?" Irving said, knowing before the voice answered who would be on the other line.

"Thank you, Eugene," Galen said. "I appreciate your helping Stone. I'm disappointed that you failed to tell us about the stakeout. But let's put that past us, shall we? To err is human. And you, unfortunately, are human. We've had our own problems here this evening, Eugene, or I'd offer to come get Stone myself. As it is, you'll need to loan him your car."

The sound of the master's voice was like the gentlest of breezes, as soft as the brush of a cotton ball. Irving suddenly wondered why he had allowed himself to get so upset at Stone. He, Irving, deserved the mild rebuke. Stone was only doing the master's work. And any friend of the master was a friend of Irving's. He told the master that he wanted to come with Stone, but the master, much to his disappointment, told him that it was more important for him to remain in his current position.

After he hung up the phone, Irving realized how happy he felt. He gave the T-shirt to Stone, who pulled it on, then retrieved his car keys from the kitchen counter.

"I just got it detailed," Irving said, dropping the keys into Stone's hand. Then, with a wink, "Try not to scratch it."

Frank sat in the passenger seat of the van as they drove north up the dark highway toward Agoura Hills. Riggs was at the wheel. Carter and Peeps sat in the back. Everyone else, with the exception of Agent Hernandez, who had accompanied the young girl and her father back to the BHA, had been too injured to join them.

Two red lights ahead of them turned out to be road flares, and Riggs slowed the van. A state trooper had his vehicle parked perpendicular to the road, blocking traffic. He waved them to stop with his flashlight, and Riggs pulled the van up next to him.

"Road's closed, sir," the trooper said. "You'll need to turn your vehicle around."

Riggs flashed his ID, and the state trooper touched the brim of his hat apologetically. "Thought you boys had all arrived. Your vehicle isn't marked or I would have waved you on through."

"How far away is the crash site?" Riggs asked.

"Not sure exactly. Your boys had us block half the county. I only know what I heard over the radio."

"Which is what?"

"Well, I'm only getting bits and pieces, mind you. You

probably know more than I do. But the way I heard it, there's two sites. One is just a body, dumped on the side of the road. And the other is the actual wreck, about two miles up from that. Grisly scene, I hear. Ambulance went right off the cliff."

"Thanks for the warning," said Riggs, putting it into gear.

The trooper put his hand on the van, stalling them. "What you suppose that ambulance was carrying, anyway? Hazardous material? Must of been something to get you all involved."

"Thanks for your help," Riggs said and drove around the flares and past the trooper's car.

Two miles later they came upon the first body. A dozen men in biosuits were hunched around the corpse, some taking photographs, others taking blood samples. Riggs stopped the van, put it in park, and slid a new biohelmet over his face. The others followed suit and checked themselves for leaks before getting out.

The agents recognized Riggs and parted as he approached. He and Frank squatted by the corpse. The EMT's face was severely burned and dotted with black splotches.

"Did you take a sample?" Riggs asked one of the agents.

"Definitely V16," the agent said. "We think he may have contracted it from whoever they were carrying in the ambulance."

"Where's the ambulance?"

"Straight that way," the agent said, pointing up the highway.

Riggs thanked them, told them to carefully bag the body, then got back into the van with Frank and the others.

Debris littered the highway ahead. Riggs had to drive slowly, weaving around the boxes and equipment that had spilled out of the ambulance.

Riggs parked the van near a large white tent set up in the middle of the highway and led Frank and Riggs inside. Peeps stayed in the van to run the video feeds.

The tent was a flurry of activity. A long row of tables had been set up directly over the yellow lines of the highway that separated the two lanes of traffic. Atop the tables were diagnostic equipment and computer terminals. A dozen agents in biosuits moved about, busy with various tasks.

A stout one with thick-rimmed glasses beneath his bio-helmet greeted Riggs as they entered.

"Where's the body?" Riggs asked.

The agent led them through the back flap of the tent to where the ambulance had launched itself into the ravine. The broken guardrail was a twisted wreck of metal and mud. Several high-wattage lights were positioned around a small crane that had been secured to the cliff face, a single black rope hanging from its end.

"Please tell me this isn't the only way down," said Carter.

The agent looked apologetic. "Winds out of this ravine are too high for a helicopter to get you down there safely. And we couldn't find an access road. For the time being, the rope is it."

Frank slowly stepped to the edge and looked over the side. It was a long way to the bottom. There were two small teams of agents already down there examining the bodies. The ambulance lay upside down, so broken and crunched it only vaguely resembled a vehicle at all.

Frank bit his bottom lip. Any height over ten feet caused the hair on the back of his neck to stand up. He backed away from the ledge, feeling dizzy.

"You okay, Frank?" Carter said.

"Fine."

Without a word Riggs grabbed a harness and began putting it on. He was rappelling down the line before Carter and Frank had their harnesses secured.

Frank was the last to go. He stood at the cliff's precipice for several minutes, gathering his courage.

The agent with the glasses stood behind him, watching and waiting. "Do you need any help, sir?" he said finally.

When Frank didn't answer, the agent poked him. "Sir? The line—do you need assistance down the line?"

Frank looked at him. "No," he said with a grin. "I'm just not a fan of heights, is all."

The agent nodded. "Nothing to be ashamed of, sir. I know the feeling. My wife is afraid of spiders. Screams like a little girl whenever she sees one."

Frank forced a smile. "Thank you. That makes me feel so much better."

He stepped over the lip of the ledge and let gravity pull him downward.

At the bottom another agent took him to where Jonathan's body had been laid. Riggs and another agent were squatting over the body when Frank arrived.

Frank had treated wounded soldiers before. In the Middle East, when the threat of biological weapons was no longer a concern, the military had put him in a triage hospital assisting surgeons. It had been squeamish work, young soldiers victimized by roadside bombs and mortar shells, and Frank had worked hard to erase the images from his memory.

All those images came back the moment Frank saw the kid in scrubs, lying there on the ravine floor in a mangled, bloody mess.

"This is nothing," the agent beside him said. "You should see the other guy." He pointed to a group of agents about twenty yards off. "Went through the windshield, then right onto the rocks. Ker-splat."

Riggs shined his penlight on the body. "You said he had a prior wound?"

The agent knelt beside him. "Yes, sir. Here in the abdomen. These bandages were still attached to his waist and look about a day old, is my guess."

Frank got down and took a closer look. "Looks like a surgical wound."

The agent nodded. "No question. You can still see the sutures." He inserted his fingers into Jonathan's side and pulled back a flap of skin. The sutures were there all right, but most were broken and hung limply from the flesh.

Carter, looking sick, turned away and walked off to watch from a distance.

"Peeps, you getting all this?" said Riggs.

"Affirmative," his voice said. "And I've lost my appetite."

Riggs turned to Frank. "Why would someone need surgery here?"

Frank snapped his flashlight to the side of his helmet and pulled the wound apart to get a look inside. It didn't take long to confirm his suspicion. "Kidney transplant," he said.

"Transplant?" said Riggs. "I thought the kidneys were higher in the abdomen."

"They are. Traditionally, we think of transplants involving the removal of one organ and replacing it with another. That's not the case with kidneys. The old kidneys remain. The new kidney is simply placed below them, closer to the groin. Look, you can see the sutures from the urethra to the bladder."

The agent took a closer look. "He's right."

Riggs looked also, then turned to the agent. "And you're sure he was infected with the virus?"

"Not just infected, sir. The kid was swimming with it. Very high concentration. I've never seen a reading like that. The ambulance drivers didn't have a chance."

Riggs stood. "What do you think, Frank?"

Frank shrugged. "It's possible he got the virus from the kidney. That happened a few years ago in Atlanta. A girl dies in an auto accident and since she was a donor, her kidneys, liver, and heart were transplanted into four people waiting for a match. A few days later one of the transplantees is dead and the other three are in critical condition. Turns out the girl was a carrier of West Nile virus but had not yet shown any of the symptoms. So her organs infected the organ recipients. Doctors were doing more harm than good."

"So whoever gave him this kidney could be a carrier of V16?"

"Maybe. But if that's true, I'd like to know how he survived this long. If the virus came from an infected donor, the kidney should have killed him almost instantly. What's more likely is that the virus he's carrying was engineered for him, since neither the kidney nor the virus seem to be the cause of death."

Riggs turned to the agent. "And he had no identification?"

"No, sir."

"What about his prints?"

"We're scanning those now, sir. If he's on any database, we'll know about it shortly."

"Good. In the meantime, I want a tissue sample from the kidney. Scan it and compare it to the other samples you've taken."

"Yes, sir."

"Then I want someone to contact every hospital in a fifty-mile radius to see if anyone is missing a transplant patient. If this kid was given a kidney in the last forty-eight hours, he should still be in the hospital. No one would have discharged him. So he's missing from somewhere. I want to know where."

"Yes, sir."

"You can check," said Frank, "but I'll be surprised if this surgery was performed at any hospital."

"What makes you say so?" said Riggs.

"Look here at his arms. These injection wounds. See the sores here? The kid was an addict, heroin probably. And some of these sores don't look very old. Few weeks, maybe."

"What are you saying, a hospital wouldn't treat a heroin addict?"

"Not for an organ transplant, it wouldn't. You've got to be clean to qualify. The demand for organs is too high to give them to people who won't take care of them properly. It's why so many people die of cirrhosis; they can't give up alcohol long enough to qualify for a new liver."

Riggs squatted in the dirt and examined the boy's arms.

"And look at his feet," said Frank. "Multiple lacerations, mud, thorns. The kid was running from something and didn't have time to grab his shoes. Who runs away from a hospital?"

Riggs looked at the agent. "Who saw the accident and called the ambulance?"

"County said a sheriff's deputy called it in."

"We got a name?" said Riggs.

The agent checked his notes. "Deputy Melvin Dixon."

"I want a written report from that guy as soon as possible. What he saw. Where this kid came from. Every detail."

"Yes, sir."

"And I want him brought in. He probably didn't contract anything, or he'd be just as dead as these two, but I want to do a full scan nonetheless. Just to be sure."

"Yes, sir."

"Wait a second," said Frank. He was kneeling over the kid. "There's something here on the back of his neck."

He turned the head further to allow Riggs and the agent to see.

Riggs got down again and shined his flashlight. "Those are stitches," he said.

The wound on the back of the boy's neck was two inches long and ran down the center, beginning just below the hair line.

"What *is* that?" the agent said.

"It's too clean a cut to be an injury," said Frank. "It looks like another surgical wound." He held out a hand. "Let me borrow your scissors."

The agent reached into his medical bag and produced a pair of surgical scissors.

Frank delicately cut away each of the sutures. The wound parted a half inch, and all three men saw it at once. Deep within the flesh of the kid's neck was a tiny blinking light.

18
BLOOD

Frank got out of the helicopter as soon as it landed at the helipad above the BHA's underground facility. Orderlies were there waiting for him, and they helped Frank pull the three gurneys out of the helicopter. Strapped to each gurney was a body bag. As the blades of the helicopter began to slow, Frank and the orderlies wheeled the gurneys to the elevator and down into Level 4.

According to the federal database, the boy's fingerprints matched those of Jonathan Fox, age fifteen. Jonathan had been arrested last year in Los Angeles for drug possession and had been ordered to serve community service. That service was never served, and the court had no address on record for the kid. Homeless, Frank figured.

Once inside Level 4, Frank asked the orderlies to take the ambulance driver and the EMT to the morgue. He wheeled Jonathan into a separate room, opened the bag, and examined the body.

With the right equipment at his disposal Frank was able to widen the wound on the back of Jonathan's neck.

The blinking light came from a computer chip attached to the base of Jonathan's brain stem. A dozen or so fiber-optic lines reached from the chip and disappeared into the neural tissue.

It took a little doing, but Frank was able to remove the chip without damaging it. He put it under a microscope and looked for manufacturing markings or anything that would help him determine the chip's origins. He found nothing helpful.

The only explanation he could think of, and it made no sense to him, was that the Healers had put this into the boy. The glaringly obvious clue was the presence of the virus. But why the Healers would transplant an organ into Jonathan or insert a computer chip into the base of his brain, Frank could only guess.

He put the chip in a small glass containment canister, then called the agency's mortician, who would conduct a more thorough examination of the body.

The next morning he placed the canister onto Peeps's desk. "You ever seen a chip like this before?"

"Please don't tell me that's what you found inside that guy."

Frank waited. Peeps sighed, took the canister, and put it under a magnifying glass attached to a swiveling arm on his desk.

"Hmm. I've never seen a design like this. Whatever it is, it looks like it holds a buttload of memory."

"You mean it stores data?" said Frank. "I thought chips were only processors."

"Shows what you know." Peeps maneuvered the canister so that the chip caught the light differently. "Wait a second," he said. "This could be a biomedical chip—you know, what you might find in a robotic prosthesis, triggered by enzymes or hormones or neural electrodes, stuff like that."

"What do you mean, 'triggered'?"

Peeps shrugged. "Well, a chip like this is normally dormant in the body. You could say it's currently turned off. It only becomes activated when it comes in contact with, for lack of a better word, a specific internal juice. If it's hit by a certain hormone, for example, it becomes operational."

"And does what?"

e a ghost, all cut up and white as death. And the
' he pointed across the clearing, "he ran off
ne trees there."

ou found the EMT also?" said Carter.

nodded. "When the ambulance didn't show up at
tal, County had me head up that way to see what
d. I found the EMT on the side of the road and
und where the ambulance drove off the cliff." He
is head. "I swear I've never had a night like that,
an I ever wanted to see."

you never touched any of the victims?" said

no," Dixon said, waving his arms quickly. "No, sir,
touched them. I knew better than that. And a good
didn't."

ter and Frank put on their biosuits and told Deputy
to wait by the roadside. Carter then unstrapped his
ninant rod and led Frank down the embankment and
s the clearing.

lidn't take long to find traces of Jonathan's infected
l in the grass. The contaminant rod beeped and
d from white to red whenever it came upon a bloody
rint.

ey followed the footprints to the tree line, unhol-
d their sidearms, and attached their contaminant gog-
to the front of their visors. With the goggles on, the
d became radioactive green. Splotches of red on the
nd indicated where Jonathan had stepped and left be-
traces of V16.

is entire area will have to be quarantined, Frank
ht, if not burned.

th the goggles to guide them, following Jonathan's
through the forest was a snap. They moved slowly
arefully, however, so the brush didn't snag and tear
iosuits. At times they lost Jonathan's tracks, and
had to double back and try a different direction be-
ey picked it up again.

"Well, that's the sixty-five-thousand-dollar question.
Chips do what they're designed for. Some chips, for example, can notify diabetics that they're running low on in-
sulin. Could be anything."

"Can you find out what's on it? Can you access the
data?"

Peeps shook his head. "Not without the trigger. I have to
turn it on first. I can hook it up to my system, but without
the trigger, it'll do nothing."

"Then we need to find the trigger."

Peeps chuckled. "That would require that we take samples of this kid, his blood or his bile or whatever, and then
drop each of those samples onto the chip in the hope that
it would do something, spark something, initiate some
process. And good luck finding someone willing to do
that."

Frank smiled and patted Peeps on the shoulder. "Thanks,
Peeps. I knew I could count on you. If you need any help,
let me know." He walked away, leaving the canister in
Peeps's hand.

Frank returned to the locker room, prepared to enter
Level 4, and found Director Irving there waiting for him.

"Frank, a moment of your time please."

"Of course, sir."

"I'd like you to go back up to the crash site this morning.
Find the deputy who saw the accident. Get a full report
from him. I'd like to know exactly where this Jonathan Fox
came from. Maybe the deputy saw something that could
lead us in the right direction."

"That's a good idea, sir, but might I suggest that another
member of the team go in my place? I was going to examine the body to—"

"Someone else can do that," Irving said impatiently.
"That kid was infected, Frank, and you're our specialist on
this V16 business. I want you handling it."

"All right. Who should I take with me, sir?"

"Take with you?"

Frank wrinkled his brow, unsure. "Would you prefer I go alone?"

"What? Alone? No, no, of course not. Take . . . Carter. Take Agent Carter with you. But just the two of you. And leave immediately. Not a word of this to anyone. This whole kidney transplant business makes me nervous, Frank. I don't want to increase the anxiety around here until we know what we're up against." He tapped his forehead with the tips of his fingers, suddenly distracted.

Frank waited a moment, expecting more instructions, as Irving stared absently at the floor. After a silence, Frank asked tentatively, "Will that be all, sir?"

Irving started, as if he had forgotten Frank was standing there. "All? Yes, yes, that will be all. Do that for me, Frank." Then without another word he walked away.

Frank watched him go, noticing a slight tremble in Irving's hands.

The Lost Hills Sheriff's Station, which had jurisdiction over Agoura Hills and was located north of Los Angeles in Calabasas, was little more than a few desks, a watercooler, and stacks of unfiled paperwork. Frank and Carter found Deputy Melvin Dixon at a table finishing off a jelly doughnut.

Carter flashed his badge. "Deputy Dixon, my name is Special Agent Carter of the Biohazard Agency. This is Agent Hartman. Do you mind if we ask you a few questions?"

Dixon wiped his hands with a napkin. "About what?"

"The accident you witnessed last night."

Dixon moved his tongue inside his mouth, dislodging a doughnut crumb wedged in his teeth, and shook his head mournfully. "Most gruesome, awful thing I ever saw in my life. Kid came out of nowhere. The truck didn't have time to swerve or anything. And the sound when the truck hit him. You know that sound, like when you got a bunch of

sticks in your hands and you b
Terrible. Just terrible."

"Why was the victim in the s

Dixon leaned back in his ch
across his stomach. "Well, I can't
uh, the victim as you call him, h
couldn't hear. I think he wanted
man might've been chasing him."

Carter perked up. "A man?"

"Big fellah. About so tall." He h
head to suggest the man's height. "

Carter and Frank exchanged glan

"You say this man was *chasing* the

"Maybe. Hard to say. They coul
can't be sure."

"What happened to him?" said Ca
what did he do after the accident?"

"Ran off into the woods. Fast as any

"Did you report any of this to the BI

Dixon wiped his face again with the
After the accident my shift ended. And
It spooked me bad, as you can guess. But
port for you, if you like."

"Tell us more about the tall man," said
follow this guy into the woods?"

Dixon blushed. "Well, I had to stay w
tim. The ambulance was on its way and
was there in the street. I had to block tr
the ambulance came and went, I figured
be long gone."

"Can you show us where this happen

Dixon grabbed his wide-brimmed hat
his police cruiser to where the truck
Dixon got out, recounted the event, and
Carter the tire marks.

"He came up right here," he said, po
the embankment where Jonathan

looked li
tall man
through
"And
Dixo
the hos
happene
then I f
shook
more t
"An
Frank
"O
I neve
thing
Ca
Dixo
conta
acro
It
bloo
turn
root
T
stere
gles
worl
grou
hind
Th
thou
W
track
and
their
twice
fore t

After twenty minutes they found a used syringe in the undergrowth. Riggs held the contaminant rod over it, and the rod's reading identified the substance as morphine.

"Anesthetic," said Frank. "If the kid just had surgery, he'd be in a lot of pain. He wouldn't be able to move without it."

They bagged the syringe and came to a creek bed. After walking up and down the opposite bank, they found Jonathan's trail again and followed it to the top of a hill. Frank was ready for a long drink of water, but didn't dare remove his helmet in an area crawling with virus.

Fifteen minutes later they reached a fence, beyond which was a wide, two-story dilapidated building.

"We should call for backup," said Frank. "I don't like the look of that."

"Me neither," said Carter.

Loud barking startled them, and Frank actually jumped. Two Dobermans charged the fence and continued barking until Carter took a small aerosol can from his hip and sprayed a mist into the dogs' faces. They immediately went limp and toppled to the ground.

"Neat trick," said Frank.

"I'd say we got about forty minutes before they wake up and start barking again."

They stood there a moment in silence. "Well," said Frank. "Go or stay?"

"We should at least know what we're calling in. This place could be empty."

"Then what are the guard dogs for?"

"Maybe it's a warehouse or a storage facility. I say we at least look around." He began climbing the fence. Frank took a deep breath, holstered his weapon, and scaled the fence after him.

When they were over, they quietly padded past the dogs and moved around to the front of the building.

Thick ivy covered most of the brick, and nearly half the windows were smashed in. Frank pulled some of the vines away from a sign near the front door to reveal the words *Happy Mountain Rest Home. Assisted Living.*

Carter pushed on the door, and it swung open with a loud rusty creak. Beyond the door was darkness. "Maybe it's empty," he said.

"Maybe it's not," said Frank.

Carter removed the penlight from his hip, turned it on, and snapped it to the side of his helmet. Frank followed suit, and their two tight beams of light shined like long white javelins into the darkness. Then, with guns at the ready, they stepped through the doorway and into the building.

Deputy Melvin Dixon was bored to the point of becoming desperate. It had been well over an hour, and the BHA agents weren't back yet. He sat on the hood of his cruiser and checked his watch for the three hundredth time. He was tempted to simply get in his car and leave.

Grunting with frustration, he hopped down from the cruiser, descended the embankment, and crossed the clearing, careful to stay clear of the spots where the bloody footprints lay.

When he reached the tree line he yelled, "Hello."

A few birds fluttered away, but otherwise it was silent.

"Hello," he yelled louder. "Can you hear me?"

Nothing.

"You BHA better get on back. I got my lunch hour soon."

The trees remained silent.

Dixon stepped over some brush and walked a little way into the forest. He could still see his police cruiser from here, but if he went any farther, he'd lose sight of it.

A twig snapped to his left.

Dixon spun around and saw no one. "Agent What's-your-name? Is that you? Hello?"

A twig snapped to his his right.

Dixon spun again. And again, there was no one. His hand fumbled for his holster. He found the leather strap that held the gun in place and unsnapped it. His eyes never stopped moving, scanning the forest, wild with fear. He pulled the gun out, hands shaking, and didn't see the figure rushing toward him before it was too late. Dixon felt a heavy fist strike the side of his head. The gun fell from his hands, and all went black.

Lichen knelt beside the body of the fallen deputy and checked the man's vitals. He didn't think he had hit the deputy too hard, but he couldn't be certain. It was difficult for Lichen to determine how much of his strength he should use in such situations. Too much and he might knock the man's head off. Too little, and he might merely anger the man and get shot.

He had done well. He found a heartbeat. The deputy was still alive.

And a good thing, too. The prophet had been very specific in his instructions.

Lichen waved to the two Healers hiding nearby, and they ran over to him.

"Take him back to the roadside. Put him in the van, but be mindful of traffic. Don't be seen. Then move the vehicles."

They nodded. One of the Healers threw Dixon over his shoulder, and they took off at a run toward the road.

Lichen removed the backpack from his shoulders. Inside were various bottles of sprays, liquids, and other decontaminants. He took one out, sniffed the air, and followed the scent until he found one of Jonathan's bloody footprints in the grass. He doused the footprint and surrounding area until he was certain the blood was diluted enough to avoid being detected on any scanner. There were hundreds of these footprints, but now that they had served their purpose (the

BHA agents' scents were still fresh in the air) Lichen began the task of decontaminating the entire area and erasing any evidence of Jonathan Fox.

So wise was the prophet. So fearless. Only he could have transformed what should have been their immediate ruin into such an opportunity. How could anyone question his greatness?

Lichen put his nose in the air and sniffed once more, searching the wind for a whiff of Jonathan Fox's blood.

19

DARKNESS

Frank and Carter stood in the lobby of the Happy Mountain Rest Home, shining their flashlights around the room.

"It ain't the Ritz Carlton," said Carter.

Frank had to agree. What was once a well-furnished and even stylishly decorated establishment was now just a dump. Graffiti covered the walls. Furniture was overturned and broken. Crushed beer cans and cigarette butts lay scattered on the floor.

"A bunch of high schoolers had their way with this place a hundred times over," said Carter.

"Doesn't look like anyone's been in here for years, though," said Frank.

They went deeper into the building and came to a set of double doors sealed shut with a rusty chain and padlock. Carter found a length of rebar on the floor, put it through one of the links of the chain, and twisted. The corroded link snapped, and Carter pulled the chain free.

"That chain might be there for a reason, you know," Frank said.

Carter winked and pushed the door open.

The room beyond the doors was even darker than the lobby. They stepped forward cautiously and swept the space with their flashlights. It was a large area, with cobwebs and dust and a wide octagonal island in the center, the kind of island that could have once served as a reception desk or a nursing station. Frank let his flashlight pass over the walls. Vandals had never gotten this far, apparently; the walls and floors were graffiti- and trash-free.

They crossed the room and found two parallel hallways leading deeper into the building's interior.

Carter's light shined on a sign on the wall. "These hallways lead to the residents' rooms. Should we check them out?"

"They look just as deserted and dark as the rest of this place. What's to check out?"

"You scared of the dark, Frank?"

"I'm scared of things that *lurk* in the dark. We shouldn't be in here alone."

Carter pointed Frank to the other hallway. "You take that one, and I'll check this one."

"You're not one to listen to reason, are you?"

"Look, I'm not thrilled about the situation here, either," said Carter, "but we got nothing yet. If we go back now and bring the team up this mountain only to find this building filled with nothing but musty smells, we're not doing anyone any favors. Now, we've only got forty minutes of oxygen left, so our time is limited. If we're going to sweep this place, we'll cover more ground if we split up."

Frank tightened his grip on his sidearm and walked to the hallway assigned him. When he looked back, Carter was already gone.

Frank moved down the dark hallway, his eyes alert. He stopped at the first resident room he came to and checked inside. It was empty and looked like all the hospital rooms he had ever seen, small with an even smaller bathroom adjacent.

Eventually the hall bent. Frank turned the corner and saw a door ahead of him with a crack of light beneath it.

Curious, he went to it. The door was locked. A small keypad on the wall had a blinking light on the side.

Frank hit his comlink. "Carter."

Carter's voice came over the frequency. "Yeah?"

"I may have found something. There's a door here. With light on the other side. And a keypad on the wall. Looks like it's got power."

"I'll come to you."

The comlink clicked as Carter released his talk button.

Frank examined the keypad closely. It was slick and modern-looking, with a digital readout screen and a polished steel design, too new to be part of the building's original security system.

Using a short, pencil-thin screwdriver from a pouch at his hip, Frank snapped off the face of the keypad, exposing the intricate circuitry underneath. Then he tapped the circuitry in just the right places with the screwdriver tip— a trick learned in the military—and the keypad sparked and short-circuited.

There was a click as the lock unlatched, and the door slid open.

Blinding white light spilled out of the room and flooded the hallway. Frank raised a hand to his helmet and shielded his eyes, allowing them to slowly adjust.

What he saw next made him shudder. This was an operating room. Various life-monitoring machines, some as big as refrigerators, sat by two sterile operating tables, positioned side by side under large shiny medical lights.

Frank entered the room and looked up. The ceiling was over twenty feet above him. Along the wall, where the second floor would be, were tall panes of glass that surrounded the room entirely. Behind the glass were rows of empty theater seats.

Cautiously, gun still in hand, Frank approached the operating tables. Everything looked fresh-out-of-the-box clean. The walls and floors were spotless, the light generous, the metal polished to a shine.

Beside the beds stood metal trays holding various surgical implements. Frank picked up the scalpel. Glints of colored light reflected off its razor-sharp edge.

Carter's voice sounded in his helmet. "Frank!"

The voice was panicked, frenzied. Behind it were the sounds of a struggle. "Help, I—"

The line went dead.

"Carter?"

There was no response.

Frank dropped the scalpel and ran from the room. He sprinted down the hallway until he reached the room with the nurse's station. He stopped, pressed himself against the wall, and listened. The building was silent.

"Carter?" he said in a whisper.

No answer.

He reached up and turned off his penlight—he'd be an easy target in the dark with it on—and the room became nearly pitch-black.

He pivoted around the corner into Carter's hallway, his gun ahead of him, prepared to fire.

The hall was empty. No sign of Carter. No sign of a struggle.

He moved down the center of the hallway, sweeping every resident's room he came to.

There was a blur of motion just as he reached one of the rooms, and the gun was suddenly wrenched from his hands.

Before Frank registered the act and moved to defend himself, massive hands grabbed him and slung him into the hallway wall opposite. Frank bounced off the wall and fell to the floor half conscious, his ears ringing.

"Don't hurt him, Stone," a voice said.

A foot rolled Frank over onto his back and planted itself squarely on his chest, pinning him to the floor.

Frank's mind cleared, and he was suddenly alert again. A dark figure stood over him. He struggled to push the foot aside and free himself, but the more he wiggled, the more pressure the foot applied until at last Frank's chest was so constricted that his lungs had no room to expand and take in air.

"That's enough, Stone," the voice said. "If you squish his chest, we can't exactly use it now, can we?"

The foot lifted, and Frank's rib cage popped back into position. The pain was excruciating. The ribs had been pressed just shy of the breaking point.

"Hit the lights," the voice said.

Frank lay on his back, still trying to normalize his breathing, when the overhead lights came on. The hallway brightened, and everything suddenly came into view. The Healer Frank had chased from the little girl's apartment, Stone, stood over him. Another man stood beside him. A much older man. White hair. White, trim beard. Frank had looked at that face in so many photographs over the past few days that he knew every feature by memory. George Galen.

The one new feature was the black headband around Galen's forehead. A small camcorder was attached to the side of it, and a red dot of light above the lens suggested that it was recording.

"Dr. Frank Hartman, I presume," said Galen, smiling. "It is an honor to meet you. Your Director Irving has said so much about you. I'm told you developed a countervirus for our healing virus. I have to admit I was both impressed and highly distressed to hear that."

Frank sat up, his chest aching. "Director Irving?"

"Oh yes, he's been most helpful as of late. Although not as helpful as we had hoped. He failed to inform us of the raid last night, for example. Stone here took quite a beating as a result. Your BHA friends shot him up pretty bad. I dare say he's still a little miffed about that. How's your chest? I hope he didn't hurt you. We need you as healthy as possible, of course."

"Where's Agent Carter?"

"The other one with you? Yes, I'm afraid he's indisposed

at the moment. But don't worry. We haven't harmed him. We're not violent people, Dr. Hartman." Then, with a wink, "Unlike certain federal agents I know who will go unnamed, but if we *were* naming them we'd use the letters B, H, and A, not necessarily in that order, of course." He elbowed Stone as if this had been a real humdinger.

Stone stared down at Frank, unsmiling.

"I hope you don't mind this," Galen said, pointing to the camcorder on his head. "I'd like to record this moment. For the good of history and such. They'll make documentaries about this one day, and I'd like to have a truthful account of the proceedings. Besides, history is more memorable if it's filmed, don't you think? We can watch the footage again and again and have the events burned so deeply into our memories that we feel as if we witnessed them ourselves. The Kennedy assassination. The space shuttle disasters. September 11." He put a finger to his mouth, reconsidering. "Of course, those are all very depressing examples. Very sad examples. I'm sure there are some good ones, too." He snapped his fingers and brightened. "The Red Sox winning the World Series. Now, that was a beautiful piece of filmed history."

"What did you do to that boy?" Frank said. "Jonathan Fox?"

The smile evaporated from Galen's face. "Jonathan's death was a tragedy. Nothing short of a tragedy. We were giving him a new life, but he wasn't ready for it. I blame myself. Had he waited the full three days, he would have seen what a marvelous gift we were giving him." He shrugged. "But alas, kids will be kids. I'm George Galen, by the way." He smiled wide again and stuck out a hand.

Frank didn't take it. "I know who you are, Mr. Galen."

Galen blushed. "Goodness. Celebrity status, already." He put his hands in his pockets. "Of course, you're the name to know around here lately." He turned and beckoned Frank to follow. "Come on, I'd like you to meet everyone."

Stone nudged Frank with his foot. Going along was not an invitation. Frank got up and followed Galen.

"You can take that silly helmet off," said Galen. "You won't need it."

Stone fell into step behind Frank, and Frank felt a light shove in the back. Removing the helmet wasn't an invitation either. Frank took it off and was immediately assaulted with the old, musty smell of the building.

"I'm told that you lost your daughter to leukemia," said Galen casually. "I'm very sorry for your loss. There is nothing worse than to see a child suffer, especially your own child. I would think that such an experience would make you more sympathetic to what we're doing. Perhaps once you see the breadth of our work and the potential we have to save so many lives, you'll be a bit more understanding. I don't mean to sound presumptive, of course, but I think you'd be a lot less hostile toward us if you knew what we were capable of. And here we are."

They had returned to the operating room, only now there were a few people inside. A woman in a blue surgical gown stood still as a statue beside the operating table. Other Healers, similarly dressed, busied themselves checking and adjusting the life-monitoring machines. They barely looked up when Frank, Galen, and Stone entered.

Galen gestured to the woman by the operating table. "Dr. Hartman, I'd like to introduce you to Dr. Monica Owens, who, you'll be pleased to hear, is as skilled as she is beautiful."

Monica had her head bowed, staring at the floor, looking ashamed.

"Skilled at what?" said Frank.

"Cardiothoracic surgery, mostly," said Galen, "but she can do pretty much anything, really. She gave Jonathan his new kidney, for example. Never done one of those in her life, but she handled it like an old pro. Her hand is very steady, Dr. Hartman, very steady. And her understanding of the human anatomy extensive. We're lucky to have her on board."

Dr. Monica Owens didn't look as if she felt very lucky.

The doors on the opposite side of the room opened, and more Healers entered, pushing four gurneys. The people on the gurneys were asleep, covered up to their chests with white sheets, and wearing paper surgical caps on their heads.

Galen pointed to each one in turn. "Dr. Hartman, I introduce you to Byron, Nick, Dolores, and Hal." Frank looked at each face. There were none he recognized. Who were these? Healers? Homeless people like Jonathan Fox?

Another man came into the room.

"And this," said Galen, "is the very talented Dr. Kouichi Yoshida. He'll be helping us today as well."

Yoshida made a beeline for Frank, a wide smile on his lips. "Dr. Hartman, a pleasure to meet you. Welcome." He took Frank's hand and shook it.

Galen said, "Dr. Yoshida, would you mind helping Dr. Owens get everyone ready?"

Yoshida seemed overly chipper. "Of course, sir. Dr. Hartman, if you'll excuse me."

Yoshida left and began examining the people asleep on the gurneys.

"I'm a very important person, Dr. Hartman," said Galen. "The work I do, the treatments I offer, it can literally heal the world. I've studied and waited for this my entire life. And as you can see, it's been a long life." He sighed sadly and patted his stomach. "I'm an old man now, Frank. I'm not as young and strong as I used to be. Well, not as young, anyway. I'm actually fairly strong. A few genetic tweaks of my own doing, but that's beside the point. The point is, I'm going to die. This old body will eventually shrivel up and call it quits. Oh sure, I've probably got a good twenty years left in me, but that's twenty years of arthritis and shuffle-board. And frankly, I'm not interested in slowly going out of this world. Old people depress me. So I've made a decision, Frank. I'm not going to die. Not permanently, anway. My mind is too valuable, my life too precious to lose forever.

"This is a new dawning, Frank. A start of a different race of man. And I'm leading it. Without me the effort will crumble, and mankind would be doomed to even greater suffering and disease. So I found a way, Frank, a way to preserve my life. To escape death. To keep me around as long as the world needs me. And I'm going to do it. And you're going to help me.

"You didn't volunteer, of course, and to be perfectly honest with you, I was going to use one of my own followers for the fifth participant. But when you came along, I had a slight change of plans. I improvised and decided to make you the fifth participant.

"And why *you,* you ask? Why should you be so lucky? Well, several reasons." He counted them off on his fingers. "Number one, you're young. You've got a good build on you, and your records show you're in the best of health. Number two, and more importantly, you've discovered a way to stop our virus. That makes you an enemy to our effort."

He smiled. "Don't get me wrong. I don't think you're a bad person. I think you're a fine man, in fact. An exemplary servant to your country. But right now, you're the biggest threat to our operation. Involving you intimately in the project is a way of dealing with that threat. If you understood what we were doing, if you knew what this was all about, you wouldn't be trying to stop us. You'd enlist in our cause immediately.

"Number three, you're a handsome devil, and I've never had much luck with the ladies. It's about time I cashed in, I'd say."

Frank looked from Stone to the exit. "What are you going to do to me?"

Galen began unbuttoning his shirt. "It's a risky procedure, yes, but it's a risk I'm willing to take. Our trial run with Jonathan was going smoothly, and had he not run off and ruined the test, I'm confident all would have gone as planned. I'm so confident in fact, that I'm staking my life on it. This time, the other person on that operating table will be me."

Galen removed his shirt and handed it to Stone, exposing a chest of white hair. "You'll be happy to know that your blood type matches mine. Everything should go smoothly."

Frank lunged. Before Stone could interfere, Frank grabbed Galen, spun him around, and put him in a choke hold.

The Healers in the room gasped. Stone moved to intervene.

"Back off!" said Frank. "Come any closer and I'll snap his neck."

Stone froze, keeping his distance.

"This is foolishness, Frank," said Galen calmly. "You're only hurting yourself. I can break free at any time. Easy as cheesy."

Frank backed away toward the exit, pulling Galen with him, using him as a shield between him and the others.

"You can't escape from here, Frank," said Galen. "It's silly to even try."

They reached the doorway.

"I won't warn you again," said Galen. "Release me or I will be forced to take action." Frank tightened his grip on Galen's throat in an effort to shut him up. Galen reached up and with a force and strength Frank didn't expect, and pulled at Frank's arms. The choke hold slipped, and Galen stepped out of it easily.

"When I said I was strong, Frank, I meant it." He grabbed Frank by the front of his suit and lifted him off the ground. "Now you try my patience."

Galen tossed Frank back into the operating room as if he weighed nothing.

Frank flew through the air, arms flailing, and crashed into

one of the metal trays by the operating tables, sending surgical tools in every direction.

Monica screamed.

Before Frank could get up, Stone had him. He lifted Frank off the ground and slammed him onto one of the operating tables. Frank kicked and struggled, but Stone's grip, like his foot, held Frank fast.

Yoshida came to the side of the table, still smiling placidly, as if this were the most pleasant exercise in which he could participate. He carried a small metal tray on which sat a single computer chip.

Monica was off to the side crying, her hands in her face.

"There, there, Dr. Owens," said Galen. "Please don't be upset. I need you in top form now. Let's not have those eyes of yours clouded with tears." He took a handkerchief from his pocket and gave it to her.

Yoshida began tightening leather restraints around Frank's ankles and wrists.

Galen came to the side of the bed. He removed the headband and camcorder and offered them to Yoshida. "Download this footage as well, will you, Dr. Yoshida? I want Frank to have a record of it. He'll appreciate it some day."

Yoshida nodded obediently. "Of course. I'll return momentarily." He took the camcorder and the metal tray holding the computer chip and exited the room.

Frank's heart was pounding. He pulled at the restraints, but they wouldn't budge.

Above him, behind the glass of the second floor, he could see Healers coming in and taking seats. They were waiting for this, witnesses to it.

Galen prepared a syringe. "I'm afraid Jonathan's escape caused all kinds of problems," he said. "We've had to step up our plans a bit, move the calendar ahead, as it were. This facility will be discovered soon, so our time is short. But don't worry, Frank, once we're finished here, we'll take you somewhere where you can rest and recuperate."

He removed the needle from a vial of medication, then pushed on the stopper to get out any bubbles. A drop of liquid escaped the needle point, and Galen turned over Frank's arm, exposing the veins on the inside of his elbow.

Frank watched him, his eyes wide. "What do you want from me?"

Galen stuck the needle into the vein and pushed down on the stopper. "Everything but your heart."

Frank felt the cold sensation of a heavy sedative rush through his bloodstream, and in seconds all went black.

20

INTERROGATION

Agent Carmen Hernandez stood in the interrogation room at the BHA, her arms folded across her chest. Sitting at the table opposite her with his arm in a sling was Roland Turner.

"I want to see my daughter," Turner said. "I want to see Kimberly."

"I'm afraid that's impossible, Mr. Turner," said Hernandez. "Kimberly is in quarantine for the time being. We need to observe her for a few days, make sure the virus inside her has been completely annihilated."

Turner's face grew angry. "You can't keep her away from me. You got no right." He turned his head and looked into the two-way mirror in front of him. "You people got no right, you hear me? She's my daughter." He looked back at Hernandez. "I want to talk to my lawyer. I want my phone call. You people can't hold me like this."

"We're only asking for your cooperation, Mr. Turner. If you cooperate, it's possible that the charges against you will be dropped."

Turner stiffened. "Charges? What charges?"

"You had a harmful, illegal substance in your home. And you were aiding a possible criminal in administering that substance to your daughter."

"It was going to heal her! Do you think I'd let him give it to her if I wasn't sure of that?"

Hernandez put her hands in her pockets and approached the table. "How are you sure?"

"What do you mean?"

"What makes you so certain? How did you know this virus was as effective as the Healers claimed it would be?"

Turner looked down at the table.

Hernandez pressed on. "You're clearly a man who loves his daughter, Mr. Turner. You wouldn't do anything that you thought might hurt her, so I believe you when you say you knew it would work. What I don't know and would like to know is what made you so sure? How did the Healers convince you?"

"I want to talk to my lawyer," said Turner, not lifting his head.

"These Healers downloaded your daughter's medical records from Children's Hospital. In other words, they acquired those records illegally. Were you aware of that?"

Turner said nothing.

"I'm sure you want to cooperate, Mr. Turner. I'm sure you want what's best for Kimberly. But unless you start talking, I'll be forced to call Social Services."

Turner's head snapped up. "Social Services?"

"Considering the threat your daughter was under, we can easily make a case with the state that you're an unfit parent."

For the first time, Turner looked afraid. "You wouldn't do that. I love my daughter. I'd do anything for her."

"I don't doubt that, Mr. Turner. But I'm not sure the state would agree, considering the seriousness of the situation."

Turner was silent a long moment. He closed his eyes and his shoulders sagged, all the fire inside him extinguished. "What do you want to know?" he said softly.

Later that afternoon Agent Hernandez stood at attention inside Director Irving's office. Irving sat behind his desk, unwrapping a stick of chewing gum and popping it in his mouth, watching her.

"You don't have to stand there like a tin soldier, Agent Hernandez," he said. "This isn't the Marines." He waved a hand. "Or wherever it was you served before coming here."

Hernandez positioned her body into a parade-rest stance, her eyes straight ahead. "Navy, sir."

Irving nodded. "Yes, yes, the Navy. Jaunty white hats and ships ahoy."

Hernandez allowed her gaze to lower for the first time and looked at the man.

Director Irving smiled. "No offense, Agent Hernandez. I have nothing but respect for our boys in green . . . or in your case, women in white." He cocked his head to the side, considering. "The Navy *do* wear white, am I right?"

The slightest hint of annoyance flickered across Hernandez's face. "Sometimes, sir."

"I thought so." Director Irving tossed the gum wrapper into the garbage can and came around to the front of his desk. "So you had a nice visit with Mr. Roland Turner, did you?"

"Yes, sir. He was most cooperative. With your permission, I'd like to see to it that the charges against him are dropped."

Irving held up a hand and chuckled. "Now, let's not get too hasty, Agent Hernandez. This Turner fellow is a criminal as much as these Healers are, in my opinion. To release him back into society is to put society at risk. Who's to say this isn't the beginning of a life of crime for this man?"

Hernandez remained silent, her eyes staring ahead, not looking at him.

"Then again," said Irving, "I do value your judgment. If you think the man should be released, I'll give that recommendation serious consideration."

"Thank you, sir."

"Now, in so many words, what did he say?"

"Healers approached him several weeks ago, sir. And

they were forthcoming in how they acquired Kimberly's medical records."

"Kimberly is the little girl in question?"

"Yes, sir."

"Go on."

"So they told Mr. Turner that they had downloaded her records from the hospital."

"And he didn't throw them out of his house straightaway? Tsk, tsk. I'm losing confidence in this recommendation of yours, Agent Hernandez. Mr. Turner sounds like a most unsound individual."

"If I could continue, sir."

Irving sat in his desk and grinned. "By all means."

"Mr. Turner also explained that Healers brought a former patient to his home. A young boy whom the Healers had already cured of sickle-cell anemia."

"Or so they said," Irving said.

"Sir?"

"Healers *said* they had cured this boy of sickle-cell anemia. Who's to say they actually did? He could have been an actor."

"To hear Mr. Turner tell it," said Hernandez, "it was a most convincing presentation."

"Oh, I have no doubt of that," said Irving. "Let me guess." He put a hand to his chin, thinking. "The Healers probably showed Mr. Turner the boy's medical records as evidence that at one time he did indeed have sickle-cell anemia. Then they showed Turner recent test results proving that the boy no longer had the disease. Then they let the boy speak, and perhaps his parents as well, giving heartfelt teary-eyed testimony that the Healers were a godsend and if not for them, poor little Timmy here would still be crippled with the disease."

Hernandez looked at him, surprised. "As a matter of fact, sir, that's precisely what happened. In a nutshell, I mean."

Director Irving stood up and shrugged. "These people are all alike, Agent Hernandez. I've seen this countless times before. They all use the same con, bait and switch. It was a sham, and gullible Mr. Turner, who, bless his heart, only wanted what was best for his daughter, was suckered in."

Agent Hernandez looked confused. "Is it not also possible, sir, that the former patient who visited him was, in fact, legitimate?"

Irving waved a hand and laughed. "Please, Agent Hernandez. These Healers are petty con men, circus performers. What they probably intended to do was return to Turner's home after, quote unquote, *treating* his daughter and politely ask for a sizable donation to their, quote unquote, *cause,* which Mr. Turner, being a naive little man, would probably have given."

"There's no evidence to substantiate that claim, sir."

"Of course not," Irving said, amused. "We caught the bastard before the Healers had a chance to sink their teeth into his wallet. He should be thanking us. Now, I want you to write a full report of your interview and give me the sole copy. Then I want Mr. Turner placed in confinement. I want him to speak to no one."

Hernandez raised an eyebrow. "Confinement?"

"Did I mispronounce the word? Confinement."

"Can we do that, sir?"

Irving stood up to his full stature and raised a finger. "You forget that I am a presidential appointee, Agent Hernandez. I have the support and protection of the president of this great nation, our commander in chief. He has given me a responsibility, and until this Healer mess is swept under the carpet, this Mr. Roland Turner, whom I consider a flight risk, will remain in our custody. Do I make myself clear?"

Hernandez looked frightened.

Director Irving felt some sense of satisfaction at this. To fill a person with fear, particularly a beautiful woman such as Agent Hernandez, was most arousing.

"Sir?" said Agent Hernandez. "Are you all right?"

Irving blinked. "What?"

"Your hands and face . . . they're trembling."

Irving stepped away from her, pocketing his hands and going to the watercooler across the room. "I'm fine. I'm fine. It's stress. These Healers, they've got me all in a fluster. You understand."

He filled a cup with water and tried to bring it to his lips. His hands were shaking so badly, he spilled much of the water in the process. "That will be all, Agent Hernandez."

She stood there, brow wrinkled, watching him.

"I said that will be *all*, Agent Hernandez."

She left.

He downed the rest of the cold water in a single swig, splashing much of it on his face in the process. He threw the paper cup to the floor and looked at his trembling hands. It was happening again. The shakes. And this time someone had noticed.

He went to his desk and opened the top drawer. The vial of Galen's saliva was exactly where he had left it. He took it out and tried to unscrew the cap. It slipped from his fingers and fell to the floor. His hands were trembling too much to hold it. He cursed aloud, then got down on all fours to retrieve it.

He had waited too long, he knew. It had been a stupid thing to do. Too much time had passed since his last treatment.

He took the vial in one hand and willed his mind to hold it steady long enough for him to get the cap off. Drops of precious saliva sloshed out and onto the floor before he was able to pour some of it into the palm of his hand.

He set the vial down, careful not to tip it over and lose the rest of its contents, closed his eyes, and pressed his wet palm to his forehead, imagining the master giving him the saliva himself.

21

HEART

Frank awoke coughing a deep phlegm-filled cough that squeezed his lungs so tightly and pained him so greatly that he was sure for a moment that he was dying. A gentle hand on his shoulder and a voice in his ear made him think otherwise.

"Cough into this," the voice said, and Frank felt a bowl at his lips.

He coughed again, a long chest-compressing cough that made his eyes water and left him gasping for breath. When it passed, he sunk back into the mattress, utterly wasted, the blood flowing back to his face.

"I know it hurts," said Monica, "but coughing expands your lungs and helps prevent infection."

Frank tried sitting up, but Monica stopped him with a delicate hand. "You need to rest. You're healing remarkably and it's probably safe to move around, but give the medication a moment to wake you thoroughly. You'll be a little unsteady on your feet if you get up too fast."

He lay back and looked up at the ceiling, planks of polished hardwood upon which danced the flicker of firelight. "Where am I?"

"Safe for now."

His mind was clearing. The operating room. The Healers. The restraints. Panicked, he lifted his arms and saw that leather straps no longer held him. He was free, but an IV tube was attached to one wrist.

"Lie still," said Monica. "Relax. Try not to excite yourself."

"Where am I?" he repeated, trying to get up again. A sharp pain in his chest hit him like a javelin and he fell back onto the bed.

"Please," she said. "You shouldn't make any sudden movements. I think the staples are nearly ready to come out, but you don't want to risk reopening the wound."

"Wound?" he said absently.

"I'll be back shortly. Do you think you can be still for a few minutes?"

He was hardly hearing her. "What? Yes. I'll be still."

"I've given you something for the pain, although if you're anything like the others, the pain should go away soon."

"Yes," he said blankly, staring up at the ceiling.

Dr. Monica Owens left him, and it was quiet for a few minutes. Frank stared up at the ceiling as his thoughts began to organize themselves. In a moment, the fog of anesthesia lifted, and he felt awake.

He turned his head to one side and saw the source of the light. A fire crackled softly in a large stone hearth nearby. The chimney above it rose a good fifteen feet before disappearing into the ceiling. The furniture around the hearth was rustic and inviting: a leather sofa, a Native American rug, an end table that appeared to be made entirely of deer antlers, a large stuffed chair with a matching ottoman. Throw blankets. Throw pillows.

It was a cabin.

Frank felt the urge to urinate and threw back the blanket that covered him. He wore a hospital gown tied loosely in the back. A catheter tube snaked out from under his gown and into a bag at his bedside. Wincing, he pulled out the catheter and slowly sat up on the side of the bed, his bare feet just touching the cool hardwood floor.

He didn't stand just yet. He still felt a little woozy.

Beside him, several medical diagnostic machines beeped and hummed, monitoring his vitals.

Looking behind him, Frank saw that he was not alone. There were four other beds in the room, each occupied with one of the persons he had seen in the operating room alseep on the gurneys. They were asleep now as well, and Frank wondered if they had remained in that state since he'd seen them last.

A night-light shining in an adjacent bathroom caught his eye.

Being careful to maintain his balance, Frank got to his feet. He took a step toward the bathroom and felt a tug at his wrist. He looked down and remembered the IV. He ripped away the medical tape and gingerly pulled the tube out of his vein. Once free of it, he dropped the tube to the floor and shuffled to the bathroom.

By the time he reached it, he was feeling steady on his feet again. His hand found the light switch, and he squinted at the sudden brightness. He moved to the toilet, urinated, then went to the sink to wash up.

The image of himself in the mirror startled him. His face was pale and thin, his eyes sunken. He hadn't shaved in days. He moved a hand over his chin, feeling the stubble. He pulled down the collar of his hospital johnny and saw that there were bandages on his chest. He pulled the gown off over his head and looked at himself again in the mirror. The bandages covered his entire torso, beginning just below the armpit and winding their way down his chest to his navel. The skin immediately above and below the bandages had been shaven, suggesting that the entire area under the bandages had been shaved recently.

He clawed at the bandage until he found the end of it, then began unraveling it.

Yards of bandage fell to his feet. And the more he un-wound, the more panicked he became, ripping it, pulling it away violently. When the last strip came free, Frank stood there naked, staring at himself.

A heavily stapled surgical wound ran down the middle of his chest, beginning at the top of his rib cage and ex-tending to the bottom of his breastbone.

Slowly Frank raised a finger and touched the red, mostly healed scar. It was real.

He reached behind his head and felt the prickly stitches of the surgical wound on the back of his neck.

He bent down, grabbed the gown, slid it back over his head, and left the bathroom.

Across the room a large wooden door with ornate carv-ings around its edges stood shut. He pulled it open. The hallway was dark and empty. Frank padded down it, mov-ing cautiously, eyes shifting.

Ahead of him a faint light spilled from a room and into the hallway. Frank stopped and listened for voices but heard nothing, then crept to the room's entrance and looked inside.

George Galen's naked body lay flat on its back atop a wide stone table. Burning candles of all shapes and sizes surrounded him, and a few sticks of incense burned in the corner—though they did little to mask the smell of a de-composing body.

Frank went to Galen's corpse. The old man's torso had been cut wide open. An incision had been made at the top of his chest and extended down past his lower abdomen to-ward his genitalia. Other perpendicular incisions had been made, allowing the surgeon to open Galen's chest like a cabinet.

Frank peeled back the flaps of skin, and it took only a moment to discover that George Galen was missing both kidneys, his liver, his right lung, and his heart.

Frank felt nauseated. He pulled down the collar of his gown and looked again at the scar on his chest. Galen had said they wanted all of Frank but his heart. Frank felt sick. They had put Galen's heart inside him.

He shook his head. Organ donors only donate when dead. Only *can* donate when dead. George Galen had been alive.

Yet here he was now, as dead as could be.

Frank hurried out of the room, breathing heavily now, desperate to find an exit and a legitimate doctor to examine him.

The front room of the cabin was just around the corner, and Frank ran to the door. He put his hand on the knob but hesitated. To his left was a window. He went to it and looked out. It was night, and Stone stood on the porch guarding the exit, a tranquilizer gun slung over his back.

Frank crouched to avoid being seen. He couldn't get out this way, not without help.

He peeked through the window again. The moonlight made it possible to see for miles beyond the porch, but the sight wasn't what Frank had expected. This was not the Happy Mountain Rest Home. Frank was somewhere else. They had moved him. And all he could see in every direction was forest. No streetlights. No homes. Just forest and mountain peaks as far as he could see.

"Thinking of taking a late-night stroll?"

Frank spun around to see a curly-haired Healer in a black cape standing behind him.

"I'm Lichen," the Healer said gently. "You shouldn't be out of your room. You need your rest."

"What did you people do to me?"

"You've had a heart transplant."

It was true, then. They had taken his heart. Frank felt unsteady, weak in the knees. "Galen's heart?"

"Yes."

"Why?"

"It was the prophecy. The prophet foretold his own death and rebirth as the beginning of the Great Healing."

Frank's knees began to wobble.

"Would you like to sit down?" Lichen said, offering a hand.

"Get away from me," Frank said ferociously, pushing the man's hand away.

Lichen remained calm, his expression blank. "You're angry now because you don't understand what the prophet has given you. You don't understand your own potential. You haven't seen what the prophet can do to people, how he empowers them, makes them stronger, more resilient, more like what we were intended to be."

"More crazy, you mean."

Lichen laughed softly. "I can see why you might think that. Had the prophet not healed me, had I not seen and felt the power he holds, I would not have believed myself. And once I was healed, he made me even stronger. Watch."

Lichen removed a penknife from his pocket. He opened the knife blade and in one swift movement sliced a deep cut across the palm of his own hand. Frank recoiled a step as Lichen held up the palm flat for Frank to see. Blood poured from the wound and dripped to the floor.

And then the bleeding stopped.

And as Frank watched, the wound somehow sealed itself shut. And then a scab formed. And in only a few seconds, the scab hardened, dried, and flaked away, leaving only a red scar. And then, the redness faded also, leaving only a thin flesh-toned scar.

Lichen took a handkerchief from his pocket and wiped away the blood that remained. "I will wear this scar all my life, Mr. Hartman, as a reminder that I was the one privileged enough to show you the prophet's power."

Frank couldn't speak. What he had seen was impossible. He looked down at the floor and, yes, the blood was still there. It was real. All he could manage to say was "How?"

"How did he do it, you mean? How did the prophet unlock the potential of our immune system? How did he learn to speak to our bodies, to tell them to strengthen themselves here, sharpen themselves there? He is the prophet, Mr.

Hartman, the means by which all who follow him *become* something greater."

The thought came to Frank and he spoke it aloud. *"The Book of Becoming."*

"Yes, the book which shows how we can become something better than human."

Frank looked again at the scar on Lichen's palm.

"And if you still doubt," said Lichen, "look at yourself. Do you think a normal heart-transplant patient can get up and move around so soon after surgery? Do you think an open chest wound would heal that fast? The virus has not completely gestated in your body, so you don't heal as quickly as the rest of us, but in a day or two the virus will have spread through your system, altered all of your DNA, and you will have the prophet's full power."

"What do you mean? How can I have the virus inside me?"

"The virus was injected into Galen's heart before it was placed inside you."

"But that's impossible," said Frank. "I can't have the virus, not if it was injected into the heart."

"Oh? And why not?"

"Because each strain of the virus must be engineered to closely match the DNA of the person receiving it. Otherwise the virus destroys cells, erodes the flesh away. If the virus was injected into the heart, it would have to match Galen's DNA. And if it did, my body would reject it. And if the virus strain had been engineered to match *my* DNA, then Galen's heart would have rejected it and shriveled up like a raisin."

Lichen laughed. "You *do* think quick on your feet, don't you? What you say is true, but that's the wonder of the prophet. He is all-wise and knows how such obstacles can be overcome. It will all be clear to you very soon. Come, it is late, and you need your rest. We can talk again tomorrow after you've had some sleep. You've already been out of bed much longer than advised."

Lichen did a half turn and waited for Frank to accompany him back toward his room.

Frank looked down at the tranquilizer gun slung over Lichen's back. Even without it, Lichen would be too much of a challenge. Frank couldn't overwhelm him, not in this condition anyway. And even if he did, the noise of a struggle would alert Stone, who stood close by on the other side of the front door. Not to mention the other Healers who might be patrolling the cabin.

They walked in silence until Frank said, "What do you intend to do to me now?"

Lichen looked surprised by the question. "*Do* to you? You misunderstand your mission, Mr. Hartman. Once you are changed, it is I who will do *your* bidding."

They had reached the door, and Lichen opened it for Frank. "Here, get some rest. More will be explained to you in the morning."

Frank went inside and the door closed behind him. He stood there and listened as Lichen fastened the deadbolt on the opposite side, locking him in. The sound of Lichen's heavy steps receded away down the hall.

"Good to see you up," a man's voice said.

Frank turned and saw that one of the other patients who had been sleeping was now up. He was kneeling at the fireplace and jabbing at a log with the poker. He gave Frank a wave, and Frank came over.

"Name's Byron," the man said, offering a hand and shaking Frank's. "Byron Pacheco. Kind of a shock, isn't it? To wake up and learn you've had an organ transplant? Not the best news to get in the morning."

Frank looked at him. He was a broad-shouldered man, curly brown hair, square jaw. He wore a hospital gown and argyle socks.

"Frank Hartman."

"Nice to meet you, Mr. Hartman. Welcome to hell." He squatted down and poked at the log again. Embers sparked and sprinkled down into the ashes. "Some of us didn't think you were going to wake up. Hal especially, he was betting against you."

Frank looked back at the other beds where people still slept.

Byron pointed with the poker. "That's Hal there. Kind of an ass, really, but I should let you form your own opinion. And that's Dolores, sweet lady. I think you'll like her. And that kid there is Nick, but I'd highly advise against calling him a kid. He's small, but he's got a temper. He hasn't had it easy, if you know what I mean. How's your chest doing? I saw the pile of bandages in the bathroom. You feeling okay?"

Frank looked at his chest but didn't answer.

Byron pulled up his gown, revealing a pair of boxers and pointed to the red scar across his abdomen. "They gave me the liver. Not as bad as the heart, I suppose, but it still burns like hell every once in a while."

"Galen's liver?"

"We all got something. Hal and Nick each got a kidney and Dolores got one of the lungs. She's had the hardest time so far. She was already sick to begin with. She hasn't been taking it well."

"Why did they do it?"

Byron laughed. "You're asking me? I've been trying to figure that out for the past two days myself."

"Two days?"

"That's when the surgeries happened." He stabbed at the fire.

Frank blinked. He'd been out for two days. And yet to be up and walking around like this only two days after a heart transplant was amazing.

Frank said, "How did you become involved?"

Byron gave the log a hard poke, then recounted to Frank how he and the others had been picked up and brought to the rest home. They were both sitting on the floor in front of the dying embers when Byron finished.

"Can the others walk?" Frank asked.

Byron shrugged. "We can get all around all right. I don't think Dolores will be running any marathons anytime soon, but she can move about okay, yeah."

"I got a good look outside earlier. I think we have at least an hour before dawn. Let's wake the others."

Byron got up immediately. "Why? What do you have in mind?"

"We're leaving."

"Leaving?"

"You're welcome to stay if you want."

Byron quickly put the poker back in its stand. "I'll wake them up."

22

PROPHECY

After meeting Byron, Frank had assumed that the other transplantees would be just as eager to mobilize; but now, with all of them all around the fireplace, he was beginning to learn how diverse and divided a group it was.

He had explained that he was with the BHA, and suggested that if they worked together, they might have a chance of escaping.

"A chance?" said Hal. "You want me to hang my life on a chance? Look, I don't know who you think you are, mister, but you're not the boss of me. I go when I say I go."

"Shut up, Hal," said Nick. "Nobody wants you coming with us anyway."

"Don't tell me to shut up. It was you who got us into trouble to begin with."

Nick made a face. "How you figure?"

"Can't we have a conversation without somebody arguing?" said Dolores.

"You and Jonathan," said Hal. "If you two hadn't made Galen so angry all the time, trying to escape, the old man might not have done this to us."

Nick sprang to his feet from his place on the couch. "Jonathan was trying to help us!"

"Let's calm down," said Byron. He had been standing beside Frank to show his support, but now moved forward to defuse the situation.

"You stay out of this," said Hal, stopping Byron with a threatening look. "This doesn't concern you."

"Jonathan risked his neck for you," said Nick.

"Not for me," said Hal. "He didn't give a damn for me."

"And why should he have? With the way you treated him."

"Nick's right," said Dolores. "We got no reason to blame Jonathan."

"No one asked you, stupid," said Hal.

"I'm not stupid," she said. "No more stupid than you. And I don't like you calling me names anyway."

"I don't care what you *do* and don't like," Hal said.

Frank tried getting their attention. "All right. Let's just all take it easy—"

"And where's Jonathan now, huh?" said Hal. "Where's Dudley Do-Right now? You see the police banging down the door here? No, you don't. And you know why? Because Jonathan didn't bother going to the police. That's why. He ditched us, all right? He saw a chance to get out and saved his *own* neck, not ours."

"You don't know that," said Nick. "You don't know nothing. I know Jonathan. He would have gone to the police. He would have found help."

"Jonathan couldn't find his own whacker with a magnifying glass. Help ain't coming."

"The police—" Nick began.

"The police nothing," said Hal. "If they were coming, they would have come by now."

"Maybe they did," said Nick. "Maybe Jonathan took them to the old place after they moved us. Anything could have happened."

Hal opened his mouth to speak, but Frank beat him to it and ended the discussion. "Jonathan's dead."

There was a long silence as they looked at him.

"What do you mean?" said Nick.

"I saw his body myself," said Frank. "I'm sorry."

"That's not true," said Nick.

"I wish it weren't, Nick. I really do. But it is. He was in an accident."

Hal looked all the more angry. "You see?" he said, throwing his hands up. "You see what trying to escape will get us? We try to walk out of here, and they'll kill us in an instant. Boom. They won't even think twice about it. And I say, anyone who tries to leave deserves exactly what's coming to them."

Nick leapt over the couch and tackled Hal. Frank and Byron wrestled him away but not before Nick got in a good punch.

Hal got to his feet, nursing a bloody lip. "You're crazy. You hear me? Every one of you is crazy."

Nick lunged again, but Byron held him fast.

"That's enough," said Byron.

Hal pointed at Frank. "Whatever you're scheming, mister, you can count me out, you hear? You want to go kill yourselves, you go right ahead. I'll be happy to be rid of you." He stormed off to the bathroom and slammed the door behind him.

The moment he was gone, Nick stopped struggling. Frank and Byron released him, and Nick crumpled to his knees and sobbed into his hands. Dolores got up and comforted him, patting him on the back and speaking gently.

"You just cry it out. You just let it come."

They stayed that way for several minutes.

"You bring us bad news, Mr. Hartman," Dolores said finally. "Bad news. Jonathan was a good boy. He might have had his issues with the drugs, but he had a good heart. And the Lord looks on the heart. Always has."

"You deserve to know the truth," Frank said. "I know Jonathan must have meant a lot to you. But if he left here to find help for you, then it seems a shame to stay here and do nothing. It would mean he died in vain."

"He's right," said Byron. "They don't watch us as closely here. They think we're too weak to get around."

"I *am* too weak to get around," said Dolores.

Byron smiled at her. "You can't fool me, Dolores. You got more fire in you than all of us combined. If anyone can do this, you can."

Dolores shook her head and blushed. "Byron, the Lord says liars will be thrust down to hell, but I do appreciate a good lie every now and again. You keep those words of yours coming."

Nick got up, and they all returned to the furniture around the fire.

"It's no use," Nick said, his face still in his hands. "They're too fast, too strong. We'd never get out. We'd only make them angrier."

Dolores sighed. "Nick's right. These boys are more than any of us can handle. No way we can outrun them. Not like this. We're still weak. Maybe it's best for us to wait here. Maybe some of your friends from that agency you work for will come."

"The BHA won't be coming," said Frank.

"How do you know?" said Dolores. "They'll be looking for you, won't they?"

"The director of the agency may have ties to Galen. He was feeding Galen information. So even if the BHA *is* looking for us, it's possible that the director would lead them off course."

There was silence as the last flicker of hope was extinguished.

"There *are* fewer guards here," said Byron. "Maybe we can slip past them."

"It doesn't matter how many there are," said Nick. "Even one is too many. We'd never get out. And if we did, what makes you think we'd find help before the Healers find us? We don't even know where we are."

"He's got a point," said Dolores.

"Look," said Nick, "I want to get out of here as much as

anyone, but if Jonathan couldn't do it, then we can't either. He was healthy. We've been operated on."

"Jonathan wasn't as healthy as you think," Frank said. "When I found him, he had undergone surgery also."

Nick got to his feet. "You mean, like us? A transplant?"

"Jonathan was a test, a dry run, to see if the transplant was possible."

"You mean a guinea pig?" said Nick, his face flushed with anger.

"Nothing you can do will bring Jonathan back. I know he was a friend, and I know his loss must be painful for you, but he's beyond your help now. As hard as it may be, you need to let it go and worry about yourself. We all do. There'll be time for mourning later."

Nick went to the fire and stared into the flames.

"There's more," said Frank. "Jonathan was carrying a virus when we found him. A virus given to him intentionally. One of the Healers here told me I'm carrying the same virus."

Dolores took a few cautionary steps away from him.

"I think *all* of us may have it," said Frank, "not just me."

"A virus?" said Nick. "You mean, like the flu or something?"

"No. Nothing like the flu. Much worse. We need to get medical attention as soon as possible."

"I don't *feel* like I got a virus," said Dolores.

"This isn't the type of virus you'd be familiar with," said Frank. "It's programmed to alter human DNA."

"I don't get it," said Nick. "Why would Galen give us a virus? Why make us sick if he was giving us his organs? Wouldn't he want us as healthy as possible?"

"We *are* healthy," said Frank. "That's why I believe each of us *has* the virus. Look at your scars. All of us underwent invasive surgery recently, but our surgical wounds are mostly healed. Medically, that's impossible. Under normal conditions, we would all still be bedridden."

"Wait a second," said Hal.

They all turned toward the bathroom, where Hal stood in the doorway, listening.

"You're saying that we all have a virus that makes us better? Makes us heal faster?"

"I can't be sure until I take us all back to the BHA for testing, but yes, it would appear that the virus is likely the reason why each of us is healing so rapidly."

Dolores laughed. "A virus that makes us healthy instead of sick?"

"In the simplest terms, yes."

"Well, what's wrong with that?" she said. "You had me worried there a minute. I thought we was all dying from typhoid or something. This virus sounds like exactly what we needed."

"Don't think of the virus as medicine. Think of it as a means of altering our genetic makeup. That's never a good idea. There could be repercussions we don't know about. Side effects. Plus, rapid healing may not be the only alteration Galen gave us."

"Alteration?" Nick said, sitting upright. "I don't like the sound of that."

"You shouldn't," said Frank. "Galen created something that he may not have fully understood or known how to control. That's why we need to get back to the BHA where we can each be properly tested and treated." He turned to Hal. "All of us."

Hal said, "But you said the director of the BHA—"

"Can't be trusted, no. But there are people there who will help us."

"Let me get this right," said Byron. "You said this virus could be programmed to alter DNA. So, is that why some of the Healers are so large, why they're so fast? Because their DNA has been altered?"

"Muscle growth isn't too difficult to initiate genetically. Livestock farmers have been doing it for years to beef up their cattle. It's a matter of turning on and off genes that produce proteins or initiate chemical reactions. Galen could have figured out how to manipulate genes to initiate any variety of genetic improvements."

"Then trying to escape is pointless," said Hal. "We're no match for these people."

"I don't know about the rest of you," Frank said calmly, "but I'm not putting my health into the hands of any doctor or Healer here. There are trained physicians at the BHA who know how to treat this virus. I'd much rather be under their care. And that means first getting out of here. And I can't get out alone. None of us can. We need to help each other."

"Somebody's coming," said Dolores.

Frank heard it too. Footsteps.

Without a word, they all hurried to their beds and lay down.

The sound stopped at the door, and the deadbolt unlocked. The heavy wooden door creaked open, and Monica entered the room, pushing a cart. On top of the cart sat several vials of medication and syringes.

With his eyes half closed, Frank watched as Monica approached his bed.

She stopped the cart beside him, lifted his arm and rotated it, looking for a vein.

"You removed your IV?" she said.

In a flash Frank was out of bed, covering Monica's mouth and stifling her scream. Her eyes widened as he picked up one of the needles off the cart and put the tip of it to her neck.

"Stick her," Hal said, jumping out of bed and rushing over. "She's the one who operated on us."

The others hurried over also. Monica's eyes shifted back and forth to each of them as they surrounded her.

"Did you hear me?" Hal said. "This is the one who cut us open. Stick her."

Frank ignored him and put his face only inches from Monica's. "I'm going to remove my hand from your mouth. You will not scream. Do you understand?"

Tears were welling up in her eyes. She nodded.

"You're not going to stick her?" Hal said incredulously.

"Quiet," said Dolores.

Hal grunted a sound of exasperation as Frank removed his hand from Monica's mouth.

"Byron, close the door," said Frank.

Byron hurried over and closed it.

"I'm going to ask you a few questions now, Doctor," said Frank, "and if you answer truthfully, no one is going to get hurt. If you do *not* answer truthfully, I'll let Hal ask the questions. Do we understand one other?"

She nodded.

"Good. Question one. What's in the syringe?"

Monica swallowed. "Antirejection drugs. You have to take them every three hours. Otherwise your body might reject the organs."

"She's lying," Hal said. "That could be arsenic for all we know."

"If she wanted to kill us, she would have done it on the operating table," said Dolores. "Now shut up and let Mr. Hartman handle this."

Frank looked intensely at Monica. "Question two. Where are we?"

Monica winced. "I don't know."

"She's lying again," said Hal. "She's one of them. I'm telling you."

"No, I swear to you. I'm a prisoner here as much as you are. Ask *them*." She pointed to Byron and Dolores.

Byron shrugged. "I used to think that, but now I'm not so sure. She didn't *seem* to be with them, but Hal's right. She's the one who operated on us."

"I had no choice."

"You had no choice?" said Hal. "Well, isn't that convenient? You had no choice. Pardon us for getting all in a tizzy, Doctor. Had we known you didn't have a *choice*—"

"Quiet," said Frank.

Hal turned to him. "Are we going to stand here and listen to this or are we going to do something about it?" He ran to fireplace and grabbed the poker.

Monica gasped but didn't flinch; the needle tip still pressed against the skin of her neck.

"Put it down, Hal," said Frank.

"I do what I please. She's going to pay for what she did to us. Now you either get out of the way or get a few whacks yourself."

"Frank is handling it," Byron said.

"Why?" Hal said. "What does he know about what we've been through, huh? Suddenly he shows up and thinks he owns the place. No, I don't take orders from nobody."

Frank spoke as calmly as possible. "Think, Hal. If you beat her to death right here and now, we'll be no better off than we were. In fact, we'll be in a much worse position because we'll have to answer for it. Now, I'm fairly certain the doctor here wants to help us. Am I right, Doctor?"

"Yes. Absolutely."

"You see? Now let's put the poker down and let her help."

"We need as much help we can get, Hal," said Dolores.

Hal's eyes narrowed at Monica. "You try anything, lady, and so help me, I'll smash your skull in."

Monica looked as if she believed him.

Frank faced her. "Now, I'm only to going to ask this once more, Doctor. Where are we?"

Monica couldn't stop the tears. "I don't know. Several hours outside LA somewhere. We drove north, I think. I couldn't tell, I was blindfolded."

Frank studied her expression and knew she wasn't lying. He put the needle down.

"You're letting her go?" said Hal.

"They took my son," said Monica. "They said they'd

harm him if I didn't do what I was told. I had no choice. I never wanted to hurt anyone."

"Never wanted to hurt anybody?" said Hal. "Here's a news flash, lady. Lots of people are hurt 'cause of you. Hurting people is all you been doing."

Monica buried her face in her hands.

"Shut up," said Nick.

Dolores took Monica's arm. "Here, sit down." She led Monica to the side of Frank's bed and sat her down. "You just cry as long as you need to." She took a napkin off the tray and gave it to Monica.

"Thank you," Monica said, wiping her eyes.

Frank said, "A Healer named Lichen said I was given a virus. He said it was injected into Galen's heart before you . . . before it was put inside me."

She nodded. "Yes. All of you. Each of the organs was injected with a high concentration of the virus before we . . . I mean, before I . . . put them in you."

"Why?" said Frank.

Monica wiped a sniffle. "Galen had altered his DNA. I know it sounds ludicrous. I didn't believe it myself until he showed me, but it's true. He changed himself. Made genetic enhancements. For himself as well as those who serve him. One of those enhancements was rapid healing. If he cut or bruised himself, the wound would heal remarkably fast."

"What does that have to do with us?" said Nick.

"You needed that healing ability. Galen had to give it to you in the same instant he gave you the virus, to counteract the virus."

"Counteract? I don't understand," said Frank.

"You all have the same strain of the virus. That's why you can interact with each other without making each other sick. Normally, when someone is given the virus, it must be engineered to closely match that person's DNA. That's why the person doesn't die. The virus is only changing a single gene usually. Everything else syncs up harmlessly. So Byron's virus would have to be different from Nick's virus, et cetera. But in this case, they're not. It's all the same strain of virus."

"But how can that be?" said Frank. "How can our bodies accept a strain of virus that doesn't closely match our DNA?"

"Because of the organs," said Monica. "The organs have Galen's healing ability. That's why you've survived the virus. He was giving you a piece of himself to protect you. The organ is rebuilding the cells in your body as quickly as the virus destroys them."

"Destroys them?" said Nick.

"Yes, but the organ rebuilds them instantaneously, so you don't feel it. Only, when the organ rebuilds the cells, it uses the DNA deposited by the virus."

"So our DNA is systematically being switched out," said Frank. "We're being given new DNA?"

"A completely different genome, yes," said Monica. "Theoretically."

"But how is that possible? The virus and the organ can't coexist. The virus should annihilate the organ. It's not Galen's DNA."

Monica looked defeated. "That's just it. They *are* the same DNA. That's why the virus and organ can coexist. The strain of virus you're carrying *is* George Galen's DNA. He engineered it to match his genome."

Byron stepped forward. "You're saying this virus is changing our DNA into George Galen's?"

"That's what I'm saying. It was Galen's goal from the beginning, to restructure an adult's entire genetic makeup to match his own, to make living copies of himself."

Suddenly it all made sense to Frank. Suddenly everything clicked into place. The prophecy in *The Book of Becoming* regarding the prophet's death and rebirth. The final illustration in the book. *The Council of the Prophets*. The five identical George Galens. They're us, thought Frank. We are the prophet reborn.

23

SUPPLIES

Everyone started speaking at once. A frenzy of conversation. Now that it was clear what Galen intended, how he planned to genetically change them into copies of himself, immediate escape was the only option. Nick and Hal argued over when would be the best time to try to leave. Byron assaulted Monica with a dozen questions. Dolores offered a vocal prayer. And Frank . . . Frank simply felt numb. Everything he had learned about Galen and the Healers now made iron-clad sense. Galen wasn't in the altruistic business of curing disease. He never had been—or at least, that wasn't his primary concern. Healing disease was only a step in his own selfish effort to cheat death. Healing had won him recruits, had earned him respect. But it wasn't what he was after. No, what Galen wanted was immortality, and in order to accomplish that impossibility, in order to alter an entire genome, he knew that he would have to do it first on a tiny scale: change the code in one place, then two, then a few genes at once, until at last he was certain that a comprehensive DNA switch was possible.

So he had formed these Healers. He had rallied these men and convinced them that they were engaged in a cause more noble than themselves, endowing them with strength and abilities. And all along it was he, this self-made prophet, who was set to reap the greatest reward.

And yet, *The Book of Becoming* had been so convincing. Galen had seemed so impassioned in his writing, so converted to his own theology. If he *was* a charlatan and if his aim was truly selfish, he was certainly a convincing liar.

Then there was his behavior following the Human Genome Project. Did that not reflect a man who truly believed much could be done to cure disease? Was it possible that Galen actually believed himself a prophet? Had he envisioned this, as he claimed, since his youth?

Frank shook his head. It didn't matter. Either way, Galen was no giver of life. He was no Healer. He was a thief. Pure and simple. And Frank was not one to be taken by thieves.

"Everyone be quiet," he said. "Let's all think for a second."

"Think?" said Hal. "We don't have time to think. You heard her."

"Your best time to go is now," said Monica with some urgency. "There are fewer Healers at night. More will come at first light."

"Just because Galen thought he could do this to us," said Frank, "doesn't mean he can. Now relax."

"But what if he can?" said Dolores. "What if we're changing like she said? I don't want that man's mind inside me."

Frank ran a hand through his hair. "That's just it. You *don't* have Galen's mind inside you. And you won't. No DNA can control how you think. Galen can't change our memories. He can alter DNA, but he can't give us his mind."

In his peripheral vision, Frank detected a subtle change in Monica's expression that made him doubt his own words, and the instant the doubt came, he knew why.

"The chip," he said.

"What chip?" said Nick.

"The stitched wound on the back of your neck," said Frank. "We all have one. So did Jonathan."

Their hands instinctively reached back behind their necks and felt the prickle of the stitches over each of their wounds.

"Care to enlighten us, Doctor?" said Frank.

Monica's gaze dropped to the floor.

"I found a chip in Jonathan," Frank said, addressing them all. "A computer chip, no bigger than a postage stamp, surgically deposited on the base of his brain stem. Whoever did it to him used an incision like the ones we have on us."

Hal's hands clenched into fists and he stepped threateningly toward Monica. "You put a chip inside us?"

"It wasn't me. It was Galen. Before he went under. *He* implanted them."

"What are they for?" said Frank.

Monica shook her head. "I don't know exactly. All I know is that Yoshida loaded them with all of Galen's research, his files, his essays, his journals, all of his knowledge. Galen even recorded much of the last few years of his life with a camcorder so that the footage could be loaded onto the chips as well. A library of data."

"But not his mind?" said Byron.

She shrugged. "I don't know. Maybe. The chip isn't only data. It also contains software Yoshida developed, software that can mimic a person's reasoning, anticipate his or her reaction to certain stimuli. The more information the software has about the person—his previous decisions, his opinions, his emotional state in various circumstances—the more able the software is to replicate the person's psychological state."

"Replicate?" said Frank. "You mean, the software can guess how Galen would think?"

"Guess and then react. It's not passive processing. Once the software chooses what it thinks will be Galen's response, it takes action. It activates neural receptors and causes the individual to act."

"I don't get it," said Dolores. "We're supposed to think differently? I don't notice anything different."

"That's because you never used your brain in the first place," said Hal.

Dolores gave him a look.

"We haven't noticed any change," said Frank, "because it's possible the chip hasn't been triggered yet."

"Triggered?" said Byron.

"Turned on," said Monica. "Activated."

"And when will that happen?" said Nick.

"The chip is triggered by the virus," said Monica. "Once the virus has spread though your system, viral genes converge on the brain stem and set off the chip."

"Set off?" said Dolores. "What's that supposed to mean?"

"We're not waiting around to find out," said Frank. "This virus has a three-day incubation period, meaning we have three days until it spreads completely through our system and does what Galen intended. Two days have already passed, so we have roughly twenty-four hours to get the countervirus in us. The BHA has developed one, and so have the Healers. Now, if we can find the Healers' version—"

Monica shook her head. "You won't. Not here. Galen kept this cabin clean. No samples of the countervirus. He knew you'd try to find it as soon as you realized what was happening, so he had it moved off-site. Your best shot is the BHA."

Hal chuckled. "Is that so?"

"Lay off," said Dolores.

"What is it with you people?" said Hal. "Am I the only person here who didn't get beat with the Stupid Stick? We shouldn't believe a word this woman says. She has every reason to lie to us. If she had this countermedicine stuff, she wouldn't give it to us anyway. Because she knows the moment we get out of here and get to the police, her ass goes to jail."

"I'm not lying. If you want to waste your time combing this cabin top to bottom, be my guest. But I'm telling you, there's none here."

Frank made an executive decision. "We're leaving. Now." He turned to Monica. "Where can we get clothes and supplies?"

"There's a storage closet in the hall where they keep extra equipment. They have clothes for you there."

Frank took her wrist. "Show us." Then, dropping his voice to a near whisper, "And if you *are* lying, if you try to alert anyone, Hal here has a poker I'm sure he's eager to use."

The corners of Hal's mouth coiled up into a grin.

Frank pulled Monica toward the door. "Wait," she said, reaching back to the cart and gathering the syringes, "you'll need these."

Frank nodded to Byron. "Byron, carry the syringes. I don't want her holding anything she could use as a weapon."

"I'm not one of them," she said.

Frank stepped close to her face. "Look, ma'am, I want to believe you. Really, I do. But right now, there's a lot of evidence stacked against you, the greatest of which is a big fat scar on each of us. Now, if you want the benefit of the doubt, if you want an ounce of trust from any of us, you're going to have to earn it. You're going to have to translate those tears into action—in other words, if I tell you to do something, you do it. No questions. No arguments. You just do it."

She nodded.

Byron held out his hands, and Monica gave him the syringes.

Frank led them across the room to the door, where he paused and looked at Monica's feet. "Take off your shoes."

Monica did so immediately.

"Carry them. I want you walking as quietly as the rest of us."

He pulled open the door. The hall was empty, still, and quiet. Monica led them through the darkness in the opposite direction Frank had gone earlier. Frank cringed at every creak of the floorboards, every heavy shuffle of their bare feet. In their room they could talk freely; they could make noise; but out here, where they were not permitted, there were those like Stone and Lichen with weapons and sensitive ears.

They reached a door, and Monica opened it. Everyone silently followed her inside. A string hung from the ceiling, and Monica pulled it. A lone, naked lightbulb illuminated.

They were in the storage room. Hal was nearest the door and shut it behind them.

A row of freestanding shelves was packed floor to ceiling with medical supplies and boxes. Monica walked to the rear of the room to the last shelf, where several matching gray suits hung in plastic dry-cleaning bags. A red necktie was draped over each hanger. Frank recognized the suits. They were identical to the one Galen had been wearing.

Monica removed one off the rack, and read the large tag that hung from it. "This one's for you, Nick."

Nick took the suit. "You got to be kidding me. We're supposed to wear this?"

Frank saw that each of the suits was tagged with a name that corresponded to one of the organ recipients. Hal found his and lifted it off the rack. "What, are we going to church or something? I'm not wearing this. I want my old clothes back."

"Your old clothes smelled like a dead dog," said Dolores. "They probably burned those the moment they took them off your drunk self."

Frank took his suit. It was just as Galen had drawn them in *The Book of Becoming*: five George Galens in gray suits and red neckties. He shook the thought from his mind. What mattered was that they were clothes; the thick material would protect them from the cold and elements. "These are the only clothes we have," he said, "so unless you want to go outside in your gowns, I say we get dressed."

Dolores dressed behind the back shelf with Monica while the men dressed toward the front of the room. Besides the suit and tie, each bag also included a white oxford shirt, a pair of undergarments, dark cotton socks, and a white handkerchief folded neatly in the breast pocket of the suit coat.

Byron examined the manufacturer's tag inside. "It's Italian." He held the coat in front of him, examining it. "Probably cost a fortune."

"The fit's pretty good, too," said Nick, bending his elbows and looking where the cuff of the coat met his sleeve. "I never had a suit before."

Frank's suit, originally intended for someone else, was a size or two too big on him. The pants were loose around the waist, but with the belt notched tight, it didn't matter.

"Do we have to wear the tie?" Nick asked.

"What kind of stupid question is that?" said Hal. "You're not going to a job interview, idiot. You don't even have to wear the coat."

Nick looked down at the coat he was wearing and did a half turn. "I like the coat."

"We should take the coats," said Frank. "It's cold out. They'll help keep us warm."

Hal looked ready to protest but instead draped his coat over one shoulder and folded his arms across his chest.

"Are you boys decent out there?" Dolores whispered.

"Yes," said Frank.

"Now I'm coming out," she said, "but if any of you laugh, I'll knock your nose so far inside you, you'll take a crap whenever you sneeze."

She stepped out. Her suit was identical to the men's, and she looked as if she'd rather be wearing anything else.

Hal stifled a laugh, and Dolores scowled.

"I know a drag queen is a man who dresses up like a woman," said Hal, "but what do call a woman who dresses up like a man? A drag king?" He laughed again.

"Leave her alone," said Nick. Then he turned to Dolores and spoke softly. "You look nice, Dolores."

"Yeah, Dolores," said Byron, "real dignified. Classy, even."

Dolores brightened for the briefest of moments until Hal giggled, "Yeah. For a guy."

Monica interrupted with a box filled with pairs of polished black wingtips. "Here. Put on your shoes."

Frank searched through the box until he found the pair labeled with his name. Not the best shoes for walking, he thought, pulling them out and bending them at the toe. But at least the soles were rubber; they'd be quiet on the floor in the hall.

They were still tying the laces when they heard the sound of heavy footsteps approaching.

Frank signaled them to move behind a shelf, and all but Monica obeyed instantly. Frank beckoned her to come, but she shook her head and shooed him into the shadows.

The door opened just as Frank and the others concealed themselves. Through the crack between the items on the shelf, Frank could see a short Healer enter the room, his face shrouded by the hood of his black cape.

"I heard voices," the Healer said. It was a voice Frank recognized but couldn't place.

"Oh, that was me," Monica said. "I was trying to reach that box up there and was cursing to myself. Do you think you could reach it for me?"

Frank watched as the Healer stepped to the shelf, his back to Frank, and reached for the box. He believed Monica. If they were still and quiet, he would leave.

Hal rotated the poker in his hand to improve his grip, and the small hook at its tip scraped against the shelf, making a grating noise.

There was a second of panic and then suddenly the Healer appeared around the corner, standing over them. Instinctively Frank lunged and tackled the Healer around the waist, slamming him roughly against the wall and causing the Healer's hood to fall back. Frank raised a fist to strike, but then saw the Healer's face and stopped.

Deputy Dixon stared back at Frank, his face showing no sign of recognition, and shoved Frank hard in the chest, sending him backward and into the others.

Hal pushed Frank aside and charged with the poker.

Dixon was faster. He dodged easily and struck Hal with an elbow in the side of the head.

Hal fell, and the poker clattered from his grip to the floor.

Dixon picked up the poker, his hands trembling noticeably, breathing hard, and looked at the others like a man only half himself. "You should not be out of your room," he said. "The master would want you all in your room."

There was a popping noise, and then Dixon's face relaxed. His eyes rolled back in his head and he fell unconscious to the floor, the poker clanging loudly beside him. Monica stood behind him, holding a tranquilizer gun, her finger still on the trigger. She looked down at the gun, covered her mouth with her one hand, and dropped the gun, suddenly repulsed by it.

Frank picked it up while Byron hurried to the door and closed it.

The gun was still loaded with several tranq darts. Frank clicked on the safety and knelt beside Dixon, checking his pulse. He was alive. "Hal, Nick, come help me get his cape off."

In minutes, Deputy Dixon lay on the floor in only a T-shirt and his boxer shorts.

"Give me your neckties," said Frank.

They handed them over.

As Frank bound and gagged Dixon, he noted how Dixon's hands trembled. After the the final knot was tied and he was certain Dixon wouldn't be able to free himself should he wake, he turned to Monica. "What did they do to him?"

"You know this guy?" said Nick.

"He's a sheriff's deputy. He witnessed the accident that killed Jonathan. He was helping us."

"Not being much of a help anymore," said Dolores.

"What did they do to him?" Frank repeated.

"Galen," said Monica, "he could control people's minds, make them bend to his will."

"How?"

She told them what she witnessed with Yoshida, how he had fallen into a seizure and how Galen had brought him back with a kiss to his forehead.

Nick said, "So the old man puckers up, kisses your forehead, and after that you're putty in his fingers?"

"I know it sounds ridiculous, but the proof is right in front of you." She pointed to Deputy Dixon. "He was brought in right before the surgeries. Galen kissed him, and the guy went blank, like his soul had been sucked out of him. I saw it myself."

"Then answer me this," said Hal. "If old geezer Galen's got magic kisses that can make a slave out of anybody, why didn't he do that to you, huh? Why didn't he just kiss you on the forehead and tell you to transplant his organs? Why go to all the trouble of threatening your son?"

"Because the trembling and seizures are side effects of the condition," said Monica, "Galen couldn't risk my hands being unsteady. He knew I was going to be operating on him, so he had to *force* me to cooperate without his . . . kiss."

Dolores cocked her head and looked down at Dixon. "Then he's a victim same as us. We can't just leave him here."

She was right, Frank knew. There was no telling what the Healers would do to Dixon once they found him here. Healers hadn't shown a particularly high regard for human life—despite their claims to the contrary—and if they blamed Dixon for the escape, ending his life might be considered an appropriate punishment and not so great a loss.

"Is there a way to reverse the effect?" said Frank. "Some antidote or medicine, maybe? Something to shake him out of it?"

"No, none that I've seen," said Monica.

"He can't go with us," said Hal. "Are you out of your mind? He's trying to kill us."

"You heard Frank," said Nick. "He's a cop."

"I don't care if he's the pope," said Hal. "There's no way we're dragging him along."

"They might hurt him," said Dolores.

"He's one of them," said Hal. "They're not going to hurt him."

"You don't know that," said Dolores.

"Well, I'm willing to take that chance, because it's him or us. We pull him along, and none of us are getting out of here."

The others exchanged glances.

"Don't seem right," said Dolores.

"What isn't right is what they did to us," said Hal. "But what's done is done. Now we got a chance of getting out of here, and we shouldn't miss it because of this guy. What are we going to do, carry him? And even when he wakes up and can walk on his own, he's not going to want to come along. He'd be nothing but trouble. They've screwed with his head. That's help we can't offer. Our best bet is to get help for *us* and then to send help back here for him. Otherwise, nobody gets help. Because we aren't getting out of here if we to try to take him along."

Frank sighed. "I don't want to leave him behind either, but Hal's right. We don't have a choice. We're in no condition to help him now. Our best option is to find someone who can and send them back here."

"Damn straight," said Hal.

Frank looked at Monica. "What about this tranquilizer gun? Are there more of these?"

She pointed to an empty peg on the wall. "It was hanging there. I didn't see any others."

"What about these antirejection drugs?"

She opened a large wooden cabinet where several vials of medication and syringes were stored. "They're all kept here."

"Pack them. We're taking them with us. And you're carrying them."

Hal waved his arms. "Whoa whoa whoa. Look, I don't care if she's a prisoner here or not, she ain't coming with us either, not after what she did to us."

"She's a doctor. We may need her help."

"To do what? Cut us open again? She put a knife to our gut and bled us. I say she finds her own way out."

Monica's jaw was set. "Hate me if you want. Turn me into the police. I don't care. But you're not leaving this cabin without me and my son."

"Your son?" said Frank. "He's here?"

"In the basement. And we're not leaving without him."

24

RESCUE

Frank could see the argument coming before it started.

"Please tell me you're not seriously considering taking this woman's child with us," said Hal.

"He's my son," said Monica. "He's only six. I'm not leaving him behind."

Hal made a face. "Six? You got to be kidding me. What, are we babysitters all of a sudden? No. No kid is coming with us. He'll only slow us down."

Monica looked at them with pleading eyes. "Please, he's only a child."

"So that gives him special treatment?" said Hal. "Just because he's younger than me?"

"He's fast for his age," said Monica. "He could keep up."

Hal narrowed his eyes at her. "Read my lips, lady. The kid stays."

"Where in the basement are they keeping him?" Frank asked.

"What difference does it make?" said Hal. "He's not coming. He'd only slow us down."

"A room, north side," said Monica. "It's guarded."

"How many guards?"

"Two, sometimes three."

"Is there a way to get outside from the basement?"

Hal stepped between them and faced Frank. "We're not taking time to get this kid. We've wasted too much time already."

Frank acknowledged Hal blankly, then looked beyond him to Monica. "Is there a way outside from the basement?"

Hal threw up his hands.

"No," said Monica. "The only way out is the front door. The back door is locked from the outside, like all the windows. But there are only a few Healers here during the night. The others come in the morning. If we can get by the ones downstairs and the ones on the porch before the others arrive, we could make it."

"Am I the only one here who thinks this woman is full of it?" said Hal. "This could be a trap. Has anyone thought of that? How do we know this kid even exists? The whole thing could be a sham to get us down into the basement where who knows what is waiting."

"He's right," said Nick. "Why should we believe a word she says? I say we go now."

"Exactly," said Hal, reaching over and patting Nick twice on the back as if they were lifelong friends who understood each other implicitly.

"No," said Frank. "This is different. The deputy we *can't* help. But a child we *can*. We're not leaving the boy behind."

Monica visibly relaxed.

"Give me the cape," said Frank.

Byron handed it to him, and Frank tied it over his shoulders, pulling the hood forward over his eyes. "I'm going to the basement. If you hear a commotion or if I'm not back in ten minutes, go without me."

"If we hear a commotion," said Nick, "then they'll know we're trying to escape. It'll be too late for us to try anything then."

"Maybe not," said Frank. "They'll think *I'm* trying to

escape. They won't know we all are. Maybe I could create a big enough distraction for you to get out the front. In the meantime, pack supplies—food, water, anything in the room you think would be useful. But no more than we would need in a day's time. Don't wear yourselves down. By the time I get back, we'll be ready."

He smiled as if it were a plan that couldn't fail, and Dolores and Byron looked as if they believed him.

"I'm going with you," Monica said.

"No," said Frank. "If you're telling the truth, I'll be back with your son. If you're not, well, then I'm out of luck."

"Leave us the gun," said Hal. "We may need it."

"He's going against guards," said Byron. "We're not."

Frank nodded his thanks to Byron. "How do I get to the basement?"

Monica told him.

"Ten minutes," said Byron.

Frank nodded. "Ten minutes."

They turned off the light before Frank opened the door, finding the hallway exactly as they had left it—dark, silent, and vacant. Frank realized he lacked one important bit of information and turned back. "What's your son's name?" he whispered.

"Wyatt," Monica said. "His name is Wyatt."

Frank hurried toward the basement, walking with a determined step so as not to arouse suspicion if he were seen. From a distance he could pass as Deputy Dixon; just keep the hood up and move like he knew where he was going.

Wyatt. I'm risking it all for a six-year-old named Wyatt.

As he moved down the hallway, Frank considered Hal's logic. Leaving the kid was indeed the most sensible thing to do. He would slow them down. And this was a window of opportunity they'd only get once. If they were caught now, the Healers would take extra precautions to make another escape attempt impossible.

And yet, Frank couldn't do it. He couldn't leave the kid.

Even if it meant not going himself. It was totally irrational, but the feeling in his gut was stronger than common sense. They weren't leaving without the kid.

Two quick turns and Frank was there at the door to the basement. It creaked when he pushed on it, a noise that echoed down the hallway and back toward the supply closet. He froze and listened, expecting Healers to materialize at any moment.

After a lengthy pause, he felt certain no one was coming.

Relieved, he put his hand back on the door and swung it open in a fast single motion so it didn't have time to squeak.

The staircase was narrow, wooden, and ancient. A few steps even showed signs of rotting. The walls were no more attractive and extended to the basement floor below, which to Frank's disappointment was flooded with light. He had been hoping for the cover of darkness. Most striking, however, was the noticeable change in temperature. The basement had no heat. And for the first time since leaving Washington, Frank could see his breath chill in front of him.

Moving slowly, he descended the stairs.

Twenty feet beyond the staircase a Healer sat sleeping in a chair beside a door. Even in a semiconscious state, with his mouth slightly agape, the Healer was physically imposing.

At least he's alone, Frank thought.

A small space heater glowed at the Healer's feet, and as Frank approached he could feel the warmth emanating from its orange, glowing coils.

Frank aimed the tranq gun and was prepared to fire when he heard a toilet flushing and a door behind him opened.

"What brings you down here, Dixon?" Lichen's voice said.

Frank continued facing forward and watched as Lichen's shadow grew in front of him as the Healer approached.

When the shadow stopped, it totally encompassed Frank's own.

Frank felt a heavy tap on his shoulder where the strap of the dart gun was positioned.

"What's this now?" said Lichen. "You carrying a dart spitter, Dixon?"

Two giant fingers pinched the tip of Frank's hood and pulled it back, exposing his head. Frank had no choice but to act. Turning abruptly, he fired directly into Lichen's gut.

Four darts sank into Lichen's stomach before he had time to flinch. If they caused him any pain, Lichen didn't show it. He looked down at the tranqs with a shocked expression, blinked, opened his mouth to speak, then fell forward to the floor, unconscious.

The noise woke the sleeping Healer, and he leapt of out his chair, disoriented.

Frank already had the gun raised. He squeezed the trigger and sent four darts into the Healer's chest.

The Healer reached down, pulled out a dart, looked at it, then fell forward onto the concrete, hitting the space heater and knocking it over so it clattered on the floor.

The struggle had been brief but loud, and Frank instinctively looked back toward the basement door, expecting it to swing open and a horde of Healers to pour through.

But the door remained closed.

He wondered if the other transplantees had heard—and if so, would they misinterpret the commotion as his attempt at a distraction and make a run for it without him?

He jumped over the Healer nearest the guarded door and pulled on the handle. It didn't open. A padlock hanging from a crude lock kept it shut tight. Moving quickly, Frank rummaged through Lichen's clothing and found the key hanging from a chain around his neck. He yanked it free, stuck the key into the padlock, and twisted. The lock snapped free.

Pushing hard on the door, Frank fell into the room.

Wyatt was sitting on a bed in the corner, his legs tucked up against his chest and his eyes wide with terror. He was smaller than Frank had expected, a skinny kid with bright green eyes like his mother's.

"I'm not going to hurt you, Wyatt. I'm a friend. I've come to help you."

The kid said nothing, only stared.

"I'm here to take you to your mother. We're going to try to leave this place." He extended a hand.

Wyatt didn't flinch. "I don't know you. You're a stranger. I'm not supposed to go with strangers."

"That's right, Wyatt. You never should. But today is the exception. Do you know what exception means?"

Wyatt raised an eyebrow. "I'm not stupid."

"Of course you're not. Listen, I know I'm a stranger, but you have to trust me."

"Are you a policeman?"

"Something like that, yes."

"Show me your badge, then."

This was insane. Healers could be coming at any moment. "I don't have a badge exactly."

"Then how do I know you're a policeman? You're dressed like one of the bad guys."

"This is a disguise," Frank said, opening the cape and showing Wyatt his suit underneath. "See?"

"You're wearing a suit. Policemen don't wear suits."

This had gone on far too long. "Kid, you're either coming now or not at all. If you still don't trust me, ask yourself, if I were one of the bad guys, would I have shot those guards in the hall?" He pointed toward the hallway, and Wyatt ran out. The Healers lay sprawled where they had fallen.

Wyatt looked up at Frank with wide eyes. "Whoa. Why didn't you say so? Let's go." He trotted off toward the staircase and, once he reached it, took two steps at a time. Frank was right at his heels. They moved down the corridor and encountered no one.

When they reached the storage closet, Monica scooped up Wyatt and held him tightly.

"What took so long?" said Hal. "It sounded like a fight. We almost left."

"If it had been up to Hal, we *would* have left," said Nick.

Byron slung a small pack over his back. "We found water bottles and a few food items. Now what? It's nearly light."

Two minutes later they were all crouched in the hallway before the front room. The porch was visible through the nearest window, and the glow of dawn could be seen creeping over the horizon. Stone was still at his post on the porch, looking out over the valley and blocking the only exit.

Frank stood up and pulled his hood over his head. Dixon was several inches shorter than he was, so he slouched his shoulders to make himself seem smaller.

Then he took the strap off the dart gun and checked the cartridge. Only four darts left. Every dart would have to count.

"What are you waiting for?" said Hal. "Hurry."

"I don't see you rushing outside to stop them," said Nick.

"It wasn't my idea," said Hal.

"Quiet," said Frank. "Stay here and stay down." He tucked the gun under his cape and, taking a deep breath, went to the front door.

A cool morning breeze hit him when the door opened. The burst of air nearly lifted the hood off his head and gave him a momentary panic. But the wind lessened once the door was opened further, and his head remained covered.

Stone was leaning against a post near the front steps. Frank couldn't see his face with his hood pulled so low, but the feet were enormous.

"Morning, Dixon," said Stone.

It was now or never. Frank raised and fired until it clicked empty. All four darts pierced Stone in the stomach, just as they had Lichen and the other.

But for Stone, a much larger, thicker, more massive target, four darts apparently weren't enough.

Frank's hood snapped back, and two massive hands shoved him hard. It felt like getting hit by a truck at high speed—all the air inside him left him at once. He flew backward, his feet completely off the ground, through the door and into the front room. Before landing against the sofa, his arm smashed through a lamp sitting on an end table. Frank felt a searing jolt of pain as something sharp cut deep into his arm, glass exploding in every direction.

Frank wanted to cry out, but he couldn't find his breath.

Suddenly Stone was over him, picking him up and bringing Frank's face to his.

"Do not make me hurt you," said Stone. Then his eyes drooped a little, and Frank knew the tranquilizers were having some effect.

Frank jerked back, and as suspected, Stone's grip was weak enough for Frank to break free. He fell to the floor and there, in a painful intake of air, got his full wind back.

Stone reached for his tranquilizer gun hanging over his back and brought it to bear on Frank. "You give me no choice."

Frank closed his eyes and waited for the inevitable popping sound of the dart discharging but heard breaking glass instead. He opened his eyes and saw Stone tip to one side before falling unconscious to the floor. Byron stood beside him, holding the remnants of another glass lamp.

Byron dropped the lamp, extended a hand, and helped Frank to his feet. "You okay?"

"I think so, yeah," Frank said, moving to dust the glass shards off himself but then wincing at the sudden pain in his arm.

"You're hurt, " said Monica, coming to him.

"You can check it later," he said. "Let's get out first. It's nearly light."

"You're bleeding."

Frank looked down at the sleeve of the robe and saw

that it was indeed wet with blood. "Outside," he said. "The other Healers could arrive any minute."

She didn't argue and went outside onto the porch, Wyatt clinging tightly to her waist and staring at Frank with what could have been awe. Frank rolled Stone over and yanked the tranquilizer gun from his grip.

Nick squatted beside Stone and dug through his pockets.

"What are you doing?" said Frank.

"Old habit. Never leave a man down." He smiled. "Or is it, never leave a downed man's wallet?" His grin left him as his hand found something in Stone's pocket. Nick pulled his hand out, holding a semiautomatic pistol.

"I'll take that," said Frank, reaching for it.

Nick gave a half turn, raising a shoulder to deflect Frank's hand. "I'm looking at it."

Frank reached again, cautiously now, and gently put a hand on Nick's arm. "It's not a toy, Nick. I should carry it."

Nick relinquished the gun, and his cheeks flushed. "I wasn't going to shoot anybody. I was curious, is all."

Frank removed the clip and pocketed it, then tucked the gun in his belt behind his back.

Outside, the blinding rays of morning were inching over the mountain range, bathing the cabin in an amber hue and reflecting off the chilled dew across the lawn.

"It's freezing out here," said Dolores, pulling her suit coat around her.

Nick descended the steps of the porch and joined the others in the yard, staring out over the valley. "We're going out in that?"

In answer, Frank walked past him and headed for the tree line south of the cabin, precisely in the direction Nick was pointing.

"But for how far?" said Nick. "I can't see anything from here. No town. No road. Nothing."

"Then I suggest we get moving," Frank said, continuing toward the trees.

Monica and Wyatt were right behind him. Hal, Byron, and Dolores glanced at one another and then hustled after Frank as well.

Nick looked back at the cabin, hesitated a moment, then hurried with the others into the forest.

25

TRAIL

Agent Riggs drove north toward Agoura Hills, his mind racing. It had been two days since Carter and Frank disappeared—two days since those two had, according to the vehicle usage records at the BHA, taken a van and left the agency. Where they had gone to and why, Riggs could only guess. It didn't make sense. Here they were, in the middle of critical investigation, gaining ground on the Healer crisis, and Carter and Frank had walked off the lot as if school were no longer in session.

"Maybe they got a call or something," said Peeps, who was sitting in the passenger seat. "Maybe someone phoned in a lead or a clue or something."

Riggs shook his head. "I checked the phone records. I didn't see anything unusual." Besides, they would have *told* me if they had found a lead."

Riggs rubbed his hand through his five o'clock shadow. Every part of him felt tired, especially his mind. For two days he had tried to find answers and for two days he had come up empty. First there was Frank and Carter, two agents who had stepped off the face of the earth without so much as a goodbye. Then there were the Healers. Jonathan Fox, who Riggs had hoped would prove to be a break in the case, turned out to be a dead end. Agents had combed every inch of roadside near where the truck had hit the boy and found nothing. No virus. No blood. Nothing. It was as if the kid had fallen out of the sky, a notion that Riggs gave more than a cursory consideration. And the deputy, the one and only witness they had in the whole ordeal, had apparently left town the morning after the accident to tend to a dying relative somewhere out of state. All attempts to contact the man had proved fruitless.

So here they were, going up to Agoura Hills yet again, this time to speak to the deputy's supervisor in person. They pulled into the parking lot of the Sheriff's Station and made their way inside. A heavyset woman in a deputy's uniform greeted them at the front desk.

"Help you, gentlemen?"

Riggs showed her his badge. "Agent Riggs of the Biohazard Agency. This is Agent Waters. We'd like to speak to Lieutenant Yontz, please."

She pointed them to an office across the room and picked up the phone. "I'll tell him you're coming."

Riggs thanked her, and they crossed to Yontz's office.

Leroy Yontz hung up his phone and welcomed them inside, inviting them to have a seat opposite his desk and offering them coffee, the latter of which they politely refused. Yontz was a slender man in his forties with a receding hairline and a gold-rimmed pair of bifocals.

"You boys have had a hard time with this one," Yontz said. "Some cases you got to give up on. That's my policy. Chase the tough ones too long, and you burn yourself out."

"I'm afraid that's not an option at this point," said Riggs.

Yontz shrugged. "Well, I told you everything I know over the phone, which isn't much. This was Deputy Dixon's thing. I don't know that I can be of much more help to you."

"Any word from Dixon?"

Yontz shook his head. "I left messages on his cell phone, but I haven't heard back from him. Some relative dying or something. I hope he knows this counts against his vacation time."

"What about the truck driver?"

"I put in a call with the trucking company. Nasty-ass lawyer called me back, said if I wanted to talk to his client, I'd have to arrange a hearing. Said no charges were made against the man; it was an accident pure and simple. Anybody could see that." Yontz put his feet up on his desk and picked at his teeth with a toothpick. "The world would be a happier place if they let us take a shot at lawyers every now and then. Nothing fatal, of course, just wing 'em."

"Could you take us to the scene of the accident?" said Riggs. "We'd like to have a look around."

Yontz put his feet down and tried not to look annoyed. "I already took your boys out there. They poked in the grass for a few hours and didn't find anything. Don't see how our going out there again is going to change that."

Riggs stood up and Peeps followed.

"Just a few minutes of your time, Lieutenant," said Riggs. "We'll be most grateful."

Yontz mumbled something under his breath and grabbed his hat.

Ten minutes later they arrived at the accident scene. Yontz parked his cruiser on the side of the road, and Riggs pulled his sedan in behind him. They got out and looked around. In the daylight, this stretch of road looked like all the miles of rural highway in this area. Had Yontz not escorted them, Riggs wasn't sure he could have found the spot.

He looked down at the clearing and the forest beyond.

"What's beyond those trees?" Riggs asked.

"More trees," said Yontz. "Not many residences or commercial properties up here anymore."

Anymore? "Were there *ever* any commercial facilities up here, any that have been abandoned?"

Yontz rubbed his chin and thought a moment. "Well, there's the old Happy Mountain Rest Home." He pointed northeast. "About two miles up that way. That place has been empty for years."

Riggs snapped his fingers at Peeps. "Notify Hernandez.

I want the assault team in a helicopter flying in this direction in two minutes."

Frank found a narrow trail not far below the tree line and decided to take it. It would lead them to civilization much faster than an aimless hike through the woods. Plus, a trail would be safer; they wouldn't have to worry about unexpected holes or gullies or invading an unfriendly animal's den. And, with fewer obstacles to watch out for, they could move faster. The morning air was cold, but the quick pace Frank had adopted was warming them. Hal had decided to wear his suit coat after all, and everyone moved with surprising ease.

Frank stepped over a log in the path and marveled. He had had surgery a little over forty-eight hours ago, and now he felt as nimble and light as ever. Wyatt was the only one who seemed to be having a bit of a struggle. He was having to take two steps for every one of Frank's. And although he was keeping up for the time being, Frank knew it wouldn't last. The kid would tire. He couldn't keep this pace up forever.

"I should look at your arm," Monica said, coming in step beside Frank.

"It doesn't hurt anymore," Frank said, still holding the arm stiff at his side. "Let's put some more distance behind us."

"We've gone almost three miles," Monica said. "We can stop long enough for me to look at it. You're no good to us if you bleed to death."

"She's right, Frank," said Byron. "Let her look at it. She's a doctor."

I'm a doctor myself, Frank wanted to point out. But he knew it was pointless to argue. They were right. Bleeding wounds needed immediate attention. Plus, his blood was contaminated. Every drop that dripped to the ground was like a seed of virus.

Frank stopped suddenly. "Wait a minute." How could he be so stupid? He must be losing his mind. "You can't look at this wound. You shouldn't be near it. I might infect you."

"It's all right," said Monica.

"No, it isn't. You don't know how virulent this is. You can't risk my blood touching you."

"I'm immune," she said. "Wyatt and me both. Galen inoculated us when he took us. He knew I'd be handling the virus, and he didn't want Wyatt becoming infected either. Let's not forget that I've had my hands inside you. Your blood has been all over me. If I could be infected, I'd have been dead a long time ago."

Frank hesitated a moment, then gave in, nodding for her to proceed.

She helped him out of the cape and suit coat. Frank was surprised that it didn't hurt him nearly as much to move his arm now. He had thought it would be a painful ordeal to get undressed and had postponed the act partially for that reason. Yet now there was no pain. Only blood. And plenty of it. The sleeve of his white shirt was red from the elbow down.

The others gathered around him. "Gross," Dolores said.

"You really cut it bad," said Nick.

Frank thought so, too, and it startled him to see so much of his own blood; he hadn't realized the cut was so deep.

"Sit down," Monica said, opening the kit of medical supplies she had taken from the storage room and pointing him to a large rock by the trail.

Frank sat and the others surrounded him. Wyatt pushed his way to the front and stared at the red sleeve. "Does it hurt?" he asked.

"No," said Frank, not looking at it. "Not really. I feel fine. Fit as a fiddle."

Monica, who was putting on rubber gloves, stopped suddenly and looked at him. "What did you say?

"I said I was fine. Fit as a fiddle."

"Why did you say it that way? Do you always say that?"

Frank wrinkled his brow. "It's just an expression."

Monica noticed all eyes on her. Even Wyatt looked concerned. She forced a smile and continued donning her gloves. "I'm sorry. It's just something Galen said to me once."

"Galen?" said Nick.

"When we first met. It's not important."

"Hell, yes, it's important," said Nick. "Maybe that chip thing is on already."

Frank shook his head. "I told you. It's just an expression. My grandfather used to say it."

Nick still looked skeptical.

"A dead old man is not controlling my speech." He turned to Monica. "Let's get this over with."

Moving quickly, Monica cut off the bottom half of the sleeve and exposed the wound, which was positioned above the elbow on the back of the upper arm. Instead of looking at it, Frank watched everyone else's reaction. Nick and Hal both winced at first, but then their faces turned to wonder.

"Would you look at that?" Hal said with a whistle.

"Looks healed already," said Nick.

Frank turned the arm over and saw that, sure enough, the wound had already sealed itself; a three-inch-long scar had formed across the muscle and stopped the flow of blood completely. It was still bright red, swollen, and sensitive to the touch, but it was not the gaping wound it must have been minutes before.

Monica wet some gauze with alcohol and cleaned the dried blood away.

"It's true, then," said Byron. "Everything you said about this virus. The rapid healing, everything."

Hal clapped his hands together loudly. "I'll be damned. The cut just up and healed itself like that."

"How does it feel?" said Monica.

Frank bent his arm. "A little tight, but other than that, fine."

"I should wrap it just in case." She ripped open a packet of bandaging and got to work.

Hal squatted down beside her as she wrapped the arm. "Now, you're a doctor, right? How long should it take a cut like that to heal, you think? Under normal circumstances, I mean."

"Difficult to say. There's no way of knowing how deep the gash was. But considering how much blood he lost, plus the fact that he cut through the triceps here, I'd say at least a few weeks. Not to mention plenty of stitches."

Hal nodded vigorously, pleased by her response. "You hear that?" he said, looking back at the others. "A few weeks. A cut like that normally takes weeks." He laughed. "And our man Frank here did it in less than ten minutes." He patted Frank on the knee as if he had done something incredibly brave.

"I don't understand," Wyatt said.

Hal was all too eager to explain. "You saw how his arm smashed through that lamp, right? Bam! Glass everywhere."

Wyatt nodded.

"Well, the glass cut through him, see? Deep. To the bone, maybe."

"Don't be so graphic," Dolores said, "he's just a boy."

"A boy who asked a question, dipstick. So cork it." He turned back to Wyatt, his face pleasant again. "So he cuts himself deep, right? But now look at it." He pointed to the wound, even though it was already covered with bandages. "It's healed and ready to go. Like magic."

Frank got to his feet. "We've stopped long enough."

Monica gathered her bag. "I should take your staples out while we're stopped," she said. "They've been in long enough. Everyone else had theirs removed before you woke up."

Frank felt the line of staples down his chest. "It can wait. We'll have time for it later."

She didn't object. "Come on, Wyatt," she said, taking his hand.

Frank put the suit coat back on and threw the cape over his shoulder, then stuffed the bloody sleeve Monica had cut away into his pocket.

They got moving again, quickly returning to their old pace. Frank felt invigorated. He knew he should be winded after having tackled three miles, but each breath came to him easily and calmly, as if he had just awoken from a deep rest.

Wyatt trotted up beside him, not having such an easy time with it. His hair was wet with sweat, and his breaths were short and labored. "What's your name?" he said.

"Frank."

"It's only fair if I know your name since you already know mine."

"I suppose."

Wyatt avoided a rock in the trail. "Are you really a policeman?"

"Not really, no."

"Didn't think so. So what are you?"

"A virologist. I study viruses."

"Like a doctor?"

"Yes, like a doctor."

"Mom's a thoracic surgeon. That means she has to cut people's chests open."

"Yes, I know. All too well." He allowed himself a glance back to see if Monica was listening. She wasn't. She was near the back, struggling more than anyone to keep up. Wyatt had found his second wind, but Monica hadn't been so lucky.

"My dad's a doctor, too," said Wyatt. "An orthopedic surgeon. That means a bone doctor."

"Well, if I break my arm, I know who to call."

"I only see him every other weekend, though," said Wyatt. "He and my mom got a divorce."

That caught Frank off guard. "I'm sorry to hear that."

Wyatt shrugged. "My dad had a girlfriend while he and my mom were still together."

Frank didn't know what to say to that one. This was getting uncomfortable.

"But I don't think I'm supposed to know that, since my mom and dad don't talk about it with me."

Kids were amazing, thought Frank. No guile. They just say it like it is, even to a total stranger.

But Frank knew he wasn't a stranger to Wyatt. Not anymore. In the hour or so since their meeting, Frank had somehow graduated to something else in the kid's eyes. Something bigger. Now Wyatt was sticking close to him, doing everything Frank did, like hopping over a log or avoiding a root, even mimicking his walk. What was it? Respect, maybe? A sense of protection, of safety? The kid had undergone quite an ordeal in the past week, something that a lot of kids might never recover from. And now here was a man who could shoot the bad guys with a tranquilizer gun and lead them all charging through the woods toward safety. No, Frank was something different to Wyatt now. And for the time being, Frank didn't mind.

Victor Owens drove north on the Pacific Coast Highway, his cell phone to his ear. After the appropriate number of rings a familiar voice said, "Hi. This is Dr. Monica Owens. I'm sorry I can't take your call right now. I'm either with a patient or on the other line. If this is an emergency—" Victor slammed his cell phone closed and tossed it into the passenger seat. It wasn't like Monica to neglect his messages. And over the past few days, he had left plenty. Yes, she was an ex-wife who believed she had plenty of reasons to hold a grudge, but that wasn't Monica's style, never had been. If Victor left a message, Monica called him back—

maybe not right away; maybe she'd let him sweat it out for a day or so. But never longer than that. And now Wyatt's school had called Victor asking him if everything was all right with Wyatt, explaining that the boy hadn't reported to class in over a week and that repeated calls to Wyatt's mother had gone unanswered.

Victor wasn't sure if he should be angry or frightened. It wasn't like Monica to pack up and take Wyatt on a vacation without first consulting Victor. They might be divorced and might not to see eye to eye on a lot of parental issues, but one thing they *had* agreed on was open communication—well, open concerning all things relating to Wyatt, anyway. The other aspects of their lives were their own business. Not that Victor suspected Monica of having *much* of a life outside of her career. She hadn't had much of a life when they were married, for the same reason.

Victor turned north on Cahuenga and sped up the hill into Pacific Palisades. What did he have left to do, then, but to go and see for himself if Monica was home? Maybe she had left a note. Maybe someone had broken in and . . . Victor put the thought out of his mind. They weren't harmed. Monica was too smart. And Victor had spent too much on that security system when they were married to let anything bad happen without raising an alarm.

The driveway was empty. Monica's SUV wasn't there. Victor wasn't sure whether to take that as a good sign or a bad one.

He parked his Mercedes at the curb, got out, and fished through his keychain for the key to the front door. To play it safe, he rang the doorbell first and was surprised when Rosa answered it almost immediately, a broom in her hand.

"Rosa."

"*Buenas tardes,* Mr. Owens." She had a peculiar smile across her face that unsettled Victor.

"Where's Monica?"

"Dr. Owens is not here," she said, as placidly as if she were getting into a warm jacuzzi.

"Well, where is she? I've left her half a dozen messages, and she hasn't called me back. I've called the clinic. No one there has seen her either."

"Dr. Owens is not here," Rosa said again.

Victor sighed irritably. Rosa's poor grasp of English was intolerable. All she could respond to were simple, curt sentences. She probably didn't even understand half of what he was saying.

He spoke slower. "Where's Wyatt? Is he with Monica?"

Rosa considered this a long moment.

Victor was getting frustrated. She didn't understand. "With, *with,*" he said with more urgency. "Do you understand the word *with*? Like, chili con carne. Monica *con* Wyatt?" He pointed two index fingers upward and then brought them together. Improvised sign language. "With. Monica with Wyatt?"

Rosa stared at him, still smiling—not amused just . . . smiling. "Dr. Owens is not here."

"Dammit, you said that already. I'm asking about Wyatt now. I want to know where—"

"Wyatt is with Dr. Owens."

Victor straightened, surprised by her sudden comprehension and a bit embarrassed that he had lost his cool. Rosa, however, didn't seem the least bit fazed by his behavior. But why had it taken her so long to respond? It was like her brain was working on a time delay.

"Wyatt is with Monica? Where? Did she tell you where they were going?"

"Dr. Owens went to the master's."

Victor raised an eyebrow. "She went to the Masters? What, the golf tournament?" Victor was no golfer, but he hadn't heard anything about the tournament in the news recently. Besides, Monica hated golf.

"Dr. Owens will be back in a few days," said Rosa. "You wants I leaves her a message?"

"Are they on vacation somewhere?"

Rosa considered that. "Yes, vacation."

Victor ran a hand through his hair, relieved. "Well, why didn't you say so? Yes, please leave her a message. Tell her to call me immediately. She's had me worried sick."

Rosa opened the door further. "I get you tea or coffee?"

"No. I need to get back to the hospital. But please tell Monica to call."

"I pass message," said Rosa, the smile still frozen on her lips.

Victor thanked her and returned to his car. Rosa stood on the porch, the broom in her hand, watching him go. Victor glanced back several times as he drove away. Rosa was still there, giving him that same vacant grin.

26

CONTACT

Lichen awoke to find himself on the cement floor of the cabin basement. He sat up, rubbed his eyes, and considered how he could have been so careless as to have fallen asleep on the floor. He yawned lazily, then spied Pine on the floor also, still sleeping. Suddenly the events came flooding back into his mind. He looked down at his stomach where four tranquilizer darts still protruded from the muscle of his gut. He sprang to his feet and pulled them out, tossing them aside.

"Wake up, Pine." He gave the giant on the floor a stiff kick in the side. Pine stirred

Lichen ran to Wyatt's room, and his worst fear became a reality. Wyatt was gone. Frank the vessel had tried to escape with the boy.

He turned back, giving Pine another kick.

"The boy's gone."

This news snapped Pine awake. His eyes widened. "Gone?"

Lichen didn't stay to explain. He bounded up the basement steps, taking four at a time. All was quiet on the ground floor, and sunlight streamed in the windows. How long had they been out?

He reached the room where the vessels were recuperating and threw open the door. The fire had died out, and the beds were empty. A thumping sound reached his sensitive ears. He cocked his head and listened. A rattling noise was coming from somewhere down the hall. Lichen lowered his shoulders, centering his body weight, getting into an attack position, and slowly moved down the hallway, following the noise.

The rattle led him to the storage closet. He pushed open the door. The man known as Dixon, who had come to them as a sheriff's deputy, lay bound and gagged on the floor, having a seizure. The noise was that of his body thrashing on the floor. Too much time had passed since his last treatment, and his body was now violently crying out for another dose.

Lichen hurried to him, grabbed the neckties that bound him, and ripped them free. Dixon continued to bang about, his head and body already bruised. Lichen held the man's head, took a vial of treatment from his pocket, unscrewed the cap, and gave Dixon what his body craved.

The man immediately began to calm. His limbs ceased thrashing and his body grew still.

Lichen gently lowered Dixon's head to the floor. He would live. How foolish of the vessels to be so cruel to one who only wanted to protect them. Lichen took one final look at the man, his heart full with compassion, then ran from the room. There was work to be done.

The front room was in shambles. Lamps had been shattered. Glass shards lay everywhere. The front door stood open. And there in the middle of the room, like a sleeping grizzly, lay Stone.

Lichen hurried to him and checked his vitals. Stone was alive. Good, thought Lichen, he'd be needed. But how to wake him up? Stone could not be stirred by a stiff slap; he had been given the greatest measure of pain resistance, and therefore pain could not arouse him.

Lichen pinched Stone's nose and put a hand over his mouth, blocking his breathing. Seconds passed, until

Stone's drooping eyes opened as his suffocating body forced itself awake.

Lichen pulled the tranquilizer darts from Stone's stomach. "The vessels, they've run off."

Pine came lumbering into the room.

Stone stood to his full height, tiny shards of the broken lamp falling from his white hair. "We must bring them back," he said simply. "The rebirth is in less than a day's time. Lichen, you're the swiftest. Run ahead and detain them. I will call the others, and we will join you in the wood. They can't have gotten far."

Lichen was out the door before Stone had even finished speaking. With a single leap he cleared the porch steps. Then he was across the yard, his legs gaining speed, his cape billowing behind him. He wouldn't need to stop and look for tracks. Their scent was still strong in the morning air.

Riggs gave the order to the pilot, and the helicopter quickly made its descent toward the dilapidated-looking Happy Mountain Rest Home. Once the helicopter touched down, the door slid open, and the assault team, suited to the hilt in biogear and armor, poured out of it, running at a crouch away from the helicopter and taking defensive positions at the building's entrance. Riggs was the last one out. He slid shut the door and tapped the side, signaling the pilot to take off again. The rotors whirred faster, and the helicopter lifted away, leaving swirling clouds of dust in its wake.

Riggs hustled to the front door and pressed against the wall beside it. He swung his assault rifle forward and cocked it. He could feel all eyes on him. The team would wait for his go before they made their advance.

The sound of barking cut through the silence. Everyone turned just in time to see two vicious-looking Doberman pinschers come bounding around the corner from the back of the building.

Agent Hernandez didn't wait for the order. She unstrapped the tranquilizer pistol at her hip and dropped both animals before they were within twenty yards of any member of the team. The Dobermans lay on their sides, eyes rolled back, tongues hanging from their mouths.

Peeps whistled from his position behind a tree in the front yard. "I don't know about you guys, but I'm glad we invited her."

There were a few chuckles broadcast over the comlink speakers until Hernandez said, "Keep making cracks, Peeps, and I might accidentally put a tranq in that skinny butt of yours."

"Sheesh," said Peeps. "Woman can't even take a compliment."

Riggs's voice silenced them. "Focus, people. There could more than Dobermans inside. And who knows what else."

They became serious again, readying their weapons.

"Lights," said Riggs.

Everyone fastened a penlight to his or her helmet.

"Lights check," said Peeps, when he had visual confirmation that every team member was ready.

Riggs gave the signal. "Move."

Staying low, Riggs ran into the littered lobby of the Happy Mountain Rest Home. The rest of the team was right behind him, staying in their preassigned formations, ready to strike at any moment.

"Peeps," Riggs said. "What you got?"

A 3-D schematic of the building appeared in Riggs's visor, and Peeps's voice sounded in his ear. "This is the lobby. The door in front of us leads to a nurses' station, beyond which are the old residents' rooms."

Riggs ordered them to follow, and he cautiously approached the open door leading into the building's interior. He pressed himself against the wall beside it, and then quickly poked his head in the doorway to peer down the corridor beyond it.

Gunfire exploded from somewhere down the corridor, and Riggs recoiled his head just as slugs sank into the door frame and blew wood chips out the other side.

"Someone's shooting at us!" one of the agents shouted.

"Someone with good aim," said Riggs, looking at the holes in the door frame where his head had just been. "'Nandez, light it up."

Agent Hernandez took a heavy glow stick from her pack, cracked it until it glowed bright green, and slung it down the corridor in the direction of the gunfire. There was a brief burst as a few more shots were fired, then all quieted. A bright green glow now emanated from the corridor.

Two agents moved to the right side of the door frame while Riggs stayed on the left. When he saw that they were ready, he nodded his head, and as one, they swung in just far enough to fire down the corridor.

The shooter was a Healer with a black hood hiding his face, crouched behind the nurses' station in the middle of the room, now well lit by the glow stick. Most of the bullets tore into the paneling in front of him, but one caught him in the shoulder and spun him away. He fell backward, and the gun flew from his hand.

Riggs and the other agents charged into the room, guns forward, prepared to fire again, but there was no retaliation. The shooter was alone. Riggs hurried to the Healer, who lay writhing on the floor, a pool of red collecting on the floor beneath his shoulder.

He was a small Healer, the size of a normal man. Riggs knelt down and pulled back the hood, exposing the man's face.

"You made me drop it," the Healer said weakly. "It was in my hand, and you made me drop it."

Stupefied, Riggs followed the Healer's gaze to a small glass vial that lay shattered on the tile floor beside the Healer's right hand. A clear, viscous liquid, not unlike human saliva, lay spilt from the vial.

Other agents gathered.

"Stop the bleeding," said Riggs.

Two agents immediately began treating the wound.

"I must protect the building," the Healer said to Riggs, his voice urgent. "I must do my duty to the master."

"Is there anyone else in the building?" said Riggs.

"Only one," said the Healer.

"Where?"

"Locked in his room. He can't get out. I see to that. The master asks me to see to that."

Riggs lifted his head. "Peeps? Get that helicopter back here with medics. The rest of you, listen up. I want this building turned inside out. If it's hot, bag it. If it moves, detain it."

Frank lay in the trail, trying to catch his breath. They had been going for two hours now without any sign of Healers or, unfortunately, help. The others were scattered nearby, leaning against a tree or sitting on a rock. Dolores lay spread-eagle on her back, fanning herself. Nick and Hal sat near a freshwater spring that trickled down the center of the granite cliff face.

Hal leaned toward the spring and allowed the water bottle to be filled again.

"Maybe it's time for someone else to have a drink," said Nick, extending a hand.

"Maybe it's time for you to shut your hole and wait your turn," Hal said.

"The rest of us are just as thirsty as you are, you know?" said Dolores.

Hal smirked. "If you know how thirsty I am, then you'll shut up and let me drink."

Dolores pursed her lips but held her tongue.

"Are you always this respectful to women?" said Monica.

Hal shrugged. "I don't see one worth respecting."

Monica looked away and put an arm around Wyatt.

Hal took another long drink, gargled a swig, then spat. "So, Dr. Owens," he said. "What do you specialize in when you're not cutting up innocent people and breaking the law?"

Monica ignored him.

"She's a thoracic surgeon," Wyatt said.

Hal smiled wild. "Thoracic? Well now, that's a big word for a six-year-old. Thoracic."

"What's that mean?" asked Dolores. "Thoracic?"

"A surgeon of the chest," said Monica. "Cardiovascular surgery, mainly."

"You mean the heart?" asked Dolores.

Monica nodded.

Dolores looked at Hal. "She's a heart doctor."

"I heard her, stupid," he said. He looked back at Monica. "So, a heart doctor, huh? Lucky for Frank here, right? New heart. Heart doctor. Nice fit. What about the rest of us? How many kidney transplants have you done?"

"Including yours and Nick's?" she said.

Hal nodded.

"Three."

"Three?" Hal got to his feet. "What kind of experience is that? You cut us up without even knowing how?"

"I did the best I could to keep you alive."

Hal grunted in disgust.

"What about a lung?" said Dolores, sitting up. "How many lungs had you done before mine?"

Monica shook her head. "None."

Dolores clutched at her chest. "None? You sure you did it right? Put all the tubes and wires back where they're supposed to go?"

"You don't have any wires, ignoramus," said Hal, "just veins and stuff."

Dolores grunted. "Listen at you, talking like you know what you're talking about."

"Hey, I know a lot more than you, all right? At least I don't talk in my sleep."

"At least I'm no drunk," Dolores fired back. Hal looked ready to make a move, but Byron interrupted. "What about liver transplants?" he said. "Ever done one of those before?"

"Once," she said, looking at the ground. "In college. On a cadaver."

"A cadaver?" said Hal.

"What's a cadaver?" said Nick.

"Man, but you are ignorant, aren't you?" said Hal.

"A dead body," said Byron, "used for research."

"Well, you're a piece of work, aren't you, Dr. Owens?" said Hal. "A real miracle worker. I guess old George Galen figured that if you could switch out a heart, then you could switch out a kidney. Lucky us, huh?"

"Who was the other kidney?" asked Nick. "You said there were three."

Monica looked at him, hesitated. "Jonathan," she said.

Nick's face reddened, and he looked away, tears welling up.

"He left before the virus had enough time to initiate the healing," said Monica. "I never wanted to hurt him."

"Well, you did, Doctor," said Hal. "And when the day comes, I'm going to watch you burn. Yes, sir. Get me a front-row seat. Maybe even throw the switch myself."

"That's enough," said Frank, standing. "Without Dr. Owens's help, we wouldn't have escaped. She deserves respect for that, at least. You want to hold ill will, fine. But for your own sake, and the sake of Wyatt, save it for another time. Right now our only concern is getting help as quickly as possible. And if we spend all of our energy arguing and bickering, we'll get nowhere. Now come on, break's over."

They all got to their feet.

"Hal, I'd like you to take point now, if you don't mind. Stick to the trail and stay with the group."

Hal looked pleased. "If you all can keep up."

Frank approached Byron. "You ever fired a gun before?" he said, offering Byron the tranquilizer gun.

Byron turned it over in his hands. "I've never shot a tranq before, but it shouldn't be too hard to figure out." In less than three seconds he checked the safety, pulled back on the hammer, stuck the butt of it flat against his shoulder, and looked down the site at some imaginary target in the distance.

"You did that a little too easily," Frank said, impressed.

"I grew up in Montana. My dad took us hunting as soon as we were old enough to tag along legally." He smiled. "And sometimes even before that."

"Let's hope you never have to use it."

Byron checked the cartridge, then snapped it back into place.

Frank said, "I'm curious—you're the only one in this group who isn't homeless, am I right?"

"Not counting yourself, the doc, or the kid."

"And yet Galen thought you were."

"I was looking pretty ragged the night he picked me up. I'd been hiking up in Los Padres National Forest and hadn't bathed or shaved in a few days. I was coming back into LA when my car broke down. Galen saw me with my thumb out and assumed . . ." He shrugged.

"Your family must be worried."

Byron held up his hand to show he wasn't wearing a ring. "Not married. And I live alone. The only people who'd notice me missing are the ones at my office. But I'm out with clients so often, I wonder if anyone there even knows I'm gone. Either way, I'd hate to see what my in-box looks like right now."

"What do you do?"

"Tax attorney. I know, it sounds incredibly boring and mundane, but believe me, you have no idea how boring it really is." He hung the strap of the gun over his shoulder. "Every quarter or so I have to get away for a few days and clear my head. It was just my luck that I chose to be away the night Galen was looking for volunteers."

"I thought we said break was over," Dolores said, her hands on her hips. "Are we moving or are we playing Getting-to-know-you?"

They got moving again, Hal on point and Frank taking up the rear. To Frank's relief, Hal chose a reasonable pace, one that wasn't too slow for their abilities or so fast that it would wear them out quickly. And now that they had rested a moment, Monica was easily keeping up again.

"How you doing?" Frank asked her. "You were struggling a bit earlier."

Monica managed a smile. "Yeah, and Wyatt is doing just fine. I was worried about him, and I'm the one slowing us down."

They walked in silence a moment. "You don't think much of me, do you?" she said finally, keeping her eyes forward. "That whole speech about cutting me some slack back there, I appreciate that, but I know you don't mean it. Not that I blame you. I don't think much of myself anymore." She pulled her coat around herself tightly and bowed her head.

Frank watched her out of the corner of his eye and slowly allowed himself to pity her. He could see that she was worn down, and not solely from the hike. She was fatigued emotionally. And why shouldn't she be? Galen had used her as much as he had used Frank and the others—more so, in fact, because Galen had forced her to *act,* to inflict pain, to threaten innocent lives, whereas Frank had only been the recipient of such actions. And wasn't that worse? Frank had been touched by evil, but Monica, she had been forced to *become* evil, committing acts that neither she nor her profession could likely ever forgive.

All for the kid.

Frank pictured Galen in his mind, dangling Wyatt in front of her, promising to squeeze the life out of him if Monica didn't cooperate. What choice did she have, really? Frank knew without even thinking that he would have done the same for Rachel. He would have killed, maimed, ripped his own heart out if it would have meant keeping her safe.

Monica reached up and wiped the sweat from her brow, or maybe she was wiping tears from her eyes. Frank couldn't tell. "I know it's a cliché," she said, "but I became a doctor because I wanted to help people. I wanted to make a difference. Make things right in people's lives. And yet, had I not been a doctor, none of this would have happened. Galen wouldn't have taken me and Wyatt, and no one would have gotten hurt."

"He would've picked someone else," said Frank, "some other doctor. It wouldn't have made a difference."

She nodded, knowing this but perhaps needing someone else to say it. "I know it will sound incredibly insufficient for me to say so," she said, "and I know it won't change the way any of you feel about me, but for what it's worth, I am sorry for everything that's happened. I wish I could simply make things right again. But I can't."

She was right, it did sound insufficient. *Sorry* is what you said to a stranger you bumped into in the supermarket or to a person you kept waiting at a lunch appointment. It wasn't what you said to someone after having nearly killed him or after taking decades off his life expectancy.

Yet there was no denying her sincerity.

Frank opened his mouth to speak consoling words when frantic shouting in the distance ahead interrupted him.

"Hey! Over here!" someone was yelling. "Help us."

"That sounded like Hal," said Monica, looking down the trail and seeing that it was empty. Their conversation had slowed them and caused them to fall behind. Now the others were calling for help.

"Over here!" Dolores's voice shouted.

Frank and Monica took off at a run down the trail. Turning a bend, they came to a wide freshwater lake. Byron, Hal, Dolores, and Wyatt were all at the bank, jumping and waving at a small fishing boat on the water a hundred yards away. Nick, on the other hand, was sitting on the ground, his head resting on his knees, looking pale and exhausted.

"Help us!" Hal shouted.

Frank squinted across the lake and saw the old man in the boat turn toward them and wave back.

"He sees us," said Hal excitedly. "Look, I think he's coming this way."

Frank watched as the old man fired up his prop engine and turned the boat in their direction. Frank felt a wave of relief, and then the reality of the situation struck him. They were all infected with the virus. Even Monica and Wyatt were likely carrying it on their clothes to some extent. It wasn't an airborne threat; it could only be passed via bodily fluids, but it was still very contagious. If they were going to ask the fisherman for help, they had to go about it carefully, making sure that the old man didn't get infected. But how? How could Frank contain the virus? The elderly were so much more susceptible to contagions than normal people. All it would take would be a single mosquito bite or a cut on the hand or maybe even a drop of sweat for the old man to contract it. No, the only option was to commandeer the boat, to take the boat and not the man, and to make sure the man got nowhere near any of them.

"Quick. Everybody get back into the woods."

They all looked at him, bewildered. "Why?" said Dolores. "The guy's got a boat. He can rescue us."

"There's no time to explain. Get back in the woods."

Nobody moved. "This is a joke, right?" said Dolores.

"Frank," said Hal. "This guy can take us to a dock or wherever it was he came from. This could be our ticket out of here."

Frank looked at the boat. It was only fifty yards away now and picking up speed. The old man made eye contact with him and waved again.

"I'll take care of it," he said, then he pulled out the pistol and held it at his side, away from the fisherman's field of vision.

"What are you going to do?" Dolores asked, fear in her voice.

Frank pointed with his free hand. "Back in the woods. Those trees over there. All of you."

Monica took Wyatt's hand. "Come on, Wyatt." She pulled him quickly over to the tree line and they crouched behind some bushes.

"You heard him," said Byron, pushing the others. "Let's go."

Hal and Dolores went reluctantly, and Byron had to practically carry Nick, who Frank noticed looked more than merely tired now; Nick's jaw was slack and his eyes bloodshot.

Frank stood alone on the shoreline as the fisherman slowed the motor and idled the boat toward him. White puffs of smoke sputtered from the engine block. The old man smiled kindly, the fishing lures pinned to his floppy hat twinkling in the sunlight.

"Heard you yelling for help," the fisherman said. "You folks need anything?"

Frank held the gun behind his back. The boat was probably close enough now.

All right, old man, let's hope you got a better heart than mine.

Hal pushed back the branches of the bush in front of him and tried to get a better look. "What's he doing? What are we hiding for? Somebody want to tell me that?"

"Quiet," said Byron. "I'm trying to listen to what they're saying."

"We're too far to hear," said Hal. "This is stupid. What's he afraid of? That we won't all fit in the boat?"

"Quiet," Byron repeated.

Hal had said it, but he hadn't really meant it. Of course, now that the boat was close enough to get a good look at, it seemed a valid concern. They wouldn't all fit. It was just a little dinghy with an outboard motor. They'd have to take several trips; that much was clear.

Well, I'm going on the first trip. You can be damn sure of that.

What happened next caused Hal to blink, just to make sure he had seen correctly: Frank whipped the gun out from behind his back and pointed it at the old man—just pointed it right at his chest like a cop cornering a crack daddy.

"What does he think he's doing?" said Byron, panicked.

"He's going to shoot him," said Dolores. "Mercy in heaven, he's going to shoot the man."

Monica clung to Wyatt and turned his head away so he wouldn't see.

Frank was saying something to the fisherman, who now had his hands raised and looked scared enough to piss himself into a raisin, but Hal couldn't hear.

"What's he doing?" said Byron again.

I know what he's doing, Hal thought. He's doing what any sensible person who values their own life would do. "He's taking the boat for himself."

The others turned to him. "For himself?" said Dolores.

"As in leaving us behind. It's a tiny boat, and he's taking it for himself. Look, he's making the old man get out now."

The others looked back at the boat, and sure enough, the old man was shuffling to the side of it, preparing to get out.

"That can't be right," said Byron.

"What, are you blind?" said Hal. "He used us to help him escape and now he's ditching us the first chance he gets." He got to his feet. "I don't know about the rest of you, but I'm not about to sit here and let him run off with our only ride out of here."

Byron reached for him. "Wait."

But it was too late. Hal was charging through the trees

toward the boat. The old man had one foot in the water when he saw Hal coming, started, and nearly fell headfirst into the lake.

Frank held up a hand. "Hal, stay back!"

Hal ran and jumped into the water. The boat was only fifteen feet out, so Hal was sure he could reach it without having to swim.

Frank yelled after him. "Hal, no! Stop!"

But Hal wasn't stopping. He charged on, waist-deep in the water, plowing through the mud that pulled and sucked at his shoes, moving toward the boat, hoping and praying Frank wouldn't shoot him in the back.

The old man's eyes widened even further when he saw Hal coming and he toppled backward into the boat.

Dolores came running out of the trees. "Wait. Wait for me." She lumbered toward the bank and tripped at the water's edge, falling face-first into the lake and sending a spray of water into the air.

"Stop!" Frank shouted. "Stay back!"

But neither Hal nor Dolores heeded. Freedom was only a few feet away. Dolores moved quickly, now up to her waist as well.

Hal's fingers were only inches from the hull when the gunshot tore through the air. For a split second Hal thought he'd been hit and instinctively looked down at his chest, expecting a pool of red to pour from it. But no blood came. He looked back toward shore. Frank was at the water's edge, pointing the gun skyward. "Get away from the boat," he said. "Both of you."

Dolores began to back off.

"He wants it for himself," Hal said, hoping she'd stay between him and Frank and take a bullet if one was fired at him. Then, turning back to the boat, Hal reached for the hull. He was touching the fiberglass surface when the engine roared to the life and the boat flew back in reverse.

"No!" Hal said.

"Wait!" Frank yelled.

But it was no use, the fisherman was too spooked. Hal made a last-ditch effort to swim for the boat, but he knew it was fruitless before he even began. He'd never been much of a swimmer. And the fisherman had the throttle wide open.

"Wait!" Frank yelled again.

When the boat was forty feet out, the fisherman jerked on the rudder, spun the boat in the right direction, then hit the gas again. The engine screamed and spat out a cloud of smoke as the boat zipped away.

Hal stood in the water watching his only chance of escape become a bouncing blip in the distance. He still hadn't moved when the wake arrived and wet him up to his neck.

27

FEVER

Riggs watched as the helicopter lifted off outside the Happy Mountain Rest Home. Inside the helicopter, a Healer lay strapped to a gurney, his shoulder wound being attended to by medics of the BHA.

"They did something to that man," said Riggs. "It's like he was in a trance or something."

Peeps stood on the ground beside Riggs, watching the helicopter ascend. "Something like that," he said.

Riggs faced him. "You know something I don't?"

Peeps passed Riggs the contaminant scanner he had been holding. "I did a scan of the liquid in that vial he was holding."

Riggs read the screen. "Human saliva?"

"Most of it. It also contained unknown substances the scanner couldn't recognize. My guess is proteins."

"Proteins?"

"Yet-undiscovered human proteins."

Riggs raised an eyebrow. "Should I get something here? I don't follow you."

"Galen's got a history of altering DNA, right? He knows how to manipulate genes in such a way that either inhibits or invigorates the production of proteins. Now, if he manipulated their production enough, if he tinkered and experimented long enough, maybe he figured out how to initiate certain biochemical reactions."

"English, Peeps."

"Drugs, man. Mind control. Maybe Galen learned how to turn saliva into a drug."

"You can't be serious."

"You got a better explanation?"

Agent Hernandez's voice crackled in their comlink speakers. "Sir! We found Agent Carter."

Riggs answered. "Where? Is he alive?"

"Alive and well. I'm sending you the location now."

The schematic of the building reappeared on Riggs's visor, and a small room toward the center of the building illuminated.

"I see it," said Riggs.

"I'm initiating the best route here," said Hernandez.

The straightest path to the destination lit up on the schematic.

"So far, the building is clean," Hernandez added. "There's plenty of equipment in here to suggest that the Healers have been a lot busier than we thought, but no Healers. It looks like the one we encountered toward the entrance was a lone leave-behind, guarding the building and Carter."

Riggs and Peeps were already running back through the rest home, following the directions to Hernandez's location. "Did you say *guarding* Carter? Was he a prisoner?"

When they reached the cell where Carter had been held, they saw the answer for themselves. The room was solid concrete, no windows, probably a janitor's closet by design. The door, which now stood open, had been reinforced recently with several deadbolts, all from the outside. A single cot sat in the room by a soiled bucket and an empty plate of food. Carter sat against the wall in the hallway, his biosuit badly torn and damaged, drinking from a water bottle one of the agents had given him.

"You look a sight for sore eyes," said Riggs.

"I was beginning to think you weren't coming," said Carter.

"Are you hurt?"

Carter shook his head and downed some more water. "I wouldn't go in my cell there, though, if I were you. Not the most pleasant of aromas."

Riggs squatted down to his level. "Where's Frank?"

Carter shook his head again. "Don't know. We found this facility. We were going to call for backup, but I thought we should get some evidence first before bringing you in. So we scoped it out. Next thing I know, someone's ripping my helmet off and knocking me on the head. A few hours later I wake up in here. They've broken my comlink, so I can't hail Frank. Then a Healer brings me food, and I know I'm in trouble. I try to fight my way out, and they teach me different. Then two days ago, I hear all the movement and commotion in the hall. From the bits and pieces I pick up, it sounds like everyone's getting out of Dodge. Next thing I know, everyone but one Healer leaves."

"We found him," said Riggs.

"So I'm told. Crazy as a squirrel, like he's under a spell or something."

"Any idea where the Healers were headed?"

"Uh-uh. I listened for a location but heard nothing. It sounded like something they had been planning for a while. It wasn't a mad rush to get out. It was a systematic packing up and leaving."

"And in all that time, you heard nothing from Frank?"

"We weren't cell mates, if that's what you're asking. I figured he must have been grabbed as well. And I thought for sure you'd come sooner than this. We left a sheriff's deputy back at the highway with the van. I thought he'd call in some backup when we didn't return."

"Deputy Dixon?" asked Riggs.

"Yeah."

"So much for a death in a family."

"What do you mean?" said Carter.

"Forget it. Deputy Dixon is apparently missing as well," said Riggs. "And if you left the BHA van by the highway, someone must have moved it, because it isn't there now."

"No wonder."

"Why did you and Frank take off without clearing it with me first?" said Riggs.

"This whole trip was Frank's thing. He said he had to check out the crash site as soon as possible and asked if I'd accompany him. I assumed he *had* cleared it with you."

"Hardly," said Riggs. He stood. "All right, everybody. Let's move. We still got two men unaccounted for.

Frank was fuming. Hal and Dolores stood dripping wet on the bank, their heads hung low. Monica, Wyatt, Byron, and Nick stood nearby, not daring to speak.

"I pulled the gun," Frank said, "because he refused to get out of the boat and loan it to us. I tried asking nicely and assuring him we'd return it, but he wouldn't go for it. I didn't want to scare him, but I had no other choice. He couldn't have come with us. We might have infected him. Our only option was to get him out of the boat completely. Then we could have taken it. All of us."

"Well, why didn't you say so?" said Dolores. "We thought you were trying to take the boat for yourself."

Frank glanced at Hal, who stood apart from the group, hands on his hips, a puddle of water forming at his feet. "I'm sorry I gave you that impression," said Frank. "I thought I made it clear before we left that this would be a group effort."

"You made it plenty clear," said Byron, scowling at Hal.

"And I believed you, too, Frank," said Dolores. "It's just that Hal here kept saying you were trying to ditch us."

Hal narrowed his eyes at her. "Why don't you stuff a wet sock in that mouth of yours? Maybe that'd shut you up for a while."

"You're the one needs shutting up," she said. "If you'd

have done what Frank told us to, we'd be halfway to the police by now."

"We can't go to the police," said Byron. "You heard what he said. We go to the BHA first."

"Whatever," said Dolores. "All I know is that we'd be in a much better place if it wasn't for hothead here."

"Hey, you were just as eager to get on that boat as I was," said Hal. "Don't try blaming this on me. If you hadn't scared the man with your splash, he might not have run off."

"My splash? Who was the one charging out of the trees?"

Hal pointed a dripping finger at Frank. "He was aiming a gun at the man. Not me."

"Yeah, but he was trying to help us. *You* were setting on taking the boat for yourself."

Frank sighed. This was useless. "Forget it," he said. "We're better off without the boat. Getting across the lake wouldn't have improved our situation much. Plus, we would have had to leave the boat somewhere, contaminated. And if someone had found it . . . trust me, we're better off not using it."

"We're better off getting rid of him," Dolores said quietly, gesturing a thumb to Hal.

Hal's face tightened and he made a move for her, but a look from Frank stopped him.

"Drop it," said Frank. "If you want to blame someone, blame me. I should have explained the virus more thoroughly."

"You should have done a lot of things more thoroughly," said Hal. "Like telling us why we had to hide in the woods." He looked Frank up and down with disgust. "You big-shot doctors are all the same, you know that? Think you can order people around like cattle, treat everybody like a bunch of schoolkids because you got a college degree and we don't. We're all just a bunch of knuckle-dragging Neanderthals, is that it? Just a bunch of stupid apes. Can't stop and explain things to us because we're too ignorant to understand."

"There wasn't time," said Frank.

Hal brushed the words aside with a wave of his hand and got right up to Frank's face. "I'm not taking a lead from you anymore. You got that? You want to go back to the BH-whatever, you go right ahead. I don't give a bunny turd where you go. As for me, I go where I choose. *When* I choose."

Frank didn't blink. "You'll stick with the rest of us. That's your only choice."

Hal sagged his shoulders as if relenting, then gut-punched Frank with a hard clenched fist. The blow caught Frank right where the bottom staples were positioned on his scar, and he felt the metal pierce deeper into his abdomen. The pain was overwhelming and he buckled, dropping the gun.

Hal was on him instantly, pinning him to the ground and throwing more punches, all aimed at Frank's chest, where his wound lay.

"Stop!" said Monica.

Byron moved closer to intervene, but Hal scooped up the gun and aimed it at him, stopping Byron cold.

Frank took advantage of the momentary distraction. He reached with one hand, found a pressure point in Hal's arm, and chopped with the other hand. The gun flew ten feet away. Hal howled, and Frank shifted his weight, rolled, and knocked Hal off of him. Hal might be strong—and likely able to hold his own in a street fight—but he wasn't a soldier. He wasn't trained in hand-to-hand combat.

Rather than make for the gun, Frank twisted Hal into a wrestler's grip and rolled with him farther away from the gun. Better to incapacitate Hal with tactical maneuvering than to risk Hal's getting the gun again and using it.

Hal kicked and twisted as Frank rolled him. But then Frank pinned him, and Hal couldn't move.

It would have been the end of the confrontation had the gun not gone off.

Frank and Hal stopped struggling and looked behind them. A bleary-eyed Nick was holding it heavenward, the faintest hint of smoke escaping from the barrel. He lowered the gun and pointed it at both of them. "Stop. Stop fighting."

Frank released Hal and slowly got to his feet. Something was wrong with Nick. He looked confused, flustered, as if he had just woken from a deep sleep. "Give me the gun, Nick," he said calmly.

"Don't give it to him," said Hal. "He's doing us wrong, don't you see? He's not letting us go to the police. He's not letting us get help."

"Shut up!" Nick screamed, his voice shrill and harsh.

The kid's about to snap, Frank thought, if he hasn't already.

"Put the gun down, Nick," Byron said, gesturing slowly with his hands.

Nick whirled around, the gun moving with him wildly, as if he hadn't known that Byron was there. Byron immediately put his hands up and backed off.

"Stay back," Nick said. "Everybody stay back." He was frantic now, confused.

Monica had Wyatt behind her, slinking slowly toward the trees over her shoulder. Dolores was less subtle. She dropped the suit coat she had been wringing out and bolted for the bushes. Nick's eyes and aim followed her, but to Frank's relief, he didn't fire.

"Give me the gun, Nick," Frank said.

Nick whirled back, his eyes wild, breathing heavily. "I'm sick."

Frank took a step closer. "I know, Nick. I can see that you're sick. I want to help."

Nick blinked, looked away, and seemed lost in thought a moment, his aim slowly sagging. Frank considered making a break for the gun but Nick snapped back and pointed his arms straight again, holding a steadier bead on Frank. "Jonathan's dead. Okay? They killed him." Tears were coming out of his eyes.

Frank took another step toward him. "If you give me the gun, Nick—"

"Shoot him!" Hal said suddenly.

Both Frank and Nick were startled, and Nick jerked the gun momentarily to Hal. "Not me," said Hal. "Him. He tried to kill me. Shoot him."

Hal pointed it back at Frank again, frantic.

"Don't!" said Byron. "Nick, listen to me."

Frank held up a hand to Byron. "Don't all talk to him at once." He lowered his voice. "Nick, you have to believe me. I want to help you."

"Don't listen to him," said Hal. "He only cares about himself. You saw him try to take the boat. He was getting it for himself."

"I want help," Nick said.

"And I want to help you, Nick," said Frank. "Just give me the gun in your hand."

Nick looked at his hands and saw the gun. He turned it sideways in his palm, lowering his aim. "It's so heavy," he said absently.

Hal and Frank both had the same idea, but Frank was closer. He charged, grabbed the gun from Nick, and turned it on Hal. Hal came to a stop, the gun inches from his nose.

"Back off," said Frank.

Hal paled and slowly shuffled backward.

Nick's knees wobbled and Frank put an arm under him to keep him upright. Monica was at his side in an instant. She put a hand to Nick's forehead. "He's burning up. He needs medication. All of you do."

"We can't stay here," said Frank. "Wherever that fisherman was headed, he may alert the police. They might come looking for us."

"He has a high fever," said Monica. "He's in no condition to move. Look at him. He can hardly stand."

It was true. Nick was leaning on Monica now. His eyes were open, but he was only partially coherent.

"I can carry him," said Byron.

Frank looked at him. "You sure?"

"You got a better idea?"

Frank didn't. Byron gently lifted Nick in the cradle position. "He's actually not that heavy. I can do this."

"Hold him still," said Monica. She removed a syringe and a bottle of medication from her pack. "Roll his sleeve back." Frank did, and Monica administered the shot. "He needs to rest," she said.

Frank nodded, then turned to Dolores, who stood nearby, shivering. "You can't stay in those wet clothes." He looked at Hal. "Neither of you can. Not in this cold. We'll have to find someplace warm where you can dry out.

"I better carry that," said Frank, motioning to the dart gun hanging over Byron's shoulder.

Byron didn't object. He glanced at Hal, and Frank knew he understood implicitly. If Frank was holding all the weapons, the chances of Hal getting hold of any were less.

Frank draped the strap over his shoulder and gripped the pistol in his hand. "All right, Hal. You lead. Straight down the trail until I tell you to stop."

Lichen made no effort to avoid the low-hanging branches on the trail. They whipped at his face and neck as he ran by them, tearing at his cheeks and sometimes cutting him deeply. Blood seeped from the cuts and dripped back toward his ears until the cuts sealed themselves and became smooth flesh again.

It pleased Lichen to know that the prophet's gift of healing was inside him. He wished he had a mirror so he could see the healings as they took place. They were testimonies, after all, visible evidence that the prophet was indeed the harbinger of a higher species, the Great Key, the way of becoming.

Lichen had not been blessed with the same gifts Stone possessed. The prophet had not given Lichen the inability to feel pain. Pain was still a part of Lichen's being. And yet, despite the pain, Lichen didn't flinch at the branches and the cuts they gave him. The sweet sting was a welcome blessing. Pain reminded Lichen that the prophet had made him unique.

"Instead of no pain, I give you speed, Lichen," the prophet had said. "Let your feet be a weapon of wonder in quickening that work which will cure a troubled world."

It had sounded like poetry to Lichen at the time, and he had accepted graciously. Combined with healing and strength, speed would make him a worthy servant. He knew his legs would not *move* faster, of course. This was impossible. But the prophet had strengthened his legs so that they would never tire. While other Healers' legs gave out from overexertion, Lichen's legs would continue to keep a quick and steady pace.

There had been times, of course, when Lichen wished he *did* have no pain.

Jonathan's death was one such instance. It had been pain that had caused Lichen to release his grip on the boy and allowed Jonathan to reach the road. Without pain, the sharp rock that Jonathan swung would have smashed the cartilage of Lichen's ear without Lichen's feeling it or caring.

And Jonathan would still be alive.

Lichen looked over his shoulder as he ran down the trail now. The other Healers were still nowhere in sight, although he was certain they couldn't be too far behind. They had had time to mobilize now, and his speed would have encouraged them to push the level of their own endurance and stay at their maximum pace.

A distant gunshot rang through the air, and Lichen stopped in his tracks to listen. It was the second shot he had heard, and this one was much closer. He scrambled up a tall sturdy tree and looked down over the treetops to the lake below.

There on the bank of the lake below him were the prophet's vessels. He could only barely make out their figures at this distance, but he was certain it was them. They seemed to be arguing.

Lichen remained in the tree and watched them until they left the lake and continued down the trail. He wanted to be certain he knew which direction they were headed.

By the time he descended the tree, the other Healers had caught up with him.

"They're down by the lake, heading east," he said.

Pine sniffed the air. "How far?"

"Close enough to catch," Lichen said, and turned on his heels and led them down the hillside, his cape billowing once again behind him.

28

PROPHET

The barn door opened with a rusty squeak, and Frank stepped inside. Cobwebs and rotted timbers hung from the rafters, and the air was thick with dust. A few rusty farming tools hung on nails in the corner, and a beam of sunlight shined through a wide hole in the roof. Frank guessed it had been deserted years ago, maybe decades.

"It's not much, but it'll get us out of the wind for a while."

The others came in behind him. Dolores waved her hand in front of her face. "Smells awful."

"Animals used to crap in here," said Hal. "What do you expect?"

Nick was asleep in Byron's arms, and Monica led them to a soft spot of ground in one of the stalls. Byron set Nick down without waking him, and Monica made sure Nick was comfortable.

"I'm starving," said Dolores.

Byron dug into his pack and found a few granola bars they had taken from the storage closet. He passed them out and Dolores devoured hers. Wyatt graciously took one and lay down to eat it but fell asleep before taking a bite. Everyone else looked just as exhausted.

Byron then passed around the water bottle, and it was quickly emptied.

Minutes later, Monica came out of the stall with her medical bag.

"How is he?" asked Frank.

"Stable. He needs to rest. I'd like his fever to go down before we move again."

"In case anyone's forgotten," said Hal, "it's very possible that these Healers are out looking for us. I suggest we don't wait around."

"We're off the trail," said Frank. "And we were careful to hide our tracks when we left it. I think we can safely rest for a few minutes."

"All we do is rest," said Hal.

"You're just as tired as the rest of us," said Dolores. "Don't be pretending you ain't."

"What I *ain't* is talking to you, so keep your comments to yourself."

Monica began preparing more syringes.

"No way," said Hal. "I don't care what it is. I'm not getting another shot from her. Period."

"They're antirejection drugs," said Monica. "I told you. Your body needs them. I should have given them to you hours ago."

"And if I was a sucker," said Hal, "I'd believe you. How do I know that's not some sleeping medicine you're trying to slip us? You all saw her. She gave the same stuff to Nick. Now look at him. He's out like a light. How do we know she isn't trying to knock us all out?" He looked at Monica. "You'd like that, wouldn't you? Get us all drugged up and sleepy. Then you and the kid could slip away without anybody being the wiser."

"You have got to be the most paranoid person I've ever met," said Byron.

"She's not one of them," said Dolores. "She's proven that. The only person nobody trusts around here is you."

Hal smiled. "All right, then. If you're so trusting, you go

first. Let her stick that arm of yours. We'll all sit here and watch. And if you don't pass out or keel over, we'll know it's legit."

Dolores looked hesitant. "Why do I have to go first?"

Hal buckled over laughing. "Stupid *and* a hypocrite. I love it."

"I'll do it," said Frank, rolling up his sleeve. "I'll go first."

Hal stopped laughing.

"And if I keel over, you can go on without me and do with the doctor as you please."

"And if you don't?" asked Dolores.

"Wait a minute," said Hal, "I like this option."

"If I don't, then you all take the shot." Frank waited for objections, but none came. He held his arm out, and Monica swabbed the area gently, then administered the shot. Dolores winced when the needle broke the skin.

When Monica pulled the needle out, Frank watched as the tiny wound sealed and became flawless skin again.

Dolores motioned for an explanation. "Well? How do you feel?"

Frank shrugged. "Fine." Then he blinked. "No, wait. I have a strange sensation." He put his hand to head, closed his eyes, and began teetering from side to side, moaning softly.

Dolores was too spooked to scream but not enough to keep still. Frantic, she scrambled back toward the barn door and only stopped because Frank became still and smiled. It wasn't until Byron started laughing that it dawned on her. "You're joking?" she said angrily.

Hal laughed, too. "Good one."

Dolores put her hands on her hips. "You think this is the time to be playing around? Woman has a new lung inside her and you want to scare her silly."

Frank's smile remained. "You're right. Sorry. The medication is fine, Dolores. You should take it. I feel better already."

It was true. Frank could feel his energy returning and the aching in his muscles subsiding.

The others took the shot without further objection.

"Now get some sleep," said Frank. "We'll stay here for an hour or so, and move again when Nick is better."

They each took a spot on the ground and lay down to rest. Frank went to Monica and asked her to speak with him outside. They moved out into the sunlight. Frank kept the barn door open and one eye on Hal.

"How is Nick, really?" said Frank.

Monica sighed. "I'm not sure. His fever is pushing a hundred and four. That's dangerously high. He wasn't very coherent even before he fell asleep."

"Heat stroke?"

She shrugged. "It's possible, but I don't think so. He's not showing the right symptoms for it."

"Will he be able to walk? We can't continue to carry him."

She looked doubtful. "You saw him. He could barely stand earlier."

"It came upon him so suddenly. He seemed to be moving just as well as the rest of us."

"He's had a transplant in the past forty-eight hours. Let's not forget that. He shouldn't have been able to run at all."

They stood there in silence. Then Monica said, "There's something else you should know. I didn't want to tell the others and frighten them, but you should know, at least. About the chip."

Frank faced her, waiting.

"I've told you what the chip contains. Galen's files, video, journals; and I've told you about the software Yoshida developed to anticipate Galen's decisions and thoughts. But what I haven't told you is how it's triggered and supposedly works together."

"Go on."

"A few years ago this Dr. Kouichi Yoshida made some

fairly significant advances in memory replication, trying to help amnesia patients regain their lost long-term memories. I assume you're familiar with genetic memory, Doctor."

"Enlighten me."

"Memories form when neurons in a circuit increase the strength of their connections. For long-term memories to develop, for example, the connection must be permanently strengthened. This is all instigated by genes inside the neuron's nucleus, which produce synapse-strengthening proteins."

"You're losing me."

"Basically, Yoshida's theory was that by manipulating neural genes, one could control the output of proteins and in turn control how they were diffused through the cell and which of the cell's thousands of synapses were strengthened. In other words, one could control which memories were formed and which were discarded, which circuits remained and which would suddenly become inactive."

"Hardwiring the brain."

"On a small scale, yes. What Galen hoped to accomplish, however, was much bigger, a universal alteration in the entire circuitry, turning billions of inactive neurons *on* and turning all currently active neurons off. In other words, if we only use ten percent of our brains, Galen wanted to switch off that ten percent and use another ten percent instead, a ten percent that he could define."

"With his own memories."

"Yes. Turn off your memories and turn on his. Don't think of it as a hard drive with all the memory stored in it, think of it as a chemical program that would generate these memories all at once, making you believe that you experienced them."

"So Galen supplied all his files and journals and data in the hope that he could convince our minds that we had experienced them, that they were our actual memories?"

"Essentially, yes. It's not a matter of uploading a few of his opinions and meshing them with your own. Like what he's doing with your DNA, Galen is switching out the old and bringing in the new."

"It's impossible," said Frank. "It could never happen."

"Whether it can or can't isn't the point," said Monica. "The point is how Galen believed it could be done."

Frank remained quiet, waiting for her to continue.

"Altering the entire active circuitry at once requires a near-lethal level of electrical shock," said Monica. "Think of it as jump-starting a car. To fire off all those synapses at once in a pattern that strengthens certain connections along a wide neural network necessitates a massive jolt of programmed energy." Her voice caught, and she stopped speaking.

Frank waited. And while he did, he felt another surge of sympathy. None of this had been her doing. And yet, because of her circumstances, she was an integral part of it.

He wanted to reach out and take her in his arms, as a friend, as a man expressing comfort to a woman, maybe rub her back gently they way he used to do with Rachel whenever she awoke in the night, frightened by a dream.

Monica composed herself. "Once the chip is triggered, its first operation is to send a massive jolt of electricity through you, a jolt that I fear might kill you should it happen."

Frank took a long moment to consider. "Then you're going to have to remove the chips."

"I'm a cardiologist, Dr. Hartman, not a neurosurgeon. I wouldn't know how."

Byron stumbled out of the barn, a bloody hand covering his forehead. "Where'd he go?" he said.

Frank looked past him. Hal was gone. Frank had taken his eyes off of him for only a moment, but Hal apparently had been waiting for it. Frank rushed inside.

"What happened?" he heard Monica ask.

"He hit me with a rock. Took the meds. He didn't come out this way?"

Frank ran to the back. A section of wall had rotted and

fallen away, leaving a wide gap in the side of the barn. He jumped through it and saw Hal, now a distance away, running back toward the trail with Monica's medical bag.

Frank looked back, drawing the gun. "Wait here." Turning, he sprinted down the hillside after Hal.

Hal looked over his shoulder, saw Frank coming, and put on a burst of speed. Frank maneuvered through the brush as quickly as possible, following Hal down and then back onto the trail. Hal stuck to the trail after that, never slowing, running in a mad sprint to get free.

Several times the trail bent sharply, and each time Hal disappeared from view as he reached the bend before Frank. Frank approached these bends cautiously, gun raised, ready for the kind of ambush a person like Hal would devise. But there never was an ambush. Hal never slowed once.

For the better part of an hour they ran, bending and twisting down the mountain, running through shallow creek beds, jumping fallen logs, dodging low-hanging branches. Slowly Frank gained, but the men were nearly equal in speed and stamina.

Finally Hal came to a skidding halt, and Frank ran up behind him and saw why. Hal was standing at the precipice of a cliff. The river raged forty feet below. Hal turned to face Frank and held the bag over the ledge.

"Stay back or I'll drop it."

Frank froze. "You need that as much as anyone, Hal."

"I'll do it. I swear to you, I'll do it."

Frank took a step closer. "Give me the bag, Hal, and we'll go back together."

Hal snorted. "Back? I'm not going back. And if you know what's good for you, neither will you. You saw Nick. He's half dead already. He'll only slow us down."

"We're not leaving Nick behind."

"So you're going to die trying to drag his corpse down the mountain? Oh, that's noble. When are you going to realize that nobody else in this world gives a damn about you and you shouldn't give a damn about them? I learned that fact a long time ago, Frank, and I'm alive today because of it. I'm a survivor. And if you want to be alive come morning, you need to start acting like a survivor, too. I'm giving you a choice. Come with me now or stay here and rot in the woods. Live or die. It's that simple."

Frank stepped closer. "I only want what's best for all of us, Hal. You know that."

Hal's arm stiffened, holding the bag farther over the side. "Stay back."

Frank aimed the pistol. "Don't."

"You and I are on the same side, Frank. You know that. The Healers, those are the bad guys. You want to point your gun at somebody, point it at them."

Frank hesitated.

Hal reached inside, grabbed several vials and syringes, and held them over the ledge. "You think I'm bluffing?"

"I think you're a smart person. You're not going to do something that will hurt yourself."

"You're wrong." Hal threw what was in his hand over the side.

"No!"

"I said, stay back."

Frank looked over the ledge and saw the vials and syringes fall into the river below and get swept away with the current.

"I'll dump the rest, Frank. Don't push me. I'll do it."

"All right. Calm down."

"Put the gun down."

"All right." Frank set the gun on the ground.

"Now kick it to me."

"So you can shoot me? I don't think so."

"Kick it over the side."

"Think what you're asking me to do, Hal. Right now there is a group of people up that road behind us, and our only defense against them is this gun, and that isn't much. If I kick it over—"

"Shut up. Just shut up, all right? You always got to play the smart guy, don't you? Always got to be the one with all the answers. Got to get the last word in? How anyone can stand you is beyond me. Here, you want the bag? Take it." He threw the bag high in the air toward Frank.

Frank's eyes followed it, and he reached out to catch it just as Hal rammed into him and tackled him to the ground. The bag fell away and rolled toward the edge as Frank struggled to get Hal off of him. The gun was still on the ground, several feet away.

Hal's face was red and furious. He grabbed Frank by the throat and squeezed. Frank pulled at Hal's hands, but they held him tight. Hal squeezed even harder, his teeth clenched.

And then Hal went rigid, put his hands to the side of his head, and screamed, as if suddenly blasted by a thousand deafening decibels. Frank scrambled out from under him as Hal fell to the ground and writhed in apparent agony. His scream continued, a deep, throat-cutting cry that echoed over the cliff face and down into the canyon.

Frank backed away in horror as Hal flopped around in the dirt, convulsing.

And then it stopped. All at once. The scream died away and Hal lay still on his back, eyes closed.

Frank waited a moment for Hal to move, and when he didn't, looked for the gun. He saw where it lay and got up to retrieve it just as Hal started laughing. Frank stopped and turned to him. Hal's laughing grew louder, a deep raucous laugh that shook his chest. He looked down at his hands and laughed, felt his face and laughed, stood up and jumped up and down and laughed.

And then he saw Frank, and a look of surprise came over him. "Frank. Look at you. You're a mess. You've got dirt all over you."

Frank didn't blink.

"You are still Frank, aren't you? You didn't beat me to it, did you?" He winked.

Frank stared at him. "Galen?"

Hal threw his arms wide. "Tada! New and improved, version two-point-oh. Goodness, I had forgotten what it felt like to be this young. Did you see how quickly I can move?" He jumped from side to side like a schoolkid trying out a new trampoline. Then he stopped. "What are we doing out here, anyway?" He looked around him, and then over the ledge. "Where's Lichen?"

"Here," a voice said. And then Lichen and three other Healers emerged from the trees at a run. Frank reached for the gun and grabbed it, but Lichen was on him in an instant and easily took it from him. The Healers pointed their tranq guns, and Frank held still.

Hal smiled. "Lichen, my boy, your sense of timing never ceases to amaze me." He looked them over. "Goodness. You're a mess, all of you. Lichen, you're worse than Frank here. Of course, I suppose I'm no better." He brushed the dirt off his jacket. "Kill him and let's get a move on."

Lichen look confused. "Sir?"

Hal became agitated. "I am your prophet, Lichen. I have given you an order. You will obey."

Lichen motioned to one of the Healers. "Check him."

Hal held out his arm and waited while the Healer produced a small scanner and placed it on Hal's arm. There was a popping noise. Hal winced as a needle pricked him, and then the scanner beeped. The Healer read the display.

"Genetic match," he said.

"Of course it's a match. Do you think I allowed myself to die only to stay that way?"

The Healer pocketed the scanner and wiped the drop of blood that remained on Hal's arm.

"You will excuse us for making certain, sir," said Lichen, bowing his head.

"You were following procedure. You need not apologize for doing precisely what I asked. Now, get rid of this one." He waved absently to Frank.

Lichen looked to Frank and then back to Galen. "I

don't understand. Our orders have never been to kill the vessels, sir."

"That's because I have never given the order. Now you will do as I direct."

Lichen still hesitated. "But, sir, the Council."

"Ah, yes, the Council," said Hal. "I had forgotten. My memories are coming back sporadically. You will be patient, gentlemen, as I organize them. Where are the others?"

"In a barn," Lichen said, "a few miles back."

Frank's heart sank. They had found Monica and the others.

Hal made a face. "A barn?"

"We tracked them there," said Lichen. "Stone is with them now, awaiting our return. I would have stayed with them also, but you and Frank, or rather Hal and Frank, ran ahead. I had to leave to catch you."

"Then we will go to this barn," said Hal. "Wait, I remember it now. A dreadful place. I sneaked out of it, didn't I? And you were trying to stop me, Frank. It's coming back to me. You wanted this." He went to Monica's medical bag and picked it up. "All that trouble for a silly little bag." He tossed it over the side.

Frank watched it fall and then disappear into the water below.

Hal took Frank's gun away from Lichen. "This one is not worthy of any council, gentlemen. He has done nothing but disrupt our work and mission. We can no longer allow ourselves to be influenced by his blatant disregard for the betterment of our species." He pointed the gun at Frank. "Not very pleasant, is it Frank? To have a gun pointed at you? A taste of your own medicine, as the saying goes." He stepped toward him. "I read your military records, you know? Incredibly boring, but if my memory serves me right, you have a nasty case of acrophobia." He stuck the gun to Frank's chest. "Amazing how thorough those records are, don't you think?"

Frank stood still and said nothing.

"It's a long way to the bottom, Frank. I imagine that makes you very nervous." He pushed Frank backward toward the edge with the gun.

"It's funny," said Hal. "I was certain that I wouldn't have any of the host's memories. But lo and behold, Hal has left me with some. A few of them not so pleasant, I'm afraid. Hal wasn't the holiest of angels, if you get my meaning. These hands have killed before, sadly."

Out of the corner of his eye, Frank could see the ledge behind him, only inches away.

"But one of the most distinct memories I have is how you treated Hal, Frank. How you treated me. Always like an imbecile."

Frank stopped. His heels were at the precipice. The churning water roared below him.

"You're sweating, Frank. I can actually see tiny beads of sweat. You're afraid, aren't you? Well, let me make it easy for you. If you're already dead, there's nothing to fear."

Frank twisted and dove backward just as Hal pulled the trigger.

The force of the bullet spun Frank around and threw him farther from the cliff face. He felt his body spinning, falling, tumbling through the air. Another shot rang out, and then he sank deep into the frigid rushing water, consciousness slipping, the world turning black.

29
FIRE

Director Irving welcomed Agent Carter into his office with a hearty pat on the back.

"Good to see you alive, Carter. You gave us all a scare. Come in, have a seat."

"Thank you, sir." He took a chair opposite Irving's desk. He was showered and changed and looked rested.

Irving went to the window, looked up and down the hallway, then closed the blinds. "Got something to eat, did you? Filled that empty stomach of yours?"

"Yes, sir. Thank you, sir."

Irving rammed his hands in pockets and shook his head sadly. "Terrible thing that happened to you. Just terrible. I'm glad you're okay. I didn't know you were in there."

Carter cocked his head. "Of course you didn't, sir."

"Hm?"

"You said, you didn't know I was in there. I assume you mean you didn't know I was in the rest home, the Healer compound?"

Irving looked momentarily shaken, then smiled again. "Did I say that?" He took quick steps to the watercooler and poured himself a drink. "What I meant was, I didn't know you were in—" He looked for the right word. "Trouble. I didn't know you were in trouble." He downed the water in a single gulp.

"Of course I was in trouble, sir," said Carter evenly. "I was missing."

Irving licked his top teeth, produced another smile, and poured himself another cup. "Of course. Of course. That's what I meant." He downed the second cup, coughing on this one. He crumpled the cup and threw it away before the coughing stopped.

"Are you all right, sir?"

"Me? I'm fine. I'm fine. Just went down the wrong pipe, is all." He pulled up a chair beside Carter and sat, looking as relaxed as possible and rubbing his hands together.

"You called me to your office, sir," said Carter expectantly.

Irving clapped his hands. "Yes, yes. I wanted to welcome you back in person and tell you myself how pleased we are to have you back."

"Thank you again, sir. . . . And is that all?"

Irving's left eye began to twitch, and he rubbed it with a finger until it stopped. Once composed again, he grinned as if nothing had happened. "No, I also called you in here for another reason." He leaned forward in his chair, looking concerned. "I wanted to assure you that I didn't know Frank would find this building when I sent him out there."

"When *you* sent him out there?"

"It seemed a good course of action to examine the scene thoroughly. But I didn't want to flood the place, you know. Two men would be enough, I said. Carter and that new one, Dr. Hartman. They'll do, I said. So that's why I sent just the two of you out there. I'm sure Frank told you it was an assignment I had given him, and I simply wanted to clarify the matter. I didn't want you thinking I had sent you there . . ." he laughed, "intentionally. I can assure you I had no idea of the danger that was waiting for you."

Carter shifted in his seat. "Actually, Director Irving, Dr.

Hartman never explained to me that the assignment had come from you. This is the first I'm hearing of it."

The grin on Irving's face waned. "I see. Well, all the same, I didn't want there to be any confusion. You understand."

"Oh, I understand, sir. I understand perfectly. You're getting sloppy."

Irving was sure he misheard. Smiling good-naturedly, he said, "Come again."

"I said you're getting sloppy, sir. Look at your hands. They're trembling. You've waited too long between treatments."

Irving paled. "What are you talking about? I don't know what you're talking about."

Carter reached into his own pocket and produced a small vial of clear, thick liquid. "Treatment, sir."

Irving suddenly stood, the back of his hand covering his mouth. "Where did you get that? I mean, what is that?"

"Look at you," said Carter, a look of disgust on his face. "You're a mess. You can't even keep your thoughts straight." He stood and went behind Irving's desk, pulling out drawers.

"What are you doing there?" said Irving. "Get away from that. Those are my things."

"Please," said Carter. "Stop whining like a baby fighting for his rattle." He opened the top drawer and found what he was looking for: a vial of liquid identical to his own. Except Irving's was nearly empty.

"You're almost empty," said Carter, holding it up. "You're using too much of it, too quickly. You have to ration it."

Irving stood like a statue, mouth agape.

"The treatment affects us all in different ways, Eugene. The weak-minded become drooling idiots while the strong ones, the ones like you and me, of course, stay cool as popsicles. Only you're not so cool anymore, Eugene, are you?"

He tossed Irving his vial, and Irving caught it. "You're melting away, Eugene. Losing it. Coming apart at the seams. And unless you wise up, you will disappoint the master. And you don't want that, Eugene. You don't want to disappoint the master."

Irving closed his eyes and cried quiet little sobs. He shook his head. He didn't want to disappoint the master.

"And that's why I'm here," said Carter. "That's why the master chose me." He sat in Director Irving's desk and put his feet up. "He's been a little displeased with your performance so far. First you fail to inform him that agents were watching the home of one of his potential clients. And Stone nearly gets shot to pieces. Then he asks you to send Dr. Hartman to the compound, and for some reason you ask me to tag along. The prophet was surprised by that and was forced to improvise. So he took me under his wing as well. And my assignment, Eugene, is to make sure you don't screw it up. Call me the prophet's insurance plan. That's like the master, isn't it? Always thinking ahead."

Irving nodded. It *was* like the master. Irving wasn't sure why he felt so certain of this—he had no evidence to support the claim—but the master was good at things, after all, so it must be true.

"I'm glad we see eye to eye, Director Irving. Because it isn't over yet." He put his feet down and picked up a pen off Irving's desk, spinning it in his fingers. "Now, about this Healer your boys shot and apprehended. Pray tell, what *are* we going to do about him?"

Frank opened his eyes and immediately vomited up water. He was still in the river, pressed against a felled tree positioned between the rocks. The current churned around him, pulling at his feet and nearly sucking him under again. But his arms were draped over the tree, and his head was up. He reached out with the one arm that didn't pain him, grabbed a tree branch, and pulled himself out of the water.

The tree surface was slick, but he steadied himself well enough to examine his shoulder. The bullet had entered just below the collarbone. An ugly circular scar was evidence of that. But the hole in the back was much larger—going out was always messier than going in—and instead of a scar, all he felt was gristle. That would take more time to heal.

At least it *was* healing. He was grateful for that. And at least the bullet went clean through—missed his lung and his clavicle, likely making it one of the luckiest point-blank wounds ever inflicted.

Looking back upstream he saw the cliff, a good half mile away. Somehow he had floated down here without drowning.

He swung one leg over and straddled the tree. It traversed the river just at its surface and acted like a filter, catching not only him but also every other scrap of debris that floated downstream. There were sticks and trash hooked in its many branches. And then he saw it—the bag—snagged on a branch nearby and bobbing in the current. He crawled to it and retrieved it. It was drenched and mostly empty, but there were a few vials of medication still inside. He zipped it up and threw it over his good shoulder.

Then, crawling along the tree, he reached the shoreline. Once on solid ground he lay back and rested, clothes dripping, muscles aching. He couldn't remember ever feeling so exhausted and wanted nothing more than to sleep.

But he knew he couldn't. There was no time.

He got to his feet. If he followed the river downstream he could probably find a road. He was at the bottom of the mountain now. Civilization had to be close. Which meant freedom and safety. As for the others, he could find a phone, contact the BHA, give them his location, and wait for reinforcements.

But how long would it take them to get here? An hour? Two? There was no way of knowing. And everything depended on his finding a phone away from civilians—not an easy task.

He looked upstream. If he followed the river that way, he could probably find the trail again. That would lead him to the barn. Back to Wyatt and Monica, who were no doubt frightened and in more danger now than ever. If not dead already.

He lifted his eyes to the sky. The sun was low in the horizon, and dark clouds were maneuvering. He had to make a choice. Upstream or down. Safety or danger.

He took off at a run, guessing that it would be dark by the time he reached the barn.

The rain fell in such heavy sheets that a steady stream of water trickled down the front of Lichen's hood. He had pulled it over his head to protect his face from the downpour, but it did little now. He was completely soaked through. And to make matters worse, the prophet was leading them up the mountain at a snail's pace, insisting on taking the lead, and refusing to allow anyone to run ahead. Lichen grunted. It felt ridiculous to move this slow.

He leaned to a Healer's ear. "I could be inside and drying right now were we not inching through the mud so slowly."

"Your place is at the prophet's side," the Healer said.

"Assuming this man *is* the prophet."

The Healers looked at him disapprovingly. "Blood doesn't lie, Lichen. He's a match. You saw so yourself."

"And yet he seems strange to me."

"Your feelings, Lichen, are of no importance to this work. It is your service to the prophet that should be your only concern."

"He took the life of another. We were to wait for all the vessels to be born again. Then they were to counsel together and disperse. All were to live. This one has disrupted that."

"The disruption, Lichen, comes from your own lack of faith. The prophet does all things for a reason."

Lichen kept quiet after that. It did no good to argue.

Soon, a faint orange glow shone in the darkness ahead of them. Lichen squinted and could see that the barn doors were open and a warm fire had been built on the earth inside. Pine stood at the doorway, saw them approaching, and waved.

Hal waved back. "See how they worship me?" he said. "Look how they welcome their prophet."

Lichen felt all the more uneasy. Even the man's speech was different. He has authority, yes, but pride also, boasting. Gone is the kindness in his voice. This was not the prophet Lichen knew.

They entered the barn and quickly surrounded the fire, grateful for the warmth of it.

Pine looked at Hal and spoke to Lichen. "Where is the other one?"

"Dead," said Hal.

Pine's face became hard. "You will not speak unless spoken to."

Hal slapped him.

Pine was so surprised that he simply stood there, slack-jawed.

"Am I a dog to you?" said Hal.

Pine looked at Lichen, begging an explanation.

"Our prophet has returned," said Lichen.

Pine looked mortified and dropped to one knee. "I beg your pardon, sir. I was unaware."

So much for waving to the prophet, thought Lichen.

"A simple mistake, Pine. I look different. I shouldn't expect you to know me by sight only. However, I cannot tolerate even mistaken defiance. You will stand in the rain for your impudence."

Pine raised his bowed head. "Sir?"

"You have insulted him who gave you Life Greater. I think your punishment especially mild. Do you disagree?"

Lichen looked at some of the other Healers and wondered if they thought this as ridiculous as he did.

"You find this amusing, Lichen?"

Lichen realized that he was smiling and stopped. "I only find it amusing, sir, that Pine would be so foolish as not to know you immediately."

Hal considered this. "Foolish indeed. Outside, Pine, before I change my mind and opt for a more humiliating form of punishment."

Pine got up, a look of bewilderment still on his face, as if he thought everyone would start laughing and tell him it had all been a practical joke. But no one spoke. And when he got out in the rain, he turned away from them and bowed his head shamefully. Almost immediately he was as drenched as those who had just come out of the rain. Lichen pitied him. The prophet would never do this, he thought. He built the species, never tore it down.

Hal removed his suit coat. "Take off your wet garments, gentlemen. Let us dry ourselves and discuss our future." He hung the coat on one of the stall walls, and his eyes met Monica's. She was huddled in the stall with Wyatt, Byron, and Dolores. Nick lay on the ground, covered with one of the Healer's capes.

"Your work is appreciated, Doctor. I never got a chance to thank you. Allow me to do so now."

Monica said nothing. She kissed Wyatt on the top of the head and held him close.

"Not even a 'You're welcome'?" said Hal. "Come now, Doctor. You and I have taken a giant leap together. Will you not at least acknowledge our achievement?"

"What are you going to do with us?" said Dolores.

Hal lowered his voice. "As much as I find you amusing, Dolores, there can be only one of us. One leader. It was a mistake of me to think otherwise. Hal's memories have been very insightful, far more than I would have suspected.

Because of him, I know now how unworthy all of you are to join me in this effort."

"You're going to kill us?" she said.

Hal frowned. "Don't be ugly, Dolores. There's a child present." He turned away from them and found a crate to stand on by the fire. "Gentlemen, I want to commend you. This day has been a long time coming. Many of you have served me faithfully for some time, and I hope you feel rewarded. Ours is a very delicate circumstance. And I don't mean cold and drenched by the rain."

Some of the men laughed, perhaps a little too eagerly, Lichen thought. He wondered if that was either because they wanted this man to be the prophet so badly that they were willing to pretend he was as charismatic as he used to be or if they were all playing along so as not to get sent out in the rain.

"I know I explained to you in detail the actions we would take following my rebirth, how we would spread the gift of healing throughout the world, stop much of human suffering, end the diseases that unnecessarily afflict us. And it was our belief that if there were five of me, five prophets engaged in that work, positioned in key locations throughout the world, then we could divide our resources and accomplish our goals more easily. 'A Council of Prophets is better than a single prophet,' I said." He paused and looked into the fire, heightening the dramatic effect, then lifted his gaze back at them. "But I was wrong."

A low murmur came from the crowd, and Hal lifted his hands to quiet them. "Our mission has not changed, brethren. Our goal has not diminished. We will achieve what we hoped to. But to suppose that a council is stronger than the man after whom it is modeled is foolishness. There can be only one prophet. One. A single leader, a single mind. What good comes from five identical minds counseling together? Is their shared knowledge and experience not the same? Is their thinking not already aligned with the others? What good does it do a man to talk to himself?

"No. The Council is unnecessary. In fact, I believe that the council is the greatest threat to our survival."

Again he paused as the Healers rustled uncomfortably. "What I tell you is hard, yes. It is different from what we have prepared for, fought for, even died for. But it is wisdom. If the world found out that five prophets have been born, those who oppress us would rise up in unison against us. We would be labeled barbarians of science, unethical monsters. Our work would grind to a halt. Those we approach to heal would reject us, and the world would linger in misery. The only hope of preserving ourselves and the good we hope to accomplish is to have one prophet. One."

"But what of the others?" a Healer asked. "They will change soon as well."

"Yes," said another. "What of them?"

Hal nodded. "Yes, what of them?" He steepled his hands and looked deep in thought, as if he hadn't considered that very question until now. "Ours is a difficult mission, brethren. In order to achieve it, a few must fall. This is unfortunate, but the fault is not our own. It cannot be helped. We have been forced to protect ourselves from those who oppress us, going so far as to destroy our own laboratories to ensure that our secrets do not fall into their hands. And as a result, some innocent lives are lost. Naturally, for every one that falls, we will heal a thousand others. But a few must fall. And as much as it saddens me, I see no other alternative for the remaining vessels. They must be ended."

There was no murmur this time, only silence.

"Remember whom we chose to be the vessels, brethren. These were those whom society had rejected. They were the least among us. We could even say that they were already dead, slaves to alcohol or drugs or ignorance. For a time we gave them a reason to live. But that reason has expired. And so they are dead again. We do them a service by releasing them from a life of suffering and pain." He held up a copy of *The Book of Becoming*. "Hear the words which have guided us, brethren, and you will see that there in wisdom is my thinking." He opened to a select passage and, in his most persuasive and holy of voices, began to read.

Frank saw the Healer standing guard out front in the rain and chose to approach the barn from the rear instead. The storm provided good cover, and he reached the back without being noticed. He looked inside. There was Hal, speaking to the Healers and holding their attention. It was as good a distraction as Frank was likely to get, so he crept inside, staying in the shadows until he reached the stall where Monica and the others were being held.

Dolores saw him and gasped, but not loud enough for anyone outside the stall to hear. And Byron, who had been digging furiously at the earth near the wall, looked up with equal surprise.

"We thought you were dead," whispered Dolores.

"We've got to hurry," Frank said. "Can he walk?" He nodded to Nick and knew the answer before Monica gave it.

"He hasn't moved since you left. And his fever's gone up."

"Here." He handed her the medical bag. She opened it and prepared a syringe. Nick took the shot and moaned in his sleep.

"You all need a dose," she said.

"Once we're in the clear," said Frank. "Byron, you think you can carry him again?"

"Beats the alternative."

"We can't outrun them," said Dolores.

"I found another way up from the river," said Frank. "If we can make it to the trees, I think we can lose them in this storm. They won't be able to track us. Wyatt, you're with me, riding piggyback."

Wyatt clung to his mother and didn't move.

"He's afraid," she said.

Frank got down to his level. "What's the matter with you? Afraid I'll drop you?"

Wyatt shook his head.

"Afraid you might not be able to hold on tight enough?"

"I can hold on tight."

"Cannot."

"Uh-huh."

"Prove it."

He wasn't falling for it. "I want to go with my mom."

"She'll be right beside us."

Wyatt looked up at his mother, considered this, then turned back at Frank. "You promise?"

"Promise."

Wyatt held up his little finger. "Pinky swear?"

Frank hooked Wyatt's finger with his own. "Pinky swear."

Wyatt climbed unto Frank's back. Byron bent down to pick up Nick, but before he touched him Nick let out a scream that ripped through the silence and filled the entire barn. Byron recoiled. And before anyone could stop him, Nick sprang to his feet and ran out of the stall.

Hal stopped speaking, and all the Healers turned as Nick stumbled toward them. A few of them backed off, startled by his crazed approach. And then all at once, Nick became still and quiet. He stood there, getting his balance and blinking his eyes, as if waking from a deep sleep. Everyone watched in silence.

And then he got his bearings and looked at their faces. "Lichen, I worried I might not see you again." He took Lichen's hands. "I hope you've been well. I've missed your company."

"The prophet," a Healer said.

"He isn't," said Hal. "He's acting."

"Check him," said Stone.

The Healer with the blood-scanner moved toward Nick.

"No!" said Hal. "I order you not to. We will dispose of this one along with the others."

The Healer with the scanner stopped and looked to Stone, unsure how to proceed.

"We must be certain, sir," said Stone. "Perhaps this one has changed also."

"Do you disobey him who gave you Life Greater? I order you to take this impostor and return him to his holding place."

"I am no impostor," said Nick.

"Silence! Stone, you will order your man to stand down."

The Healer with the scanner waited.

"There can be only one prophet," said Hal. "One. Nick is nothing but an insolent child."

"I am no child," said Nick, standing erect, his voice booming.

"You will not speak!" Hal shouted. "Stone, your man will stand down."

Stone nodded for the Healer with the scanner to obey.

"No," said Lichen, and he grabbed the scanner.

"You will stand down as well, Lichen," said Stone.

"And turn my back on what we've built? No. If there is a charlatan among us, it is this one." He pointed at Hal. There were gasps from the others.

"How dare you?" said Hal, seething.

"He gives us orders contrary to those given by the prophet. What greater evidence do we need?"

"I am blood of his blood," said Hal. "Flesh of his flesh."

Nick grabbed the scanner and pressed it against his arm. It popped and beeped, and then he held it high for all to see. "As am I."

Lichen read the display. "It's true. Look."

"It's a trick," said Hal. "Stone, restrain them both."

Nick smiled and spoke pleasantly. "Don't bother, Stone. I think we can all clearly see who's acting here and who's not."

"I am George Galen!" said Hal.

"No," said Nick. "You are Galen and Hal. Which means

you're stained. The memories of the one have influenced the memories of the other. You're nothing more than a sad imitation of me."

"And you are nothing but a boy," said Hal, "weak and foolish, just like Jonathan."

"You will not speak his name!" said Nick, suddenly fierce. "Jonathan was more a man and friend than you'll ever be."

Hal smiled. "Really? I don't recall ever thinking that. It seems as if you're the one who's stained, not me."

Nick reached down and picked up a heavy stick, whose end burned in the fire, and raised it like a torch. "You're so smug, Hal. Everybody's wrong but you. The only person worth listening to is yourself. Funny way to think, for a slobbering drunk."

"You shut your mouth."

"Of course, what really tickles me is that if you do have all my memories, then you must remember how pathetic you looked when I found you in the playground. Reeking of vomit and cheap liquor. Lying in the sand, red-eyed and drooling. I could have whizzed in your ear and you wouldn't have even batted an eye."

Hal went rigid and clenched his fists.

"And despite all that, despite being quite possibly the saddest excuse for a human being I've ever seen, you still have the gall to bully people, to treat them like they're below *you*." He laughed. "That takes balls, Hal. Real *cojones*. Either that, or you're even more of a—what's the word you like to use—dipstick than I thought."

Hal charged, but Nick was waiting for it. He stepped aside and swung the stick like a bat, striking Hal in the back as he ran past and leaving scorch marks on his wet white shirt. Hal fell to the dirt in a heap.

Stone ran to intervene, but Hal held up a hand. "Stay back. This is between crybaby and me."

He got up and Nick came at him with the stick. Hal ducked, and the stick struck a support beam instead. Hot ash and embers burst from its tip, falling among the rotting hay and, in a flash, igniting it.

With Nick now off balance, Hal kicked high and hard. There was a loud crack as ribs broke, and Nick flew backward, breaking through the wall of one stall and landing in another. The torch flew from his hand and fell against the wall. Even with moisture in the air, the timbers took to the flame. Fire shot up the barn's interior like it'd been sprayed with kerosene.

Nick got to his feet, cracked his neck, and smiled. "All my best moves, but none of my good sense. I have to give you some credit, though, Hal. You were right about one thing. There can be only one prophet. But it certainly isn't you."

He ran at Hal, then launched himself in the air, feet first and together. He hit him with such force that Hal buckled and broke through the wall and fell flat on his back outside in the rain. Before he had even stopped sliding through the mud, Hal was struggling to get to his feet again. He ran back inside, his jaw set. Pine came in behind him, looking shocked.

"All my best moves indeed," said Hal, grabbing another stick from the fire. He swung it repeatedly at Nick, who ducked and dodged every blow, then hit the stick away. It spun through the air and fell in the dirt, still burning.

"What do we do?" asked Lichen.

Stone stood frozen.

Frank crouched at the stall entrance and motioned the others to follow. "Come on." He ran along the wall, keeping low, Wyatt on his back. They could make it out the back if they hurried.

Flames were spreading everywhere fast. Black smoke billowed up into the rafters.

"They're getting away," said Hal.

"Don't let them get away," said Nick simultaneously,

pointing to Frank and the others as they scurried toward the back exit.

Several Healers, Lichen among them, took the order and ran ahead of Frank, blocking the exit. Frank stopped, Monica beside him.

Lichen swung down to grab them, but Frank pivoted and pushed Monica away so that Lichen grabbed nothing but air.

Wyatt's arms tightened around Frank's neck as he hung on for dear life.

"Go back," Frank called over his shoulder. "Out the front."

Byron and Dolores turned and ran in the opposite direction, toward the open barn doors.

Frank took Monica's hand and tried retreating as well, but two Healers stepped behind them and blocked their path. They were surrounded.

Dolores saw them trapped and stopped.

Frank waved her on. "Go."

Byron grabbed Dolores's arm. "Come on!" He pulled her out the doors and into the rain.

Four Healers closed in on Frank, Wyatt, and Monica. The burning stick was at Frank's feet. "Lock your feet around my waist," he said to Wyatt.

Wyatt obeyed, and Frank was able to let go of Wyatt's legs long enough to reach down and pick up the stick. He waved it threateningly at those around him.

"Fire does not hurt us," said a Healer.

"Yeah, but it leaves nasty scars," said Frank. "You may not feel it, but I'll make you ugly."

Behind him, Monica said, "Can you heal faster than fire burns?"

"We do not want to harm you, vessel," said Lichen. He stepped forward, but then quickly retreated when Frank waved the flame. Monica's question was having its effect.

For the moment Frank had them at bay. But he knew it

wouldn't last. Eventually one of them would get close enough. And then it would all be over.

Hal hit Nick with a blow that knocked him against one of the support beams. It cracked under Nick's weight, and Nick cried out, bloody and broken.

Hal, sporting as many cuts and bruises, grabbed Nick by the collar before the younger prophet could counter and shoved him back into the beam a second time. The wood cracked again. Another shove. And another crack. The whole structure shivered from the blows.

Up in the burning rafters timbers crackled and snapped, weakening the roof supports and sending clouds of smoke up through the holes in the ceiling.

Desperate to get free, Nick reached out and took Hal by the throat. Then he lifted his knee and found Hal's groin. Hal immediately stopped shoving, and his legs gave out beneath him. He hung limply in Nick's hands as Nick squeezed his windpipe.

Hal's face turned red, then purple. He waved frantically to Stone, "Help me," he gasped.

Stone ran to him, grabbed Nick's hands and tried prying them away. Nick didn't budge. His face was set and determined. He wasn't letting go. Hal would die.

Frank swung the flaming stick wide again, driving the Healers back. Monica stood behind him, her back to his and Wyatt's, rotating with him so they moved as one.

Another Healer charged, and this was the one Frank was waiting for, the one with the dry cape, the one who hadn't been out in the rain. Instead of swinging aimlessly, Frank lunged, stabbing the man in the side.

The Healer stumbled backward in a panic as his cape caught fire. He dropped to the ground and rolled frantically, trying to smother the fire. But all he accomplished was to spread the fire to the structure immediately around him.

The other Healers watched in horror and backed off Frank even more. Frank took advantage. He waved the stick in wide arcs and backed out of the center of the circle, clinging with one hand to Wyatt and keeping Monica protectively behind him.

"Help me," said Stone, as he struggled to pry Nick's hands from Hal's neck.

Lichen ran to assist him, and the other Healers trying to seize Frank, Monica, and Wyatt followed after him.

Unimpeded, Frank, Wyatt, and Monica bolted out the back of the barn and into the rain. Byron and Dolores were out there waiting for them.

"This way," said Frank, leading them toward the path he had taken up from the river.

"What about Nick?" asked Dolores.

"Nick isn't Nick," said Frank.

She stopped. "So we're leaving him?"

In answer, Frank took her hand and pulled her until she was running again—with Monica right beside him and Byron close behind.

"Pull his hands away," ordered Stone.

The Healer nearest him took Nick's hands and with Stone's help pried them free from Hal's throat. Hal fell to the ground, gasping and coughing.

"Hold him back," said Stone.

Nick pushed the Healers away. "Don't touch me."

Hal was up in an instant, knocking Stone to the side and tackling Nick. The Healers scrambled to separate them, but the two rolled away from them and disappeared into a cloud of black smoke.

"Find them," said Stone, coughing and covering his mouth with his cloak.

The Healers dispersed into the blackness, coughing and waving the smoke and cinders from their faces.

And then Hal appeared, soaring backward in the air and striking the support beam with such force that Stone wasn't sure if the cracking sound had come from the wood or Hal's spine.

A second later the beam snapped, and the burning roof collapsed, thick flaming timbers that crashed down into a massive raging heap.

Stone felt his body jerk to one side as a Healer pushed him clear of the falling debris.

Then, as if taking a cue from the roof, the rest of the structure crumbled, adding more timbers to the growing pile and throwing up a thick cloud of burning embers.

Stone rolled over and pushed aside the wood that covered him. "Galen!"

There was no answer, just the sizzle of the rain on the burning pile. He got up, wiped the soot from his eyes, and began making his way back to where Nick and Hal lay covered.

One by one other Healers came and helped him, but by the time they got the top third of the rubble away, Stone knew it would be too late.

When they finally reached them, the wood was all black and soaked from the rain. Hal and Nick were burned beyond recognition, lying beside each other, one still choking the other.

"The others have taken to the forest," Lichen said. "Should we divide the men?"

Stone wiped the rain off his face, smearing some of the soot onto his checks. "No. We bury our dead."

"But unless we move—"

"We show our master the respect he deserves," Stone said. "Then we retrieve Byron and Dolores."

"And Frank Hartman?" asked Lichen.

"He is not worthy of the office," said Stone. "He has

proved a threatening obstacle. He must be removed to prevent any further losses."

"Then we should hurry," said Lichen. "We may still be able to track them.

"There's no need to track them," said Stone, opening his cell phone. "We now know where he's taking them."

30

VESSELS

Runoff from the mountain had transformed the already fast-moving river into a violent torrent of rushing water. Frank stayed a safe distance from the bank but always kept the water in sight. There was no trail here, and he couldn't risk getting lost by venturing too far from the waterline.

They passed the spot where the felled tree had traversed the river, but the tree itself was gone, no doubt flushed downstream by the elevated current.

Wyatt clung to Frank's neck, bouncing up and down as Frank carried him through the brush. Monica and Byron kept up, but Dolores lagged considerably. They had already stopped three times to wait for her.

"Don't wait for me," she had told them. "Keep moving. I'll get there eventually."

But they always waited. And during their last wait the rain stopped.

"Hey," said Byron, looking up at the night sky. "It stopped."

"What difference does it make?" said Monica. "We can't get any wetter."

It was true. Their clothes were soaked through, their hair wet and limp. Frank was just as wet now as he had been in the river.

"Look at the stars," said Wyatt.

They looked up. The rain clouds had parted, revealing countless tiny lights against a sweeping black canvas.

"Wow," said Monica. "You live in LA, you forget what real sky looks like."

"It's like this every night in Montana," said Byron. "Nothing but stars."

"How many are up there, you think?" asked Wyatt.

"Oh, about a bajillion," said Byron.

Wyatt made a face. "A *bajillion*?"

"What, you never heard of a bajillion before? It's one step above a trillion. You know, million billion trillion bajillion. And then of course there's foobajillion."

Wyatt looked skeptical. "Uh-uh."

"No, it's true. Ask Frank."

They both looked at Frank. Byron winked.

"Um, yeah," said Frank. "That's right. Foobajillion. And after that is . . . oh, what do you call it?"

"Fooba-doobajillion," said Byron, keeping a straight face.

"Right, fooba-doobajillion," said Frank. "How could I forget fooba-doobajillion?"

"You're making that up," said Wyatt.

"Oh no," said Frank. "In fact, I read recently that scientists have determined that there are exactly six fooba-doobajillion and one grains of sand on the earth."

"Really?" said Byron.

"Yeah, scientific fact. Well, actually, that's not completely accurate. Last time I was at the beach I accidentally swallowed a grain of sand, so now I guess there's only six fooba-doobajillion even."

Monica laughed.

"I knew you were teasing," said Wyatt.

"Fooba-doobajillion?" she said. "Sounds like a Hawaiian fruit smoothie."

They all laughed then, even Wyatt, who probably didn't get the joke but knew it was one. It felt good to laugh; a release, almost, allowing them to forget for a moment what had happened at the barn. They were still laughing when Dolores arrived, tired and breathless.

"Y'all could wake the dead with all the noise you're making. What's going on? We celebrating? Healers decided to leave us alone or something?"

Mentioning the Healers dampened the mood in an instant.

"We should keep moving," said Frank.

After another mile they found a paved road. They followed it for a few hundred yards and came to a privately owned campground. The sign by the gate said *Closed,* but they went in anyway.

The office was locked. Frank looked in through the window but didn't see a phone.

They went around back and saw that most of the campsites were empty. Either it was off-season or people had left when the rain hit.

A small cinder-block building nearby turned out to be a laundromat for campers. Nobody was inside, but two of the dryers were spinning and filled with clothes. Frank ushered everyone in and locked the door behind them; he couldn't risk someone coming in unexpectedly.

The clothes in the dryers were dry and hot to the touch. Frank took everything out and threw it onto the counter. It all belonged to a couple, it seemed, a man and a woman of medium build and height. There was enough for everyone to have a new shirt. And everyone but Frank got new pants.

"Where do we change?" asked Monica.

"We'll turn around," said Frank. "Women change first. Put your wet clothes in a pile here."

"If you think I can fit in these pants," said Dolores, holding up the ones Frank had given her, "you're smoking something green and illegal. Ain't no way in heaven my butt is getting in these. Not unless you take out all the other organs inside me."

Frank took them and tore slits in the waistline. "Here."

She took them back but still looked doubtful. "Well, turn around, then. A woman needs her privacy."

The boys sat down on the floor behind the washers. After a minute, Dolores reappeared. "What do you think?"

"Dashing," said Byron. "Definitely better than a man's suit."

She grinned. "Thought so myself. You all can change now."

When the boys got up to get their clothes, Monica was towel-drying her hair and wearing a long-sleeved pullover and a khaki pair of capri pants. She saw Frank watching her and stopped toweling.

"Done with that?" he asked quickly.

She tossed it to him.

"Thanks."

Wyatt put on a sweatshirt that hung to his knees and a pair of men's shorts that hung to his ankles. Dolores gave him her belt, and Frank made a hole in it so that it fit Wyatt snugly.

"I look stupid," he said.

"No you don't," said Frank. "You look cool. Baggy is in."

"This isn't baggy," he said. "This is a bedsheet."

"Hey, too big is better than too small," said Byron. "I can hardly breathe in this thing."

Dolores took one look at Byron's T-shirt and smiled. "You look like one of those muscle guys on Venice Beach."

"Except without the muscles," he said.

"Please. You got muscle. Just not toned, is all. Ten push-ups a day for a week and you'll be turning heads."

Byron smiled. "You're a physical trainer all of a sudden?"

"Ha. That would be the day. Me with a job."

He shrugged. "Why not?"

"Cause I'm a homeless woman, that's why."

"Whatever you think you are, you're right."

She made a face. "Who said that? The president? Please, thinking you're somebody and being somebody is two different things. Just because I think I'm a supermodel doesn't make me one."

He made a face of disbelief. "You mean you're not a supermodel?"

She shoved him.

"I'm serious. There's got to be a job out there for someone as stubborn as you."

"There ain't. I got nothing nobody wants."

"Ever tried to get a job?"

She put her hands on her hips. "What is this? Oprah? Homeless people can't get a job. What's the first thing they ask for on a job application? Huh? I bet you don't even know. You've probably never had to fill one out before."

"I'm going out on a limb on this one . . . uh, name."

"Right. And after that I got nothing to write down. No address."

"What about family?" Byron asked. "Is there a relative you could stay with?"

She smacked her forehead. "Now, why didn't I think of that? I'll just pick up the phone and call my rich brother in Beverly Hills. I'm sure he's got an extra room in that mansion of his."

"Sorry. I just meant—"

"Nobody chooses to be homeless, Byron. If you're homeless, it means you got nobody, or at least nobody who claims you. Only friend I got is Jesus. And he does me just fine."

"You sure he's your only friend?"

"He's never forgotten me. When I'm hungry he feeds me, when I'm naked, he clothes me." She motioned to her new outfit. "See?"

"What I mean is, maybe there's other people who want to be your friend."

She snorted. "Like who?"

"Like me."

She looked at him, surprised. "You?"

"Is that so hard to believe?"

"You want to be my friend?"

"Yeah. I kind of thought we already *were* friends."

She looked surprised. "But I'm ugly."

He could only laugh. "No, you're not. You've helped all of us through this. Monica, don't you think Dolores is a beautiful person?"

"The most beautiful."

"See? Frank, what about you?"

"One in a million. Gem of a woman."

"See?"

"*I* like you," said Wyatt.

Byron laughed. "See? Even Wyatt likes you, and he's an incredibly tough judge of character."

"Ya'll just trying to be nice because you feel sorry for me."

"If people tell you they want to be your friend, Dolores," said Byron, "you either tell them yes or no."

"We waited for you, Dolores, because you're one of us," said Frank. "You want to belong to somebody, you belong to us."

"That's right," said Byron.

She looked at each of them, then nodded, beaming. "All right. Sounds good to me."

Frank gathered their wet clothes once they were finished, as well as everything else they had touched, and threw them in the trash. Then he tied off the trash bag, took three more bags from the utility closet, and put each bag inside another until he was certain it wouldn't break open if snagged. Then he threw it in the Dumpster out back.

When he came back inside Monica was preparing more syringes.

"Again?" said Dolores. But she didn't put up a fight. In fact, she even rolled up sleeve without being asked.

Once everyone had received a dose, Monica got the tweezers out of the bag. "I need to take out those staples," she said.

"It can wait," said Frank.

"It's waited long enough. Take your shirt off."

He removed his shirt and lay on the cold concrete. She knelt beside him and delicately pinched each staple before pulling it out. Frank felt awkward there on the floor with her so close to him. Rather than look at her while she worked, he looked just past her up at the ceiling tiles.

"There," she said, removing the last one. "That should feel better."

"Thank you." He got up and quickly put his shirt back on. It did feel better. Much better. In fact, he realized that most of the discomfort he had been feeling was from the staples and not from the wound itself.

"Now what?" said Byron.

"Dinner," said Frank. He walked to the junk-food vending machine in the corner and kicked in the Plexiglas. It took three sturdy kicks to make a hole big enough to reach everything. The machine hadn't been stocked in some time, but there were enough potato chips and candy bars to go around. Wyatt and Dolores couldn't have been happier.

After fifteen minutes, Frank was wishing he hadn't eaten so many.

"Who wants the last Snickers bar?" asked Dolores.

"It's all yours," he said.

She tore into it while he went back to the utility closet for more trash bags. He filled them with the Plexiglas shards and the food wrappers. Then he emptied the bottle of spray glass-cleaner and filled it with bleach. While the others watched, he sprayed down everything they had touched: the dryer, the vending machine, the countertops. He even went back to the office and sprayed the window he had looked through and the door he had knocked on.

The remainder of the bleach bucket was emptied onto

the floor. When he was done, the laundromat smelled so strongly, it was doubtful anyone would enter without hosing the place down first.

The others were waiting outside. "Any luck finding a car?" he asked.

"One," said Byron. "Over at that campsite. Man and a woman. I think these are their clothes."

Frank spotted the tent and car in the distance.

"But they're sleeping in it," said Byron. "Tent must have flooded in the rain."

"No good then. We can't risk infecting them. We'll have to keep looking. Meanwhile, we stay off the road. They might be looking for us. Wyatt, you want piggyback or are you walking?"

"Are you kidding?" said Monica. "He's on a sugar high. He could carry *us* on his back."

"I'll walk," he said.

They stuck to the woods but stayed close to the road. Occasionally a car would pass. "Why don't we flag one down?" asked Dolores.

"Same reason we shouldn't have flagged down the boat," said Frank.

"So we have to find a car with nobody in it? Oh, that'll be a cinch out here in the middle of nowhere. People are always abandoning perfectly good cars on the side of the road."

"You're a woman of faith, Dolores," said Frank. "Pray for a miracle."

"Oh, I'm praying already. Trust me. And when this car magically falls from the sky, then what? You going to break inside and jump it? Or should I also pray that the key be in the ignition?"

"Key in the ignition is preferable," said Frank.

Dolores grunted in exasperation.

They passed a road sign, and Byron went up to the street and read it. "Says we've been in Kings Canyon National Park."

"Where's that?" asked Frank.

"Couple hours north of LA along the Sierra Nevada."

"Couple hours in a car, maybe" said Dolores. "Not on foot."

"Then I suggest you keep praying," said Frank. She gave him a look that said she was half annoyed and half amused.

They got moving again, and no one said another word for two miles. Finally Wyatt came and walked beside Frank and broke the silence. "Where'd you learn to shoot a gun?" he asked.

Frank looked at him. He looked like an adult who'd been hit with a shrink ray in those clothes. "In the Army," he said.

"I thought you said you were a doctor?"

"I am. I work for the military."

"Oh. Is that where you learned how to fight?"

"I suppose so."

"Think you can teach me a few moves?"

Frank raised an eyebrow. "Why do you ask?"

"There's this boy in my class. Keener Kiner. Big guy, total jerk. He picks on me and my friends."

"Anyone with a name like Keener Kiner has no right to pick on anyone."

"That's what I told him."

"What did he say?"

"He punched me in the stomach."

"Oh. So you want learn how to punch him back?"

Wyatt shrugged.

"Did you tell your teacher he picks on you?"

"That's what my mom said. But it doesn't work. If I told, then he'd really come after me."

"Hitting someone isn't easy, you know? It's not like in the movies. It really hurts your hand. It's like hitting a tree."

"So you're not going to teach me?"

"I could, but I don't think it's a good idea."

"Let me guess. Now you're going to lecture me on how it's wrong to fight."

Frank smiled. "No, I'm going to give you a dose of reality. Let's say Keener the wiener corners you, and you sock him one. And let's even assume it's a really good punch. What's going to happen next?"

"Um, he's going to hit me back?"

"Right. And if he hits you, and remember he's really ticked at this point, what's that going to feel like?"

"It's going to hurt," said Wyatt.

"Right. And probably a lot. And then what are you going to do?"

"Um, hit him again?"

"OK, so you hit him again. Now you're hitting each other. Boom boom boom. How is this going to end?"

"Me getting my butt kicked?"

"No offense, but probably so."

"Well, at least I stood up to him. That's something, right?"

"What good will it have done you? Do you think Keener is going to suddenly leave you alone? No, now he's proven he can kick your butt. He's even more confident than he was before. And while your friends might be impressed that you got in a few good punches, that doesn't change the fact that you got your butt kicked."

"But what if I did beat him? It's possible."

"OK, let's assume you beat him. Bloody lip, the works. All your friends put you on their shoulders, and you're a hero for a day. But what happens tomorrow? You think Keener is going to play fair? No, he's a creep. He's got to save face. So he's going to get his buddies, or worse, some older kids, and they're going to ambush you. And then you'll really get your butt kicked."

"So what do I do?"

"Ignore him. Never be alone. If you see him coming for you, go hang with an adult."

"So I run?"

"Running from a fight you can't win doesn't mean you're a coward. It means you're smart. What do you think we're doing now? You think I should have stayed in the barn and fought all those Healer guys, stuck it out, showed them that I wasn't a coward?"

"That's different."

"Why? They're bigger than me, stronger than me, like Keener is to you."

"But you did fight some of them."

"Only because I had no choice. Only because the other option was much worse. Every other time I ran. I got out of there. You think that makes me a coward?"

"No. But even if I'm not a coward the other kids will still call me one."

"Maybe. Do you care?"

Wyatt shrugged.

"Well, that's the question you have to ask yourself. What's more important to you, getting called a coward by some snot-nosed wienies who are no braver than you, or getting your butt kicked repeatedly until you graduate from high school?"

"My dad would probably say getting called a coward."

"Well, your dad is entitled to his opinion. As for me, I have better things to do than get pummeled every day. They can call me whatever they like."

The forest suddenly opened to a wide field beyond which were acres of fruit trees lined in neat rows. The road curved sharply to the south. Frank and Wyatt stopped and waited for the others.

"Well, what do you think?" said Byron. "Should we stick with the road?"

"This orchard belongs to someone," said Frank. "I say we check it out."

No one objected. They walked down the nearest furrow and soon reached a dirt road that divided the orchard and led to a small farmhouse. All the lights were off, but a beat-up white pickup sat parked out front.

"It's quiet," said Monica.

"Do you think anyone's home?" said Byron.

"Let's hope not," said Frank. "Stay here."

Monica crouched by the road behind some trees with the others while Frank snuck up to the house. When he was only a few feet from the truck, a dog chained to a post in the yard sprang to life from the shadows and began barking loudly.

"Shut up, dog," Dolores whispered.

"It's going to wake them," said Byron.

Sure enough, the front porch light came on. Frank hid behind the truck just before the front door opened.

A middle-aged man in an undershirt and boxers shuffled outside. He yawned, scratched his backside, saw nothing of interest in the yard, then told the dog to shut up. When it didn't, he picked up one of the shoes by the doormat and pitched it. It hit the dog unawares, and the dog retreated and fell silent.

"Well, that's not very nice," said Dolores.

"Shh," said Byron.

The man mumbled a few obscenities and disappeared inside.

Frank went around to the passenger door—opposite the dog—peeked inside, then opened the door and crawled in. The dog went berserk, barking, pulling at his chain, pawing to get free.

"What's he doing?" said Byron. "They're awake. He can't jump it that fast."

The truck engine roared to life.

"Okay, maybe he can."

The truck peeled out of the yard in reverse just as the man in boxers came running out of the house yelling. Frank spun the wheel, and the truck spun with him. There was a grinding of gears, and the truck shot forward and bounced up onto the dirt road. The man in boxers ran after it, while the dog pulled vainly at his chain. Monica and the others scrambled to the roadside, and Frank skidded to a stop, reached across the cab, and threw wide the passenger door. "Get in."

They didn't need to be told twice. Monica and Wyatt climbed in first, followed by Dolores and then Byron. Frank floored it before Byron had the door closed.

"How the hell did you do that?" said Byron, yelling over the engine.

"Thank Dolores," said Frank. "The key was in the ignition."

Frank stuck to the rural roads, always driving in a southeasterly direction—the bobbing compass on the dashboard proved useful in that regard. The LCD display on the radio said it was one in the morning, which explained the light traffic.

The cab was unmercifully cramped. What was intended to seat three, now accommodated four and a half. It helped that Wyatt sat on Monica's lap, but it didn't make Monica any more comfortable. And when Wyatt fell asleep, it became even more awkward as she tried to cradle him without invading anyone else's space.

The heater worked, at least, much to Dolores's delight. And moments after Frank turned it on the lowest setting, Dolores slumped onto Byron's shoulder, fast asleep. Wedged against the window Byron had little else to do but join her, and shortly fell asleep as well.

"You think you can stay awake?" said Monica.

Frank rubbed his eyes. "If I was driving alone I'd have the radio blasting and the windows down."

"You want me to drive?"

"No, I'm good." He tried to press himself more into the driver's side door to give her another inch of room. "You can't be comfortable holding him that way. Why don't you lay him across everyone's lap?"

"I don't want to disturb them," she said.

"An atom bomb wouldn't disturb them. Go ahead."

She bent forward and lifted Wyatt's legs gingerly onto Byron and Dolores's lap. Then she sighed and wiggled her leg. "My leg fell asleep."

"It's all the rage," he said. "Sleep, I mean."

"Right."

He had meant it as a joke, but knew it was a stupid thing to say as soon as the words came out. Classy.

"I hope he didn't talk your ear off back there," she said.

"Wyatt? No, not at all. After everything he's been through, it's good for him to talk."

"I think he's kind of taken by you."

"Well, I hear he's a tough judge of character, so I'll take that as a compliment."

She smiled. "You have any kids?"

Once again, the question had snuck up on him. "A daughter," he said finally.

"How old is she?"

"She would have been eight this year. She died about a year and a half ago."

There was a brief silence. "I'm so sorry. I didn't mean to—"

"No, it's okay."

"I can't imagine how difficult that must have been."

"It wasn't sudden. She'd been sick for a long time."

"I'm so sorry," she repeated.

"Don't be. She made me very happy." He smiled to himself. "You would have liked her. She was a crazy kid. Loved the Bee Gees."

"The Bee Gees?"

He laughed. "I know, what six-year-old loves the Bee Gees? My father was to blame. He brought an old record player and a bunch of albums for her hospital room. She really got a kick out of it. Most of the nurses had never even heard of *Saturday Night Fever*. She even did this little dance in her bed with her hips and her hand. Cracked me up."

Wyatt squirmed a bit to reposition himself, then lay still.

"What was her name?" Monica asked.

"Rachel. Rachel Evelyn."

"Pretty."

"Names from my wife's family"

"And what's your wife's name?"

"*Ex*-wife, actually. We divorced shortly after Rachel died."

"Oh. I'm sorry to hear that."

"Rachel was kind of the glue holding us together. When she was gone—I don't know, if we had had other children, maybe it would have been different. But she was so sick, even early on, that more children was the farthest thing from our minds. Not because we were disappointed with her. Not at all. She just needed all of our attention. You know what I mean?"

She nodded.

"That's probably more information than you wanted to hear," he said.

"No, I don't mind. In fact, it's almost therapeutic to hear someone else talk about their divorce. It seems like that's all I've been doing for the past year, getting a divorce."

He glanced at her.

"It was all finalized a few months ago. Kind of a surreal experience. Just sign your name on some legal document and *whoosh,* everything you thought you had structured in your life is suddenly gone." She became quiet, and after a moment, she reached up and wiped her eyes. "You'll have to excuse me. I'm sort of an emotional wreck. And not about my divorce, either. About everything."

Frank kept his eyes on the road. He wouldn't disturb her. Let her have her cry.

"You never met Jonathan," she said, sounding calm

again. "Not alive, I mean. He was good kid—misguided, maybe, but a good kid. With a little help, a kid with a future, maybe. And now, nothing."

"You can't blame yourself for—"

"Why not? It was my doing, wasn't it? I killed somebody else's kid to save my own, didn't I? And Hal and Nick. You saw the barn fall. They couldn't have survived that."

"Then the fire killed them, not you." He said it as convincingly as possible, even though he didn't fully believe it himself.

"Don't be nice to me. Please. I don't think I can handle that." She was quiet for a long time after that, staring out the windshield as if in a trance, the only sound coming from the hum of the engine and the low purr of the heater fan. "I never thanked you," she said. "For getting Wyatt. Before you left. You risked your life. After everything I did to you. I'm grateful for that."

"I didn't do it for you," he said. "I did it for Wyatt."

"I know," she said. "That's what makes it all the more wonderful."

He said nothing, only nodded his head slightly. Then she leaned against Dolores's shoulder and in moments fell asleep.

The tapping on the driver's side window woke Frank. It was morning. He sat up and saw the old man in coveralls standing outside the truck, smiling. They were parked in a field. Frank vaguely remembered pulling off the road after nearly falling asleep at the wheel.

"You folks all right?" the man said.

"Where are we?" said Dolores, coming to.

Frank turned the ignition and started the truck, startling the old man. He backed up as Frank waved politely and put the truck in reverse.

"What's happening?" said Byron.

"Where are we?" Dolores said again.

Monica and Wyatt woke as Frank bounced back onto the road again. How long had he been asleep? Two hours? Three? It couldn't have been long. Dawn was just breaking. Frank shook his head. Stupid. Shouldn't have pulled over.

Soon they were among the early commuters creeping into LA from the San Fernando Valley.

By eight o'clock they were taking the Wilshire exit and circling back toward the Federal Building. As they turned right onto Veteran Avenue to head for the Federal Building's parking lot, a line of congested traffic brought them to a stop. A roadblock had been set up ahead, manned by half a dozen BHA agents in biocontainment suits. The agents stopped each car that approached and looked inside it before waving it on.

"They're looking for something," said Monica.

Three cars up, an agent squatted down next to the driver's window and looked inside. In his hand was a piece of paper featuring the photo of a person's face.

"Not some*thing*," said Frank. "They're looking for some*one*."

The agent determined the car he was inspecting was clean and told the driver to continue on.

"I got a bad feeling about this," said Monica.

"Yeah," said Frank, "me too."

The agent moved to the next car, leaving only one car between him and the truck. He motioned for the driver to roll down the window, and then Frank saw the face on the photo.

"Hey, that's you," said Monica.

"Then they're looking for us," said Dolores. "We're saved."

"Hold on," said Frank. He backed up a foot, cranked the wheel, and gunned it. The truck did a U-turn, narrowly missing a car headed north, and turned east onto Wilshire.

"What are you doing?" said Dolores.

"Are they following us?" said Frank.

"No," said Monica, "I don't think so. Another car turned around also."

"Hold up," said Dolores. "Somebody want to tell me what's going on? I thought we were going *to* the BHA. Now we're running away from it?"

"They were looking for me," said Frank. "They knew I was trying to come back to the BHA and were trying to stop me."

"But why would they want to do that?"

And the answer came to him the instant the question was posed. "Irving," said Frank. "Of course. Has to be."

"Who?"

"Director Irving, head of the BHA. Galen said that Director Irving had been helping him. Maybe the Healers are still in contact with Irving. If so, they could have informed him of our escape and asked him to use the BHA to stop us from reaching the countervirus."

"Wait a second," said Dolores. "*You* said the BHA was the one place on earth where we would be safe. And now you're driving away from it? No, let me out of this truck." She reached for the passenger door handle, but it was locked.

"Stop," said Frank. "Just relax. Let me think."

"Think?" she said. "Think? All we been doing is walking and thinking."

Frank accelerated, weaving among the traffic heading east on Wilshire Boulevard.

"But I don't get it," said Byron. "How did this director mobilize the entire BHA against you?"

"I don't know," said Frank. "He could've told them anything, made up all kinds of incriminating intel against me. He's the director. Who would disbelieve him?"

"Maybe we're being paranoid," said Monica. "Maybe we're getting upset over nothing. Maybe they were looking for you because they want to help you."

"If they wanted to help me," said Frank, "they'd be

looking anywhere *but* the BHA. The Healers are the only people who knew we were headed back to the BHA this morning. And that roadblock was expecting me."

Monica rubbed her eyes, looking defeated. She knew he was right.

"But what if you talk to them?" said Byron. "What if you tell them you're innocent of whatever it is you're being accused of? Maybe all you need to do is give your side of the story."

"And what if that doesn't work?" said Frank. "Who's to say they'll even permit me to *give* my side of the story? They could be under orders to detain me immediately. Maybe Irving told them I'm a bio risk and should be quarantined. I *do* have the virus. That would be an easy story to prove." He shook his head. "No, Director Irving's too smart. He would have anticipated my trying to exonerate myself. Count on him having a plan for it."

"He's right," said Monica. "There's no time to take that risk. Your chips could be triggered at any moment."

There was a silence. To mention the chips was to mention Nick and Hal. And no one seemed ready to broach that subject. Frank had said it before: there'd be time for mourning later.

"What if we all go in together?" said Byron. "It'll be our word against his. There's four of us and only one of him."

"Galen only mentioned Irving," said Frank. "There could be others. I have no way of knowing how deep the Healers' penetration is."

Byron pounded a fist onto the dashboard, startling everyone. "Then we got no options. There's nothing left we can do."

"Hold on," said Frank. He took a sharp right and began a wide loop that took him to Westwood Park, a lavish city park behind the Federal Building. He found a parking space in the back corner away from other cars and killed the engine. "Stay here. Don't get out for any reason."

"Where are you going?" said Byron.

"Inside. If I can get to the countervirus—"

"Whoa whoa whoa," Byron said. "Inside? Are you out of your mind? You just can't waltz into the Federal Building. You said they were looking for you. If the director is working for the Healers, he'll have the entire agency against you. Besides, how can you possibly get in and out without infecting anyone?"

"I'm open to other ideas."

No one had any.

"Then stay here. I'll be back as soon as I can."

Frank got out, scaled the park fence, and dropped into the back of the Federal Building's expansive parking lot. Taking a breath to steel himself, he ran toward the back entrance, not having the slightest clue how to get inside.

330   NALE AND JOHN SON

"Where are you, one?" said Blount.
"Inside. If I can get to that county tower."

31

INFILTRATION

The Federal Building parking lot was six acres of tightly packed vehicles. Frank ran behind a row of cars, keeping low and using them for cover. He paused once he had the building's back doors in sight. Getting in, he realized, would be impossible. There were six agents standing guard at the rear entrance. Each agent wore an armored biocontainment suit and carried heavy weaponry. Two more agents stood beside a BHA assault van parked along the entrance road. Plus, there were the six or so agents still manning the roadblock on the east end of the parking lot along Veteran Avenue. It was a fortress.

Frank crouched behind a car, his mind racing. There was no way he was getting inside.

The back doors of the building opened, and Frank squinted, trying to get a better look.

Agent Carter exited the building, his helmet tucked under his arm. The other agents greeted him, and Carter snapped his helmet into place and cocked his weapon.

Of course, thought Frank. Carter. Galen had apprehended him in the rest home before taking me.

Frank had assumed that Carter had been disposed of, that Galen would consider him an obstacle best removed. But Galen had seized control of Deputy Dixon's mind, hadn't he? What would stop him from seizing control of Carter's as well? Frank had only been spared the same fate because Galen had bigger plans for him.

And what about Riggs? Where was he? Was he under Galen's control, too? There was no way to be certain. The only safe assumption at this point was that all this firepower was intentional. Frank was a target. Healers had lost confidence in him as one of Galen's successors and now were using the BHA to have him removed.

Frank looked down at the gray suit he was wearing. He looked a mess—torn, muddy, and grass-stained. He wouldn't get past the agents dressed like this. But if he had a biosuit, he could contain the virus inside *and* use the suit as cover to get in the building.

The BHA van was parked forty yards from the rear entrance. There would be a spare biosuit in it. The only problem was, there was no way to get in the van without the two agents currently crowding it noticing.

What he needed was a distraction.

He looked at the car beside him. It was heavily dented, and a sheet of plastic was taped where the passenger window should have been. He maneuvered around to the passenger side, ripped away the plastic, unlocked the door, and crawled inside.

It was a stick-shift. He got into the driver's seat, opened the driver-side door, and put it in neutral. Then, pushing off the asphalt with his left leg, he slowly backed the car out of the parking space and turned it ninety degrees. The van and agents were another row of cars over, so he was still obscured from their view.

Leaving the car in neutral and staying low, he straightened the steering wheel, got out, and crouched at the front bumper.

Then he pushed.

It took a few yards for the car to pick up speed, but soon it was going without his help. He moved away and hid behind another car as the five-speed rolled down the row at a brisk clip.

It smashed into a Mercedes parked fifty yards away, and a car alarm went off. It couldn't have been more perfect.

Several agents ran by as Frank remained hidden. Then, when it was clear no others were coming to investigate, he crept to the van. Both agents were gone, and from this side of the van he was hidden from the building. He opened the back door and crept inside.

The spare biosuits were kept in an emergency containment kit in the rear. He put one on, snapped on the helmet, and fastened the utility belt. It had the standard accouterments: an aerosol sedative, a box of small plastic containment bags, a small first-aid kit, an empty holster. He looked for a gun but didn't find one, then switched on his comlink.

An agent's voice, shouting over the whine of the car alarm, sounded in his ear. "—inside the car, sir."

"Are you sure?" Carter's voice said.

"Affirmative. Rods are red, sir. No question. I'm getting V16 all over the interior."

Frank shuddered. He was still hot with the virus.

"Roger that," Carter's voice said. "I'm on my way."

Frank watched through the windshield as Carter and three more agents ran down to the crash site, leaving only four agents at the front entrance. It was now or never.

He went out the back of the van and then jogged with confidence around it toward the building, giving the illusion that he was running up from the crash site. The four agents seemed to pay him no mind and in fact were leaving their posts to get a look at the commotion in the parking lot. Frank kept his head down and stayed a distance from them without giving the impression that he was doing so intentionally.

One of them spotted him. "Hey."

Frank stopped, his heart pounding.

"What's going on down there?"

Frank rested his hands on his knees, pretending to be out of breath, but mostly keeping his face out of sight. "V16," he said in a slightly deeper voice. "Think I got a leak in my suit. Need to check it out." Hoping that was a sufficient response, he jogged to the door and went inside, relieved that no one tried to stop him.

A particularly jumpy security guard greeted him in the lobby. "What's going on out there? Is it him?"

Frank kept his head down and turned on his exterior mike. "Sir, please stand back. I have a biohazard here." He held out a closed fist, and the security guard recoiled, eyes wide with terror.

Frank hustled to the elevator and pushed the button. The door opened, and he stepped inside, realizing instantly that he didn't have the key the elevator required.

The security guard watched him with pained fascination from the farthest point in the lobby.

"Officer," Frank boomed. "I don't have my key. I need to use yours."

"I can't do that without clearance," the guard shouted back weakly.

"Then let me put it this way. In my hand is a Level 4 pathogen capable of instigating an epidemic not seen on this planet since the black plague. Now, unless you don't mind your eyeballs turning to jelly while we wait for this clearance, I suggest you give me your damn key."

A bulky ring of keys slid across the waxed tile floor and stopped at the elevator. Frank reached down and picked it up. "Thank you."

He inserted the correct key, and the doors shut. As the elevator descended he realized he needed to do a little more planning. What was next? A BHA security guard with a contaminant rod. And beyond him, what? A door that required both a card key and retinal scan. And beyond that, a room filled with fifty people and the director of the agency. Perfect.

Okay, you have no weapon. No card key. And two useless retinas. Think.

The elevator stopped, and the doors opened. A smiling guard turned to face him.

"Before you do anything," said Frank. "Hear me out."

The guard started, jumped back, and scrambled for his radio. Frank had no choice but to snap the aerosol can from his hip and spray him in the face. The guard's eyes rolled back and he crumpled to the floor.

Frank found the guard's card key, then dragged him by the ankles down the corridor to the BHA entrance. He swiped the card key and then got his hands under the guard's arms to lift him.

A red light emitted from the retinal scan, and a computerized female voice said, "Error. No retina detected." Then the light shut off.

Great. So he'd have to get the guy up there and *then* swipe the card.

With great effort, he hefted the guard to a semi-standing position. But he needed both his hands to do so, and the guard's head kept lolling to the side, away from the scanner. Finally he opted for pressing the guard against the wall and holding his head in place with his own head. Then, using his knees for additional support, he swiped the card and quickly reached up and pulled the guard's eyelids open.

The red light emitted and the female voice said, "Error. Please look directly into the light."

Frank pulled the head away and saw that the man's eyes were still rolled back. Damn.

He shook the man's head. That didn't work. Then he delicately put his gloved finger to the man's eyes and moved them manually. The guard looked straight ahead with a deathly stare. Frank pressed the head against the wall again and swiped the card. The light emitted and the door opened.

Frank gently lowered the body to the floor then stepped

through the doorway. There was a buzz of activity in the command center, as always. If he kept his head down, maybe they would ignore him, maybe he could blend in.

Frank descended the stairs and soon realized that an agent in full biogear was too unnatural a sight here in the command center to avoid notice. The agents here were analysts, dressed in conservative business suits, not biogear. Right now Frank stuck out like a sore thumb.

One by one the analysts looked up from the computer terminals as he passed. A few stepped out of his way. They were all watching him.

Head still bowed and moving briskly, Frank saw one of the analysts run into Director Irving's office. A moment later Irving himself emerged, hands in his pockets, standing in Frank's path.

"Dr. Hartman, this is a surprise. I can only assume you're here to turn yourself in."

Frank looked up. The room was quiet. Everyone stared at him.

"I know about you, Irving. You gave the Healers information. You set me up to be taken."

Irving laughed. "Do you really think anyone in this room is going to believe a word you say, Dr. Hartman? After all the evidence we've gathered against you?"

"What evidence?"

"That you were assisting the Healers. George Galen made you an offer you couldn't refuse. It must have been quite a sum for a man of your talents."

"You said evidence, not baseless accusations."

"We took a Healer into custody," Irving said, his voice rising. "He's been quite a source of information. He told us how you murdered those two homeless men, how you burned them alive just because George Galen instructed you to. What had he called it, a test of your allegiance? And he told us where we could find the bodies, too. We brought them back to the morgue. I could take you to them now, but something tells me you wouldn't be too surprised by the sight of them, having set them ablaze yourself."

Frank was stunned. The Healers were laying it on thick, using Hal's and Nick's corpses to their advantage.

"You've made a mockery of this agency, Dr. Hartman. May God have mercy on your soul. Agent Atkins."

To Frank's right, Agent Atkins raised a pistol. Frank didn't move.

"Escort Dr. Hartman topside where Agent Carter will take him for further questioning."

Frank held up a hand up to Atkins. "Wait. Listen to me. Carter and Director Irving are working for the Healers."

"Agent Atkins," Irving said. "Remove this man from the premises, by extreme force if necessary."

Atkins advanced.

"Look at his hands," said Frank, pointing. "See how he's shaking? He's drugged. Galen has been manipulating him."

Atkins shot a glance at Irving. Other agents were looking, too.

"You're pulling at straws, Dr. Hartman," Irving said. "My medical condition doesn't make you innocent."

"He's working for Galen," said Frank. "Him and Carter both."

"Enough!" shouted Irving, a little more frantically than necessary. Some of the analysts near him started, then backed away from him cautiously. Irving straightened, trying to compose himself.

"Galen infected me with V16," said Frank, "along with five other people. He was trying to create genetic copies of himself by implanting his organs in us."

Irving's face reddened. "Agent Atkins, take this man into custody."

Atkins didn't move.

"The doctor who performed the surgeries, a cardiologist, is probably on the missing person's list. You don't believe me, check it out."

"Another one of your victims, no doubt," said Irving. "Agent Atkins, I will not ask you again. You will remove Dr. Hartman or shoot him should he show further resistance."

Frank looked at Atkins. "I can prove it. Dr. Owens is right outside and will confirm everything I've told you."

Irving turned white. "She's outside?"

"As well as three other people who will testify on my behalf, two of whom are also infected."

Irving ran to a phone and picked up the receiver. "Get me Carter."

"No," said Frank.

Atkins pointed the gun at Director Irving. "Wait. Put the phone down."

Irving stared. "Are you a fool?"

"You said *she*," said Atkins.

"What?"

"You said, 'She's outside.' You knew this doctor was a woman."

"He said it was a woman," offered Irving.

"No I didn't," said Frank.

"Put the phone down," said Atkins.

"I will do nothing of the sort. And you, sir, are guilty of insubordination." His attention turned to the phone. "Carter, it's Director Irving. I—hello?" He looked down at the base of the phone, where a young female analyst had her finger pressed on the button, cutting the line.

Atkins advanced slowly. "If this is a misunderstanding, then we'll resolve it without Agent Carter's assistance. And without yours."

"This is insane. What's the matter with you people?" He backed away from the desk. "You're going to believe a murderer, before you believe your own superior. I am a presidential appointee!"

He was floundering now, backing away from them toward his office. He bumped into an agent, turned, reached into the agent's suit coat, and pulled out a gun. Before the agent could respond, Irving had the barrel pointed at the man's head. "Stay back," he said.

Everyone froze. "Put the gun down," said Atkins.

"I told him not to involve you, Dr. Hartman," Irving said. "I knew you'd be trouble. But he wouldn't listen to me. And now you've gone and made a mess of everything."

"Put it down," repeated Atkins.

"You think I'm going to let you get the countervirus? You think I'm going to let you stop it?" He pointed the gun at Frank and fired. Bullets ricocheted off the wall behind Frank as he dove for cover behind a desk. Two more bullets splintered the edge of the desk, not far from Frank's head.

People screamed and dived for cover.

"Stop," said Atkins, running toward the back of the room.

Frank peeked over the desk and saw Atkins chasing Irving down the back corridor. Frank raced after them.

He caught up to Atkins at the door that led to the subway line. It was sealed tight.

"He went inside," said Atkins.

"Open it."

"I can't. Analysts don't have access to T4."

Frank pounded the door once with his fist. This couldn't be happening. Irving was headed to the subway line. And from there to T4, where the only vials of countervirus were kept. And unless Frank stopped him, he was certain Irving would try to destroy the vials. Now that his cover was blown, Irving had nothing to lose. He'd do whatever was necessary to keep Frank and the others from eradicating the virus and stopping the transformation.

"We have to open it," Frank said. He looked around him, desperate for a wedge to slide the doors open. He saw a fire hose coiled behind some glass on the wall. "Break the glass," he said.

"Why?"

"Because I can't. I might cut my suit. Just do it."

Atkins brought his elbow hard against the glass, shattering it. Frank reached in, took the long nozzle, and quickly unscrewed it. Then he held the nozzle like a hammer and hit the space where the two sliding doors met. The clang echoed through the chamber but made only a small dent in the surface.

"You're wasting your time," said Atkins.

But Frank continued pounding, hitting the same spot with explosive force over and over again, gradually increasing the dent until the metal was pressed in far enough that Frank could wedge his fingers inside.

"You'll never get it open that way," said Atkins.

Frank strained and the doors parted a few inches.

Atkins looked stunned. "How'd you do that?"

Frank pulled again. Gears creaked as he slid the door a foot wide. Then he squeezed himself through just as the subway car was pulling out of the station. He jumped over the subway attendant, now lying facedown on the platform, and ran toward the car as it pulled away.

Frank put on a burst of speed. The car was only a few feet away but quickly getting faster. Just before it disappeared into the tunnel and just before Frank ran full speed into the concrete wall that marked the end of the platform, he launched himself into the air, arms fully extended, reaching for the ladder rungs on the back of the car.

He caught one and swung painfully down against the rear of the car, his dangling feet only inches from the track below. The force of his landing rocked the subway car.

A shot rang out, and a bullet ripped a hole through the metal a foot to Frank's right. He pulled himself up to the rung above him and kicked his feet until they found purchase.

Just as he was reaching for the third rung, the car banked hard to the left. Frank felt himself swinging away from the ladder and slamming back against the car, holding on with one hand and kicking desperately to right himself again.

Another shot and another hole, this one dead center on

the ladder, precisely where he had clung to the ladder only a second before.

The track became straight again, and Frank swung back into the rungs. He quickly got his footing and scurried up the ladder to the top of the car. The tunnel walls and ceiling whipped past, and Frank felt the wind push at him fiercely as the car picked up speed.

He lay on his stomach and clung to the small rivets on the car's exterior, hoping Irving hadn't heard him.

He apparently had.

Glass shattered as Irving smashed out the subway car window. Then Irving's head emerged from it. He turned and looked up onto the roof. He saw Frank and raised the pistol just as Frank kicked out with his leg, catching Irving's arm and sending it swinging back in an arc against the tunnel wall. There was a brief flash of sparks as the gun scraped the wall and was torn from Irving's grip. Irving cried out and pulled a bloody hand from the wall as the gun bounced and disappeared onto the track behind them.

Irving looked at Frank, his face trembling and twisted with anger, then disappeared inside.

But only for a moment. When he reappeared, he was no longer wearing his suit coat. And as he climbed out of the window and crawled up to the roof, Frank could see why. Irving had wrapped the coat repeatedly around his hand, not to make a bandage but a glove. Gripped in that hand was a foot-long shard of glass from the shattered window.

"You could've been the master, Frank. You could've done great things. But you went off and made a mess of it, made a mess of everything. Stone was right. You are no longer worthy."

Frank kicked out to disarm him, but Irving was waiting for it. He dodged and lashed out with the glass, slicing through the biosuit and cutting Frank's leg.

Frank winced. The cut wasn't deep, but the look in Irving's eyes told him it was just a taste of things to come.

Frank clawed his way forward, pulling himself against the wind, trying to put some distance between them.

Suddenly the car shot forward, increasing its speed.

Irving flattened himself against the roof and grabbed hold as the wind pushed harder against them. Then, once steadied, Irving pushed off with his feet and forced himself slowly forward despite the gale, coming for Frank.

Frank clung to the rooftop, unable to move any farther. The wind was too strong now. It was all he could do to keep from sliding backward. He turned his head just enough to look behind him. Irving was in his airflow and therefore still crawling forward.

In a second he'll be on me, he thought.

He turned his head back to the front and saw the bend in the tunnel just before the car banked hard again to the left. The force of it ripped his hands from their holds, and he felt himself sliding off the roof.

He caught the bar on the edge of the roof just as his body tumbled over the side. Now he was hanging, the track racing below him, the tunnel wall only inches behind him. He looked back as Irving tumbled off the roof as well, catching the bar and nearly falling away from the car.

They hung side by side, Irving within striking distance. Before Frank could stop him, Irving lashed out with the glass and sliced Frank across the arm.

Frank cried out. Blood poured from the wound, spilling out of the biosuit.

A glint of victory twinkled in Irving's eye. He reared back the knife again, but Frank was faster. He swung his body hard to the side and rammed Irving with his shoulder. Irving's head snapped back from the blow, and when he looked up again his face was covered in blood. But not his own blood. Frank's blood. Blood from the cut on his arm.

The virus attacked instantly, boring into and searing Irving's skin. He screamed, dropped the glass, and wiped at his face furiously with his free hand. But it did little good. In a second, the virus was spreading down his hand and across his face.

He looked up at Frank, his face blotchy and black. "I have failed the master."

And let go.

Frank watched as Irving's body dropped into the darkness and disappeared from sight. Dead. Or as good as dead. If the fall at this speed didn't kill him, the virus shortly would. Frank felt sick. He had never intended to kill. He only wanted to be whole again. But Irving wouldn't allow it. Frank was a threat to the master's plan. Master. The master of what? Deceit? Manipulation? Selfishness? I didn't kill Irving, Frank realized. Eugene Irving died the moment he lost his will to George Galen. Galen was the killer, the master of death, even after he was dead himself. And Frank could easily turn into Galen at any time.

Fatigued and aching, Frank pulled himself back up to the roof and lay flat. In moments the car began to slow. When it came to a stop on the platform, an armed agent in a biosuit was waiting. "Don't shoot," Frank said.

"It's me. Hernandez. Atkins called ahead. He explained everything."

Frank slid off the roof and onto the platform. "Let me see your hands," he said.

"My hands?"

"Hold them out."

She did. Her gloved hands were calm and steady. "You going to read my palm or something?" she asked.

She wasn't part of it. "Why didn't you stop the car?" he asked.

"I tried. Irving must have overridden the system on the other end. You okay? You're bleeding."

"It'll heal itself. Just keep your distance." He pulled a bandage from the first-aid kit at his hip and began wrapping his arm, covering the blood and containing the virus.

She looked in the car. "Where's Irving?"

"About a half mile back. You have a key to that door?"

She led him to the entry and swiped her card key. The retinal scan confirmed her identity, then the door opened. Two agents lay on the floor in the corridor ahead of them, darts protruding from their backs. Frank and Hernandez ran to them.

"What happened in here?" he said.

"I don't know. I've been on the platform all morning. Before that it was peace and quiet. Are they—?"

Frank found a pulse. "No, sedated. These are Healer darts. You didn't hear anything?"

"The doors are too thick."

"Who else has come through here?"

"No one. Not down the subway line. Not since Carter left."

He took one of the agent's sidearms. "Call Atkins. Have him look for a white pickup truck at Westwood Park. Tell him the site is hot and requires maximum containment. There are people inside who need immediate attention."

"I think Atkins has his hands full engaging Carter, but I'll tell him. What are you going to do?"

"Retrieve samples of the countervirus."

"From the infirmary? Not alone, you're not. I'm coming with you. I'll radio Atkins on the way." She put in the call and led Frank through the labyrinth that was T4. He was grateful to have her. They passed more sedated agents along the way, all lying helplessly at their desks or on the floor in the corridors. There were no signs of resistance; the attack appeared to have happened all at once and caught everyone unawares.

They rounded a corner close to the infirmary and stopped in their tracks.

"Did you hear that?" she said.

"Sounded like a child screaming."

They listened and heard it again. Definitely a child. A little girl.

"Come on," she said.

They burst into the locker room, guns at the ready. On the

far side of the room were the doors to Level 4, now wide open. Cautiously Frank and Hernandez approached them. It was silent inside. They went through another series of doors and into the infirmary. The doors to the patient rooms were open as well.

"This one's empty," Hernandez said, checking a room.

"This one, too. How many people were still in here?"

"Seven or eight."

Frank ran down the line. Every room was unoccupied, and the tousled bedsheets and scattered personal items suggested that they had left in a hurry. He ran to the nurses' station, grabbed a syringe, then ran to the spot where he had left the metal trunk.

The trunk was gone. No countervirus.

In the distance, a child screamed.

Frank stuffed the syringe into a pouch on his hip as he and Hernandez rushed out of the infirmary and toward the elevator, where the sound had originated. As they rounded the corner they saw Stone carrying the trunk of countervirus into the elevator. Lichen was behind them, carrying the young Turner girl, Kimberly, who was crying and looking distraught. Several more frightened patients were waiting inside the elevator.

"Stop!" Frank said.

Stone saw them, turned with his dart gun, and fired. Frank pushed Hernandez away and took cover as a hail of darts dotted the wall where they'd been standing.

"We can't let them get away," she said.

"We can't risk hitting the patients."

The elevator doors closed. Frank and Hernandez sprang to their feet and ran to the elevator.

"Can you stop it?" he said, pushing the elevator call button.

"No. But here." She pointed to a ventilation grill on the wall. With a single kick, she knocked the grill inward, exposing a wide air shaft. "The chimney," she said. "It circulates the air up to the surface. Without it, we'd all suffocate."

She climbed into the hole.

Frank followed her inside and looked up. Sunlight shone into the shaft from the open grate at least sixty feet above them. Huge fan blades spun above the grate, sucking out the stale air. A line of ladder rungs in the wall of the shaft began where they stood and ascended to the surface. Hernandez grabbed and began climbing. "Come on."

Frank sighed. More heights and narrow spaces. He holstered his weapon and climbed after her.

Halfway up, they heard the helicopter engine start and the blades begin to spin. "Hurry," she said. But Frank was already moving as fast as he was able, constantly convincing himself not to look down. The engine roared to full power before they reached the top. And when Frank finally pulled himself up and onto the helipad, the helicopter was well out of range and banking south toward LA.

Hernandez crawled back into the chimney. "Come on. If we hurry, we can track it."

Frank didn't move, couldn't move. His only hope of beating Galen, the only hope for Dolores and Byron, was now a disappearing speck on the horizon. Why had they taken it? To keep it from me? And why take the patients?

"Frank," Hernandez called out. He turned to her wearily. "Are you going to stand there? Or are you going to help me catch a helicopter?"

He didn't answer but instead took the syringe from the pouch at his hip—a syringe that should have been holding countervirus—and felt despair.

And then it happened.

A volt of electricity shot through him, so powerful and so relentless that he could do nothing except drop to his knees and scream. Every muscle in his body constricted as images flashed through his mind at blinding speed, faces he had never seen but now recognized, places he had never visited but now knew well, events he had never experienced but that now felt familiar to him.

He is taking my mind. He is taking the last bit of me.

Forcing himself to move despite the current surging through him, Frank uncapped the syringe, reached behind his neck until he found the small surgical scar, then rammed the needle into it. The added pain was like another bolt of electricity. Frank's back arched. His scream intensified. But still he pressed down, forcing the needle deeper into his flesh.

Suddenly the needle tip struck something hard and pierced it. And all at once, the electricity stopped.

Frank collapsed forward onto the helipad, and in an instant Hernandez was beside him, pulling the needle out and rolling him over.

"Frank?"

He wasn't dead. "Yeah, it's me."

She looked at the needle. "Are you out of your mind?"

"Not completely."

She helped him up.

"Don't bother tracking the helicopter," he said. "I know exactly where it's going."

32

DISPERSION

Agent Atkins stayed crouched behind the Audi as a hail of bullets shattered what was left of the windshield. Glass shards rained down around him. He couldn't stay here. Carter was better trained, a better shot, and clearly not intimidated by Atkins's little band of analysts who had come out to apprehend him. Each of the analysts had taken cover behind various cars and were now as pinned down and helpless as Atkins was.

He looked to his right. An agent in a biocontainment suit lay face-down on the asphalt, not moving. Carter had shot him. Put the gun to his back and shot him—had shot every armed agent out here. And did so so quickly that Atkins hadn't even fired his weapon. Once Carter knew he was compromised, all hell broke loose.

An analyst two cars over poked his gun around the bumper and fired off two rounds. Brave soul. Little good it did, except give Carter another target to shoot at. Headlights exploded and tires popped as Carter laid down machine-gun fire into the car.

The voice of one of the analysts sounded in Atkins's earpiece. "We need backup, some armor."

"We need to find that truck," said Atkins. "Hernandez said a white pickup."

"We won't find anything if we're dead."

Point taken. Atkins got on the radio and called for backup again. He wished Agent Riggs were here, he and his assualt team. They would know how to handle this. They could take Carter. But Director Irving had sent all of them off on some mission this morning—probably to get them away from the building and allow him and Carter to run things unhindered. It was all a scheme. That was glaringly obvious now.

Another volley of bullets sank into the Audi, and Atkins pulled himself up into a tight ball as glass and shrapnel rained all around him.

Where the hell was backup?

The sound of an approaching helicopter was music to Atkins's ears. About time. He crawled along the car until he could see the helicopter coming in from the north. It was the BHA's, flying low. But who was flying it? Hernandez?

It flew overhead and began a rapid descent toward Carter. The door slid open, and Atkins saw the billowing black cape of a Healer. Atkins raised his weapon and fired, but Carter was already climbing inside. Atkins ran out from behind the car and sank two shots into the back of the helicopter, but it was too late. It was already ascending again. When it reached a safe height, it thrust forward and accelerated toward the south.

Monica and Wyatt were squeezed against the floorboard as far as they could go. Byron sat huddled by the passenger door, and Dolores lay sleeping across the seat. The gunfire had been deafening. And close. Monica couldn't see through the vines that covered the fence to the Federal Building, but the shots were clearly coming from that direction. How Dolores had slept through it was mystifying.

"I hear a helicopter," said Byron.

Monica heard it, too, then saw it, over the fence. It descended quickly into the Federal Building parking lot and momentarily disappeared from sight. Then, as quickly as it went down, the helicopter was up again. There was brief gunfire and then quiet.

"I think it's over," said Byron.

They waited, and the silence continued.

"What should we do?" he said.

"Frank told us to stay here."

"And if something happened to Frank and he's not coming back? Or if they're looking for us? Are we going to sit here and wait for them?"

"I'm scared," said Wyatt.

She held him closer. "I know, sweetheart. Me too."

Dolores's whole body stiffened. Her eyes shot open. And she screamed.

The others covered their ears as the piercing, anguished cry reverberated inside the truck's cab.

Monica threw her arm around Wyatt to protect him, and then the screaming stopped and Dolores passed out.

Byron discovered he had been screaming as well only when Dolores stopped. He silenced himself, put a hand over his heart, and tried to slow his breathing.

Monica's heart was racing. Every nerve in her body was on alert. Wyatt continued to bury his face into her stomach.

Dolores stirred, batting her eyes open.

"She waking up," said Byron.

Dolores jerked awake suddenly, startling everyone. She sat up and rubbed her eyes, looking confused.

"Dolores?" said Monica.

Dolores put her hand to her head, still drowsy, and looked at herself in the rearview mirror. "What happened?"

"You fell asleep. Then you started screaming."

"Screaming?" She looked at Monica with a blank expression. "Sorry. Sometimes I get nightmares. I didn't mean to scare you."

"It's all right. You're safe now."

"Where are we?"

"Behind the Federal Building. Frank went to get help."

"He hasn't come back yet?"

Monica shook her head.

"We can't stay here. They might find us." She reached for the wheel.

Monica stopped her. "You're in no condition to drive. And Frank told us to stay put."

"It's been almost an hour," said Byron. "There was a lot of gunfire. What if. . . . How long are we going to wait?"

Monica glanced at Wyatt and saw that he was twisting his right forefinger nervously. "And where would we go?" she said. "Who could help us?"

Byron didn't answer. There was no answer.

A BHA van bounced into the parking lot from Sepulveda. It idled for a few paces, then—as if searching for the truck and suddenly spotting it—turned on its siren and shot toward them.

"They found us," Dolores said in a panic. "We got to get out of here." She reached for the steering wheel. Monica didn't know whether to stop her or to help her. It didn't matter. Neither would have made much difference. The van skidded to a halt near them, and four agents in biosuits got out and surrounded the truck. They didn't draw their weapons, but their hands were on them, ready to do so if needed.

"Dr. Owens?" one of them said.

Monica felt panicked. How to respond? She nodded.

"I'm Agent Atkins, a friend of Dr. Frank Hartman. I'm here to help."

"Don't believe them," said Dolores.

"Unlock the door and come out of the truck," he said.

"Don't do it," said Dolores. "It's a trick."

Monica reached for the door lock.

"Mom."

"It's okay, sweetheart. It's going to be fine." She unlocked and opened the door. Agent Atkins offered a hand

and helped her down. Then he reached in and lifted Wyatt out. Monica knew then. They were sincere. They were here to help. She took Wyatt in her arms and cried.

On the other side of the truck, another agent helped Byron out. Byron thanked him profusely and even patted the man on the back. The agent then offered a hand up to Dolores. She reached out a hand to accept it, but instead grabbed the man's wrist, spun him around and kicked him in the back, sending him to the asphalt.

"Dolores!" screamed Monica.

Agents rushed over to subdue Dolores, but she climbed back in the truck and closed the doors before they reached her. The engine revved to life, and Dolores threw it into reverse, causing a few agents to jump out of the way to avoid being hit. Dolores rammed the gearshift into drive and hit the gas, charging straight at Monica. Monica froze, unable to move. Agent Atkins dove to the side, and at the last second, Dolores swerved, pulling right up next to Monica instead of running over her. She rolled down the window long enough to say, "Your work is appreciated, Doctor. I never got a chance to thank you . . . then again, maybe another one of me already did."

Agents rushed over, but Dolores was already peeling away. She shot out of the parking lot, narrowly avoiding an accident on Sepulveda, and sped away out of sight.

B   n ran to Monica. "Are you all right?"

She looked at him with a dazed expression, then nodded. For those few moments in the truck, she hadn't been talking to Dolores; she'd been talking to Galen. She looked at Wyatt. "Are you hurt?"

He shook his head.

Agent Atkins got to his feet. "There's a reason I'm not a field agent. Everybody okay?"

Another siren sounded, then several BHA vans raced into the parking lot. Before the lead van had stopped, Frank jumped out and ran to Monica.

Relief washed over her. He was alive. She had imagined

a hundred different things happening to him, but he was alive.

He reached her, his face taught, a look of concern.

"I'm all right," she said. "Wyatt and Byron are fine. But Dolores, she . . . she took the truck. She . . . transformed."

He nodded. He understood.

Agents hurried out of the vehicles and urged the gathering bystanders to get back while they contained the area.

"You have the countervirus?" she asked.

He sighed. "There's no time to explain. Stay with Wyatt."

"Why? Where are you going?"

"To end this." He turned to Byron. "You're with me. The moment we have the countervirus, you need to be on hand to receive it."

"You're hurt," she said, noticing the red bandage on his arm.

"I heal fast, remember?"

She didn't laugh.

He took both of her arms, and she looked into his eyes. She could see that he wanted to say something to her—to reassure her, maybe, calm her, perhaps. Or was it something else? A part of her wanted it to be. A part of her wanted to hear him talk about anything other than this, something normal, even something they had talked about already. But he said nothing. He merely smiled weakly and climbed into the van.

"Don't go," said Wyatt.

"I need you to take care of your mom. Can you do that?"

Wyatt took his mother's hand and nodded. An agent helped Byron into the rear of the van, and the doors closed. She stood there and watched it turn out of the park.

"Dr. Owens?"

She turned around to face an agent. "Yes?"

"Ma'am, I need you and your son to put these bags on until we can get you inside to decon."

She wiped her eyes and took the bags. "Of course. Thank you." She looked back toward Sepulveda, but Frank's van was already gone.

"Let me get this straight. You have some of Galen's memories," said Byron, "but not all of them?" He was bouncing in the back of the van, wiggling into a biosuit.

"I broke the circuit before everything was hardwired," said Frank.

"Then do the same to me. Now. Break it so the change can't happen."

"And risk missing the chip? This is your brain stem we're talking about. I did it to myself because I had no other choice. It could have killed me or left me brain-dead. I'd rather not risk doing that to you. If we can get the countervirus inside you first, the reaction won't occur."

"But what if we don't get the countervirus in time? I'd rather be dead than him."

"That's why Agent Hernandez here is preparing an EMP collar. The moment you feel a jolt of abnormal energy levels on your body, it will hit you with an electromagnetic pulse, which we hope will short-circuit the chip and stop it."

"Can't you just do it now and get it over with?"

"There's also the possibility that the EMP will stop your heart. So, no, the countervirus is our best option. The collar is a contingency plan."

Hernandez held up a crude-looking collar with a small device attached to the back. She fastened it around Byron's neck and flipped the switch. "Try not to generate too much static electricity or you might set it off inadvertently. And don't plug anything into electrical sockets or get too close to power lines."

"I'll keep that in mind," he said a little uneasily.

"And don't rub your hands together quickly or take clothes out of the dryer," said Frank.

"I'm glad you find this amusing," said Byron.

Frank helped him secure his helmet and got his air flowing. Then he hit his comlink. "You look a little too comfortable in that biosuit, Byron. Career change, perhaps?"

"And have people shoot at me every day? No thanks. I'll take a boring desk job and die of natural causes."

The driver called back from the front. "Approaching the airfield, sir."

"We're getting on an airplane?" asked Byron.

"No, we're stopping people from getting on airplanes. Galen planned an exodus. He was making copies of himself to form what he called the Council of Prophets. Each of the five members of the Council was supposed to lead a group of Healers to a densely populated city; Paris, London, Tokyo, São Paulo, and Beijing were the first wave."

"To do what?"

"Continue healings, spread the virus, generate recruits. Each group was to consist of ten Healers, so you can imagine how quickly the virus would spread."

"That's fifty Healers. Please tell me there aren't that many where we're going."

"There will be at noon today, once the recruits arrive."

"Recruits?"

"Galen wasn't healing people out of the goodness of his heart, Byron. He was building an army. Every person healed in Southern California thought they were being given a free cure, but they weren't. It came with a heavy price: enlistment."

"He's forcing all of his former patients to become Healers?"

"None of them know this, of course. They think they're gathering for a routine medical checkup. When they hear they've been drafted, I daresay they'll be surprised."

They turned west onto a poorly paved road leading into an abandoned airfield. Most of the land had been stripped, including the runway; all that remained now was a hangar, a large airplane-assembly building, and a smattering of smaller, single-story structures in various stages of disrepair.

"This is the old Hughes Airport," said Byron. "No one can get a plane out of here. They tore up the runway years ago."

"Galen never planned on flying from here," said Frank. "They're flying out of LAX, a mile north of here. Hughes is a meeting place—not only because it's inconspicuous and conveniently close to the airport, but also because Galen needed a building large enough to hide two stolen city buses."

Byron raised an eyebrow.

"Once all the recruits are gathered, they'll be drugged, given boarding passes, loaded onto the buses, and taken to LAX—seen by all but noticed by no one, just folks taking the bus to the airport. Then they'll board planes to any one of the five cities."

"But why are Healers going through with this? There is no Council of Prophets. It failed."

"Not completely. There's currently one member."

"You mean Dolores? You think she's coming here?"

"If she's Galen, she'll play it as planned. She'll be here." He looked out the windshield and spoke to the driver. "Park behind that building there, and stay out of sight of the hangar."

They parked and got out. Frank had them hide behind a few old storage crates while he looked at the hangar through binoculars. The white pickup was parked out front.

"Dolores is inside," he said. "We can safely assume Carter and the others are as well. Now we wait for the recruits."

"And you're sure all of them are coming?" said Byron.

"We're counting on it," said Hernandez. "This may be our only chance to identify everyone Galen's treated."

"He left specific instructions that no one be left behind," said Frank. "It's why the patients were taken from the infirmary. Everybody goes. Trust me, they'll be here."

"So this is it?" said Byron. "Two little vans of BHA agents against the entire Healer army? No offense, but that's a little David-and-Goliath, don't you think?"

"We're going into a hot zone," said Hernandez. "A place loaded with virus. You can't just send in the cavalry. We have to contain the place first."

"You say that as if you were throwing a sheet over a table. These are Healers. I've seen what they can do to people. They don't give up easily."

"Not all of the Healers have been genetically altered," said Frank. "Those who haven't will be of little concern."

"Yeah, and those who have will be a very big concern."

"What're you worried about?" said Hernandez. "We've got Frank." She winked at Frank, and they both smiled. Byron failed to see the humor.

Frank lifted the binoculars and watched the road by which they had entered. After a few minutes, a car pulled in. "I think our first recruit is arriving," he said.

The sedan drove onto the airfield, approached the hangar, and parked. A woman in conservative business attire got out. A side door to the hangar opened, and Stone ushered her in. Soon, another car came. Then another. And finally a congestion of cars entered the airfield and headed toward the hangar. Two Healers went outside to direct the traffic. Stone stayed at the hangar door, checking names off a list as they entered.

"Where's this cavalry you mentioned?" said Byron. "When do you call for backup?"

"If we put in the call now," said Frank, "this place will be flooded with sirens; Healers will know we're on to them. Then we'll have a hostage situation. For our plan to work, we wait."

"I don't suppose I should know what this plan is?"

"Don't worry. Your job is to stay here out of sight. As soon as we get the countervirus, we'll come back with it." He turned to Hernandez. "Remember, Galen planned to store the samples of virus and his countervirus in two separate duffel bags. They also have the trunk of *my* countervirus. We don't call until we've secured it all."

She nodded.

"Shouldn't we at least call the airlines?" said Byron. "Warn them ahead of time?"

"The FAA is alerted," said Frank. "But hopefully they won't have to become involved. The plan is to stop the Healers here. No one reaches the airport."

Soon the traffic slowed, and finally the last car parked. Stone checked the name off the list and waved for the Healers who'd been directing traffic to come inside.

"That's everyone," said Frank, handing the binoculars to Hernandez. "Wish me luck."

"Wait, you're going by yourself?" said Byron. "That's the plan?"

Frank answered with a wink, then got up and walked alone toward the hangar.

Lichen tried to hide his disappointment. Of all the vessels to become the prophet, Dolores was the one who made him feel the most uneasy, and not because she was a woman, though that was a big part of it. It just didn't feel right. Galen had always been a father figure, and now to have him suddenly be a mother figure who acted like a father figure felt more weird than Lichen cared to admit.

"You're staring again, Lichen," said Dolores. She was looking at one of the buses parked inside the hangar and had seen Lichen's reflection on its surface as he stood behind her.

"Forgive me, sir. I am merely overcome with gratitude that you have returned."

She laughed. "No, you're not. You're wondering why I'm a woman."

Lichen said nothing.

She turned and faced him. "All is well, Lichen. Have faith. I can see now that this was the best course of action.

I have no regrets. My eyes have been opened, in fact. Until now, I only understood half the members of our species. Now I get the whole picture. Women are fascinating."

Carter approached. "They're ready for you, sir."

"Thank you, Carter." She patted Lichen's arm. "Faith, Lichen."

Lichen didn't shudder at the touch, but he wanted to. There was no doubt she was the prophet—he had checked the blood himself. The question was whether or not she *should* be the prophet.

He followed her to the open space where all the recruits were waiting. It was a big crowd, and all were accounted for, even those who had been inside the BHA infirmary. It hadn't been an easy task extracting them, and Lichen felt a measure of pride in knowing he had done something right for a change. He spotted the little black girl toward the front and smiled at her. She saw him, but didn't smile back.

As instructed, each of the recruits stood on one of the circles painted on the floor, which arranged them into rows. They were an army in formation, even if they didn't know it yet.

"I am George Galen," Dolores said loud enough for all to hear. "I know I may not look like a George, but we are not always what we seem, are we? Consider yourselves. Until recently, each of you seemed a lost cause. Your doctors had written you off; many of your families had given up hope. Friends all looked at you with pity. But to me you seemed different; to me you always seemed full of life. I looked at you and saw years yet to be lived, memories yet to be made. And so my associates and I have given you a second chance at life and put an end to the suffering which so unfairly beset you." She smiled. "It makes me happy to see you all so healthy now. Your bodies so strong and able to do so much. I want to wish each one of you well." She went to the first person in line and kissed him on the forehead. Then she went to the next and kissed him, and so on down the line.

Lichen noticed how some of the people exchanged glances. This wasn't what they had expected. But once she kissed them, their faces relaxed.

When Dolores finished giving a kiss to them all, she walked back to the front. "Now I ask something of *you*," she said. "*The Book of Becoming* teaches us that when our lives have been lifted, it behooves us to lift others. You will continue this effort, multiply it, carry it forth, help those of our brothers and sisters who are without hope in the world. What I ask of you is a sacrifice, to leave your lives and move to a greater calling. Is there a one among you who objects?" No one made a sound. "Good. Now, hop on one foot." Everyone did. Dolores giggled.

Lichen felt annoyed. To make light of their sacrifice seemed inappropriate. Was this Galen? Or the remnant of the women Dolores?

"Touch your nose," she said. Everyone did. Some of them continued hopping on one foot as well.

"Okay, Simon says stop." They stopped, and she laughed again.

There was a sound of commotion at the door, and Lichen looked to see a Healer roughly escorting Frank inside. Dolores stopped laughing. Everyone stared.

Frank snapped off his helmet. "Wonderful. We're all here."

Carter rushed over and grabbed him threateningly.

"Come now, Carter, is this the respect you give me now?"

"You deserve none," said Carter.

"I am here for the Council. Am I not welcome?"

Carter released him. "Council?"

Frank pulled down his collar, exposing his neck. "Lichen, prove to this unbeliever that I am who I say I am."

Lichen looked at Carter, hesitated, then came over with

the box and placed it against Frank's neck. He took a blood sample, and the box beeped. Everyone waited while Lichen looked at the reading. "It's a match," he said.

Carter took the box from him. "I don't believe it."

"Let me see that," said Dolores.

Carter gave it to her. She looked at it, then lifted her eyes to Frank, studying him. "He's tricking us somehow. That's just like him."

Frank smiled. "Are you saying that because, like Hal and Nick, you believe there can be only one prophet, or is this simply cautious skepticism?"

"It's a trick," said Dolores.

Frank sighed. "I'd rather not waste time squabbling. We have too much work to do. You want proof that I'm Galen? Fine, ask me anything. Ask me something only Galen would know."

"What gift did you give me?" said Lichen, surprising everyone for speaking out of turn. He couldn't help it. The prospect of a man, a sane man, being Galen was too exciting.

Frank made a face. "Lichen, even Frank knew that. Your gift is speed, among others. Maybe it would be more convincing if I told you which underpass I found you at three years ago, skinny, homeless, half starved, with only a ragged blanket to warm yourself."

Lichen's eyes widen. No one but Galen knew that.

"You want more proof?" said Frank. "Behind that building to the east are two vans of BHA agents watching this hangar."

Several Healers became alarmed. Carter looked out the window.

"I've convinced them that I'm still Frank," he went on. "When the chip switched on, Frank tried stopping it by ramming a needle into the back of my neck, but fortunately he hit it an instant too late. I had already become who I am." He laughed to himself. "What's funny is that the

BHA believe that Frank was successful and that I'm still Frank with some of Galen's memories. It was so easy to convince them. They simply took me at my word."

Lichen was beaming.

"If that's true," said Carter, "then why did you bring them here? Why give away our location? Why threaten the dispersion?"

"Because it was the only way for *me* to get here. Had they known who I was, they would have stopped me. Plus, I had to get Byron here. He hasn't transitioned yet. With Hal and Nick gone, we can't risk losing another Council member. Three will have to suffice."

"Byron is here?" said Carter.

"Am I talking to myself? Yes, Byron is among them. He thinks he's along because the countervirus is close. Incidentally, we have it, don't we?"

"Yes, sir," Lichen said, pointing to the trunk. "The version Galen . . . I mean, *you* created. And the version Dr. Hartman created in that trunk over there."

"Wonderful," said Frank.

"Wait," said Carter, still looking skeptical. "How do we know there aren't a thousand federal agents out there, waiting for us to leave the hangar?"

Frank rolled his eyes. "Must you always be so melodramatic, Carter? There are two vans. Two. I wouldn't allow them to call for backup. I made the excuse that it would have alarmed you. If you want proof, send Stone over there—quietly, I'd advise—and apprehend them. We need Byron anyway. The rest of us will wait here. If I'm lying and they're not back in a few minutes, you can shoot me."

Carter considered this.

"Do it," said Dolores.

"But I'd recommend you take their weapons and bind their hands," said Frank, "not tranquilize them."

"Why not?" said Carter.

"Because we'll need to cover our tracks once we've dispersed, and unless we make them subservient, they'll alert the authorities to our intentions. If that happens, we'll have federal agents boarding our planes in London or Tokyo or wherever the moment we land." He pointed to the crowd of people still standing inside their individual little circles. "These will prove to be effective companions. Why not add to their numbers? The more the merrier. And look at Carter. He's proven to be a most effective tool. These BHA agents could prove equally helpful."

Carter and Dolores exchanged glances.

"Or if you think that a bad idea," said Frank, "or are still convinced that I'm trying to hoodwink you somehow, then by all means sedate them. But *you'll* have to deal with the bodies, not me. I'm not in the mood. But under no circumstances should you sedate Byron. We'll need him the moment he's reborn. I'm not waiting for a sedative to wear off. We all have planes to catch."

Dolores snapped her fingers at Stone. "No tranqs," she said. "Bind them if you must, but leave them awake."

"I would go out the back if I were you," said Frank, "and go in a wide circle and approach them from the rear. They're watching the front. If they see you coming, they'll call for backup. Total surprise is the only assurance we have that they won't alert others."

"And how do we know you haven't already alerted others?" said Carter.

Frank sighed. "You *are* a worrier, aren't you? Ask yourself, Carter, if I had alerted the authorities and was planning a massive siege on this compound, would I bother to come in here now? No, I'd come with the siege. Well, actually, I'd probably wait until after the siege and come when the smoke cleared." He smiled. "I did pretend to alert the airlines, though. That was fun. I acted as if I was calling the FAA, but of course I was actually calling information and checking the weather. Expect sunshine, by the way." He laughed. Lichen joined in.

Ten minutes later the Healers returned with the vans. Lichen opened the hangar door wide enough for them to drive in. The van doors opened, and then Stone pushed the agents out. There were six agents total, including Hernandez, and Byron, all with their hands tied behind their backs.

"See?" said Frank. "Delivered as promised."

"You lied to us!" said Hernandez. She charged, but a Healer stopped her.

"Don't be angry with me, Agent Hernandez," said Frank. "It was you who was naïve enough to believe me." He looked at Carter. "And if you're still not convinced that I am who I say I am, remove Byron's helmet. You'll find an EMP charge around his neck intended to disrupt the chip, should it initiate."

"Take off his helmet," said Dolores.

The Healer unsnapped Byron's helmet and removed the collar.

"You crooked little bastard," said Byron.

Frank frowned. "Such language, Byron. I hope that when you are me, you'll show a little more decorum." He went to Hernandez, spun her around, and checked the cords that bound her hands. "Did you secure these tightly? I don't want them wiggling their hands free."

"Yes, sir," said the Healer.

"Good. Put them in the corner there and watch them closely." He turned to Carter. "There you have it, Mr. Paranoid. Are we going to waste any more time questioning my allegiance or shall we proceed with the dispersion?"

Carter bowed his head. "My apologies."

Frank clapped his hands and rubbed them together. "All right, let's do inventory. What have I missed? Do we have the boarding passes?"

"Yes, sir," said Stone, getting the box of them.

"Wonderful. What about the virus and countervirus? I want to see both of those duffel bags with my own beady eyes."

"Here, sir," Lichen said, bringing the duffel bags over. Frank unzipped them and saw that they were full of vials of V16 and the Healer-manufactured countervirus. "Excellent. Please be careful with these. Now, show me the trunk."

Lichen unlatched the trunk's fasteners and lifted the lid. The red vials of countervirus Frank had created were lined neatly in rows inside the black foam.

"All safe and snug," said Lichen.

"Marvelous. Thank you."

"You're a dirty coward!" said Hernandez. "You know that? A dirty stinking coward!"

Frank slammed down the lid to the countervirus trunk, stormed over to Hernandez, put a hand on her back and another on her helmet, and jerked her head back. "And you, good woman, forget that I have the power to take your life, should I choose." He released her, and she kept quiet.

He stood erect and straightened his hair. "Now, where were we?"

"Inventory," said Lichen.

"Ah yes, inventory." He looked at Dolores. "Unless a member of the Council dissents, let us distribute the boarding passes."

"Agreed," said Dolores.

"Very well," said Frank. "Stone."

Stone took the boarding passes and went up and down the aisle giving them to the appropriate individuals. Frank went to inspect the buses. "Are we sure these will hold all the recruits?"

"Yes, sir," said Lichen. "We counted the seats. We'll pull into the terminal, leave them at their gates, then pull away."

"Easy as cheesy," said Frank.

Lichen smiled, recognizing the phrase. It was the prophet, no question. "Yes, sir. Easy as cheesy."

Byron heard Hernandez's voice in his ear. "Don't move," she said. "This is going to sting."

She was right. Byron felt the needle stick him in the

neck and then the cold fluid as it entered his bloodstream. As asked, he didn't flinch, nor did he take his eyes off the Healer ten paces away, his back to them.

Hernandez removed the needle.

"What was that?" he whispered.

"Put your helmet back on. Quietly. I'll put one on as well. We can speak freely that way."

Byron did as he was told. Once the helmet was in place, he heard Hernandez's voice loud and clear through his comlink.

"Congratulations," she said. "You've just been given a healthy dose of countervirus."

He looked at her. "How?"

"Keep your eyes to the front."

He turned back.

"Frank gave it to me," she said.

"How?"

"This is the plan, Byron. Sorry you weren't privy to it, but we didn't know how good an actor you were."

He felt the cords around his hands cut loose. "Keep your hands behind you," she said.

"Frank's acting?"

"We had to get a sample for you and we knew we weren't going to get it in a fight."

"He slipped it to you?"

"I called him a coward, which was enough of a distraction for him to grab a vial. Then he jerked my head back and dropped it into my hand. We practiced the move before we picked you up."

"How did you get your hands free?"

"He slipped me the knife when he checked my cords. Not a bad plan, really. I'm just amazed it worked."

"You almost gave yourself away with that 'dirty stinking coward' line."

"Too much?"

"I thought I was in a bad western. And the EMP charge?"

"An excuse to get your helmet off so I could give you the shot. The charge is actually a scrap computer part."

"Cute. Now what?"

"When I say 'move,' you get on that first bus there and hold tight. Now take your helmet back off before anyone notices."

Frank remained as casual as possible as he inspected the two buses. He surreptitiously glanced in Hernandez's direction, and she nodded discreetly, giving him the signal. It was done. She'd given Byron the countervirus. Frank felt his shoulders relax.

"They meet your approval?" said Lichen.

"The finest buses in Los Angeles," said Frank. "My only question: what will we do if someone is waiting at the bus stop?" Then he laughed so Lichen would know it was a joke, and Lichen laughed with him.

Stone approached. "The boarding passes are distributed, sir."

"Good. And the trunks?"

"On the buses and ready for transport."

"Excellent. Let's put the people on the buses, too. Byron's taking his time, and I don't want them standing forever. That is, if the good member of the Council agrees?"

"If I agree with what?" said Dolores, joining them.

"I suggest we put everyone on the bus. Why keep them standing? We'll move the moment Byron transitions."

"Very well." She turned to Lichen. "Load them onto the buses."

Lichen directed the crowd onto the buses.

When everyone was on board, Frank put an arm around Dolores. "Why don't you tell them to relax? They've got a long journey ahead of them, and some of them look a little nervous."

She agreed. She went on each bus and told them to relax. Many of the passengers fell asleep immediately.

When she was done, Frank praised her for her generosity.

"You're only complimenting yourself," she said with a smile.

He laughed. "So I am." He scratched his chin. "Now, we should discuss temporary alternates to take Hal's and Nick's places on the Council. Assuming all goes well with Byron, we'll have three. That leaves two vacancies. Let's gather the Healers and discuss it."

She agreed.

Frank made a megaphone with his hands. "Can I have everyone's attention please? Can we all gather over here please? Healers only, please." He led them to the other side of the hangar, as far from the buses as possible without it being obvious that this was his intent.

The only Healer who didn't come was the one guarding the agents. Frank positioned himself so that the Healers' backs were to the buses and their attention on him. "As you all know, we don't have a full Council." He put his hand to his forehead. It was the signal; he only hoped Hernandez had seen it. She apparently had. He saw her unsnap the aerosol sedative from her hip. Frank said, "I propose that we elect among ourselves two who can take the places of Nick and Hal on the Council."

Hernandez stealthily approached the Healer guarding them and sprayed him in the face. Four agents were there to catch him silently and drag him out of sight.

"This will be a temporary assignment, of course," said Frank, holding the Healers' attention. "We will make two more copies of George Galen as soon as possible. But we need a leader for each of the five groups until then."

The agents split up and silently got on the two buses. Hernandez got behind the wheel of one, and Byron positioned himself in the seat behind her. She looked out the window at the second bus. An agent was at the wheel, giving her a thumbs up.

Frank saw that the agents were ready, and addressed the

Healers. "I'd like to nominate Stone and Lichen as possible replacements. They've served me faithfully for a long time. Does anyone object to these nominations?"

The Healers seemed content with this suggestion, and no one more so than Lichen.

Frank held out his hand. "Stone, relinquish your weapon. As a Council member, weapons are below you."

Stone, the largest and strongest of all those gathered, slung the tranquilizer gun off his shoulder and handed it to Frank. Frank checked the cartridge and saw that it was full of darts, then shot five darts into Stone's gut.

Stunned and confused, the Healers gasped, recoiled. Stone stiffened, then the tranquilizers took him, and he fell unconscious to the floor. It was the final signal, and Hernandez must have seen it, because a second later, both buses roared to life. The Healers stumbled backward as Frank continued firing, taking down three more before the others realized the buses were escaping.

Byron was thrown forward as his bus slammed into the hangar door and ripped it off its track. Bus windows shattered. People screamed. The hangar door fell atop the buses, then slid off their roofs as the buses surged forward.

"Hold onto something," said Hernandez.

Byron steadied himself and grabbed the pole behind the driver's seat. He looked out the window just as a Healer jumped onto the side of the bus, smashing his hands through the windows to get a hold. Another Healer joined him, and the bus leaned to the side from their weight. Hernandez swerved with the wheel to compensate.

A third Healer exploded through the door of the bus, landing on the steps near the meter and showering Byron and the first few rows of passengers with broken glass. With one hand on the wheel, Hernandez drew her weapon and fired repeatedly into the Healer's chest, sending him back out the door and rolling away onto the dirt.

Passengers continued screaming as Hernandez shoved the weapon at Byron. "Make yourself useful."

He gripped it, stumbled down the steps, held the doorway with one hand, and leaned out of the vehicle.

The Healers hanging by the side of the bus saw the gun and dropped away.

With all the excess weight now gone, the bus rocked straight again, jerking Byron and nearly causing him to lose his footing. He gripped the doorway and steadied himself.

A chorus of sirens sounded ahead of them, and Byron looked in their direction. A row of law enforcement vehicles was speeding toward them—squad cars, unmarked cars, BHA vans, SWAT Humvees.

"There's your cavalry," said Hernandez.

"You called them already?" said Byron.

"We called them before we left. You think we would have tried this alone? They've been out of sight, waiting for us to remove the hostages and virus."

Using her comlink, she told the other driver to stop. The buses slowed, and agents in biosuits hustled out of the BHA vans and loaded the buses, confiscating the two trunks and calming the passengers.

Byron followed Hernandez out. She took an assault rifle from one of the agents and climbed into the back of a van.

"You're leaving?" he asked.

"We still have a man inside."

Byron climbed in beside her. "I'm coming with you."

"Not this time. Help calm those civilians."

She closed the door and the van sped away.

Frank continued firing into the crowd of Healers until the gun was empty. The plan had been to take out the most threatening Healer first. And that had worked flawlessly; Stone lay unconscious at his feet. And since no other Healer had been armed when Frank started firing, he had easily picked off several others. A few had run after the buses, and a few had run outside, trying to simply escape. They had no chance of getting away, Frank knew; the entire airfield should be surrounded by now. And this time the authorities knew what they were up against. If they had followed Frank's advice, they had come equipped.

Carter ran for cover behind a stack of discarded debris, and Frank put three tranqs in his back, knocking him out and sending him crashing to the floor unconscious.

Out of the corner of his eye, Frank saw Dolores duck into a side room. He hurried after her. He had to sedate her before an overly eager police officer took a shot at her or before, acting as Galen, she did something drastic in the face of defeat.

He ran through the doorway and entered a poorly lighted metal workshop where spare plane parts were once made or repaired. Several rusted lathes were positioned around the room, as well as other large iron machines for shaping and cutting metal. Everything was decades old. There was a flash of movement to Frank's right, then something hard and metallic struck him. He felt himself break in several places and then crash into some shelves along the opposite wall.

The shelves crumpled on impact, and heavy tools fell all around him.

He lay there a moment, trying to orient himself. His head throbbed. It hurt to breathe. He tried to get up but couldn't. The pain was too intense. He lifted his head and spat blood.

Dolores emerged from the shadows.

"I've tried to consider your point of view, Frank," she said. "I really have. I've racked my brain a hundred times, and I still can't get a handle on you BHA people. Do you have any idea how many hundreds of people we could have cured every day together as the Council? How many lives we could have bettered?"

She made a face. "Does it please you to know there are

sick children in this world? Is that it? Is that what you want? Are you some kind of sadist or something? You get a kick out of seeing people die slowly of fatal diseases? I'm changing the world, Frank. I'm empowering people. You may not agree with our religion, but you can't deny the fact that we're doing good. And now you've wasted it. You took something good and you destroyed it. You took the last hope for millions of people and flushed it down the toilet. I don't care what you think about me, Frank, but that makes *you* the bad guy."

Frank struggled to all fours.

"Science saves, Frank," said Dolores. "Always has. And yet, whenever that spark of discovery appears, civilization also poops out someone like you, someone who crashes the whole thing to hell, and people who didn't have to die, do." She put her hands on her hips. "Your daughter would be real proud of you right now, wouldn't she? Daddy just screwed the world."

"Stop talking like you're him," said Frank weakly.

"I *am* him!" said Dolores. "I am George Galen."

Frank pushed himself up to his knees. "No, you're not. You only think you are. Your real name is Dolores Arlington, and you're one of the bravest women I know."

"Dolores Arlington is dead."

"You don't look dead to me. Come on, Dolores, you think I just fell off the turnip truck? I know a living person when I see one. Trust me, you're nothing like George Galen. And a good thing, too."

"Oh yeah? And why is that?"

"Because George Galen, Dolores, is a phony, a snake-oil salesman, a big bag of gas. He pretends to be this great savior of the people, this harbinger of health, this cure for human suffering. But in reality, George Galen cares about none of those things. All George Galen cares about is George Galen. Heal the world? Please. More like heal George Galen's incredibly low self-esteem. He's so unsure of himself, so insecure in his ability to persuade people to his way of thinking that he makes a way to *force* people to obey him. He talks about healing children, but what he's really doing is making slaves."

"But Lichen and Stone and—"

"Oh sure, he's got a few friends who follow him around because they choose to and not because they're coerced, but so did Adolf Hitler." Despite the pain, Frank managed a grin. "And the funny part about the whole thing, the real knee-slapper of this whole affair, is that old George Galen worked so long and so hard at his con that he began to believe the lie himself. He actually fell for his own scam. He convinced himself that he really was a savior. But that's not you, Dolores, is it?"

"I . . . I don't know."

"No, that's not you. Dolores, you're different than that. You care about people. You're genuine. George Galen thought he could take your mind away. He thought he could replace it with his own. But he didn't. He can't swipe your mind. All he did was add some of his memories to yours. That's why Hal was still Hal, even when George Galen convinced him that he wasn't Hal anymore. Galen can't take our minds, Dolores, not if we don't let him. Look at your hands."

She looked down at her hands.

"Are those George Galen's hands? No, they're not. Now touch that face. Is that George Galen's face? No, it isn't. He's trying to push your mind aside, Dolores. Now you have to push back."

The pain had subsided enough for Frank to stand. "You remember the laundromat? You remember what Byron said? He said you were one of us. And he's right. You're still one of us, Dolores. But George Galen? He's one of nobody. Because he doesn't exist anymore. His time is up. He had a chance, but then he blew it. There is no George Galen. George Galen is dead."

She stared at him a long while, her bottom lip quivering. Then she buried her face in her hands and cried. "I got bad luck," she said through tears. "Nothing but bad luck."

Frank went to her and put his arms around her.

BHA agents stormed into the room, guns drawn, but Frank gave them an all clear and they lowered their weapons. After that, he just held Dolores and let her cry.

33
AGENT

Dr. Kouichi Yoshida walked into the lobby of the US Bank
Tower in downtown Los Angeles wearing a navy, pin-
striped suit and carrying a wicker picnic basket. He had
bought the suit only minutes before, at a men's clothing
store around the corner, for eleven hundred dollars. It was
a ridiculous price, especially for a man still up to his neck
in student loans and credit card debt, but Yoshida felt it
appropriate for the occasion and hadn't batted an eye at
the price tag. He had paid in cash and tipped the clerk a
crisp one-hundred-dollar bill.

To the people in the lobby, Yoshida appeared to be just
another young, sharply dressed investment banker. Thousands of men in similar attire came and went from this
building every day, and to everyone here, Yoshida was
simply another face in the crowd. This was how Yoshida
wanted it, of course. He wanted to blend in. It was un-
likely that his face had shown up on any wanted poster so
soon after the ordeal—and even less likely that anyone
here would have noticed such a poster even if one had
been posted—but Yoshida wasn't one to take chances. He
left his sunglasses on and walked toward the elevators
with a determined step—as if he knew exactly where he
was going and made the trip every day.

The security guard seated behind the marble counter didn't look up from his sports magazine as Yoshida passed. It was a tiny victory, but still Yoshida felt a rush of adrenaline as he realized one hurdle had been cleared. Yoshida had decided before entering the building that if the security guard did indeed recognize him, Yoshida wouldn't run. He would simply submit and allow himself to be arrested. He had never been a fighter—or a runner— and now wasn't the time to start.

Only, Yoshida didn't want to be arrested. He couldn't endure the humiliation. There would be a media frenzy, with flashing cameras and microphones thrust in his face as federal agents escorted him to and from the courtroom every day. Then CNN would, no doubt, interview all his past mentors and professors and ask them if they had believed Yoshida was a monster when he had been under their tutelage and, if not, how in the world could a man of such promise go so bad so quickly?

No, Yoshida couldn't stomach it. *Wouldn't* stomach it. He was guilty, yes, but he would decide his own destiny.

In the elevator, a few people looked suspiciously at the wicker basket, but Yoshida returned their inquisitive glances with a friendly smile. He had tied a red ribbon onto the handle in the hope that it would lead people to believe that the basket was a gift, filled with fruit, perhaps, or cheeses. The guise must have worked, because no one said a word, and Yoshida made the ascent without incident.

The top floor was the seventy-third, and when Yoshida reached it, he was alone. He stepped off the elevator and found the nearest window. The view was breathtaking. It was sunset, and Yoshida was on the highest floor of the tallest building in all of Los Angeles. Below him, cars crept up the 405 like a long line of army ants.

He left the window and meandered through the halls until he found the door marked *Roof Access*. The door was locked, of course, but Yoshida had anticipated that. He removed a pouch from his pocket and opened it in his hand to reveal various picklocks. Yoshida chose two of appropriate length and design, and after a little tinkering, the lock snapped free and the door opened. A short flight of metal stairs took him up to the roof.

The view from the roof was even better. To the west, the sun was disappearing into the horizon, dipping into the ocean like a giant orange out for a swim and laying a white shimmering glow across the surface of the water. It was beautiful, and Yoshida felt his eyes tear up despite himself. He stood there, unmoving, taking in the wind and the sight and the smell of the city until the afterglow faded and night came.

Now Los Angeles was a blanket of twinkling lights in every direction. Yoshida gazed up at the sky and marveled at the faint stars. Light from the city made it difficult to make out many constellations, but Yoshida was able to identify a few and felt content at having done so.

Finally he sat and opened the wicker basket. Inside was a takeout box of Mongolian beef from PF Chang's, his favorite restaurant, and a bottle of expensive wine. Yoshida rarely drank wine, but it seemed to fit the occasion. He ate slowly, savoring the flavor, and drank only half a glass of wine before corking the bottle and setting it aside. A fortune cookie came with his take-out order, and Yoshida cracked the cookie and unfolded the thin rectangular piece of paper.

You are destined for great things.

Yoshida smiled, folded the paper neatly, and tucked it in the breast pocket of his coat. Inside that same pocket was a small vial. Yoshida pulled it out and held it close to his face. The vial was empty and had been for several hours. It shook slightly in his trembling hands. The trembling would get worse, Yoshida knew. Much worse. It always did. And Yoshida had tired of it. He had tired of many things—most of all, the master. He hated the master. He despised him. And when he had heard that the surviving vessels had been found and treated, Yoshida had felt a deep relief. They deserved their lives.

Yoshida wanted his life as well. But not badly enough, not enough to go to the BHA. Some of the people the prophet had taken advantage of were being treated there, but Yoshida knew he didn't belong among them. He had done too much, wronged too heavily.

He tucked the vial back into his breast pocket, wiped his mouth with a napkin, stood, and straightened the knot in his brand-new two-hundred-dollar necktie. There was no wall at the roof's edge. The roof floor simply ended, a straight drop to the bottom. Yoshida looked west again, toward the ocean. There, the black water melded with a black horizon, looking to him like the end of the world and the beginning of space. Filling his lungs with a final breath of high-altitude air, Yoshida ran toward that space. As fast as his legs could carry him.

Frank drove to the Federal Building and entered through the rear entrance without the security guards even asking for his ID. The jumpy one insisted on escorting him to the elevator and even pushed the button *for* him. Other people in the lobby watched him as he passed and then whispered to one another when they thought him out of earshot.

Frank thanked the guard politely and rode the elevator alone to the bottom.

Ten minutes later he was being ushered into the director's office, the new director, who had wisely chosen a new space for her office, far from where Irving had had his. She apparently didn't want any of his negative influence hanging over her.

It had surprised Frank that a new director was chosen so quickly; it had only been a few days since Irving's unfortunate demise, but already the boys on Capitol Hill were trying to rectify the media disaster that was the BHA.

"Dr. Hartman, I'm Director Nichols. Please have a seat."

He did, noticing new furniture also. There was not the faintest hint of Irving in the room.

She leaned forward from behind her desk and smiled politely. "Agent Atkins informed me of your honorable discharge from the military. Should I offer my condolences or my congratulations?"

Frank, who had been taking in his surroundings, looked at her intently for the first time. She was the kind of woman who wore clothing that accentuated nothing except the fact that she didn't want you looking. Dark heavy fabric that showed little skin yet plenty of poise. It didn't make her unattractive. It simply communicated that she wasn't interested in using her appearance as a weapon of influence. She was saying, Yes I'm a woman, but that's not why I have your attention. Simple brown hair. Thin face. Tight lips. Not a scrap of jewelry.

"I loved my job, ma'am. Serving my country has been rewarding. It's not something I part with happily, if that's what you're asking."

"Then I give you my condolences, and as a citizen of this country, thank you for your service."

It wasn't lip service, he knew. What the woman spoke, she meant.

"Thank you," he said.

She went to the window and looked out at the analysts buzzing busily at their workstations. "It's I who should be thanking you, Doctor. Because of you we've successfully found and destroyed all of the Healer labs hidden throughout the city."

"Thank George Galen. He put the locations in my head."

She turned to him. "Yes, he put a great many things in your head, didn't he?" She folded her arms. "Tell me, what's it like to have two memories?"

"I wouldn't recommend it. Your employer will fire you and you'll suddenly feel as if you've lived enough years to be a hundred and twenty."

She smiled, which surprised him a little and relaxed him even more. She sat in the chair beside him. "The military was wise to release you, Dr. Hartman."

"I agree."

"But I also think that the military's loss can be our gain. I'd like to offer you a position here. We'd have you under heavy surveillance for a while to ensure that you're . . ."

"Stable?"

"Up to the task, let's say. And if you are, we'd be foolish not to have you. You already know the extent of this agency's operations even more than I do, and you possess two of the greatest medical minds alive. Not many people can say that." She smiled again.

"That's very generous of you."

"I don't operate by generosity, Dr. Hartman. I make decisions based on what I believe will fulfill the purpose of this agency, which is to protect the American people."

He believed her. "Are you sure it's politically wise to make such an offer? The BHA isn't the most popular of federal agencies at the moment. Taking me in wouldn't exactly help your cause."

She laughed. "Smart and politically minded. Some might find that a threatening combination." She patted his arm. He didn't mind. "Let me worry about Washington," she said. "The president feels that an incident such as this one is evidence that the BHA is a necessary component of our national defense. We're not going anywhere."

"That sounds like a rehearsed response."

"I've been practicing. You think the media will buy it?"

"Coming from you, who could doubt it?"

She smiled wider this time. "I like you, Dr. Hartman. I'm glad you're joining our team."

"I haven't yet accepted your offer."

"No, but you will." She winked. "And to help convince you of that fact, I've arranged for you to visit T4 and see precisely what it is I'm offering. I'll have Agent Pacheco escort you. He's been eager to see you." She got up and buzzed the secretary.

A minute later Byron appeared at the door in a dark

conservative suit with a flashy ID card pinned to his coat. He nodded. "Hello, Frank."

Frank took his hand. "You clean up well."

Byron didn't waste any time. "Shall we?"

They took the subway car. Frank noticed that the agency had already patched it up nicely and put in a new window.

"So you opted for a career change after all," said Frank.

"It's still a desk job. No one's shooting at me."

"What does a tax attorney do for the BHA, exactly?"

"I'm too green to do much of anything. Right now I tell a lot of stories around the watercooler in an effort to impress women. Other than that, I'm in training. I won't bore you with the details. Benefits are great, though. Good dental."

"So they sent you to convince me to accept their offer?"

"You want the straight answer?"

"I expect nothing less from you."

Byron loosened his tie and sat forward. "There are two philosophies. Half the people here are crapping their pants thinking you could go all psycho-Galen on us at any minute. So *they* want you here to keep a close eye on you. The other half are crapping their pants at the thought of all the good you can do for the agency with your mind and Galen's working together."

"That's a lot of crap. Where does the director fall?"

"Definitely the latter. She's an optimist."

"And you?"

"Do you have to ask?"

He didn't.

"So, how do you feel?" Byron asked. "There was some worry around here that once we had the countervirus in us, our bodies would reject the organs."

Frank shook his head. "The countervirus merely stops the replication. It doesn't reverse it. My DNA matches Galen's now, so the heart has no reason to reject it. Dolores is the same. It's you I'm worried about."

"Me?"

"The virus didn't spread completely through you. Otherwise the chip on your brain stem would have been triggered."

"So some of me is Galen and some of me is myself?"

"Only genetically," said Frank. "You still have your mind. Be glad of that."

"So if you were to stick around, you might be able to get rid of the Galen in me?"

"Is this an attempt to make me take the job?"

Byron laughed. "No, this is purely selfish. Even if you don't take the job, I want to be made right again. You can set up a lab at my apartment if that's what it would take. Then again, it's not a very big apartment, so yeah, you taking the job would be preferable."

The car reached the loading dock, and Agent Hernandez was at the platform to greet them. "Good to see you, Frank."

She took them inside T4. All was orderly. There were no agents on the floor with darts in their backs. In fact, Frank recognized a few people they passed as those he had seen sedated that day. It was a little inspiring—these were people who had dusted themselves off, cracked their knuckles, and got back to work.

"Well, look what the cat dragged up," said Peeps, coming out of an office to greet them. "Riggs, come look who decided to grace us with his presence."

Riggs came out, and they exchanged pleasantries. "Sorry we missed all the action that morning."

"I'm not," said Peeps.

"Irving had sent us on some search-and-rescue op, said he had gathered new intel on your location. It was all to get us away from the building, of course."

"So I heard," said Frank. "Don't worry, you didn't miss much."

"Maybe we'll see you around here more often," said Peeps, raising an eyebrow.

"Maybe," said Frank.

Peeps and Riggs said their farewells and left them.

Byron and Hernandez then took Frank into Level 2, where Dolores was staying. She was sitting up in her bed, eating a plate of fried chicken.

"You look awful," she said.

"It's raining out," said Frank.

"Then I'm glad I'm in here. The only thing worse than a cold sidewalk is a cold, wet sidewalk."

"They feed you well, I see."

She took a bite of a drumstick and smiled. "It ain't Kentucky Fried, but it ain't half eaten either. At least I'm not pulling it out of the trash." She finished the drumstick in two more bites. "They told me you might start working here on a permanent basis."

"Word travels fast, apparently."

She frowned. "Don't seem fair to me. I get a hospital bed, and you get a job. Where's the justice in that? You're just as crazy as I am."

He grinned. "More so, I think."

"They also say you might be able to help me get of rid of, you know, the old man's memories."

"I'd like that very much."

"The sooner the better, I say. Byron says he's going to help me get my own place once I get out of here. Might even be able to help me get a job. Said he'd be a reference for me."

"I'm glad to hear it," said Frank. "I'll be a second reference if you need one."

"Good. I need at least three, I'm told."

"We should get going," said Hernandez, moving toward the door.

Frank squeezed Dolores's hand. "It was good to see you," he said.

"You say that like this is good-bye," she said. "But you'll be seeing a whole lot of me in the near future."

"I can't think of anywhere I'd rather be," he said.

She blushed. "That's a lie, I know, but I sure do love a good lie every now and again."

He patted her hand and followed Byron and Hernandez out. They went to Level 3 next, where all Galen's recruits were being housed. Frank was surprised to see Lichen sweeping the floor—he had assumed that the Healers would be incarcerated somewhere, under lock and key, as Carter had been.

"Shouldn't you be in a cell?" Frank said coolly.

Lichen stopped sweeping and looked to Hernandez for permission to speak. Hernandez nodded. "I'm being co-operative," Lichen said.

Frank felt relieved, partially to see Lichen unhurt and partially to see a Healer trying to rectify what he and the others had done. But Frank was bothered by his feelings. The part of him that was happy to see Lichen was the Galen part of him, the part that crept so subtly into the real part of him that it was impossible to distinguish at times. Galen had a presence in his thoughts and feelings, and Frank cringed at moments like these.

"I have made grave mistakes," Lichen said. "I believed I was doing good, but I was not. It is only right that I try to undo the damage I've done."

Had anyone else said it, Frank would have written it off as a lie, a criminal playing nicey-nice in the hopes of special privileges. But this was Lichen, a man who didn't lie, a man who was never insincere. He truly hoped to correct a mistake.

"He's tagged," Hernandez said. "If he tries to leave the room, he'll get a rather large jolt of electricity through his body. It's as good as any cell."

"It's unnecessary," Frank said. "He's not going to try to escape."

Hernandez looked as surprised as Lichen did.

"Thank you, sir," Lichen said, bowing his head slightly. Frank then took a quick tour of the holding cells. The

Turner girl was recuperating in one of them. Her father was
with her. There were others Frank recognized as well, including Deputy Dixon and Wyatt's nanny, Rosa. They were
all alive, at least. That was something.

"They're waiting to have Galen's obedience drug removed
from their system," Byron explained. "It would be your first
assignment if you decided to stick around. We've got them
on some medication that's keeping them stable, but they
need a lot more than that. They need someone who can help
them, someone who understands what it was that Galen
gave them."

"You're really building your case, aren't you?" said
Frank.

"The BHA needs Galen as much as it needs you,
Frank," said Hernandez.

"That rest home is a nice pile of rubble," said Byron.
"That should make you happy. We confiscated all of
Galen's and Yoshida's equipment first, of course. That
wasn't destroyed. It's all in Level 4. You'd have access to
it."

"Under heavy surveillance," said Frank.

"Very heavy, I'm afraid," said Hernandez.

"Beats unemployment," said Byron.

Frank nodded. It did indeed.

"Think what this is, Frank," said Hernandez. "Galen had
some wonderful ideas. If even half of what he started is
possible and can be done safely, it will change everything.
You have a chance to do things right, help a lot of people.
Think about that."

Monica's house was easy to find. The address was listed.

Frank hadn't called first. He probably should have, he
knew—it was the gentlemanly thing to do—but he wasn't
a phone talker. Phones were awkward.

The doorbell had a nice ring to it, one of those multi-
toned half-songs. A rich person's ring.

A middle-aged man in a bathrobe answered the door. "Can I help you?"

Frank suddenly wished he had called first. "I'm Frank Hartman. I'm not even sure if I'm at the right house. I'm a friend of Wyatt and Monica Owens."

The man looked embarrassed. "Of course." He stuck out a hand. "I'm Victor Owens. I'm Wyatt's—"

"Daddy, who is it?" said Wyatt, squeezing his way past his father and coming out onto the porch. "Frank! You came to our house."

Frank wished he hadn't. "Yeah, I hope that's okay."

Victor took Frank's hand. "Thank you. Thank you for helping Monica and my son. They told me everything. I can't tell you how grateful I am."

This was going from awkward to extremely awkward. Every response Frank could think of felt contrived, so he merely smiled and let the man shake his hand, which went on for far longer than Frank would have liked.

"Wyatt won't stop talking about you," said Victor. "Frank this and Frank that."

Frank looked down at Wyatt, who if he grinned any wider might split his cheeks. "Well, I have plenty to say about him as well," said Frank. "He's a very brave young man."

"Yes he is. Please won't you come inside?"

"No, thank you. That's very kind. But I was just passing through. I can't stay. I just wanted to say hello."

"Monica will be sad she missed you."

"Yes, tell her that we all said hello. All of us. There were a few of us involved, you know. Not just me."

"I'll tell her, yes."

"Thank you."

"You're leaving?" said Wyatt, looking crestfallen.

Frank squatted to his level. "Yeah, I've got to get going. It was good to see you, though."

"When are you coming back?"

Frank stole a glance to Victor. "Oh, I don't know. I'm a busy guy these days."

Wyatt looked over Frank's shoulder and brightened. "Mom's home."

Frank turned around to see Monica's SUV pull into the driveway beside his rental car. Why oh why hadn't he called first?

She got out and put her sunglasses on top of her head, holding her hair back.

"Mom, look who's here!"

"I can see that," she said. "Hello, Frank."

"Hello." He didn't know if he should go to her or wait there on the porch. What he wanted to do was dash to his car and peel out of the driveway.

She reached into the SUV and came out with a sack of groceries. "Victor, there are a few more bags in the back. Do you mind?"

Wyatt's father hopped to it. He grabbed the sacks, then disappeared back into the house.

Monica paused at the porch. "Did Victor not invite you inside?"

"No, he did," said Frank. "I told him I had to get going. I only came by to say hello."

She looked disappointed. "Oh. You sure you don't want to come in?"

"No, I don't want to intrude. I was just in the neighborhood." He had forgotten how striking her eyes were.

"I'll walk you to your car," she said. Before Frank could object, she passed Wyatt the sack of groceries. "Take that inside, will you, squirt?"

"See you, Frank," said Wyatt, hefting the sack and leaving Frank and Monica alone on the porch. They walked toward the driveway.

"I'm glad you came by," she said.

"I should have called first."

"You don't have to. Come by whenever."

"That's nice of you. Thank you."

"Wyatt would want to see you."

"Yeah. I would like that."

They stood by his car. "You look good," she said. "I didn't see you after everything. I'm glad you're okay."

"Same. I was glad to hear you both checked out okay. You know, virus free."

"Yes, that was a relief. And you as well."

"Right. No more virus."

She sighed. "Listen, about Victor. This whole thing really shook him up. The thought of losing Wyatt . . . he hasn't stopped spending time with him since we got back. It's more time than he's *ever* spent with him, actually. He even insisted on sleeping here a few days so he can put Wyatt to bed and get up before he wakes."

"That's great. A boy needs his father."

"I just didn't want you to think that he and I, you know . . ." She searched for the word. "We're not getting back together or anything. I mean, not that you care, but he has his girlfriend at his house."

"Oh. Well, that's great that he wants to spend time with Wyatt."

"Yes, I only hope it lasts."

"Me too."

"But that doesn't mean that Wyatt won't want to see you, of course. He would. That is, if you're not leaving town."

"No, I'll be here now," he said.

"Permanently?"

"For now, anyway."

She nodded. "Good. So we'll see you again, then."

"Yes." He got his keys out of his pocket and fiddled with them until he found the one he needed. When he looked up at her again she was smiling, not a neighborly, polite smile but an I-enjoy-your-company smile. Or at least that's what he hoped.

"Good-bye," he said.

"For now," she said.

He unlocked the door and got inside. She watched him pull out and away, waving twice before his car disappeared down the hill, heading back into Los Angeles.

AFTERWORD

by Orson Scott Card

Back in 1976, I was working as a staff editor at *The Ensign* magazine in Salt Lake City, where fellow editors Jay Parry and Lane Johnson and I ate lunch together and talked through our ideas for science fiction stories. I had shown them my short story "Ender's Game," which I had recently revised and sent off to Ben Bova at *Analog,* and we were all excited by the possibilities that science fiction offered to us as writers.

Then came the day that I came to work brandishing Ben Bova's response to my second pass at "Ender's Game"—a check for $300. Suddenly it wasn't just a dream—one of us had actually *sold* a story. Everything seemed possible. And the ideas we talked about began to seem like they might lead somewhere in the real world.

It was in those conversations that the story ideas emerged that became my second novel, *A Planet Called Treason,* and many of my early short stories—including my collaboration with Jay Parry, "In the Doghouse," and a few stories that have never been published.

We all talked to one another as if we knew something about professional writing. All we *really* knew was how to get excited about each other's ideas, giving each other the courage to sit down and write.

Since I was the one who had sold a story, though, the burden was on me to produce. The next story I sent to *Analog* was sent back with Ben's advice that what I had was the beginning of a story, and now I needed to finish it. I was stunned—after all, I sent it to him because I thought I *had* ended it. But I was not so stupid that I couldn't listen to good advice, and I found more things to do with what eventually became "Follower."

Ironically, several people told me that they guessed the ending right from the start. I thought that was crazy, since I hadn't even known the ending when I wrote the beginning of the story; later, though, I realized they were right: when I was flailing about for an ending, I hit upon one of the most obvious ways to take the story and used it. So of course it was predictable; I had taken it from page 5 of volume I of my Mental Cliché Shelf.

(And no, I won't send you a copy of that collection. You have to build your own. In fact, you already have.)

Ben bought the revised version of "Follower." Thus encouraged, I settled down to work on yet another idea I had batted around with Jay and Lane at those lunchtime writing workshops. This was the era when vital-organ transplants were still news, and I did a fairly standard paranoid what-if: What if you got an organ transplant you didn't want, and the implanted organ started taking over your body?

Once again, Ben Bova rejected my first version. It wasn't enough to have something horrible happen. He asked some pertinent questions: *Why* does the heart take over the hero's body? Whose heart was it? What happens because he was taken over? Why was the hero chosen to receive this heart? Who did the transplanting?

Reading over this list, one can only wonder what in the world was in the story I originally submitted. The answer is: It was a very short, icky little story that I thought of, in my delusional new-writer state, as being "Poe-ish." Sort of a modern "Tell-Tale Heart." Except that even Poe made sure we knew why the hero would hear the thumping of the dead heart. I had given the reader nothing.

Following Ben's lead, I came up with answers to those questions, and the result was my third sale, "Malpractice."

But by now it should be obvious that I was *not* working alone. My ideas were all being tried out on two bright and talented friends, whose encouragement showed me which stories were most likely to be worth pursuing. And then I had an editor who, detecting more promise in my work than others saw, helped guide me into discovering what it takes to make an idea into a story.

Fiction writers do not work alone. Even those who hole up in an attic or take their laptop to the park and work on stories they have never discussed with a soul are still drawing from the experience of reading other stories and from the ideas other people gave them about which stories matter enough to be worth telling.

Storytelling is a communitarian act: Every story creates a community, and arises under the influence of the communities the writer has been part of. (This is the great but obvious "insight" that remains the only useful concept to emerge from the blather of Deconstructionism.) "Malpractice" was most definitely my story—every word was mine, every story decision was my own. And yet it reflects the responses of three collaborators who listened and read and made suggestions.

Skip nearly thirty years, and guess what—I'm still a supplicant, a novice writer trying to break in. Oh, sure, I have fifty-plus books published, but that's yesterday's news. Now I'm trying to break into the film industry in Los Angeles. I have the help of a brilliantly talented young writer, actor, and comic named Aaron Johnston, who is running the LA office of Taleswapper (the film company I formed with director Peter Johnson).

On the theory that we shouldn't wait for me to learn how to write successful screenplays, we decided that Aaron should look over my short stories and see if there were any he'd be interested in adapting as screenplays. The plan was that we would pay him scab-labor wages as an advance against the *real* money he'd make when somebody funded the development of the picture.

So Aaron pored over my published story collections and chose a couple of projects—a story called "Fat Farm" and one of my oldest ones, "Malpractice." For various reasons—not least of them the likely budget of the resulting film—we settled on "Malpractice" as the starting point.

The short story contained enough plot to get us through about twenty minutes of film. Plus, the climax of "Malpractice" is still simply finding out what's happening, which is pretty much where a movie thriller really gets moving. Obviously the story would have to grow considerably and become much more intense.

Thus Aaron and I began sessions reminiscent of what I used to do with Lane and Jay. The danger was that because I was an established writer (of fiction, not screenplays), Aaron would take my ideas as dicta that had to be followed. The result would have been a story that I believed in and he didn't—which would guarantee that he could not write it well.

Fortunately, Aaron was too smart and too honest to let anybody else force their ideas on him. Despite the difference in our ages (he was young enough to be my son) and whatever authority my list of publications might give me, Aaron took nothing I said as a final answer. Instead, he responded to ideas with more ideas, and when I brought up problems with the story as it was developing, he thought of solutions faster than I could. (In *Storytelling: The Videogame*, as with all other videogames, youth has its advantages.)

The result was a very good screenplay, entirely of Aaron's writing, but thick with story ideas that came from both of us. It had been a true collaboration. It had also been great fun for me, and not just because Aaron was doing all the *hard* work.

I liked the result so well, in fact, that I pitched the screenplay to my editor at Tor Books, Beth Meacham, as a collaborative novel based on Aaron's screenplay based on our collaborative conversations based on my short story. She read the screenplay and took our bet.

(That's what publishers do, of course—they bet thousands of dollars that the writer can actually produce a novel, and many thousands more that readers will actually buy it. And when they lose that bet, I don't see many writers taking up collections to make up their losses. That's why I don't understand the writers who get angry or resentful when publishers reject their manuscripts. It's the publishers' money, and so the publishers get to decide which horse to bet on in the race. If you're a writer and nobody bets on your manuscript, the answer isn't to whine and complain, or even to start your own race; the answer is to get another horse—to write another book or story. And another. And another, until somebody's willing to bet on one of them.)

Once again Aaron and I plunged into outlining the novel version—which had to be even longer and more complicated than the screenplay. Movies have to communicate instantly with their audience, which means that there's a sort of thinness required in the writing—even of the most arty and "dense" movies. It's simply a thinner medium. There's not as much time to explain things. And you can't get inside the characters' heads.

This time around, though, Aaron and I had not only each other and the normal list of friends and relatives we involve in our creative processes, we also had Beth Meacham. Inevitably, once the screenplay existed, Aaron and I became inadvertently trapped inside the decisions we had made for that version of the story. Beth helped us find our way outside, to broaden the novel and make it better. The things we learned from working with her on that project also helped me as I worked on my solo thriller, *Empire*—though that was also a collaboration.

Heck, it's all collaboration, to one degree or another.

It's a great thing to write a solo novel, where I get to make all the decisions and mine is the only name on the cover.

But it's also a great thing to collaborate. That's how I began, after all, in the collaborative world of the theatre. When I was a playwright, the scripts I wrote were never more than the *plans* for plays. I couldn't know what I'd written until actors stood up and said the lines and did the actions. Working with Aaron was a return to those days— and to the days in the cafeteria at 50 East North Temple Street in Salt Lake City, where Jay and Lane and I batted ideas around like badminton birdies.

We're already at work on a collaborative thriller based on my short story "Fat Farm."

And Aaron is well along on his first solo novel. Because that's where this sort of thing leads. Some hotshot young genius gets a taste for fiction writing, and he wants to turn it into a career. The only thing I ask of him is that he wait at least five years before his books surpass mine on the best-seller lists. It's what they called, in the Vietnam War era, a "decent interval."

—*Lexington, Virginia, February 2007*

TOR

Award-winning authors
Compelling stories

Please join us at the website
below for more information
about this author and other great
Tor selections, and to sign up for
our monthly newsletter!